HELTER SKELTER

ELIZABETH YOUNG

http://lizy-writes.blogspot.co.uk

HELTER-SKELTER

CHAPTER ONE – FRANCE 1940

Corporal Albert Smith and the pitiful remains of his squad were heading for the coast, a scant hour ahead of the enemy, when Albie, from his seat in the cab beside Private "Tommy" Thompson, saw the helter-skelter. It was far off to the right, blackened and smoking rather than clean red and white stripes, but the truncated-cone shape was unmistakable. He clutched Tommy's arm. "Tommy! Look at that – I don't bloody believe it!"

Tommy steered round yet another bomb-crater, gripping the juddering steering-wheel of the van as he fought to control it. "What, Corp? I don't see nothing."

"Over there," Albie insisted, "By that house."

Tommy risked a quick glance and then turned his attention back to the road. "It's only a windmill," he said, "What's so special about that?"

Of course — only a windmill with the sails gone, the canvas blown away in the wind, but for a moment Albie had been back on the pier, a skinny kid with empty pockets yearning for a ride on the helter-skelter. Shaking his head at his own stupidity, he reminded himself he was a soldier with men relying on him to get them home alive. He lit two cigarettes and placed one between Tommy's lips. "Never mind me, Tommy — I'm that tired I'm seeing things."

"You ain't the only one, Albie - sorry, I mean Corp," said a voice behind him, "I could've swore I seen the sea just then."

Albie peered through the streaks of mud on the windscreen and caught a glimpse of shining water. "You're right, Bert, that's the Channel — and on the other side of that's England — we're nearly home."

A ragged cheer erupted in the back but Tommy didn't join in — he had seen ruins ahead. "Another town, Corp, although it looks deserted — there's not much of it left."

"You'd better stop anyhow," Albie told him, "Some Jerries might've got there first."

"I'll never get this old cow started again," Tommy warned, so Albie told him to keep the engine ticking over and took two of his men to reconnoitre.

Bert Daly and Albie Smith were old friends who had joined up together eight months earlier, and to who's apparently charmed lives the other men in the squad attributed their own survival. Together with Ratty Green, Albie and Bert clambered over the familiar mountains of rubble, checking behind pock-marked walls and doorways that opened onto nothing, and moved warily along the main street to a cobbled square that was surprisingly untouched. They waited tensely for one of the tall wooden shutters to burst open and a German to spray them with bullets, but the place was as it seemed - totally deserted. A tricolour hung limply from the Hotel de Ville's stone balcony — a cast-iron table sat on the pavement outside a café, its three chairs at odd angles as if the customers had left only moments earlier — a window-box of blue flowers looked recently watered — but there wasn't a soul in sight. They found the door to the bakery open and liberated some long loaves.

"Like concrete, these are," Ratty complained, stuffing the front of his jacket. Bert forced the lock on the café door and emerged triumphantly waving some bottles. "These'll soften them up," he said, but then a stray breeze lifted the flag and a shutter banged, sending all three men scuttling for cover beneath an archway big enough to drive a truck through. Tree branches creaked and blossom dropped like snow, twirling across the cobbles to float on the shallow water round the fountain, but nothing else stirred. Albie was flooded with a sense of foreboding and whispered, as if afraid of breaking the spell, "There should at least be a dog."

Bert shivered, clutching his wine-stuffed jacket, and looked at Albie. "It's spooky, Corp – can we go back?" Until the sergeant had copped it, Bert's mate Albie had been taking orders, not giving them, but now he was all that stood between seven men and disorganized panic. Albie looked round the peaceful courtyard, thinking that the folk who had lived here must have been terrified if they'd left this lovely place — but he was wasting time. Stepping out into the square he shaded his eyes and looked north towards the sea. "The road ahead's clear," he said to the others, "But the van'll never get past that rubble - we'll have to find another way through. Let's take a road each and whoever gets to the van can bring Tommy back to this square."

Bert and Ratty ran down two of the side roads, leaving Albie alone in the weird silence. He took the third road round behind the Hotel de Ville and found himself in a smaller square - one surrounded by houses rather than public buildings and bars - and there, smack-bang in the middle, was the roundabout from the pier. French words were painted round the canopy, the gilding was a bit battered and a few sections were missing from the step that ran round the ride, but it was the same set of Gallopers right down to the colours of the horses. Albie gaped at it — first the helter-skelter that wasn't, and now this. He walked forward one step at a time, half-expecting it to disappear before his eyes, and put out a tentative hand to touch the flared nostril of his favourite horse Blaze. To his relief it was undoubtedly solid and real, not a figment of his over-strained imagination, and he forgot his duty for a moment to climb into the saddle. There was a whine as if the silent motor was about to start up and he gripped the twisted pole in anticipation of that first jerk of movement, but then there was an almighty bang and an explosion blew him, the horse and the entire roundabout into a dark, swirling funnel of unconsciousness.

*

A wave of pain washed Albie up from the depths but he couldn't hear a sound. There should be music pumping its oompah beat from the Gallopers to draw the crowds and drown out the swoosh of waves through the girders under the pier. There should be lights too, flashing red, green, blue and yellow, swirling into a rainbow streak as the ride picked up speed, but he couldn't see them. He tried to touch his face to check his eyes were open – sometimes the darkness of his tent could be as thick as a blanket – but his arm was stuck and he couldn't move. He panicked briefly, but then he realised that Maria must have gone to sleep on it again, so he kissed her ear to get her to move. Her ear was cold and he thought they should have filled the hot water bottle before they came to bed – he ought to do it now but he couldn't be bothered to get up. He slid back into unconsciousness.

A little while later he woke again to the thump of an engine ticking over — that would be John and Bert with the van and he was still in bed. He could hear Bert yelling, "Albie, where are you? We gotta go!" Bert was bloody noisy this morning - if he wasn't careful he'd wake Abuela. Sure enough, she called from the wagon steps, sharply commanding. "Albert! Albert – wake up!" but he was too tired to move. Sleep claimed him again.

A warm damp patch had spread under his back and he woke to the knowledge that he'd wet the bed again and Mum would be mad at him. A light came on and he flinched when someone slapped his face and a voice said, "Corp! Corp! He's alive — I saw him move." His eyes fluttered open – it was a different uncle this morning so Mum must've dumped the last one. He shut his eyes, hoping he'd go away. Another slap jerked his eyes open. He saw a pony's head moving away and wondered who'd let Blossom loose. A weight left his chest and he could breathe again. His arm came back to life and his eyes snapped wide open - shit, that fucking hurts! Then there were arms lifting him, a sharp jab in the thigh, and he began the long slide down, round and down the helter-skelter with Dad waiting at the bottom – "Want another go, lad?" – and a soft landing into sleep.

*

Beneath the roar and scream of German planes, Tommy Thompson got them there, barrelling through debris with scant regard for his tyres — he'd drive on the wheel-rims if he had to as long as the engine kept going. Auntie Jones the medic and Bert had made Albie as comfortable as they could in the back, and their unlikely transport was weighed down with soldiers clinging to both sides, grimly determined not to be left behind. At times they were forced to leave the road to skirt bomb craters or burning and abandoned vehicles — on a couple of occasions they even seemed to be doubling back — but Tommy kept the old Renault going by sheer will-power and a lot of swearing and, slowly but surely, the sea came nearer.

"We're heading for trouble," said 'Joan' Darby, peering through the smeared windscreen.

"Looks that way," agreed Tommy, "Bloody Jerries don't want us to leave their party!" He spotted a gap between the dunes that was momentarily clear of men, shouted, "Hang on, you lot!" and put his foot down. Sheer momentum took them almost to the crest, but then two tyres burst on metal spikes and the van lurched sideways and buried its nose in the sand — it would take them no further. Tommy climbed stiffly from the cab and patted the over-heated bonnet affectionately. "You're a good old girl really – sorry I swore." Joan Darby shook his head but made no comment as they crawled the last few yards over the sharp-edged grass to peer over the crest of the dunes.

"Jesus wept! Look at that fucking mess," Tommy yelled over the continuous thump of falling bombs.

"Not much point in rushing, was there?" Joan replied

almost philosophically. "We'll never get out of that lot alive."

Beyond the dunes the beach stretched for miles in both directions, every square yard of it covered with men crouching vainly in the only cover available – burnt-out vehicles or the bodies of those already killed — while sand fountained up as the Germans tried to bomb them off the beach. Between each deafening explosion the air was thick with screams and the parade-ground bellows of sergeants trying to keep their men together, but under these sounds lurked a strange hush. Tommy frowned until he realised what it was — no-one was talking. You put thousands of men this close together and normally they'd be chatting and telling jokes, but every man down there was huddled in his own fragile bubble of terrified silence.

*

Albie thought he was in Mum's kitchen listening to the howl of the storm and the shriek of wind round the chimney-pots. He wondered if the pier would survive and said to Dad nervously, "We'd better go and check."

"No-one in their right mind would go out in this," Dad replied and Albie knew he was right — best to stay indoors with a cuppa. Then he heard the baby crying and someone shook him saying, "Come on, Corp, time to go." He fought as someone tried to lift his fourteen stone – he wasn't going out in that storm with chimneys crashing down onto the street – but the voice insisted, "Corp, we need you!" so he struggled to his knees — "That you, Bert?" - and the men sighed with relief. When Bert Daly had screamed at them that he knew his best mate was alive, the squad had dug desperately to get the Corp out from under that roundabout, because without his luck they were doomed. 'Gyppo' some of them called him – behind his back, of course, because he had a fist like a sledgehammer - but his gypsy magic had got him this far even after the Sarge was blown to bits, and they were going to stick with him like fleas on a dog.

Leaning heavily on Bert, Albie managed the climb down from the back of the vehicle. He felt like a wrung-out dishrag, but with the remnants of morphine dulling the pain in his shattered and bandaged shoulder, he rallied the men — now increased to fourteen in number by the strays they'd collected on the road – and they slithered onto the beach where they dug themselves into the foot of the dunes. Auntie Jones claimed the rear of this makeshift shelter and, with Paddy O'Brien's large frame blocking out most of the noise and dirt, he strapped up a broken leg and patched a few relatively minor injuries. In the terrified chaos of Dunkirk beach, where every man alternated between watching the sky for planes or the sea for the promised rescue, nobody noticed the small, trembling goat that peered occasionally out of Paddy's battledress blouse, or the even smaller baby that Auntie kept hidden in his kitbag. Albie, as one of Auntie's patients, could lie with his head near the baby's, and every time she opened her puzzled blue eyes she was reassured by the sight of his sea-grey ones looking back.

All afternoon the squad huddled there, watching in horror as hundreds of their fellow soldiers died of their wounds or from the relentless fire that rained down on the scene. Night brought some relief from the onslaught, so Bert and Ratty dashed back to the van to retrieve the bread and wine that had been forgotten in the terror of the drive west. Albie made them share the booty, which didn't go far divided among fourteen men, but Bert raised a smile by remarking, "It's like Jesus feeding the five thousand."

'We'll need a bloody miracle to get out of this,' thought Albie, but he kept quiet as Joan cut the bread and Bert soaked each lump with wine and handed it round. Each man sucked his piece dry and held it out for more of the sour wine that shone black as blood in the moonlight, and their little feast put new heart into them.

By the next night, though, what they desperately

needed was water. When the baby had taken her share, Paddy milked his goat into a mess-tin and gave the two seriously injured men a cupful each, but it was nowhere near enough. Auntie divided the last shot of morphine between Albie and the other man and when the pain eased, Albie sank back against his pack and closed his eyes.

The flashes that lit up the night sky danced outside his eyelids, comforting him with a familiar glow, and he floated away on the thought that there was no need to put more wood on the fire – the pot of water would still be hot in the morning. A salty breeze whispered over his face, wafting him back fifteen years to the ragged kid he'd been then, nipping onto Thambay Pier when the gateman's back was turned. He would stand by the toffee apple stall, watching the other kids zoom shrieking with delight down the final curve of the helter-skelter, longing with every cell in his skinny body to join them. A tear trickled onto the pack he was using as a pillow, but then the old man beside the ride beckoned, saying, "You here again?" and when Auntie checked on his charges, Albie's pulse was beating steadily and his lips were curved in a smile.

CHAPTER TWO – 1925 — GEORGE

"You here again?" George had seen the boy sidling round the curved wall of the helter-skelter, his evident desire to remain unseen making him conspicuous. He'd been hanging round for a week or more but George hadn't spoken to him before.

"Just looking, Mister! No law against looking."

Cheeky little sod, but his wide grin was engaging — reminded George of his own boy, now grown and gone to work in a factory. A factory! Standing at a bench, day after boring day under electric light in the racket of machines, when he could have been out here in the open, watching the excitement on kids' faces and listening to their shrieks of delighted terror. Still, Eric had a wife and two kiddies to support and he'd never loved the ride like his dad did.

"You painted it since last year, Mister." Albie spat on his hand and wiped it on his skinny chest before stroking the red and white curve. George swallowed a sudden lump in his throat — his Eric had never had that look on his face — one of adoration that twanged an answering chord in his own breast. So the boy had been here last year too - he vaguely remembered him now - he must love the pier. "Want a ride, lad?" he found himself saying.

Albie's eyes lit up briefly before his face fell. "Ain't got no money."

"Did you hear me ask for any? Go on, quick, before I change me mind!" Albie couldn't believe his ears and picked up a mat hesitantly, watching George out of the corner of his eye as he stepped through the small arched doorway, but then he realised the bloke really meant it, shouldered the heavy, slightly damp mat, and started up the winding stairs. They were very steep, but he could run up the loft ladder in a flash when one of his 'uncles' got too free with his fists, and the lovely smell of dust, wood, sea and excitement was better than that of mouldy mattress and mice that filled the loft.

He climbed steadily towards the soft light that beckoned from the tiny doorway at the top, not rushing, trying to stretch the treat out as long as possible. Albie had seen so many other kids take this wonderful ride — had watched from the shelter of the toffee apple kiosk as they slid yelling round its ridged spiral to land on the pad at the bottom in a heap of arms and legs, and then drag their mats back round for another go, their mums and dads handing over the pennies with indulgent smiles. It had never occurred to him to envy them their parents – where parents were concerned you got what you were given – but with every quivering fibre of his being he envied them the rides on the helter-skelter.

Suddenly he couldn't delay it any longer and took the last flight at a run, the heavy mat banging against his back, and burst into the sunlight to stand on the little platform and gaze. You could see the whole of Thambay from here! The people right below him were just hats, moving at that half-speed that stepping onto the slats of the pier seemed to force on all grown-ups, but one kid was running, chasing a big beach-ball that was blowing away. He watched until the ball was caught then shifted his eyes to the prom. Back there the figures were tiny — flowing around each other like oil on a puddle when you stirred it with a stick — and how did all those carts and motor-cars and bikes miss running into each other?

Turning round slowly, he was dazzled by the shine of last night's rain on the brightly painted roofs of the kiosks and the gold on the theatre at the end of the pier. Albie shaded his eyes to look further, all the way to where the sea dropped off the world – his gaze retreated rapidly. This side of the helter-skelter was right on the edge of the pier and the waves were rolling underneath — it was an awfully long way down! Albie clutched at the warm smooth wooden rail and dropped his mat — he had to grab the handle to stop it sliding away without him. God, that was close! He took a few deep breaths to steady himself and then lowered his bottom carefully onto the mat, still holding onto the rail. The bristles stuck into his skin through his threadbare trousers and it was tricky trying to sit straight, but he knew the position he must get into – he'd seen it often enough – and finally he was settled to his own satisfaction. He eased an inch at a time onto the slide and hovered there on the brink, holding back with both hands and braced knees to savour the moment. It was just him and the helter-skelter — all he could see was that shining polished curve – then with all his strength he pushed off and he was on his way down.

He was surprised how slowly he was moving — he could see the sections of wall pass one at a time, was he doing it wrong? — but gradually he picked up speed, holding onto the edges of the mat and leaning instinctively into the curve. He scraped his elbow and both knees before he learned to tuck them in, then he leaned back and the clouds whirled over his head as he went even faster, and he was flying! He opened his mouth to let out a great yell of sheer joy as the red and white paint blurred — round and round and down and down, until the breath was knocked out of him when he landed on the pad and the world went still.

Albie lay there with his eyes shut, thinking he would be happy to die right now with this memory the last thing in his head, but his body had other ideas. As his lungs sucked in a great gasp of air he looked up to see George towering over him. "You all right?"

"Oh yes!" Albie breathed, "Oh yes."

An enormous hand reached down, and George noted with no surprise that the lad flinched — he'd spotted the bruises, fresh ones overlaid on old, and wondered what sort of life the poor kid had. George backed off a step to give him room and time to recover his senses — with that shine on his face you'd think he'd been to the moon and back. "You watch these mats while I grab a cuppa and you can have another go, all right?" he said and walked off to the tea-rooms without a backward glance. Bursting with pride, Albie scrambled to his feet and pulled his mat round to the pile by George's stool. When George returned with two cups of tea and packets of sandwiches, Albie was standing by a stack of mats you could have sworn he'd squared up with a ruler. "Here you are – hope you like cheese and chutney?" George didn't know what had come over him, feeding the young scruff - must be going soft - but the lad said thanks nice enough before wolfing down his sandwich — he'd obviously not had any breakfast, let alone dinner.

Ten minutes later the afternoon crowd was queuing up, and Albie earned more than his sandwich, running round the red and white wall dozens of times an hour, hauling the mats while George dealt with the customers. No-one left the queue that afternoon because they got tired of waiting — in fact there were seldom more than half a dozen in line — but at six o'clock, when the last stragglers had been herded off the pier, George had taken more money than ever before. As Albie heaved the final mat onto the pile George asked him, "All done?" Albie nodded, his eyes as big as saucers. "Go on then — up you go!"

Albie raced up the stairs this time, his tiredness forgotten in his haste, and in the soft peace of the summer evening he lived once again those short, endless moments of pure weightless ecstasy. As he placed his mat with meticulous neatness on the pile he didn't say a word, but the hope was pouring out of him in waves. George pulled a tanner out of his pocket and pressed it into Albie's grubby palm. "You've earned that today, lad — see you tomorrow?"

*

Albie was waiting at the barrier when George arrived the next day. His clothes were the same ones, but his face had been scrubbed and his hair slicked down with water. When they went through the barrier together Albie grinned at the gateman. "Told you I work here!" he said, and walked proudly down the pier beside George, trying to look as if he'd done this for years.

Every day he worked tirelessly, every day he wolfed down his sandwiches, and every evening he climbed up the slide with a big tin of beeswax to polish it, and rode down again on the last mat of the day before taking his wages with a cheerful, "Ta, Mister Smith," and disappearing into the town. During the quiet moments – dinner-times and days when the weather kept people inside the penny arcade or the tea-rooms – George and Albie talked. George never asked any questions, but the occasional unguarded remark told him that no-one cared about Albie except for him. He did his best to keep clean, but his clothes were never washed and the musty smell told George all he needed to know about Albie's home.

One day, when Albie bent down to pick up a pile of mats, his shirt ripped clear across his back and George seized his chance. Handing him some coins he said, "Time you had some new stuff, Albie. Go down the market and get some trousers and a couple of shirts."

"I can't have nothing new, Mister Smith."

"Why not? You've worn those out working for me — you're entitled."

"It's me mum — she'll think I nicked 'em."

"You not told her you're working?"

"Well… not exactly… I don't see her much… she's out most nights… you know…"

George was pretty sure he did know. "Tell you what — I'll ask the missus if she kept any of our Eric's things — would that do you?"

"Much better, Mister Smith, much better."

*

One damp day in early October George looked at Albie and thought no-one would know he was the same kid. He was as clean as a cold tap could make him and he'd shot up like a weed — he'd filled out nicely too on a sandwich and six-penn'orth of food a day. This was going to be hard. "Albie, winter's coming."

"It is that, Mister Smith." Albie had dreaded this day but in a way it was a relief to have it out in the open. "You'll be closing for the winter, then?"

"End of this week, Albie — it's hardly worth opening now. Will you be all right?" With no wages all winter, how would he manage?

"I'll get by, Mister Smith. You'll be back next year, won't you?"

"Easter week — I'll look out for you, so make sure you're here."

The next few days were soft and warm, but on the Saturday afternoon the weather turned mean and a chilly wind blew chip papers around.

"Lazy wind," George commented as the pair of them wrapped their hands round the welcome warmth of their tea, "Too lazy to go round so it blows straight through." Albie did his best to smile but it was a poor effort, and after a day with only two intrepid customers they packed up early.

*

Sunday was the last day, and if it hadn't been for Albie George wouldn't have bothered, but he was glad he did because the boy was a mess. One eye was swollen almost shut, his shirt was ripped and he winced when he bent to pull the mats outside.

"Leave 'em, lad — let's go inside for a cuppa," said George, and when they were sitting in the steamy warmth of the tea room Albie, comfortable in George's steady familiar presence, told his friend all about it.

"Landlord slung us out," he said. "Mum said we was going to stay with Nan, but Nan wouldn't have us so we went to the pub, and this bloke hit Mum. When I tried to help Mum he back-handed me, but Mum laughed and kissed him and then she said ..." Albie tailed off, fighting back tears.

George unclenched his fist to reach over the table and put his big hand on the boy's arm. "Come on Albie, spit it out."

Albie stared at the tattoo on the back of George's wrist and spoke so softly that George could only just hear. "Mum told me to eff off. She was going to stay with this bloke, she said – the one what hit her – and they didn't want a gyppo bastard tagging along." He stirred his tea savagely. "She's always calling me that – says a gypsy got her in the club. Anyhow, I'd fed meself for months, she said, so I could carry on doing it. Then they both laughed, so I effed off." He sniffed and poured more sugar into his tea while George took several deep breaths.

"Where did you sleep?" he asked gruffly.

"Under the pier — it weren't too bad."

But it was more than enough for George. "Right!" he said, "No lad of mine sleeps under the pier. Drink your tea and help me close up proper. You're coming home with me."

"But what will Missus Smith say?"

"Give her someone to feed and she's happy — you leave her to me."

So Albie finished his tea, helped to close up proper, and went home with George, where Dot Smith took one look at him and declared he could do with feeding up.

*

From the moment Albie trailed uncertainly behind George into her kitchen Dot mothered him. He had a jam sandwich to keep him going while she peeled half a dozen more potatoes, then he shared their meat pie and mash and cabbage. No meal had ever tasted so good.

The moment it was over Dot said, "George – you get him clean while I get the bed made up."

"I stuck me head under the tap this morning," Albie protested, but it made no difference. While Dot made up a bed for him in Eric's old room, George scrubbed him at the sink – with several changes of hot water and soap, to Albie's astonishment – then he sat by the range cocooned in a towel while his hair dried. The old pyjamas Dot produced were another shock – fancy having clothes just to sleep in! – and when he woke the next morning in a bed that smelled of soap-flakes and lavender he rubbed his eyes hard to make sure it wasn't a dream. After a lifetime of dirt and fists and neglect he had landed in heaven.

For the first few days Albie behaved angelically, desperate to fit into this household where food was plentiful and he felt safe, then one evening George said, "Now we've got you permanent you'll have to go to school."

"I can read," Albie said in a panic, but George stuck the Daily Mirror under his nose.

"What's that say then?" he asked, pointing at the headline.

"Man – something – by horse," Albie read slowly and smiled uncertainly, "That other word's a long one."

"'Trampled'," read George. "And how about what's next?"

"How much more do I need to know?" But Albie's cheeky grin, that had averted a deal of trouble in the past, cut no ice with George.

"A lot more than that, my lad, and school's the place to learn it."

"Not before I've cut his hair," said Dot. "Fetch that old towel, Albie, and I'll do it now." But as she started combing his thick hair she shrieked, "He's got nits! George Smith — you brought nits into my nice clean house! Albie, don't move an inch." She rushed to cover the floor with newspaper and started hacking at Albie's hair.

"It ain't surprising, Dot, the life he led before," George said soothingly, "And his gypsy curls make nits hard to spot."

"Gypsy? You never said he was a gypsy!"

Albie cowered while they fought over him, wondering if he'd be back sleeping under the pier tonight, but slowly George managed to calm Dot down and took over the removal of his hair, using an old razor to shave him almost to the bone.

*

The next Monday, with Albie's head covered only by a layer of stubble, George marched him along to the local school. Albie's eyes bulged with apprehension when the tall yellow brick building loomed and swallowed them, but with George's big hand clamped on his bony shoulder he stood bravely in front of the headmaster's desk while his name was added to the roll.

"Albert Smith, age twelve," he heard George say. "Adopted him, haven't we — my cousin's boy from out of town."

"Lost his father in the Great War, did he?" asked the headmaster and Albie tensed, but George didn't hesitate. "That's right — his mum couldn't cope and it's put his learning a bit behind, but he'll soon catch up, won't you son?"

Albie stood up taller - if Mister Smith was ready to tell lies for him he'd not let him down. "I'll work ever so hard," he promised.

The headmaster pinned him with a glare. "Mr Fletcher will make sure of that. Right, Mr Smith, leave him with me. Say goodbye to your father, Albert."

Father! For the first time in his life Albie had a father! George's hand rested briefly on Albie's shorn scalp. "See you at teatime, son — make sure you behave, now."

Albie swallowed the lump in his throat and watched George's broad back in its tight suit disappear through the door. "Bye Dad," he whispered under his breath, but George heard him.

*

Mr Fletcher was a thin man with a gammy leg and gas-damaged lungs who taught with a distracted air, but his hearing was acute and his aim with a piece of chalk uncanny. Twice during Albie's first morning, Mr Fletcher spun round from the blackboard and his chalk hit a chatterer square on the forehead. Once, when a lumpish boy at the back used a swearword, the heavy wooden blackboard rubber whizzed the length of the room and the sinner only just ducked in time.

When the big brass bell clanged for dinner-time Albie joined the dash for the door, but Mr Fletcher called out, "You – new boy – stay!" Smirks from the other boys convinced Albie he must have broken a rule already, but it was worse than that – it was a reading test.

"How old are you, Smith?" asked Mr Fletcher when Albie had stammered to a halt.

"Twelve, Sir."

"You're small for twelve — have you actually been to school at all?"

Albie's voice rose indignantly. "Course I been to school!"

"Obviously not often enough — a six-year-old can read better than you. I really should send you to Mrs Baines in the Infants." Albie flushed scarlet and clenched his fists, but Mr Fletcher had dealt with truculent soldiers for four years and knew his men. "Listen, Smith, I'll strike a bargain with you. If you can bring your reading up to scratch by Easter, it will remain between the two of us and no-one else needs to know — how does that sound?"

Relief surged through Albie and spilled over in a grin. "You're on, Sir! You give us the lend of a book and I'll start tonight." He spat on his palm and stuck his hand out and Mr Fletcher, to his eternal credit, shook it firmly, only wiping his hand on his handkerchief when Albie had gone.

Five minutes later Albie was eating his bread and jam in the playground, thinking it might not be too bad at school after all, when another boy leaned against the wall next to him. "Me name's Bert, what's yours?"

"Albie."

"Short for Albert, same as me?"

"Yeah."

"Don't say much, do you?"

"Do when I've got summink to say."

There was a thoughtful pause. "Got nits too, 'ave you?"

Albie was about to throw a punch when he saw that Bert's head was as bare as his own, so he merely tapped Bert's chest with his fist. "Nits knows quality hair when they sees it."

Bert laughed out loud. "Nice one! I'll remember that when the nit-nurse comes round." He gazed hungrily at the paper package in Albie's hand and added, "Your mum figuring on feeding the whole school? Can't eat all that, can you?"

Albie knew that look. Before last week he would have hidden in a corner and crammed the lot down, away from other kids with eyes just like Bert's. Even now he had to force his arm to hold out the packet. "Help yourself," he said and the next words came easier. "Take two – I'll be having tea when I gets home."

George 'just happened' to pass the playground at lunch-times that first week, although careful not to let Albie spot him, and he noted his growing friendship with Bert. On Friday there were two slices of cake alongside the bread and jam as a treat, and Albie was handing over one slice to Bert when he looked up to see they were surrounded. Walter Biggins' bullet head and thick shoulders blotted out the watery sun, and his gang of half-a-dozen formed a semi-circle cutting off any chance of escape, while ranged behind them were the fifty or so other boys of the Upper School.

"Ain't that sweet!" sneered Wally. "Two nit-heads sharing a bit of cake — where's mine then?" and with a hand like a bunch of sausages he whipped the slice of fruit cake from Bert's hand and stuffed it into his own mouth. While Wally chewed noisily, enjoying his audience's sycophantic laughter, Bert shrank back into the wall – he'd been at the receiving end of Wally's brand of humour for years – but Albie had grown up fighting for every scrap of food, and Bert was his first real friend – he put his head down and charged. With a 'whoof' of expelled air, a mixture of cake and Wally's spit sprayed over Albie's back, and a moment later Wally's fist slammed into his side. A collective gasp from the onlookers was followed by a second of silence, but when Albie was seen to be still upright the playground erupted and the fight was on.

Albie ignored the blows that should have floored him – he'd weathered worse in his short life – and a couple of weeks of Dot's cooking had put new strength into him. His sharp fists pummelled Wally's stomach, preventing him from recovering fully that first expulsion of breath; he kicked Wally's shins with his hard new boots; he ducked and dodged and weaved with a speed and agility that Wally's overfed bulk couldn't hope to match, and the shouts of "Get 'im Wally!" began to be interspersed with "Good on yer, Albie!"

Mr Fletcher stood smoking a cigarette on the back steps of the school, and the Headmaster sucked a light into his pipe by his first floor study window, both of them wondering whether the new boy was about to give Biggins his long-overdue come-uppance. Then Wally shoved Albie hard enough in the chest to send him staggering into the circle of spectators and snarled, "You had enough yet, shrimp?"

"I ain't even got started, fatso!" Albie parried and Wally came in for the kill.

Bert, held in his ring-side position as much by the one-on-one rule as by the hands gripping him, feared Albie was going to get a thrashing. But Wally's reputation – and his attendant gang – had kept him out of fights for a long while, and he was too mad that this new boy had hurt him to think straight. On top of that he wasn't very bright, and he opted for the classic move of holding a smaller kid at arm's length and pounding his head with a fist. When his hand found no hair to grab he was caught off balance, and in that split second Albie clutched his opponent's protruding ears, pulled him in sharply and head-butted him.

Wally writhed in the dirt with blood pouring through his fingers while the crowd stood stunned at the turn of events, then a cheer echoed round the playground and a whistle blew. Mr Fletcher pushed through to the front and hauled Wally to his feet, pulled his hands away from his face and inspected him. "I think you have a broken nose, Biggins — let me look at it." Holding Wally's head with one hand, he moved the other to Wally's nose and, without giving the boy time to think about it, tweaked the bone back into position with an audible scrape. Wally let out a yell of pain but Mr Fletcher merely said, "That will save your father a doctor's fee — now wash your face and report to the headmaster."

Albie was bending over with his hands on his scraped knees while Bert thumped his back, crying triumphantly, "You beat 'im, Albie, you bloodied 'is nose!" and neither of them noticed the dispersal of the crowd until Mr Fletcher pulled Albie upright by his collar. "You too, Smith."

"Me too what, Sir?"

"Headmaster's study, quick as you like."

"But he ain't done nothing wrong, Sir! Wally started it!" Bert protested.

"I dare say, but the rule is no fighting, so up you go, Smith."

Ten minutes later Albie eased his bottom gingerly onto the bench.

"Six?" Bert whispered.

"It weren't so bad," Albie said and glanced over his shoulder at Wally, who was standing against the wall at the back. "At least I didn't blub." Bert's eyes widened, but a cough from Mr Fletcher warned him that the full story would have to wait until home time.

*

"Your new jacket!" Dot shrieked when Albie got home, and as he tried to sneak upstairs she caught his arm. "And what's wrong with your face? You've been fighting!"

George looked up from behind his newspaper. "Leave him be, Dot — the other boy's worse," he said and winked at Albie. "You did good, son — that Biggins lad has had it coming for years."

Albie grinned, bringing another shriek when Dot noticed his bleeding tooth. "Couldn't let him take your cake without a fight, could I?" Then a thought struck him. "What was you doing there, anyhow?"

"Just happened by, son, and heard the racket — never could resist a good scrap."

Albie returned somewhat apprehensively to school on Monday but he needn't have worried. While his vivid shiner attracted an admiring circle of boys, Wally's huge and already filthy bandage was studiously ignored and his gang had shrunk to two diehards. When dinner-time presented no further entertainment the boys milled about uncertainly, missing the familiar hierarchy, but by Wednesday dinner-time things had settled down. When Albie and Bert ran down the back steps into the rain-swept playground they were greeted with a chorus of "Al-Bertie, Al-Bertie" and the friendship between the two former outcasts was established with this accolade of a shared nickname.

*

Once Albie had mastered the shamefully babyish reading books under Dot's relentless tuition, George took over the task of teaching him, and in the long winter evenings he and Albie would sit by the range in the flickering gaslight with the Daily Mirror. With Dot crocheting steadily in her rocking chair, George's thick finger would follow the lines of print while Albie read. "'Unemployment Insurance Act' and 'British Women Seek Vote'. What's a vote, Dad?" So George would launch into a working man's dissertation on politics until Dot intervened. "Save that for the pub, George — Albie's trying to put you off," and George would pick up the paper, Albie's tongue would poke out of the corner of his mouth again and the lesson would continue.

<u>CHAPTER THREE – 1925 — CHRISTMAS</u>

Albie woke up with a fizzing in his stomach and pulled back the curtain, wondering why he was awake when it was still dark. Then he remembered. He scrambled to the foot of his bed and there it was — the stocking! One of George's old socks — that Dot had declared last night was more darn than sock - bulged lumpily at the foot of his bed.

His mother had pooh-poohed Father Christmas, saying it was just a fairy-tale for kids with parents who'd more dosh than sense, and he'd never had a present before. He hadn't expected anything this year either until he'd heard Dot's voice raised at George the other day. "Albie's ours now, and Eric had a stocking till he was twelve!"

Then George's deep chuckle. "Which was when he told you he didn't believe in Father Christmas any more."

"Well, Albie's getting one till he tells me the same," Dot had retorted. "I've been saving bits for weeks."

Albie had crept away and breezed into the kitchen noisily ten minutes later saying, "Mum – Bert says his mum's making paper-chains – can we have some?" Dot had stared at him silently for a moment, her lip trembling slightly.

"That's the first time you've called me 'Mum', Albie – of course we can make some," and right after tea she'd got out the scissors and glue and a pile of old newspapers.

Now the kitchen, festooned with paper-chains and with a tree standing by the dresser hung with decorations from a box under the stairs, awaited the festive dinner. Albie could smell the rich scent of the pudding that was already steaming on the range, so Mum was up, but it was too early for him to go downstairs so he pulled his stocking towards him.

His fingers explored through the wool of the sock, prolonging for as long as possible the moment when he would open his first ever Christmas stocking. He found the unmistakable rubbery resistance of a ball that'd fit nicely in a pocket on school-days, but Mum had been sneaky and disguised the other packages with many layers of newspaper.

Albie extracted one small present at a time, opening each one as slowly as in a game of pass-the-parcel. The ball was black in the moonlight but he guessed it was red — he bounced it a couple of times before remembering Dad was still snoring on the other side of the thin wall. A box opened to reveal a model car, all shiny paint and bulbous headlamps with a real driver you could take out. There was a catapult he'd lay odds Dad had slipped in when Mum wasn't looking, and which he hid behind one of the small drawers in his chest. A bag of toffees and a sugar mouse came next — he dangled the mouse by its tail so he could bite the head off — and then, right in the toe of the sock, he found an orange and a tanner.

He laid it all out on the worn eiderdown and gazed at the little heap, then wiped his cheeks angrily. He must be turning soft, blubbing over a few bits and bobs from Woolworth's – he'd nicked better stuff than this in his time. He stretched his feet out and kicked a heavy parcel which he'd missed earlier, but it was obviously a book so he left it – he didn't need any more bloody reading. Lying back against his pillow, he scraped his teeth slowly over the sugar mouse, savouring the sweetness that Mum usually banned until after tea.

When the smell of bacon wafted upstairs he pulled his clothes on and thundered down to the kitchen.

"Did Father Christmas come?" Dot asked immediately.

"Give me a ball and a car and a bag of toffees, he did," said Albie, grinning at her pretended surprise, "All wrapped up in newspaper, too – he reads the Daily Mirror, just like Dad."

"Does he now?" said George, "Man with some sense, then. Happy Christmas, son."

"You too, Dad, and Mum of course, and ta very much for the book."

"You'll enjoy that when you get into it," George said, grinning. "I read it myself in the 'Young Folks' magazine when I were your age."

"You read it?" That was different, and Albie tore the wrapping from the book. 'Treasure Island' he read on the cover and opened it. There, on the flyleaf in Mum's round hand, were the words, 'To our Son Albie with Love from Dad and Mum Christmas 1925'. George saw him swallow hard and said quickly, "New out, it were when I were a lad, and I nearly ran off to sea because of it. Then I met Mum and realised I'd found my treasure right here at home."

"Get away, you great softie!" said Dot, blushing and clipping him with the tea towel, "Now eat your breakfast, you two, or we won't find a seat in church."

The Christmas joint of beef was in the oven when Dot pinned her hat on for church. Albie looked away, afraid that one day she'd stick the pin straight through. He had his jacket on and was heading for the door when she handed him a parcel. "Dad got you the book — this is from me."

"More presents!" Albie breathed, clutching the squashy package.

"Don't stand there gawping, lad — open it!" laughed George, and when Albie ripped off the paper a heap of striped wool tumbled out onto the rag rug.

"I never seen you doing this!" he exclaimed, wrapping the scarf round his neck and chest.

Dot beamed at the success of her surprise and turned him round to tuck the ends into his belt. "Did it while you were at school. It's not new wool, mind — I unpicked some old jumpers."

"It's great, Mum – lovely and warm," Albie said, pleased with the red and blue stripes, and to Dot's surprise he kissed her cheek.

"Get on with you!" she said, "You get a cold and who'd have to nurse you?"

After church, George and Dot's son Eric came round with his family and, while Hilda helped her mother-in-law with the dinner, George gave his grandchildren their presents from under the small tree. Young Georgie opened a huge parcel to reveal a lorry big enough to sit in, and his little sister Daisy squealed with delight at her doll with eyes that shut when it lay down. Then George picked up another parcel and squinted at the label. "'Albie', it says — anyone here called Albie?"

"But I got a book and a scarf already," said Albie.

"Must be your lucky day, then," smiled George. Albie ripped off the paper to discover a box of Meccano complete with its own set of spanners, but as he stammered his thanks, Eric scowled.

All through dinner Eric hardly said a word, and although young Georgie and Daisy chattered enough to cover his silence, George watched him thoughtfully. After the pudding, in which all three children had miraculously found a thrupenny bit, Eric tilted his chair back and patted his stomach. "Lovely dinner, Mum — I'm stuffed."

"Chairs were made with four legs for a reason!" Dot snapped, and Eric grimaced and dropped his chair back down. "Does Mum nag you like this, Albie?"

"All the time."

"Good – can't have you getting off lighter than me." He leaned his elbows on the table and fixed Albie with a glare. "You'll be leaving school in three years — how are you planning to earn your way? I could have a word with Mr Evans at the works."

"Me – work in a factory? No thanks," said Albie and Eric's fists clenched, but Albie lifted guileless eyes to his face. "I couldn't stand being indoors – I'm going to work on the pier with Dad."

"You three youngsters can get down now," George said hastily, and while the children played with their toys, Dot and

Hilda cleared the table and made a pot of tea.

"You spoil that boy, Dad," Eric said abruptly, "I never got three presents at his age."

"He never had any up till now," George replied, shocked at Eric's vehemence.

"Then he should be grateful for anything."

George took his time rolling a cigarette and leaned over the range to light it before saying quietly, "He *is* grateful, Eric. Now leave it – I don't want to fall out with you on Christmas Day."

After Eric had taken his family home, George and Dot put their feet up and listened while Albie began to read Treasure Island aloud. When it was time for bed he closed the book reluctantly, his mind already picturing a seaman with a scarred face, sitting in a pub remarkably like the Kings Head down the road.

*

Boxing Day was a Saturday that dawned cold and blustery but dry. Albie was still eating his breakfast when Bert arrived and asked breathlessly, "You ready? We'll miss the best spot if we're not quick."

"Come in and shut that door," Dot scolded, so Bert did as he was told, sniffing appreciatively at the fragrant air while Albie got his scarf and jacket.

"Here, Bert, there's a sausage left over," Dot said in feigned surprise, "Could you manage it if I wrap it in a bit of bread?"

"Shame to waste it — ta, Missus Smith." Bert was happy to help out with the leftovers that always seemed to need eating up when he came round — with his Dad out of work there was never enough to eat at home.

With Albie's old scarf wound round Bert's neck and a jam sandwich in each pocket the friends raced to the pier. Albie patted the shuttered helter-skelter affectionately on his way past but they didn't stop — the pier was filling up rapidly. They had to use their elbows to get through to the iron steps down to the fishing platform at the far end. The studded metal under their boots was slick with rime and the railing cold enough to burn, but this favoured spot was packed. They defended their pitch manfully against all comers for almost an hour before they heard the cheers and catcalls from up top that greeted the appearance of the competitors. Peering at the heaving green water beneath him, Albie shuddered. "Must be bloody mad!" he yelled in Bert's ear, "Dad says they rub pig fat all over like a roast dinner."

"Bet they'd sooner be in an oven than out there," Bert responded as the whistle blew and the shout went up, "They're off!" A minute later the first swimmer appeared, his black costume in stark contrast to his winter-white shoulders that were shiny with grease. He powered through the wind-whipped breakers with awe-inspiring speed, closely followed by a dozen other men in their bright team colours. Albie and Bert cheered them all, having no special allegiance and, as the leaders rounded the marker-buoy, cheered even harder for the line of stragglers who had no chance in hell of winning but were determined enough – or had been drunk enough last night – to brave the sea on Boxing Day.

The two boys had chosen their spot with care, and when the crowd surged left to get a good view of the landing-beach, the boys went right, scrambled up the slippery steps and ran along the pier to the prom. They wriggled ruthlessly through the press of coats and stopped, with their noses a whisker away from a policeman's blue serge bulk, in front of the lido. When the winner – unsurprisingly the man in black – trotted athletically through the crowd towards the relative warmth of the Lido's indoor pool, Albie ducked under the policeman's outstretched arm.

"Good swim, mister!" he said cheekily, standing right in the man's path, and before the long arm of the Law could haul him back and clip his ear he had not only shaken the winner's hand, he had also patted his back.

"What you got there?" asked Bert when they'd escaped. Albie opened his fist and licked his palm. "Dad was right – it is pig fat – and like Mum says, it's better for a bit of salt!"

The leading swimmers were all inside the lido and Albie and Bert were heading for the chestnut-seller's barrow when the sound from the prom altered. Encouraging cheers for the stragglers faltered and died and a low moan built up, then an isolated scream was echoed by several others and the boys ran back.

On the beach stood most of the last-minute race entrants, swathed in towels and coats. When the boys stood on the bottom railing they were in time to see two tail-end competitors emerge shivering from the waves, but one group of supporters stood at the water's edge surrounding a weeping woman, and she was still holding a towel — one swimmer hadn't made it. "Look there!" someone yelled when a dark head showed in the underside of a wave. There was a brief surge of hope, but the head vanished beneath the foam and the crowd fell silent as the wave rolled greasily between the girders. Several life-belts were dangled from the pier but no hand reached up from the sea towards them, and the men on the beach shucked off their towels to begin the search.

Then a commotion rippled across the prom, and on a wave of encouragement the team swimmers burst onto the beach to plunge back into the sea, battling the breakers and diving repeatedly while others waded under the pier.

After an endless few minutes there was a shout, "They've got him!" but the body that the barnacle-scratched men carried onto the beach was limp, and the towel on which they stretchered it was stained bright red before they reached the prom. The crowd parted to let them through only yards from Albie and Bert, and they caught a glimpse of the face before someone covered it.

Shaken and subdued, the boys wandered off to spend

Albie's stocking money, but even a paper cone of hot chestnuts failed to lift their spirits.

"Reckon he were dead, Albie?" asked Bert eventually.

"Got to be with his head bashed in like that," said Albie.

"But his eyes was open," Bert argued hopefully.

"So? I seen eyes like that once after a pub fight," Albie told him, "Dead as a doornail, those eyes was."

"I ought to tell Mum," Bert said, and they trailed miserably away from the promenade.

Albie had never been to Bert's home, and when they entered the yard and ducked under the lines of soot-streaked washing that hadn't dried in a week, he cringed at the memory of his life before George and Dot adopted him. As they climbed the malodorous stairs even the smell was the same, and for the first time in three months he thought about his real mum.

"Here we are," said Bert, pushing open one of two doors on the second landing, and they entered a room that was only a few degrees warmer than outside. A man who was clearly Bert's father looked up from his seat at the bare table. "This must be Albie," he said with a smile, "But what're you two doing back so quick? I thought you'd be gone till dark."

"Oh Dad, it were awful!"

Bert's mother listened with her hands over her mouth as the boys related the tragedy. "Who was it – anyone we know?" was Gladys's first question. When the boys couldn't tell her she took her shawl off its peg, saying to her husband, "I've got to find out," and hurried off to discover which poor woman had been widowed on Boxing Day.

"Makes our troubles look small, don't it?" said John Daly. Albie looked at the tiny fire smoking in the grate, the ragged apron on Bert's sister May, and the four smaller children – two of them with Bert's red hair — tucked together in a bed in the corner of the room. It was worse than the place he used to live in – there was even ice on the inside of the window – but it still felt like a home.

Then he noticed the children's wide eyes and said to Bert, "Reckon we scared the babies with that story. You tell 'em a more cheerful one while I go and tell Dad and Mum about the drowning." He stood up to leave and there was a rustle of paper from his pocket. "Hey, Bert – we never ate our jam butties! Those'll cheer your babies up — makes good jam, my Mum does."

When he left the room with a wave and "See you later" John Daly could have wept with gratitude — the children had had no food at all today and here were two fat packages oozing jam. "Get a knife, Bert — these'll feed you all."

"You eat mine, Dad — Missus Smith give me a sausage."

Albie walked home slowly. The Daly's kitchen had brought back unpleasant memories of cold and hunger, but it was Christmas, and he couldn't help wondering if his mother was all right. Besides – she might be drunk enough to tell him where to start looking for his gypsy father. After telling George and Dot about the swimming tragedy he slipped out again, and made his way through the back streets beneath a sky that was beginning to leak snow.

The double row of tenements still crouched between the scrap yard and the timber yard that belonged to Wilson's furniture factory. Albie's footsteps seemed over-loud until he realised that his sturdy boots were ringing on the cobbles as his bare feet never had. He stopped to look around — in only three months the narrow street seemed to have sunk further into the ground, as if weighed down by poverty and misery. Two ragged children stared at him from the front step when he squeezed past them into the hallway.

Then the smell hit him – a combination of rats and bugs and an outhouse shared by too many people. He'd lived with the smell for twelve years and never noticed it before. What the hell was he doing here? What if his mother wanted him back? He turned to flee and one of the children whined, "Spare a penny, mister?" Mister! Did he really look like a grown-up to them? He fished in his pocket and found the last of his roast chestnuts which he dropped into the grubby palm.

"Thanks, mister," the child said, and an upstairs window banged open – his mother's window. Albie looked up – but it wasn't his mother.

"What are you after?" the woman called.

"I used to live here."

"Well, anything you left behind is mine now, so you can bugger off."

Albie retreated at a run and didn't stop until he got to the Market Square, where he leaned against a shop front under the arches and asked himself what he'd hoped to gain by going back. If his mother *had* still lived there she wouldn't have welcomed him, and she definitely wouldn't have told him who his father was, even if she knew.

"Sod her!" he yelled into the deserted square, and a clatter of pigeons took off above his head and circled the square before wheeling back to their roosts. Albie grinned and then shivered. His bum was freezing to the stone sill and the snow was getting thicker by the minute. He stamped a track of boot-prints all round the square through the pristine snow, then ran down beside the Town Hall and threw a snowball at an angel in the churchyard. Then he scuttled home to his new parents to get warm, and spent the afternoon alternating between building a Meccano model of the pier and reading more of Treasure Island.

<u>CHAPTER FOUR – 1925/6 – ALBERTIE</u>

The next morning Bert was on his way to Albie's when he saw a line of men outside the Town Hall. After reading the notice on the door he raced back home and burst into his kitchen. "Dad – they're taking on men to shovel snow!" John Daly was on his feet and out of the door in a second with Bert close on his heels. "Here, Dad – take my scarf – you could be out all day."

His father smiled his thanks before running through the streets to the Town Hall, and Bert was soon sitting by the Smith's range with some bread and dripping in his hand. "They wouldn't take boys," he told Albie.

"We could do something else though."

"You could clear the path to the lavvy," said Dot, "There's a shovel in the shed."

Albie pulled a face — he'd been hoping to earn some money — but Bert looked at the food he was holding and stood up. "All right, Missus Smith — come on, Albie, it won't take long."

The path was soon clear and the boys were spreading ashes on it when old Mr Evans leaned over the wall to ask, "You two want to earn a penny each doing mine?" Word went down the street ahead of them, and when the short day ended they sat in Albie's kitchen and emptied their pockets onto the table-cloth. Four wrinkled apples and a handful of toffees lay there among the coppers.

"We ate the biscuits," Albie told Dot, "They'd only be crumbs if we'd kept 'em." Then they counted the pennies. "Two shillings and fourpence!" Albie's cheeks glowed with more than the cold, "It would've been more, but there was two old dears who didn't have no money. Two and fourpence – that's one and tuppence each! What you going to do with yours, Bert?"

"Give it to Mum," Bert said at once, "She does a good

meat pud when she's got the makings." He wrapped his coins carefully in a bit of rag from his pocket, "Best I go now before the shop shuts. You on for the next street tomorrow, Albie?"

"Might as well while the snow lasts," Albie replied and added in a burst of generosity, "Take the toffees and apples for your babies."

Bert shoved his spoils deep inside his pocket and ran home, leaving Albie staring thoughtfully at his own pennies. What was it Eric had said at Christmas? He should be grateful for his home and pay his way. With a sudden movement he pushed the money towards Dot. "Here, Mum, you take it to help pay for me keep."

Dot tucked her hands under her apron, saying, "We don't need …" but George interrupted loudly enough to drown her words. "We don't need it like Bert's mum does but it will come in handy, 'specially as it's winter. Mum will take a shilling. You got a spare jam-jar, Dot?" Wordlessly, Dot found one under the stairs and banged it down on the table. "This can be your savings jar, Albie," said George, taking two pennies off the pile, "And this'll start you off." He dropped the pennies into the jar and placed it ceremoniously on the mantelpiece beside the clock.

Albie gazed at it beaming happily. "Wonder how long it'll take to fill?"

The snow couldn't last forever, of course, but from their snow-clearing efforts Albie and Bert became known throughout the streets between their homes as willing and trustworthy. By patrolling their patch regularly they picked up a steady trickle of other odd jobs for after school and weekends.

Halfway through January, when they were fetching a parcel of fish from a kiosk under the prom, Albie spotted an old pram wedged between the girders of the pier. They hadn't been down to the beach since Boxing Day — the dank area beneath the pier still held the echoes of the Boxing Day widow's screams — but that pram was a major find.

"We could carry a sack of spuds in that," Albie said.

"It's a bit of a wreck."

"It's got four wheels – we can fix the rest."

For two nimble boys it was a matter of moments to retrieve the battered pram. The paintwork was blistered and peeling and the handle missing but the wheels still turned, and after they'd tipped out the sand and seaweed the bodywork looked sound, so they dragged it home.

George was on his way back from his winter job of keeping the boiler going in the Kings Head and met them at the door. "Transport?" he guessed at once, "Good idea – need some help?"

That weekend they oiled the wheels and replaced the handle with a broomstick, then the boys rubbed it down and painted their school nickname 'ALBERTIE' on both sides in big red letters. At the ceremonial unveiling George commented, "All them curly letters could be on the side of a gypsy wagon," and Dot snorted in disgust, but the words echoed through Albie's head all day. 'Gypsy brat' his mother had called him, and perhaps her angry outbursts had held the truth. After that, whenever they used the pram for carrying potatoes or boxes of bottles, or for taking the heavy wireless accumulators to be refilled, he watched the wheels turning and wondered how he could possibly track down a travelling man.

At weekends the two young entrepreneurs began venturing further afield to scour the out-of-town roadsides and ditches for anything that would burn, then carried it home, chopped it up in Albie's back yard and sold it door-to-door. Albie loved their country jaunts, and even more so when spring began to show in a misting of green in the hedges, but Bert wasn't so keen. One day in February, spotting a patch of snowdrops under a tree, Albie flung his arms wide in a gesture of sheer joy. "Look at that, Bert – it's lovely out here, ain't it?"

"Too quiet for me and too cold," Bert answered, pulling his cap down over his ears – one good thing about wearing Dad's cast-offs was the size of this cap. "Prefer streets and houses meself." He bent down by a five-bar gate to pick up a bit of wood, and a snort inches from his head knocked him back on his bottom. "Shit! What was that?"

Albie clutched his sides with laughter at the sight of Bert sprawled in the mud. "It's only a horse — seen one before, ain't yer?"

"Fixed to a cart, yes, but not blowing in me ear!" said Bert, backing away from the head towering above him, but Albie was enthralled. He approached the horse slowly, murmuring a string of sounds that weren't exactly words, and it responded by twitching its ears towards him as if it was listening. Albie pulled a fistful of grass from the hedgerow and offered it to the creature with the huge gentle eyes. The horse's warm breath and soft lips caressed his hand as his offering was accepted, and for a brief moment he saw the flicker of firelight on painted wagons hidden in shady woods, but Bert broke into his reverie. "Come on, Albie, we got work to do." Albie dragged his mind back into the here and now, patted the horse's neck, and turned away to help Bert push the pram further along the lane.

"What was you saying to him?" Bert asked once they were well clear of the horse.

"Dunno," said Albie, "Horse talk, I suppose. Maybe my dad really was a gypsy."

Bert stopped dead. "What d'you mean – ain't Mister Smith your dad?"

Albie chewed his lip and kicked the toe of his boot against the pram wheel. "Well, he is now, but he didn't used to be – I'm adopted."

"So you don't know who your parents are? You could be a prince or anything!"

"Not with a mum like I had," Albie said, suddenly deciding to trust Bert with his shameful secret. "I'm not sure she knows who my dad was, but she called me a gypsy bastard."

"Your own mum?" Bert gasped, "That's awful. I'd hate not knowing who my dad was," but as Albie continued to kick the pram wheel, Bert tugged his friend's cap over his eyes and said, "Just don't try reading my mind, all right?" and sped away with the pram, laughing.

Albie adjusted his cap and chased after him. "Don't go telling no-one, will you?"

"Not me, mate, but you better not let Wally Biggins find out – he's mouthy enough as it is."

It ain't fair, Albie thought — even fat Wally knows who his dad is — but then the lane petered out to a muddy track and he had to concentrate on pushing the pram. They were about to turn back when Albie spotted the huge branch lying half-hidden in the ditch. "We'd make a few bob with that," he said, but Bert shook his head. "Can't fit it in — we'll have to come back tomorrow." They looked at each other as the same fear struck them both — what if someone else found it? Hoping to hide it in the trees, they got behind the branch and heaved, but although they felt it give, hauling it out of the ditch was beyond them.

"We'll have to leave it," said Albie, but Bert was reluctant to give up. "I know!" he cried, "Dad can help — we'll get Dad." They raced home at breakneck speed, and while Albie dumped the pram's load in his back yard, Bert went to fetch his father.

John Daly was only one amongst thousands during the Depression who sat day after purposeless day in a cold house watching his children slowly fade through hunger. Although grateful for the food that Bert's money put on the table, John resented the fact that Bert could do it when he couldn't. To save his pride he insisted on viewing the fetching and carrying as just a boys' lark, so when Bert barrelled into the kitchen with some garbled story of needing his help, John was reluctant to move. But Bert insisted, and before his father realized it he was running down the country lane behind the boys.

Between them they managed to balance the branch precariously across the long-suffering pram, and as they wheeled it home John felt his spirits lift for the first time in months. By the time they reached the back yard they had collected a considerable crowd, and before they had reduced their find to manageable logs they had sold half of it to local housewives. As he helped to stack the remainder against the side wall of the lavatory, John said, "You've got quite a little business going here."

"It'd go better if we didn't have to go to school," said Bert hopefully.

"No chance, son — schooling will get you a gaffer's job," said John.

"What would we want that for?" asked Albie.

"So you don't end up sitting at home week after week with empty pockets like me," John answered bitterly.

The boys fell silent — they hadn't thought of school as actually being useful – and then Bert said suddenly, "Tell you what, Dad — why don't you do it in the week and we'll do it weekends?"

"What – me — collect wood with a pram?"

"It's *our* pram," Albie said indignantly, and when neither Bert nor his father seemed to have heard him he added, "It's hard work, all that collecting and cutting up," but that was the wrong thing to say because John Daly snapped, "I'm not afraid of hard work!" and the decision was made.

When Bert and his father had gone home, George tackled Albie. "I heard what you said to Mister Daly. It was rude and I ain't too happy about it."

"And I ain't too happy neither – but Bert didn't seem to

mind him muscling in."

"Of course he wants to help his dad — blood's thicker than water."

"So why did my mother dump me, then?" George looked at Albie's mutinous expression and sighed. "I know it ain't fair, Albie, but some women shouldn't have kids. My own mum was a hard woman – I never knew much love till I met Dot." He cleared his throat and ruffled Albie's short curls. "But that's all water under the bridge now. What's important is to help people worse off than us, and John Daly's kids are starving."

*

Soon John Daly pushing the pram was a common sight on the streets of Thambay, and within a month he had picked up enough regular jobs to keep him busy, but after George had a quiet word with him he was careful not to encroach on the boys' small errands. When Albie realised his savings jars were filling up at the same rate as before, he reluctantly accepted that 'Albertie' was now a three-man team.

He also became resigned to attending school regularly, particularly when he learned that any absences would be reported back to George. The hour after supper was still devoted to his reading lessons with George, though he needed little persuasion to follow the adventures of Jim Hawkins and Long John Silver, and the nursery books of six months ago were a distant memory.

In the last week of term Mr Fletcher, who had received a clandestine visit from George, held up his own newspaper and said to the class, "I have here an article about Ireland that will interest those of you with relatives over there. Smith, will you read it to us?"

"What, me, Sir?"

"Yes, you, Smith."

In an audible aside Walter Biggins scoffed, "He couldn't read a comic," and a few boys sniggered, but Albie walked straight up to the platform by Mr Fetcher's high desk and, with only a little help with the long words, read the article on the troubles in Ireland. When he had finished, Mr Fletcher took the paper saying, "Thank you, Smith, well read," and Albie returned to his desk with a noticeable swagger.

*

"Easter's next weekend, Albie," George said the next day, "Should I get another lad to help me with the helter-skelter?"

Albie almost choked on his toast and marmalade. "Don't you dare – that's my job, that is!"

"I thought you'd be out running errands with Bert," George said slyly.

"Huh! Bert's going to work with his dad over the holidays. He'll only need me in the evenings."

"Well, if you're working the ride you won't be free till then anyway," said George, "Now get your jacket and we'll start cleaning it today."

Half an hour later, armed with buckets and brushes, George and Albie began the mammoth task of scrubbing down the sixty-foot tower. George was happy to delegate the job of negotiating the slippery climb up the slide to Albie, but he insisted he took his boots off to avoid scratching the surface. After a whole day of hanging onto the rail with one hand and wielding a soapy scrubbing brush in the other, Albie ached all over. "I should've stuck to chopping wood," he complained to Bert that evening.

"There's not so much call for wood now it's warmer," Bert told him, "Me and Dad were talking about that today — we've started looking for stuff to sell to the rag-and-bone man as well."

"Found any slip-proof boots?" joked Albie, massaging his calves.

"Now you mention it," grinned Bert, "I might have found just the thing."

The next day George was amused to see Albie tying

onto his feet two bits of rubber cut from an old motor tyre, and when the pier officially opened for the season, the red and white stripes of the helter-skelter gleamed as good as new.

The advent of the trippers gave the boys a new way to make money. During the Easter holiday, and later after school each day, Bert raced round their regular customers while Albie worked with George, and when the last train of the day had taken its load of pink, sand-encrusted passengers home, Albie joined him to scour the beach for what he dubbed 'pirate treasure'. They searched under and around the pier, collecting all kinds of abandoned items which they sold to the rag-and-bone man, and beer bottles to take back to the pub for the deposit.

George would sit on his stool outside the helter-skelter, leaning back against the warm wood with a flask of tea, smoking and contemplating the beach while the boys scavenged. Trippers never saw this aspect of a seaside town – the part George loved the best. Seagulls strutted the sands and fought over dropped sandwiches; local men leaned on the prom railings for a smoke and a chat and a sight of the sea after a day at work; fishermen called to each other as they prepared their boats for the night, and kids from rich homes and poor ones had the entire beach as their playground. George had heard folk in the pubs singing the praises of London, where wages were better and you might see the King, and you could go to the cinema or a music-hall, but he'd take the seaside every time. Even in winter, when the gales howled and you couldn't walk along the prom without bending double, the pounding waves were better entertainment than any film or variety act.

Albie and Bert had been in the beach-combing business for about a week when opposition arrived in the form of Wally Biggins and his two side-kicks.

"This is our pitch!" Wally yelled from a hundred yards away. At the sound of Wally's half-broken voice George leaned over the rail, wondering if he'd have to intervene, but Albie answered from beneath the pier, "Not any more, it ain't — we been here months and not seen you."

"What do you mean - months?" Wally sneered, "It's been too bloody cold to be on the beach till now."

"We found this pram under the pier just after Christmas. Four months working this pitch makes it ours now."

George smiled to himself as a scuffle broke out beneath his feet, and when the scrap spilled into view he saw that Albie and Bert were holding their own against Wally and another lad. The fight almost covered the squeak of the pram wheels, but George recognized the sound and reacted in time to see the third boy pushing it across the damp sand on the other side of the pier. The thief had bounced it up the steps and reached the prom when George's meaty hand grabbed his collar and he growled, "Got you, my lad — thieving's a crime."

"It were only a joke, mister."

"You see me laughing? You'd better hope you ain't damaged it."

"Damaged it? It's just a rubbishy old pram."

"Rubbish or not, it ain't yours," said George, shaking his captive, "What's your name?"

"I ain't telling," the boy said but just then Albie and Bert arrived and Albie said, "That's Terry White - him and Fred Kelly are all that's left of Wally's gang."

"In that case I know all their dads," said George with a smile that made Terry cringe, "Any more trouble and I'll be round to see 'em, so bugger off and don't come back!"

CHAPTER FIVE – 1926 – BIKES

As spring moved into summer, Albie and Bert's daily scavenging yielded a richer harvest. Wally and his friends had obviously decided that with George a constant presence it would be wise to steer clear of their area of beach, and the months passed peacefully. With the aid of a garden sieve and two kiddies' spades, Albie and Bert sifted the sand around marks left by deck-chairs, unearthing coins and cigarette boxes, jewellery, and even the occasional pocket-watch or wallet. George made them hand in the wallets at the police station, but they turned anything else of value into cash at the pawn-broker and their saving jars filled up rapidly. By the time school opened again Albie was as brown as a hazelnut and Bert, cursed with the pale skin of a redhead, was sporting a healthy glow.

Even John Daly looked like a different man – tanned and weather-beaten from being out in all weathers. During the fruit-picking season he made an arrangement with a farmer to take away broken hop-poles for firewood in exchange for bringing groceries from town. When the coal miners stayed out long after the General Strike was over the demand for his supply of wood increased, and he found transporting the hop-poles in the pram a laborious business.

One warm September evening he called round to the Smiths' house breathless with excitement, saying, "I need to talk to the boys," and George and Dot listened with amusement when he addressed Albie and Bert as equals. "I've got the chance of buying a hand-cart. It's old but sound and I've beaten the price down, but I'm still a pound short. What would you say to selling the pram?"

"It's full of sand and all scratched," Albie said quickly, "It won't fetch a pound."

"It might if we do it up," said Bert, "And it's mostly Dad who uses it now – a hand-cart would be much better."

"I've got half a tin of red paint left from the ride," George offered and Albie was out-voted, but even after a good going-over and two coats of paint, the pram that had served them faithfully all spring and summer only fetched twelve shillings. The boys were at Bert's when his father came in with the bad news.

"Eight bob to find," he moaned, "And the man won't hold the cart for me much longer."

"I must have more than eight bob here," said Bert, emptying his savings jars onto the table, and when they counted up the coppers, Bert had nearly two pounds.

"We could've kept the pram after all," Albie said sulkily, "That was a handy size."

"Dad needs something bigger," Bert said, pushing a heap of coins across the table, and John scooped the money into his pocket and dashed off again to close the deal.

A couple of days later he and Bert wheeled the cart round to the Smiths' house. The wood had faded to grey but it was solid enough, and painted on the sides with the last of the red paint was the legend, 'DALY DELIVERIES'. George clapped John on the shoulder and laughed. "Daly Deliveries — that's a good one – folk'll find it hard to forget that name!"

"That's the idea," said John, "Can't take the credit though — our Bert dreamed it up."

Albie stared at the new name and said to Bert, "So we're not Albertie no more?"

"It's only a name, Albie – we've still got our own customers."

Albie shoved his hands deep into his pockets and slouched indoors, refusing to look any longer at the cart that Bert and his dad had painted without him, but then he saw his jam-jars on the mantelpiece and had a brainwave. He ran outside again and grabbed Bert's arm. "Tell you what, Bert — if you put the rest of your money in with mine we could ask the rag-and-bone man to look out for a couple of bikes —

Albertie will have its own transport after all."

*

By the end of the tripper season, when the wind whipped the
sand horizontal and no-one came down to sit on the sands, the
boys were the proud owners of two old bikes. Bert had the
smaller bike with a metal basket on the front that could hold a
whole box of groceries, and Albie, who was now several
inches taller than his friend, rode the larger one. George
helped him to fit a wooden box to the rack over the rear wheel,
and they soon learned to ride them.

The bikes meant that they got through their errands in
half the time, which was how Albie came home one day much
earlier than Dot had expected. As he took off his dirty boots on
a sheet of newspaper he sniffed appreciatively – Mum was
always cooking but a cake was a rare treat. "That smells
good!"

"You're not supposed to be home yet!" Dot cried,
standing with her back to the table and spreading her arms to
hide the ingredients, but Albie had already seen them. "Icing
an' all! What's that for?"

"Well, you've seen it now so I might as well tell you,"
Dot sighed, "It's a birthday cake."

"Who for?"

"For you, of course. Seeing as you don't know when
you were born, Dad and me decided on tomorrow — October
the eleventh – the day you came to live with us."

"Aw, Mum! I never had a birthday before, let alone a
cake!" Albie reached past Dot to wipe a none-too-clean finger
round the mixing bowl. "Icing tastes lovely — slap plenty on
won't yer?"

"I'll slap you if you don't go and wash your hands this
minute!"

At breakfast the next day Albie found two parcels
beside his plate — George had bought him a puncture-repair
kit to strap on his handlebars, and Dot had knitted him a

sleeveless pullover to go under his jacket. After school Bert came round for tea bringing a newspaper-wrapped parcel containing a water-proof cover for Albie's bicycle box.

"Mum made it out of an old mac Dad found," Bert told him, "I've got one too — we might need 'em now the rains have started."

The cake with its thirteen waxed candles was declared Dot's best ever, and when Bert went home she gave him the remainder, saying, "Your little ones can wish our Albie a happy birthday too."

"You're a star, Missus Smith," Bert said and pecked her cheek, but she pushed him away. "Get on with you! If Albie and George ate all that cake I'd have to let out their trousers!"

Later that night, lying on George's broad shoulder under their cosy eiderdown, Dot said, "You'd think Albie's mother would've marked his birthday at least. If I knew who she was I'd go round and give her a good slap."

"Then it's a good thing you don't know," George replied, kissing the top of Dot's head. He was grateful for the darkness that hid his guilty flush, but the next weekend his secret was revealed anyway.

He and Albie had gone to close up the helter-skelter securely for the winter, and were sheltering from the rain, sitting inside the ride on the pile of coir mats. When George struck a match to light a cigarette, the contrast was so stark that Albie remarked, "We could use a proper light in here."

"Can't think why," George replied, "We'd have to pay electric."

"My mum used to bypass the meter," Albie said, and then clapped his hand over his mouth. "Sorry, Dad – my *first* mum."

"No need to apologize, Albie — you had twelve years with her, when all's said and done." George pinched Albie's shoulder and added, "At least you've got some flesh on your bones now."

Albie shifted closer to George's comforting bulk and threw an arm across his legs, saying, "That's down to this Mum's cooking." The sound of rain on the wooden wall was loud in the dusty space, and his thoughts went their own way. "She moved out of the yard, you know – I went round at Christmas and someone else was living there – I wonder where she is now."

George took a deep breath and said, "She went off to London with some bloke. I asked around and the landlord at the Kings Head told me."

Every muscle in Albie's body tensed, catapulting him out of the doorway to cling to the pier rail with white-knuckled hands. George stayed put with an effort – the woman had been Albie's mother, after all, and he had a right to be upset – but after a while he called, "You all right, son?"

"She just effed off and never give me another thought – I could of been dead for all she cared!" Albie yelled, and dashed off to the promenade and away.

"Bloody hell!" George swore. He waited until it was clear Albie wasn't coming back before locking up and then went into the tea-rooms. He nursed one cup of tea after another, sitting by the window and wiping the steam away every few minutes to peer towards the town, but there was no sign of Albie all afternoon. At four o'clock the pier manager closed up and George trailed home, as reluctantly as a schoolboy with a bad report, to be met at the door by Dot.

"What did you say to him?" she hissed, jerking her thumb at Albie slumped by the range swathed in a blanket, "He come in soaked through and wouldn't say a word."

George glanced up at the dryer where Albie's clothes still dripped. "He asked about his first mum," he said, his face purple with guilt, "And I said she'd gone to London."

"You never told me that, so why did you have to go and tell him?" Dot's voice rose with indignation and Albie lifted his head. "I had to find out one day, Mum, and it ain't

Dad's fault – I did ask."

"But that was hours ago, son," said George, "Where've you been all this time?"

"Went to Nan's, didn't I," Albie mumbled, "Thought she might know who my dad was – my *first* dad, I mean."

George was relieved to spot the glimmer of a smile when Albie corrected himself, and although he dreaded the answer he had to ask, "What did she say?"

"Not much," Albie shrugged, "She wouldn't let me in the door – but she did tell me my mum got me off a gypsy at hop-picking time."

"We'll have no more talk of gypsies in this house," Dot said severely, "You're ours now, so you can forget about anything else."

Albie's eyes lit up with pure mischief. "When's hop-picking, Dad?"

"August time usually – why?"

"Bert says it takes nine months to grow a baby so that would make my birthday in May."

"Well, we're not about to change it now," Dot snapped, "October it is and October it stays. And you and Bert have got no business talking about babies at your age – whatever next!"

*

Albie and Bert had bought the bikes to use as delivery vehicles, but on the occasional dry Sunday that winter they began exploring further afield. Thambay was surrounded by fields full of food crops and hop vines, with farming hamlets and little villages tucked into odd corners, and the gentle hills of north Kent were easy to negotiate. Bert viewed these excursions as fact-finding missions – his choice of reading material always involved soldiers or spies – but Albie simply loved the outdoors. He felt his soul expanding every time they left the streets of town behind them, and he was very glum when the snow forced them to put their bikes away and get out the shovels.

It was February before they got them out again, and with tyres newly pumped up and chains freshly oiled they covered their regular round quickly once more. On their first Sunday afternoon George assured them he couldn't smell rain, so Albie persuaded Bert to cycle out between the bare hedges and into the countryside. Albie led the way, and after twenty minutes or so Bert said, "This is the road where we found that big branch — the one that started Daly Deliveries."

"Is it?" said Albie with an air of innocence, "Maybe the winter storms have brought down some more," but then he stopped suddenly, dismounted and disappeared behind a tall hedge saying, "Won't be a sec!"

"Come over shy, have you?" Bert laughed, but Albie swiftly reappeared with an armful of hay which he stuffed into the box on his bike-rack. "Thought I remembered seeing a haystack there," he said and cycled off. Bert followed him, puzzled, but a minute later Albie stopped again beside a five-bar gate and dismounted.

"Oh no!" Bert groaned as light dawned, "You've come to see that horse."

"It might not be here," Albie said, climbing onto the gate, but a 'harrumph' came from the far side of the field and the shaggy horse cantered into view over a rise, making straight for him. It was moving so fast that it looked ready to jump the gate and Bert backed away, but the horse slowed to a walk and then stopped with its nose against Albie's chest, blowing damply into his shirt-front. Balancing on the gate with the top bar digging into his hips, Albie murmured softly into its ear while the long yellow teeth tugged at the bundle of hay under his arm. He ran his free hand confidently up the side of the big black head and pulled on an ear, then wove his fingers through the coarse mane. The horse was small compared with the carthorse that delivered barrels of ale to the Kings Head but it was still enormous, and Bert trembled when Albie rested his forehead against the hard square face.

"Come on, Albie, what if someone sees us?" Bert said, and Albie withdrew his hand reluctantly from the horse's mane. As he did so he smelled smoke and heard the crackle of burning wood. Perhaps this is a gypsy horse, he thought with a surge of excitement, but Bert hissed, "A motorcar's coming!" and he jumped down. Holding their bikes, they stood looking innocent and the driver acknowledged them with a wave.

When Albie turned round the horse had gone. He slumped with disappointment, but then he caught another whiff of smoke and he was half-way over the gate when Bert asked, "Where you going?"

"To find the gypsy camp – I can smell smoke."

"I can't smell any," Bert said, "And what if they kidnap you? My mum says they steal kids."

"You can stop here, then, and hold the bikes."

"Not blooming likely! You ain't leaving me alone in all this countryside." Bert was obviously scared, so Albie climbed reluctantly down from the gate.

He came back the next day after school but the horse didn't appear again, and although he searched everywhere there was neither sign nor smell of a camp-fire.

*

A few weekends later Bert arrived at Albie's with his basket overflowing. "Dad says we've got to take these groceries to Pinetree Farm — he's having a lie-in 'cause he were out all night."

Dot's ears pricked up at the hint of a bit of gossip. "Your dad out all night? That ain't like him."

Bert didn't disappoint her. Tapping the side of his nose conspiratorially he said, "Missus Timson had to move a bit sudden-like, but don't let on Dad helped her."

"Mum's the word," Dot said, her eyes gleaming with malice – a moonlight flit was wonderful fuel for a good gossip.

"The landlord says we can have her place," Bert added, "Mum went round this morning. We'll be two streets nearer you and we'll have all the downstairs and a yard for Dad's stuff." This was good news indeed – since John Daly had begun working with the boys, the amount of wood and scrap stored in the Smiths' yard had increased enormously and Dot would be glad to see the back of it. "When are you moving?" she asked.

"Next weekend. Mum told the landlord Missus Timson was a slovenly cow, and she'll only take the place if she can go in and scrub it all out first."

Leaving Dot and George to chew over Gladys Daly's nerve at talking to the powerful landlord in such a fashion, the boys divided the groceries between them and set off.

"Pinetree Farm's not far from your horse," Bert said and Albie rode faster, but the wind and rain were sweeping across the open fields and it was too cold to stop. They pedalled hard with heads down, sheltering their eyes under the peaks of their caps, but by the time they reached Pinetree Farm they were soaked — only the waterproof covers had saved the bags of sugar and currants from the same fate.

Ruth Finch the farmer's wife was used to worse than water dripping on the flags of her kitchen and she beckoned the boys into the steamy warmth, where a small blond boy looked up from a jigsaw puzzle."Hello, I'm Luke – who are you?"

"They've brought the groceries, love," Ruth said. "Leave those bicycles in the porch, boys — I expect you could use a hot drink?" and then she raised her voice to a shout that Albie reckoned would reach across several fields. "Bessie!" As she put two mugs on the scrubbed table in front of them, a girl wearing a pinafore over her dress came running in and Mrs Finch told her to take the shopping through to the larder.

Bessie pouted, "Luke could've done that," but she did as she was told and then sat on the form opposite Albie. "Bert was here last year fruit-picking, but why ain't I seen you before?"

"I were helping Dad on the pier all summer," Albie said, and as Luke's mouth dropped open in envy, Bessie cried theatrically, "Oh! I love the pier! My favourite's the roundabout."

"That's all right, I s'pose, but our helter-skelter's the best ride."

"But it's so high up! I'd be scared to death."

Young Luke rolled his eyes at Bert – it was so obvious Bessie was hoping Albie would offer to share a mat with her — but to their amusement Albie didn't take the hint. "Best stick to the roundabout, then," he said dismissively and put his mug down, "Ta for the tea, missus — just the job, that were. Come on, Bert, we got work waiting."

"But it's still raining," Bessie said, "Won't you stay till it eases off?"

Mrs Finch glanced sharply at her daughter – it wasn't like Bessie to be this thoughtful – and got her purse out to pay. Picking up the grocer's bill she exclaimed, "Nearly a shilling for sugar! I thought prices were supposed to have come down!" and she was so incensed that she forgot to add the usual delivery charge. Bert hesitated with the cash on his open palm, unsure how to ask, but Mrs Finch realized her mistake. "Eeh, Bert, I'm sorry! Here's yours. Wait a minute – have a slice of cake as well." The boys returned to their bikes each clutching wedge of fruit cake that must have weighed a good half pound, and as they negotiated the puddles and cowpats of the farmyard, Bert said to Albie, "That Bessie fancies you!"

"Don't talk rot! What would I want with a girl?"

"You could do worse," Bert said seriously, "Farmer's daughter an' all – always plenty to eat on a farm."

"Girls are silly," said Albie, "We get 'em round the ride all giggling and screaming and fretting about their hair. You can keep 'em."

"Just you wait!" said Bert with elderly wisdom, "If she wants you she'll be round."

CHAPTER SIX – BESSIE

Bessie Finch was fourteen and a half – a year older than the boys – and almost a woman. As well as Luke she had two older brothers, and spent her days helping her mother cater for the needs of a household of men. Together they prepared meals for the family and for farmhands, some of whom slept in the barn loft and needed feeding at night as well as midday. They washed clothes made filthy by farm-work and fought a constant battle, with the help of a part-time maid, against the dirt that invaded the house.

Bessie always looked forward to the weekly trip to market as a change of scene, but the Saturday after Bert and Albie's visit she braided her hair with more care than usual before climbing onto the cart beside her mother.

Setting up the trestles under the arches round the Market Hall, Bessie joined in with the usual banter between the stall-holders, and when the son of their nearest neighbours tugged her pigtail and asked, "Who're you all prettied up for, Bessie?" she tossed her head and shot back, "Not you, that's for sure, Timmy Coppin!"

"Ooh – hoity-toity miss!" laughed Timmy, not a bit abashed, "I'll have a kiss off you before summer, you see if I don't!"

Hiding her blushes, Bessie climbed into the cart to unload the butter and cheeses and eggs, telling herself she wasn't 'prettied up' for anyone in particular, but between customers she watched the four roads that led into the square, hoping for a glimpse of the tall boy with the grey eyes.

The early rush was over and Ruth Finch had gone for a cup of tea in the tea-shop when Bessie spotted two bikes entering the square. As Albie and Bert skidded to a halt on the cobbles, Bessie smoothed her braids and practised her pout, but then a woman asked her for a pound of cheese, and Bessie was so intent on watching Albie that she cut her hand with the cheese-wire.

"Careful there, my girl!" her customer exclaimed, "My old man won't eat it if it's all bloody!" When the cheese was wrapped and stowed in her capacious basket the woman wanted butter and eggs, and by the time she'd gone, so had Albie.

Ruth returned to find Bessie in a foul mood, and she sighed at the thought of how much easier it was bringing up boys. "It's not too busy at the moment, dear," she said, "You have a look round for ten minutes," and Bessie shot off without even asking for her usual shilling. She peered down each street in turn and searched between the stalls, all without success, and she was on her way back to their own stall when Timmy Coppin blocked her path and asked, "Do you want a ride in my dad's motor?" Bessie was instantly diverted – her brothers couldn't stop talking about Farmer Coppin's motor car — but she scoffed, "You can't drive a motor!"

"Can too!" Timmy retorted, "Not on the main road, mind – not yet — but I've been driving it around the farm lanes. Come up tomorrow afternoon and I'll show you." He winked suggestively and Bessie was suddenly aware of how big and handsome he was.

"I'll have to ask my mum," she said, pleating her apron with her fingers.

"That's up to you," Timmy shrugged, "I'll be by the copse in Bottom Meadow after dinner tomorrow — see you there?"

"I'm not sure," said Bessie, edging towards her mother and safety, but Timmy said, "Suit yourself – there's plenty of others I could ask," and Bessie was hooked.

It was easy to slip away after Sunday dinner because Sunday afternoons were when Dad and Mum disappeared upstairs for 'a bit of a lie-down'. Growing up on a farm had left Bessie with few illusions as to what that meant. Her own ripening body had begun to form images of that 'lie-down' –

images which embarrassed yet excited her and which only escape from the house could dispel.

She thought no-one had seen her and nearly jumped out of her skin when her little brother yelled from the home barn, "Where are you going, Bessie?"

"None of your business!" she snapped, "Just going for a walk."

"Can I come?" Luke pleaded — Sunday afternoons were boring.

"No you can't, and stop pestering me," Bessie snarled over her shoulder and hurried on, careful to watch where she was walking — she didn't want to turn up for a ride in a motor car with cow-muck on her boots.

Luke was just seven, born after Adam Finch came back from the trenches to pick up the reins of the farm with only half the workforce he had had in 1914 – and most of them old or lame or both. His two older sons had still been schoolboys then, and Bessie a spoilt five-year-old who barely recognized her father. The birth of Luke, conceived in the passion of relief to be home safe and whole, had come as a shock, but was ultimately of less consequence than the births of the calves and lambs that would put the farm back on a sound footing.

Pete and Brian were big strapping lads now and the farm was prospering, and Ruth had Bessie to help in the house, but the habit of treating Luke like one of the orphan lambs was ingrained in the entire family. He was kept warm and fed but otherwise generally ignored and left to his own devices.

Until he went to school Luke's only playmate had been Bessie, and over this past year even she had begun to shut him out. He fed the chickens and knew all the corners they were likely to lay their eggs: the farm cats tolerated his handling of their kittens in exchange for the bits of meat he brought them: the huge brindled sow recognized his step and would rear up for him to scratch between her ears with a stick. Starved of human company, Luke made friends with every animal on the farm, and from playing his solitary games he knew every corner – not much escaped his sharp little eyes.

He had been building a fort to defend against Indians when he saw Bessie scuttling across the yard looking furtive, and at her rebuff he went back to it, but then he changed his mind. In an instant he was no longer the Fastest Gun in the West but a Faithful Indian Scout with the eyes of a hawk, tracking a Band of Outlaws. He stuck a pigeon feather into the back of his cap and ran to the gate, noting a fresh boot-print at the base of the wall and some mud stuck to the bottom bar. "Bad men go this way," he muttered and slipped through the gate. He found another print on the clump of grass and tracked the Outlaws round the barn, across the field and through a gap in the hedge just as the last Outlaw left the second field over a stile.

The Indian Scout patted his mouth and whispered a war-cry then slid like a shadow along the hedge, unseen by the herd of buffalo which would trample him to death if they decided to charge. There was a footprint right in the middle of the stile and he peered up and down the lane – mustn't be spotted by their lookouts – before running across in a crouch and squirming under the second stile to lie safely hidden in the long grass. His hand closed on a piece of wood and, armed now with his trusty tomahawk, he lifted his head just in time to see the Outlaw disappear into the copse on the far side of the field. So their hideout was in the forest, was it?

Keeping his eyes on the forest in case of ambush, he held his tomahawk ready to fight off any attack and ran, swift and silent as a coyote, to the edge of the copse. When he paused to listen, something nudged his shoulder and he jumped violently, but it was only an inquisitive horse. He rubbed its nose and put his fingers to his lips. "Shush, Brother Horse — if bad men come, you warn?" he whispered, and then he was among the trees and undergrowth and had to place his moccasins extra carefully, testing the ground for twigs, for an incautious step would earn him a painful death over a slow fire.

Bessie was in a high old state of nerves. She was sure Mum hadn't seen her, but she'd forgotten that Luke saw everything, and he knew she wasn't supposed to leave their farm without telling Mum. Still, she'd sort him out later — a bribe and a threat combined usually did the trick. She checked her boots again for cow-muck and scraped them on a fallen branch just to make sure. The copse was very quiet and she moved faster, suddenly afraid she might be late. What if Timmy wasn't there? She'd feel a fool for walking across Coppin land if he hadn't meant it. And she'd said she'd have to ask her Mum! She squirmed with embarrassment at the memory. Timmy Coppin was seventeen and she'd bet the other girls he asked out didn't have to ask their mums first.

Bessie shivered, wondering if he'd try to kiss her today and unsure whether she wanted him to. Alice, one of the dairymaids, said you had to put your head on one side or you'd bump noses and sometimes they put their tongue in your mouth. Bessie didn't like the sound of that at all but she'd practised last night on her hand just in case. And did you keep your eyes open or shut them? With a tight knot in the pit of her stomach she walked through the copse to the lane that bisected it and hesitated on the grass verge – had Timmy meant her to meet him here or in Bottom Meadow? She was just about to go and look in the meadow when she heard the clatter and bang of a motorcar and froze.

Peering round a tree-trunk, Luke froze too. He knew that sound – it was Farmer Coppin's motor car! The wonderful contraption pulled up only yards away, just beside Bessie, but it wasn't Farmer Coppin who leaned from the driver's seat.

"I can't stop or I'll never get her going again!" Luke heard Timmy Coppin shout over the noise of the engine, then Bessie put her foot on the running-board, took Timmy's out-stretched hand, and climbed in beside him. As the motorcar juddered off down the farm track, Luke was left gasping with jealousy. Of all the mean things his sister had done, this was the meanest. He dashed his fists across his face to wipe off the angry tears and plodded back home plotting revenge. Bessie'd be in really hot water when he told Mum and Dad about this.

By the time he was back in the home barn his anger had cooled and hardened and he'd decided to keep his mouth shut. If Bessie could get a ride in the motor car, then the threat of Mum and Dad finding out should be enough to make her take him next time. He demolished the fort and built a motor car, turned his cap backwards so it wouldn't blow off in the rush of air over his windshield, and when the bell rang for tea he drove into the kitchen at a splendid twenty miles an hour.

Bessie *had* been kissed — an awkward affair of bumped noses and intruding gear-sticks and the need to keep the engine running. She hadn't liked it much but it was her first kiss. She was too distracted to eat her tea, nibbling at her food and dropping most of it under the table for the old house dog. Her mother was in too mellow a mood after the long afternoon of loving to notice how quiet Bessie was, and her big brothers — who had cycled into town to play football and drink a few pints – filled the kitchen with enough noise for a whole football team. Bessie slipped away to her bedroom early without causing comment, but Luke smiled to himself and hugged his secret knowledge.

*

When Bessie sneaked out the next Sunday Luke followed her again, but to his intense disappointment Timmy Coppin didn't bring the motor car – he just grabbed Bessie and kissed her before leading her further into the copse. Luke pulled a face – if they were going to be kissing he didn't want to be anywhere near them – so he emerged from his hiding-place and mooched back to the barn to play with the latest batch of kittens.

The next week though, when Bessie went to meet Timmy for the third time, Luke couldn't resist the challenge. Tracking her was easy because he knew where she was going, but remaining undetected was tricky; several times Bessie turned round suddenly and almost caught him out in the open. Luke wasn't surprised she was nervous – if either of them were caught leaving the farm there'd be trouble – but he had to trail so far behind that he nearly missed their meeting. He looked away while they kissed, but when Timmy pulled Bessie into Bottom Meadow and inside the barn, Luke camouflaged his cap with some greenery and crawled through the new grass to the barn wall. He pressed his ear to a crack between the boards just in time to hear Timmy say, "Take your coat off, Bessie." Luke frowned – it was too cold for taking coats off – but then Bessie said, "No – and leave my buttons alone," and then there were kissing noises, so Luke retreated to the trees.

Bessie would never have known he'd been there if he hadn't stepped on a dead branch – the crack as it snapped sent an entire rookery cawing into the sky. Luke made a dash for it, but as luck would have it, Farmer Coppin was driving his motor car along the lane. As Luke ducked back into the hedge Bessie's arm snaked round his neck, half-choking him. "What are you up to, you little monster? I'll tell Mum you left the farm."

Luke raked his boots down Bessie's shins and she dropped him. He raced across the lane and dived through a small hole in the other hedge before Bessie could climb the stile, and he was well out of her reach in the cow pasture before he turned and yelled, "You tell Mum on me and I'll tell her you went in their barn."

Bessie stopped dead. She didn't know what Luke had seen that afternoon and she was afraid to ask, but the fear of her mother finding out was enough to make her mind up. She had got used to the strange feeling of Timmy's tongue in her mouth, but the only thrill she got from their meetings was their clandestine nature – if there was any danger of her mother finding out, they would have to stop. She was surprised to discover she was more relieved than disappointed once the decision was made.

After lunch the following Sunday she made a big production of collecting the ingredients to make a cake and spent the whole afternoon in the kitchen, even going so far as to call Luke inside to lick out the bowl.

"You not going for a walk today, Bessie?" he asked slyly.

"Can't be bothered. You want this or shall I let Ben have it?" and Luke snatched the bowl before she could put it on the floor for the old sheepdog. He drew a spiral pattern in the creamy brown mixture and licked his finger with slow relish. "Look, Bessie – I've drawn a helter-skelter!"

Bessie's hands stopped in the act of closing a packet of currants as she remembered unpacking them from the box on Albie's bike. "Tell you what, Luke – shall we ask Mum and Dad to take us on the pier next week?"

*

For a family that lived only a few miles inland, the Finches saw the sea less often than the weekend trippers. The pier was humming with activity when they arrived, and Bessie spent the first few minutes simply revelling in the bustle and colour, then Timmy waved and called her name and she was so pleased that she forgot all about Albie and ran to join him.

Luke went to the railing to watch the line of men fishing from the lower level, while Adam and Ruth Finch linked arms and strolled along the boardwalk. They stopped every few yards to talk to friends and acquaintances, Adam to discuss Russia and politics while the women criticised the London fashions that the sun had brought out.

As they walked away from the third such conversation Ruth said, "I'd never get into one of those straight-up-and-down dresses!"

Adam slipped his arm round her waist and squeezed. "No flesh on them at all, these modern women — I prefer something I can get hold of." Ruth blushed scarlet and slid out of his embrace. "Adam Finch – we're right out in the open!" She looked round to make sure no-one was watching and murmured, "We'll go upstairs after tea if you like. Now where's Luke got to?"

Adam pecked her cheek and went to join Luke at the rail. "Which ride do you fancy, son? You can have three goes."

Luke was overwhelmed by the choice of rides. The Gallopers looked exciting, but Bessie had got there first and she scowled at him to go away. There was another roundabout with a giant teapot in the middle surrounded by teacups which he would have dismissed as too babyish if he hadn't seen one of his school-mates in the queue. "I'll go on this one first," he decided and Adam handed over the money.

The ride *was* a bit tame, but Luke and Gerald pretended they were driving a lorry which made it better, and after that they went on the Gallopers together. Bessie was round the other side so she couldn't see them, and Luke and Gerald rode Blaze and Hercules as hard as they could, Cowboys chasing Indians.

When Gerald's mum took him off for an icecream, Luke had used up two of his rides and the afternoon had only just started. He stood hopefully beside the Chair-O-Planes that swung their occupants right out over the sea, but the man said he was too small for the chairs. Still trying to make up his mind, he watched Dad have a go at the Shooting Gallery and win a vase for Mum, but after he won a cowboy hat and plonked it on Luke's head the man refused to take his money any more, saying, "You're a farmer, aincher? Been shooting rabbits for years, I shouldn't wonder, and I've got a living to make," and Luke's small chest swelled with pride — his Dad was too good a shot for the pier! He begged his last pennies from Dad, shoved them in the pocket that didn't have a hole, and went back to the Gallopers, but Bessie was still on them — Timmy must have paid for her to stay on the roundabout. Timmy was holding on with only one hand and Luke thought he'd try doing that next time, but when the roundabout stopped his mother called, "Bessie – Luke — time to start back."

"We can't go yet," Luke wailed, "Dad said I could have three goes and I've only had two!"

"We're going home for tea, dear," his mother said, catching her husband's eye.

"Fair's fair, Ruth, I did promise," said Adam, "The helter-skelter's right here, Luke — have a go on that — but it's straight home afterwards."

When Luke joined the queue Bessie remembered it was Albie she'd come here to see, and found him tidying the mats by George's stool. "So this is where you've been hiding!" she said archly.

"I ain't hiding – I work here," said Albie, "Where else would I be?"

"Bert's been back twice with groceries but you didn't come with him."

"Didn't come where?"

"To the farm, of course!" said Bessie impatiently.

"Oh, that farm – I remember now — your mum give us cake."

"I helped make that cake — did you like it?"

"Never had any — Bert took it home." Albie caught George's look, interpreted it as a reminder that there were mats to fetch, and went to get them.

Bessie flounced off thinking that if Albie wouldn't notice her she'd try Timmy again, but she was too late – he was already sharing some candyfloss bite for bite with another girl. When Luke's mat shot off the end of the slide Bessie was waiting for him, and it was with something approaching relief that George watched them leave. That Finch girl must be a good year older than Albie but she was obviously setting her cap at him. He'd lay odds she'd be back — when Albie started noticing girls, Bessie Finch could spell trouble.

*

The candyfloss machine had been imported from America by the toffee apple man whose kiosk was directly opposite the helter-skelter. It attracted a huge crowd, some actually to buy and bury their faces in the sweet balls of fluff, but many more simply to watch and marvel at the magical transformation of a jug of sugar into fine-spun gossamer threads. This new attraction also increased George's trade and, with more sunny days than cloudy ones, April and May were busy months.

One day Albie was collecting mats from the bottom cushion, wondering why there were no more coming down, when a chorus of shouts and screams from above alerted him to trouble. George was herding the queue back outside when Albie reached the door. "Nip up top and see what's happening, Albie, but for heaven's sake don't start a panic."

Albie had difficulty squeezing past the customers who were packed tight on the narrow stairs. Only those near the bottom were responding to George's instructions to "Come out of there" — the rest of them continued to push upwards. Tempers began to fray in the thick heat, people started shouting, and several mats were dropped. When someone almost toppled Albie over the handrail he'd had enough. "There's trouble up top," he yelled, "So all of you stop shoving and let me past to sort it!"

A few people muttered "Cheeky young bugger!" but they let him past and Albie finally managed to reach the platform. There were six people standing in the tiny space, each one holding a bulky coir mat, and one boy was sitting at the top of the slide with his feet on the next boy's back. Albie peered round the curve and saw the head of a girl in front of him and another boy beyond her. "Gawd, what a mess!" he muttered under his breath.

"That's my sister Bessie down there," said a large young man, "What're you going to do? She's too scared to move."

Albie grabbed the top boy and hauled him back onto the platform, told the next boy to crawl past him, and then slid onto his mat behind the blonde curls. A tear-stained face looked round and Albie recognized the girl from Pinetree Farm – now he thought about it, she seemed to have been around a lot lately – and he said quietly, "Bessie, you've got to crawl over me," but she gripped her mat with white-knuckled fists and shook her head. Her brother called, "Come on Bessie," but still she wouldn't move, so Albie leaned forward and prised her fingers open, then held her tight and wriggled backwards until her brother could take her. Albie tapped the broad shoulder of the last customer. "Come on, mate – let me see what the problem is," he said, and the boy turned his head and sneered, "My mat's stuck, and if you looked after the ride proper it wouldn't've happened."

Albie clenched his jaw – it *would* be Wally Biggins, wouldn't it – but he merely said, "You going to climb back and let me look at it or what?"

"What – climb over you? No thanks!"

"It's that or slide down on your bum," Albie said impatiently, and finally Wally wriggled past him, contriving to dig his heel into his crotch as he went. Albie peeled Wally's mat upwards and groaned when a hundred sticky threads stretched between it and the slide – someone had dropped candyfloss. Even if he removed the mat the slide would still be too sticky for the crowd on the platform to ride down. He crawled back to be confronted by a sea of angry faces.

"Last time I come on this bloody ride!" Bessie's brother said, and Wally's voice led a chorus of agreement. Albie knew this could ruin them — all it took was a rumour of bad maintenance to kill a ride stone dead. Then he spotted a sticky residue round Wally's mouth, grabbed him by the shirt-front and turned him to face the others. "Look at his face! Wally dropped his candyfloss and stuck his own mat to the slide — it says on the entrance no food's allowed."

Wally squirmed free of Albie's grip and retorted, "Candyfloss ain't food!" but Bessie's brother growled, "So it's your fault my sister's been scared out of her wits, is it?" In a calmer voice he asked Albie, "Can you fix it? I don't fancy backing down the stairs."

Albie thought fast — what he really needed was a bucket of soapy water but that would take too long to fetch – then inspiration struck. "Won't take a minute then you can follow me down," he said cheerfully and slid back down over the line of mats until he was far enough round the curve to be invisible from the platform. Grinning at his own nerve, he un-buttoned his fly and soaked Wally's mat with as much piss as he could squeeze out, braced his feet against the sides and used the soggy mat to scrub vigorously. When he yelled, "Done it!" Bessie's brother pulled back all the other mats and Albie let himself go, clutching the ruined mat to his chest and polishing the slide with the seat of his short trousers as he went. George waited at the bottom until all the customers had ridden down safely, but Wally ran off before he could grab him to exact revenge.

"I'll watch those kids like a hawk after this," said George, "Candyfloss, toffee apples, sandwiches – I'll frisk 'em myself if I have to." He grinned at Albie, "You done a good job there, son, but you'd best not tell Mum how you did it – she'd throw a fit."

CHAPTER SEVEN – 1927 – GYPSIES

Albie and Bert still went foraging on their area of the sands each evening but at weekends, while Albie was with George, Bert went out with his dad. When the six-week summer break was a few days away, he told Albie, "You'll have to do the beach on your own in the holidays — I won't be back before dark."

"You going fruit picking again?"

"Got to be done," said Bert, kicking a sand-castle over, "We need the money – my sister May's coming too."

"Any gypsies arrived yet?" Albie asked casually.

"There's some camping on Pinetree land by the cherry orchard," Bert said and grinned wickedly. "None of 'em look like you, but you could always come picking and see for yourself."

"Couldn't leave Dad on his own," Albie said with a tinge of regret, "And I know you think it's stupid but it bugs me not knowing who I am."

"You're Albie Smith and my best mate," said Bert, punching Albie on the arm, "I'll give your love to Bessie Finch, shall I?"

"Don't you dare! She's enough of a pain as it is, hanging round here every Sunday."

*

Partly out of a sense of loyalty to George and Dot but chiefly out of nervousness, Albie resisted the lure of the gypsies for a week, but eventually the need to find out overcame his reservations and one evening he rode out to Pinetree Farm. The scent of a bonfire told him he had found the campsite, so he hid his bike in a hedge and crept closer, his footsteps muffled by the long grass. He was amazed to hear a man's voice murmuring the same sounds he had used to the carthorse. Horse-talk, Bert had called it, and this man was using it too, which must prove Albie was a gypsy. His gasp of astonishment alerted the man, who moved swiftly to bar his way. "What do you want, boy?"

Albie stared at the man dumbly. Hair as dark as his own curled over black eyes set in a brown face, and more curls showed in the open neck of the man's collarless shirt. Past his shoulder Albie saw a woman stirring a pot suspended over a fire, and two small children stared at him wide-eyed.

"Cat got your tongue, boy? Run away from home to join the gypsies, have you?" The sneer in the man's voice brought the blood rushing to Albie's cheeks and he blurted out, "I'm looking for my father – I think he was a gypsy."

The man barked a laugh. "Well, you're too old to be mine." His hand shot out to grasp Albie's arm. "But if you're looking for a home…"

"I've got a home," Albie said hurriedly, tore his arm free, and ran off followed by the sound of mocking laughter. He rode home through a mist of tears. That had been a waste of time. He'd hoped for a look of recognition on someone's face — a sense of belonging. George and Dot were Dad and Mum now and they loved him, but they weren't his own blood. His real mum had abandoned him and all he wanted was for his real dad to acknowledge him. Was that too much to ask? But that man had nearly kidnapped him – he'd have to be more careful. He pedalled back to Thambay as if the Devil was after him, burst into the kitchen and surprised Dot with a hug. She sniffed his hair and said, "You smell of bonfires – what have you been up to?"

Albie slipped out of her embrace. "Nothing, Mum – a farmer was burning leaves," he said, and George, who was sitting by the range with his paper, smiled and said nothing – Albie was a growing lad, and as long as he stayed out of trouble he was entitled to a few secrets.

Albie thought about that meeting for days afterwards, and finally came to the conclusion that he'd just picked the wrong set of gypsies – he'd have to widen his search. Every so often after that, when Bert was helping his father with Daly Deliveries, Albie would cycle off in a new direction. Usually he would simply ride, bowling along the gently sloping lanes of Kent between fields and orchards, but if he smelled smoke he would track it down like a hungry boy following the scent of baking. Often he found only a gardener burning weeds; or he'd watch a sickle of fire creeping across a field of stubble. Once he clung to a hedge while a fire-engine clanged past and then pedalled furiously behind it to watch the volunteer firemen extinguish a thatch fire.

But occasionally he came across a circle of wagons and tents where a group of dark-faced people would stop what they were doing to stare at him. He never saw the same group twice, but at one camp – the fifth or sixth one he had found — a man actually talked to him; at another a man asked his name, and at a different camp he was startled when a man called him 'young Smith' when he shooed him away. As he rode off it occurred to Albie that gossip and rumour spread through the separate camps just like in a town, and the gypsies were telling each other about him.

His mind was buzzing too loudly for him to go straight home that day. Seeking a sympathetic ear, he went to the field where the horse lived, stood on the gate and whistled, hoping he hadn't picked a day when it wasn't there, but he didn't have to wait long before the warm nose was nuzzling the hay from beneath his arm. "One of these days I'm going to find my real dad," he confided in one sensitive ear. The horse snorted and Albie laughed, "You don't believe me, do you? I got gypsy blood, I tell you. I just got this feeling if I don't look too hard he'll turn up." He waited until his friend had eaten every wisp of hay and then rode home contentedly — talking to the horse always helped him sort out his thoughts.

*

That evening, knowing that Albie would be out for at least an hour, George and Dot had taken the opportunity for a proper all-over wash in the tin bath in front of the range. George was sitting with his knees up to his chin, thinking about Albie. The lad was officially approaching fourteen, but he looked older. His voice had broken and he had more than a hint of bum-fluff on his chin. He was already as tall as George, and the boy who had struggled to haul two mats with his skinny arms two years ago now picked up a pile of them without even breaking into a sweat. He was beginning to attract the girls, too. When the hop-pickers had arrived a couple of weeks ago, George noticed quite a few of the London girls hanging round the helter-skelter trying to catch Albie's attention. It was good for business of course, but their presence kept George and Albie on their toes, for these Londoners tried every trick in the book to sneak in without paying.

George thought sometimes that even one of the sharp-tongued Londoners would be preferable to Bessie Finch, who turned up on the pier practically every weekend. She'd arrive on her bike and somehow it had become his job to make sure no-one nicked it while she wandered round. The girl was turning into a right little hussy too, because when she rode the helter-skelter she never tucked her skirt between her legs, and lay sprawled with her knickers showing for much longer than necessary. George would have said something if Albie had shown the slightest interest, but he didn't even look and besides, what was there to say?

Dot took the flannel out of his hand to wash his back. "What's bothering you, love? You ain't said a word since you got in the bath."

As George relaxed under her ministrations he told her all about Bessie's behaviour.

"You want my advice," Dot said as she rinsed off the soap with a jug of fresh water, "You won't say nothing to Albie. It's hard enough growing up these days with everything changing so quick – motorcars and now aeroplanes going faster than is natural – Albie don't need you to point him to trouble. You just keep an eye open and your mouth shut."

George stepped out onto the rag rug in front of the range, and when Dot wrapped the towel round his middle he slid his wet arms round her waist. "I can't help fretting, love. Albie saw more than a kid should before he came to us." He didn't need to elaborate – Dot knew exactly what he meant but she had a different slant on it. "Probably put him off – have you thought of that?"

"Now you've given me summat else to fret over," said George and pulled on his pyjamas while Dot washed quickly, afraid Albie would be home before she was decent.

They were sitting over a pot of tea when Albie came in and Dot sniffed as he wheeled his bike through. "You smell of beer – you've not been in the pub, have you?"

"Only taking bottles back – one weren't empty and it spilled."

"Well, you leave that shirt in the sink and get in the bath before you go anywhere near my nice clean sheets!"

Albie grinned at her cheerfully. "Not with you in the kitchen, Mum. You go on up – I'll empty it when I'm done."

Dot went upstairs, but George lingered over the dregs of his tea, chatting idly while Albie bathed in the luke-warm water, and he noted without actually staring that the boy had become a man. "You got a girl-friend yet, Albie?" he asked with studied carelessness.

"Me? When would I get the time? Couple of them hop-pickers offered, mind." Albie laughed at George's horrified expression. "Thought that'd get you going! Don't you fret, Dad, none of 'em's my type — too pushy by half."

As they emptied the tin bath George concluded that Albie would probably be all right. At least he'd started looking, and if he didn't like pushy girls, Bessie hadn't a hope.

CHAPTER EIGHT – 1927 — HERO

Working all summer on the farm was sending Bessie nearly mad with boredom. Every Sunday afternoon – her only time off – she cycled into town to meet her friends on the pier where she tried to flirt with Albie, but his lack of response was depressing. She was just setting off one week when she met Timmy Coppin driving his cart. "Where are you off to, Bessie?" he asked and she replied quickly, "Nowhere special — give me a ride?"

This chimed so perfectly with Timmy's own darker thoughts that he said, "Leave your bike in the hedge," and held his hand out. Bessie put her boot on the wheel-hub so he could pull her onto the foot-board, and a moment later she was sitting beside him adjusting her sun-bonnet. "If you're going to town will you buy me a cream cake?"

"I might," said Timmy, "What will you give me for one?"

Bessie shrugged and blushed, but he was big and handsome and smiling at her, and as she watched his hands on the reins she shivered at the memory of them fumbling with her coat buttons.

Timmy took her to a cottage tearoom for their cakes, which seemed awfully grown-up to Bessie, and when he stopped the cart on the way home and kissed her, there was only her thin summer dress between his wandering hands and her body.

After that clandestine outing, Bessie yielded to Timmy's blandishments to renew their trysts in the barn in Bottom Meadow, where his kisses became more demanding and his hands less easy to push away. As summer progressed she began to like those kisses and the sensations his hands aroused on her sun-browned skin.

It was clear to Timmy that he could have her if he pushed a bit harder, but he was afraid to while she was under age. Bessie wouldn't be sixteen for another year and although he'd wanted her willing, he hadn't expected her to be this enthusiastic so soon. If he didn't watch it he'd forget himself and go too far one day, and if word got back to their parents there'd be hell to pay.

*

One Sunday evening Luke Finch taxied his aeroplane across the farmyard, through the gate and behind the barn. He was Charles Lindburgh today, setting off on a round-the-world flight. He licked his finger and held it up to test the wind – coming from the north – then revved his engine and glanced at each wing – all the struts in good order. "Chocks away!" he shouted, pulled his flying helmet firmly over his ears and started down the runway. The track across the field was only a couple of feet wide and his wing-tips brushed the crops as he flew. When he reached the hedge he made a fuel-stop, and decided to go straight on rather than right to the field where Dad had gone after tea to plant winter cabbage. The cows were used to Luke, but today they scattered as he raced through them with arms spread wide, emitting a loud nasal whine. Lindburgh hovered at the stile – crossing the Atlantic was a major undertaking. Nothing was coming down the lane so he took a deep breath and zoomed across, over the second stile, through the field of horses and into the copse. He'd made it – he'd landed on foreign soil!

Under the trees the air was violet with evening and insects danced in the low slants of light. The intrepid flyer bowed to acknowledge the congratulations of the French crowd and left his aeroplane to be checked over by the mechanics while he explored. Every step had to be taken with care in these foreign forests because the undergrowth hid a thousand dangers. Poisonous snakes could drop from the branches overhead, wild boar might charge and gore him with their curved tusks, or man-eating tigers could be lurking in the purple shadows waiting to pounce on the unwary.

At the edge of the forest there was more light, but was that a tropical breeze ruffling the spring grass on the prairie, or savage natives armed with blow-pipes? Luke darted back into the forest and re-emerged with a rifle. He crept along silently just under cover of the trees until he could dash across a few yards of open ground and flatten himself against the wall of a native hut. He inched along and risked a peep round the corner-post only to be blinded by the orange ball of the setting sun, and then he heard noises and froze with all senses alert.

It sounded like animals fighting – a big one grunting and a smaller one whimpering amid the rustle of dried grass. He gripped his trusty rifle firmly as he poked his head cautiously further round the post. There, on the edge of the hay that was piled rafter-high in the small thatched barn, two people were wrestling. He was about to move closer to watch when a stray sunbeam shone through a gap between the boards onto the familiar pattern of his sister Bessie's frock. One more second and he would have rushed to her rescue armed with only a stick, but then he saw her brown arm reach up to pull her attacker towards her and heard her murmur, "Don't go, Timmy." The deep voice of their neighbour's son answered, "I've got to, Bessie — you ain't sixteen yet."

Instinct told Luke he'd cop it if Bessie knew he'd seen her so he crept quietly away, and then ran through copse and field and over the lane until he was safely on Pinetree Farm. Only then did he remember his aeroplane, but it was a half-hearted flight he made back to land in the home barn.

Half an hour later Bessie slipped into the home barn to make sure all her buttons were done up, and was horribly startled when Luke jumped down from the hay bales.

"What are you doing in here?" she snapped.

"Building a den – what about you?"

"I came to find you – it's your bed-time."

Luke opened his mouth to call her a fibber, but he

decided it wasn't worth the trouble and followed her indoors, where their parents were relaxing by the range with a glass of cider.

Ruth looked sharply at her daughter — there was something going on with Bessie that she couldn't quite put her finger on — but all she said was, "You've got straw in your hair."

Bessie's hands flew to pull the evidence out of her curls, hoping the dim light hid her guilty flush. "I've been in the barn with Luke," she said, crossing her fingers behind her back and fixing Luke with a glare. Luke stared back — if Bessie wanted to wrestle with Timmy Coppin then let her, but he knew her secret and it might come in useful one day.

"That's nice, Bessie," Adam smiled, "He's got no-one else to play with. Tell you what – now the potatoes are all in I'll treat you both to rides on the pier on Sunday – how does that sound?"

"Yes please, Dad — perhaps I'm big enough now for the Chair-O-Planes!" Luke cried, and only Ruth noticed that Bessie didn't seem over-enthusiastic.

*

Bessie hadn't been able to come up with an excuse not to go to the pier, and Luke was dismayed to discover he was still not tall enough for the Chair-O-Planes. Even standing on tip-toe he couldn't reach the necessary mark on the wall – and the man patting his head kindly and saying "Maybe next year, sonny" only added insult to injury. He scuffed miserably along until he met Gerald and they secured two of the fastest horses on the Gallopers. Timmy Coppin was on the roundabout with a crowd of girls, and Luke thought it was odd that Bessie didn't talk to him although she was only two horses behind him. Clinging to their horses' necks and leaning sideways, he and Gerald shot every girl in sight, and Luke paid particular attention to Bessie — when she got off the ride she was bleeding from a dozen bullet-holes.

Bessie trailed despondently away from the Gallopers. She had imagined Timmy waiting for her in the barn, and had anticipated their next conversation starting with him demanding to know why she hadn't turned up. He couldn't have waited long before driving into town with those tarty girls from the dairy. What was worse, he hadn't even seen her, let alone said hello. Suddenly she brightened up at the sight of Albie, as tall as Timmy and even better-looking, and carrying a pile of mats with his muscles showing below rolled-up shirt-sleeves. He always seemed too busy to talk but she'd make him notice her today — that would show Timmy Coppin he wasn't the only boy in the world.

Albie sat on the pile of mats, watching a couple of kids playing on the beach. The sea was high today in the blustery wind and their parents were huddled on a rug with their coats on, but the two boys had taken off their shoes and socks to paddle, running in and out playing tag with the waves. In a way he wished he was still young enough to join them. George had gone for a cup of tea and a sit-down in the warm, so Albie was alone when Bessie insinuated herself between him and the view. "Hello Albie, all on your own?" she cooed, leaning her elbows on the rail and pushing her bosom forward.

Albie looked all round with exaggerated movements. "Seems like it."

"I seen you out our way on your bike, but you never come to see me."

"Got no reason to."

Bessie twirled one of her curls round her finger. "Who needs a reason? I could give you a cup of tea – or something. What do you want down that lane anyway?"

Albie wriggled uncomfortably on the scratchy mats – no-one but Bert knew he visited the black horse and Bessie Finch was the last person he was about to tell. "Just errands and stuff," he muttered.

Bessie could think of only one explanation for his evident discomfiture. "I reckon you've got a girl-friend. Who is she then? Is she prettier than me?"

Albie was saved from the impossibility of answering by shouts from below and he jumped up to look down at the beach. The two little boys were gesticulating wildly at the pier, and when Albie leaned further out he saw a child on the steps from which passengers boarded the pleasure-boats, and a second child further down, clinging on by one arm while heavy waves battered his body.

Luke and Gerald had gone down the steps to play at dodging the waves, but Luke had misjudged his third dash, slipped on the treacherous ironwork, and a wave had swept his feet from under him. His desperate grab had connected with the rusty railing and he'd managed to get his elbow round a strut, but he couldn't regain his footing and the next wave had soaked him. Now his whole arm was wedged in the rail and he couldn't get it out, he was shivering violently, the tide was coming in, and he was too terrified even to yell.

As Albie raced along the boardwalk the usual shrieks of delight from the rides masked Gerald's cries for help – Albie was the only one on the pier who knew the boys were in trouble. He cut a swathe through the crowd and swung down the ladder, then hauled Gerald off the lower steps and onto the fishing platform just as another wave swamped Luke. When the sea retreated, Luke's arm began to slide out of the rail, then another wave surged in to lift him like a piece of flotsam. Knowing that the next wave would take him, Albie jumped half a dozen steps in one leap and made a desperate lunge, just catching Luke's jacket in time. Wrapping the soaked, sobbing child inside his own jacket, he climbed the step to the upper level.

By now the drama had brought every ride and sideshow to a halt, and there were as many people hanging over the rail as at the Boxing Day swim. There was such a crush that Albie struggled to get through, but Fred Ford the strongman bellowed "Give 'em room!" and parted the crowd with a single sweep of his powerful arms. Fred's daughter Ellen scooped up the sodden, weeping Gerald and ran after Albie to the shelter of the tea-rooms.

Adam Finch had been enjoying a chat with George over tea and cakes when Bessie ran in screaming that Luke had drowned. He dashed to the door fearing the worst, to be met by Albie coming in carrying Luke's limp body.

Bessie shrieked hysterically, "He's dead, ain't he?"

Adam didn't even hear her. He had saved calves and lambs born as limp as this and he wasn't about to give up on his own son. Snatching Luke from Albie he held him upside-down, thumping his back until water ran out of him and then, to everyone's astonishment, covered his son's mouth with his own and blew. After a few breaths he thumped the child's back again, and this time Luke vomited up a great gush of seawater and coughed back into life. Adam hugged him in an ecstasy of relief, and sat on the nearest chair to strip him bare and wrap him in a blanket someone thrust into his hands.

Next to them, Ellen Ford rubbed Gerald vigorously with a tea-towel and wrapped him in another blanket, and at this happy outcome to what could have been a tragedy, the crowd spread out among the tables demanding cups of tea. Albie endured dozens of congratulatory hand-shakes until George saw the pleading in his eyes and secured a corner table, where he fended people off with his broad back saying, "Let him drink his tea in peace."

Adam stopped briefly beside them with Luke, still shivering and pale green but alive, held against his chest and said, "I don't know how to thank you."

"No need, Mister Finch," Albie said, "I'm just glad I seen him in time."

"I'm taking him to the doctor now," Adam said, "But I won't forget what you did today." He nodded at George, "Boy to be proud of, your son," and he headed for the door.

Bessie hurried after them, but on her way out she paused by Albie's table. Planting a kiss full on his mouth she gushed, "You're my hero!" before following her father, well-pleased with her dramatic exit.

When Doctor Jenkins heard how Adam had brought his drowned son back to life, he wrote down every detail for future reference. Vigorous pumping of the casualty's arms was the accepted method of resuscitation, but the farmer's trick of using his own breath to re-inflate the lungs was well worth noting — he might even send a paper to a medical journal. There was a slight rattle in Luke's lungs that the doctor told Adam would take a while to disperse.

"Keep him at home for a few weeks and tell his mother to feed him up — he's thin for a farmer's boy."

Adam looked at the son he had so nearly lost and realised the doctor was right. If he saw a lamb that scrawny he'd think it was a weakling, and he was ashamed he hadn't noticed. "Ruth will make sure he eats - don't you worry about that."

Doctor Jenkins whipped the bowl across to catch yet another offering of vomit from his small patient. "We'd better get rid of that seawater — it could be full of all kinds of muck."

So poor little Luke, who felt dreadful enough already, had to swallow a dose of castor oil.

As Adam paid the fee, the doctor told him, "Keep him in bed for a day or two — I'll come over in the week to see how he is." He ruffled Luke's damp hair. "You're a very lucky boy — you need to be a lot bigger before you try to swim the Channel."

Luke grimaced and vowed, "I ain't going near the sea ever again!"

*

A few mornings later Doctor Jenkins drove to the farm,

listened carefully to Luke's chest and declared him to be on the mend. "A couple more weeks at home, young man, and plenty of fresh air when it's not raining, then you should be fit for school."

"Will our Luke really be all right?" Ruth Finch asked a few minutes later in the kitchen.

"He'll be fine — he just needs fattening up a bit," Doctor Jenkins assured her.

"If you see Albie Smith will you ask him to pop in and see us next weekend? I'd like to thank him for saving my boy's life."

When Doctor Jenkins passed the message on, Albie said the pier was too busy and he couldn't spare the time, but George said, "No use you trying to duck out of it — I can manage a couple of hours without you."

"You've got to give Luke and his mum a chance to thank you," added Dot.

"I don't need no thanks," Albie protested, but Dot said severely, "What you need ain't the point — they need to say it, so you're going."

So the next Sunday Albie rode to Pinetree Farm, accompanied by Bert for moral support, and found the entire Finch family waiting in the big farmhouse kitchen. Adam Finch and his two grown sons shook his hand with vigorous two-handed grips and Ruth gave him a hug. Albie bore all this stoically, but when Bessie clung to his neck and kissed him for longer than was necessary, he was uncomfortably aware of Bert smirking in the background.

Luke rescued him by pushing Bessie aside and offering his own small hand. "Thank you for saving my life," he said solemnly, and then the family spread out to reveal a table groaning with food. "Mum's made a special tea."

When the boys left the farm, stuffed to the gills with ham, fried potatoes and fruit cake, their bicycle baskets were crammed with more ham, cheese and butter, and only lack of space had prevented Ruth Finch from packing in more.

"Told you there's good eating on a farm," Bert said, "You're well in there — and I thought that Bessie was never going to let go of you!"

"Oh shut up, Bert – I'd sooner have one of them noisy London girls. They might be tarty but you know where you are with them."

<u>CHAPTER NINE – GROWING UP</u>

By October all the fruit was in and the Londoners had returned to the dirty, grey, smog-bound city, leaving Thambay to the locals. The stall-owners on the pier each scrubbed their own patch clear of the sticky residue of ice-creams, lollipops, candyfloss and drinks. Over winter the salt spray would mist it over with rime which they'd scrub off next spring before the fresh paint went on.

Then this unique set of people, who knew each other so well yet scarcely exchanged more than a greeting during the frantic summer months, held their customary end-of-season party in the tea-rooms.

The elegant ex-soldier who played tinkly-sweet tunes for the tea-drinking trippers struck up something more lively, and with the tables stacked up against the windows the dancing began. When George took Dot for a turn round the floor, the strongman's daughter Ellen pulled Albie into the crowd, and after a few moments of stumbling embarrassment he began to enjoy himself.

Cheerful and full of energy after a few drinks, George and Dot left the pier at nine o'clock to walk home along the promenade.

"I always feel the town's ours again after that party," George observed, slowing his steps to prolong the peaceful stroll.

Dot looked over her shoulder. "I can't see our Albie – thought he was coming too."

George laughed softly and put his arm round her waist. "He might be courting. Remember when we was courting, Dot? We used to walk like this."

Dot smiled and George thought she looked nineteen again in the moonlight as she answered, "The way I remember it, you held more than just my middle."

"Is this what you mean?" asked George, stirred by the

memory, the moonlight and the ale, and he swung Dot back against the railing, put a large warm hand on her bosom and kissed her like a young and eager lover.

When they came up for air Dot snatched his hand away, scolding, "George Smith! What will people think?" but her eyes were glowing and her smile soft. George tucked her hand into the crook of his arm and started walking again. "I don't give a damn, and anyway there's no-one around."

A quick check assured Dot this was true but renewed her concern. "Where *is* our Albie? It's getting late."

George chuckled, "It ain't that late, and he's probably doing the same as us with Ellen Ford. I don't think we need to fret about Albie and girls – that Ellen'll learn him what it's all about!"

Ellen Ford had done pretty much as George surmised. She'd had her eye on Albie all summer, and tonight she'd decided he'd do nicely. When Albie had only one beer mixed with lemonade she guessed he was younger than he looked, but no-one else at the party had taken her fancy, so after that first dance she stuck with him.

Ellen was a good-natured girl who lived with her strongman father, took the money in the ticket-booth, and ejected any rowdy elements with more strength than they expected in a girl. During the cold winter months she and her father travelled with a small circus to Spain, where Fred worked as a rigger and took on the locals in a boxing booth.

Ellen's big blonde body attracted quite a few Spaniards, but the presence of her large father kept most of them at a respectful distance. Besides that, Ellen didn't fancy the small, dark foreigners. Albie was English and good-looking and the right size for her and, after downing a second glass of shandy, was more than willing to walk her home to the boarding-house on the edge of town.

When Ellen stopped at the end of the back alley and said, "It's only a minute from here," Albie offered her his hand to shake. Ellen was momentarily taken aback, but then realised she would have to take the initiative. She pulled him closer and pressed her lips against his. For a second he didn't respond, and Ellen wondered if she'd taken too much for granted, but then his arms slid round her and tightened.

It was a boy's kiss and Ellen would have left it at that, but Albie drew back a few inches, gazed into her eyes and asked with stunning simplicity, "Am I doing it right? I've never kissed no-one before."

Ellen was touched and thrilled. "Lovely kiss that was," she assured him, "Your lips are so soft. Can I have another one?"

Albie didn't need asking twice. He drew her close again and Ellen held his head and increased the pressure of her kiss until his lips parted. When she felt his breathing quicken she gave him one last squeeze and took a small, slightly unsteady step back. "Lovely," she said again, "I'll see you next season and have a few more of those," and a minute later she had vanished along the unlit alley towards her door. Albie walked home in a daze of happiness. He'd kissed a girl at last and he'd got it right!

*

A week later Albie came down to breakfast to find a large parcel covering his plate and big grins on George and Dot's faces. "Happy birthday, son," they said in unison.

Albie kissed Dot, shook George's hand, and tore the parcel open to reveal a pair of long trousers. "Ta very much," he said, "Does this mean I'm a man now?"

"We only got you them 'cause you're getting too big for short trousers," Dot said repressively, "You're a boy while you're still at school."

"But now I'm fourteen I can leave school."

"Not till Christmas, Albie — you know that," said George, "And besides, Bert can't leave before Easter – why not wait till then and leave together?"

"I s'pose I oughtn't to leave him to deal with Wally on his own."

"Is that lout still giving you trouble? I thought that was over last year."

"It's nothing I can't handle, Dad, but he's got it in for us. Bert's dad caught him nicking something off his cart and told the coppers."

"That don't sound too good. And another thing – staying at school a bit longer will give you time to find work."

Albie choked on his fried bread. "But Dad — I work with you!"

"The ride don't pay enough for two men's wages, son."

"Then I'll carry on just for pocket money."

George hardened his heart — and his tone of voice. "Your mum needs proper wages from you, Albie – you eat like a man already."

Albie dropped his knife as if it had suddenly become red hot and turned pleading eyes on Dot, but she said firmly, "Your dad's right, Albie - you need to pay your way."

"But what about the ride? Dad *needs* me!"

"I'll manage," said George, "And in the summer I might get young Georgie to help after school."

In the playground later, Albie responded to Bert's boisterous "Happy birthday!" with a scowl. "Fine birthday this is turning out to be. Dad wants his grandson to work the helter-skelter instead of me."

"Well, he'll need someone else when you start work, won't he?"

"God! Not you an' all!" Albie moaned, "I got no idea where to start looking."

"Why don't you talk to my dad? He needs help now the business is growing."

"Ain't you doing it? It *is* called Daly Deliveries, after all."

"I'm going to be delivery boy for the butcher — Dad

6

needs someone stronger than me."

Albie felt strange approaching John Daly with cap in hand – after all, it was less than two years since he and Bert started the business – but John put him at ease immediately. "I should've thought of you myself. Your strong back is just what I need."

"I can only do mornings in the summer season, mind — Dad ain't getting any younger and afternoons on the pier can get a bit hectic."

"I'm sure we can work something out — George and Dot have been more than good to my family."

*

So Albie and Bert left school together at the end of the spring term and moved from boyhood to manhood in the space of a day.

Dot cooked her Easter dinner a week early, knowing that George and Albie would be too busy the next weekend, and as usual they invited Eric and his family to share it. Eric offered again to put in a word for Albie at the factory and again he refused to consider it. "They wouldn't let me have afternoons to help Dad," he said, "And Georgie's only ten – he's too young to do it yet."

"Georgie won't be working on the pier at all," snapped his mother, "I'm not having him mixing with those people."

Dot glared at George to remind him he had promised not to lose his temper with Hilda today – but then Eric made matters worse by asking Albie, "Why did you wait till Easter to leave school and earn proper money? You were fourteen before Christmas but you let Mum and Dad carry on supporting you."

"That's enough!" George thundered, "Albie's got a proper job now, but he's been earning his keep since we took him in. And Hilda's got no business being snooty about the helter-skelter. It kept you in food and clothes even though you never helped me much."

Into the pool of silence that followed, young Georgie dropped his own pebble. "I'd like to help Grandad on the pier."

His mother clipped his ear. "You'll speak when you're spoken to, young man, and you're not going near the helter-skelter while this gypsy's working there."

"Hilda Smith! You take that back!" Dot shrieked, "Our Albie ain't a gypsy."

"Well, Pauline Biggins says she knew his mum when they were younger, and saw her going with a gypsy in the hop-fields."

"That Pauline Biggins always did have a mean mouth!" Dot exclaimed, "I've a good mind to go round and give her the sharp edge of my tongue!" She started removing her apron, clearly intending to set off that minute, but George caught her wrist. "Leave it, Dot – you can't go storming round like that. Besides, what if it's true? Look at all that curly hair, and Albie's dark enough for a gypsy."

"He's outside all the time – of course he's brown."

"Mum – it don't matter – and I ain't about to let Hilda wind me up. If I *have* got gypsy blood in me, one of these days I'm going to find out for sure."

"Why would you want to do that – ain't we good enough?"

"Aw, Mum, you and Dad are more than good enough. I just want to know if the man who made me was a decent one, 'cause the woman who had me sure as hell wasn't."

"And there's no call for language at my table neither," Dot snapped, and got up to make the tea.

George winked at Albie – the boy had learned a thing or two over the years, one of which was that the best way to distract Dot was to give her a reason to scold.

*

Bert had secured the regular job as delivery boy for the local butcher mainly by virtue of his readiness over the past two years to turn out in all weathers. The position came with a bicycle, and Bert's thirteen-year-old sister May, after a fierce argument with her mother, took over his old bike and his round of small errands – the Albertie partnership had ended with the boys' schooldays.

Once Albie had cleaned the helter-skelter and worked on the pier through the Easter rush, he began working with John Daly, arranging the larger deliveries so that Albie's afternoons were still free to help George. Now there were two of them to lift heavier items onto the hand-cart, Daly Deliveries could handle whole hundredweights of coal or huge sacks of potatoes. They also shifted beds and wardrobes when people left one rented house for another – occasionally under cover of darkness. This always made Albie nervous, for the landlord's collection men could turn up at any time and they took a dim view of a moonlight flit.

Taking bales of hay to the dray-horses was Albie's favourite job. The sound of the cart-wheels brought every horse to its half door, and Albie always lingered to talk to them, sometimes slipping inside their stables for a few minutes, unfazed by their size. They delivered loads of manure to the allotments from the stables, and John kept a tarpaulin and an old sheet for the cleaner jobs, such as taking bags of washing to and from the laundry – the last thing they needed was for it to pick up the stink.

As word spread of Daly Deliveries' readiness to take on any job, they began getting the occasional call to help out in the evenings by taking a particularly well-oiled customer home from one of the town's pubs. Albie asked one landlord why he bothered and the man explained, "It'd give the pub a bad name if anyone was robbed leaving here." John always had a pail of water handy to swill the cart out after these late calls.

One evening John knocked on the Smith's door asking for Albie. "The landlord of the Station Arms sent the potman to fetch us."

"I'll get me jacket."

There was quite a crowd waiting when Albie and John pushed the cart into the pub yard, and before they could raise any objections, three bodies were lifted in, two of them moaning in pain and one unconscious.

"What's going on here?" John demanded as a lantern flared briefly on blood stains.

"Been a bit of a fight," the landlord said in a low voice, "Didn't want to get the Law involved but they need to go straight to hospital."

"We ain't taking three on our own," Albie said. John tried to shut him up with a glare but Albie insisted. "What if they start fighting again?"

"These two'll come along to help you sort them out," the landlord said quickly, beckoning a couple of men from the crowd and pressing a folded paper into Albie's hand, "Mum's the word."

Albie found he was holding a rather grubby five pound note, and raised no more objections as he and John pushed their barrow out of the inn-yard. It wasn't until they crossed the well-lit Market Square that Albie realised their unconscious passenger was Walter Biggins. So Wally had started going to pubs already, had he?

John caught sight of Albie's expression and asked, "Is something the matter?" but Albie remembered the fiver in his pocket and turned his grimace into a smile. "Just thinking that if we keep on at this rate we'll be buying a van!"

"Not a bad idea – these three are damned heavy."

Their two 'bodyguards' were too drunk themselves to be much help, but they got to the hospital along the Whitstable Road without incident. After handing the patients over to the hospital porter and a doctor who was clearly expecting them, Albie asked John, "How are they going to get treatment without being reported for fighting?"

One of the helpers turned on him. "None of your business – you've been paid to keep your mouth shut."

"And you'd better watch your mouth too, Timmy Coppin," John retorted, "Your father's a friend of mine – and a magistrate."

Timmy backed off, holding his hands up apologetically, and the four of them lounged against a wall in virtual silence for over an hour, smoking and listening to the small sounds of the warm summer night, until a nurse came out and said, "Your friends need help."

The pain of treatment had sobered the patients up but shortened their tempers — one had a bandage on his head, another wore a splint on one arm, and Wally had his leg in plaster. When he saw Albie he snarled through gritted teeth, "What the hell you doing here, Gyppo?"

"Fetching your miserable body home, Fatso, unless you'd rather walk?"

Wally started to say something else but Timmy told him wearily, "Shut up, Wally – you're in enough trouble as it is. You're dad's going to pay through the nose to keep the landlord sweet."

Wally subsided, muttering, and allowed Timmy to help him into the cart, but he groaned at every bump in the road and accused Albie of doing it on purpose. Albie was heartily sick of the sight of him when they eventually left him with his mother, whose grim expression promised that Wally was going to get it in the neck after all. Even more cheering was the fact that each man gave them five shillings for their trouble and the promise of silence.

John spread the five pound note reverently on the table the following evening. The entire Daly family gazed at it in awe as he put his hand over it and looked at Albie.

"Did you mean what you said about saving for a van, Albie? Half of this money is yours – but you're too young to drive."

"You can teach me on the back roads," Albie said, "How much is a second hand one?"

"More than we can afford yet – twenty quid or more."

"If Mum goes fruit-picking this summer it would bring in more," Bert suggested but Gladys pulled her youngest onto her lap and said, "Jimmy's not at school yet — how can I take him?" Like many other families, there was a gap after their first two children because of the war, but John and Gladys had made up for that by having four more babies in four years.

"Take a rug for him to sit on and a sandwich for his dinner," said Bert, "It'll do him good to be out in the fresh air."

*

The idea of buying a van took hold of everyone, and the knowledge that Gladys Daly was working towards it spurred Albie on. When requests for the services of Daly Deliveries were slack, he took casual jobs wherever he could find them. He spent many mornings unloading crates and barrels at the pubs, packing chairs and tables in the furniture factory or shifting timber in the yard by the railway line – any job where his strength and ready smile could earn him enough money to pay his way at home and hold his head up when Eric came to dinner. Sometimes the jobs he did even led to more work for Daly Deliveries, and the business that was started by two boys with a pram was supporting the entire Daly family, as well as paying Albie a wage.

Mr Wallace the butcher worked long hours, so Bert was seldom free until late. As the hours of daylight lengthened, Albie often rode out in the early evenings to visit 'his' horse. One June morning he woke up on the tail-end of a dream that haunted him all day, and when the last customer left the pier, Albie was close behind. He cycled quickly through the summer evening. The planting and hoeing had finished weeks ago and it was too early for harvest, so he thought his chances of finding the working horse in its field were better than average.

Dismounting by the gate, he whistled as usual, and the horse thundered across the field to greet him. As it crunched its customary carrot Albie stroked the velvety nose and threaded his hand through the coarse mane. When he had first seen the horse he'd had to stand on the gate, but now their heads were the same height.

Albie's mouth was dry — he'd imagined this moment so many times in the past two years and never had the nerve to carry it out, but this morning's dream had shown him the way and given him courage. Talking softly, he climbed the gate, sat astride the top bar with his fingers clutching the mane, and asked, "You going to let me ride you?"

An ear twitched, so Albie slid his arm round its neck. The horse shifted so that its broad back was parallel with the gate, inviting Albie to mount. Still murmuring his horse talk, Albie swung his leg over the black back and allowed his weight to settle slowly. Now came the moment of truth. Would this animal, more used to pulling wagons and ploughs than to carrying people, accept him or toss him to the ground?

The enormous feet shifted restlessly but Albie reached forward and pulled one of its ears. The horse shivered as if to seat him more securely, then shook its head and moved forward. Albie had only ridden roundabout horses before today, and the strong muscles and wide back felt enormous, but he squeezed his knees together instinctively and gripped the long mane. He swayed with the roll of the body beneath him, inhaling the warm scent of horse mingled with the smell of grass crushed by the huge feet. As they walked along the edge of the field he could see clear over the hedge to the empty lane, and to the lush green of the cherry orchard on the far side, where the pea-sized green fruit hung quietly fattening in the summer air. It was very peaceful.

But then he saw the fork in the lane and thought of the farm traffic that could appear at any moment. He didn't know who owned the carthorse — both Pinetree and Coppin Farms were nearby and it could belong to either. He tensed ready to slide off its back, but the horse turned of its own accord and took him back to the gate, where it stood steady as an armchair until he had climbed off. Albie rubbed the big black face, murmuring his thanks, and the horse put its nose against his chest and pushed him, gently but firmly, off the gate. As his bottom landed on the grass verge the horse let out a snort of laughter. Albie chuckled, "You had enough of me, have you?" and the horse tossed its head and cantered out of sight over the rise.

As Albie pedalled up the lane through clouds of midges he sensed he was being watched, but no-one shouted at him for riding the horse. Ever since he started looking for his father Albie had often felt eyes on him when there was nobody in sight, and he had learned not to be disturbed by it. Today's watcher felt different but still not threatening, and Albie relaxed — if anyone *did* ask what he was doing here, he was just out for a bike ride.

*

Bessie Finch had heard the bicycle coming up the lane and only just ducked behind the hedge in time – in another second she would have been caught leaving Bottom Meadow, where she had been canoodling with Timmy Coppin among the hay-bales in the barn. Bessie would be sixteen in August and Timmy knew it – their barn sessions were getting closer and closer to the point of no return. The trouble was, although Bessie's body clamoured for release from the tension that his long seduction had built up, she wasn't sure that he was the one she wanted.

Ever since she had kissed Albie at Luke's thank-you tea her obsession with him had grown. If she went to the pier she always left her bike by the helter-skelter, but Albie ignored her – he seemed more interested in the strongman's daughter. At least Timmy wanted her, which he demonstrated each time they met with an ardour that Bessie believed could only be fuelled by love. But often while Timmy's hands wandered she imagined Albie's grey eyes close to her own, and pretended it was his muscular arms pressing her down into the sweet hay. Then, thinking about Albie, she would return Timmy's kisses with a passion that aroused him even further.

This had been one of those evenings, and with Albie on her mind Bessie thought she must have imagined him, but when she got home she couldn't help asking her mother, "Was Albie Smith here? I thought I saw him at the fork."

"Haven't seen him, love – why didn't you say hello?"

"I couldn't be sure it was him in this light."

"You shouldn't be out this late if it's too dark to recognize a friend."

Luke kept his head down, pretending to concentrate on the wood-block fort he was building. He knew where Bessie had been — and who with - no mere girl could outwit the Master Spy. But he had an even better secret that that — he had been hunting wild boar in the cherry orchard and had seen his hero Albie ride the big carthorse bareback.

CHAPTER TEN – 1928 – FIRST LOVE

The next evening Albie raced round to the Daly's, eager to tell Bert about his ride, and met his friend just coming out of the door. "I've got something to tell you!" Albie said.

"Not now, mate — come round tomorrow," Bert said and dashed off.

Albie stood in the street gaping. Bert had polished his shoes, his hair was all slicked down with Brylcreem and he'd even scrubbed the meat-blood out of his nails - what was all that in aid of? Then the truth struck him like a fist. It was Saturday night - courting night - and there was only one reason for Bert to be all dressed up — he had a sweetheart. Even so, he was his best friend — he could have listened for five minutes, couldn't he?

Albie thrust his hands savagely into his pockets and mooched along in no particular direction, lonely and disgruntled at having no-one to share his excitement. He kicked a stone down the road for a while, but when that palled he slumped moodily against a wall, watching couples stroll by arm in arm. A trio of girls gave him speculative looks but were repelled by his scowl and went on their way giggling. A group of lads went past him laughing and scuffling, obviously on their way for a friendly night out, making him feel even worse. Bert hadn't even told him about his girl - fine sort of friend he was! He pushed his shoulders off the wall and started walking again, then a street sign showed him he was nearly at Ellen's lodgings, and on an impulse he went to the door and knocked. When the landlady shouted, "Ellen — there's a lad wants you!" Ellen appeared at the top of the stairs. "What are you doing here, Albie — is something wrong?"

Albie stood awkwardly on the step, very conscious of the landlady listening from behind her half-open door. "Nothing's wrong - I just wanted to see you."

Ellen came down to the hall shrugging into a cardigan. "Let's go for a walk."

"Be in before eleven or you'll be locked out," the landlady warned as Ellen pulled the door closed.

"Miserable cow!" Ellen hissed, linking arms with Albie. "Now tell me why you've come all the way out here. Have you fallen out with Bert?"

"Hardly seen him all week," Albie muttered sulkily, "Reckon he's got a girl."

"And what's wrong with that?"

"Could have told me, couldn't he?"

Ellen sat on a low wall and tugged Albie down beside her. "Don't be silly, Albie — he'd have told you if he'd got a proper sweetheart."

"But I wanted to talk to him tonight and he practically ran right past me."

"If he *is* meeting a girl it'll be a new one, so of course he was in a hurry," Ellen said, hiding a smile, "I expect he'll tell you about it tomorrow."

"I suppose so," said Albie, "But I had something to tell him."

"Then tell me instead," Ellen coaxed and kissed his cheek.

So Albie told her all about it. About the first time he saw the horse and how it had towered over his undernourished frame. He told her about returning every so often with hay or a carrot as a gift, and the thrill of yesterday when he'd fulfilled his dream by riding it. "Not that I did much, mind — just sat on its back while it walked - but it were magic!" Albie's eyes gleamed in the darkness.

Ellen twined her fingers through his. "Are you satisfied now you've ridden your horse?"

"Satisfied? You mean have I had enough?" Albie stared at the pale sliver of moon just beginning to appear over the roof-tops, "I won't be satisfied till I've galloped." On a surge of energy he pulled Ellen along the road and into the darkness of a stable-yard so that he could kiss her in private, spreading his jacket over a bale of hay for them to sit on. With the evocative smell of horse in his nostrils he told Ellen the secret that only Bert knew — the strange sense of familiarity with horses that he couldn't explain, and the 'horse-talk' he used to communicate.

Ellen was silent for so long he was afraid he'd revealed too much, but then he heard the smile in her voice when she said, "I've heard Spanish gypsies talk to their horses like that – maybe you're a gypsy."

Learning that other gypsies talked to their horses was comforting, even if they *were* foreign, and Albie felt better for having confided in Ellen. He twisted her hair into a rope round his hand and drew her in for a kiss of gratitude that swiftly changed to passion. A minute later, when she put her hands on his chest to push him away, he chuckled, "Reckon I've got gypsy blood, eh? I'll show you," and he tightened his embrace to kiss her again. This was much better than snatched kisses inside the helter-skelter, and Ellen's last coherent thought was that Albie had grown from a boy to a man in half an hour.

The warm darkness combined with genuine fondness and bodily urges into a heady mixture that fired Albie's blood. He kissed Ellen's mouth deeply, then his lips slid down to her throat while his fingers undid the buttons of her dress. He stroked her breasts gently, thrilled by the soft skin he had never touched before, and when he cupped their weight her nipples stiffened against his palms. He hardened in response and groaned, moving his head to kiss her mouth again. Ellen tugged his shirt free so that she could knead the strong muscles of his back, and Albie pushed her deeper into the hay. Unbuttoning her dress even further, he kissed her bare stomach and murmured, "You taste of honey," and ran his tongue up her ribs as if he was licking an ice-cream cone.

Ellen writhed with pleasure, the little voice that strove to remind her of Albie's youth being shouted down by the clamour of her body. When he took hold of the hem of her dress and whispered, "Ellen – are you going to let me?" she undid his buttons to release him from the confinement of trousers and pants and grasped him in her warm hands. "Oh God!" he moaned, growing even harder, and Ellen could resist no longer. She caught hold of his shoulders and lay back, wrapped her legs around him and guided him inside her.

Albie froze in astonished delight. For a second he simply held still with his hands on either side of her head, and in years to come he would never forget that moment. A shaft of moonlight shone through a gap in the plank wall onto Ellen's thick blonde hair and wide, welcoming smile, and the sensation of being enclosed in the heat of her body was amazing. Then Ellen lifted her hips and he could hold still no longer. He plunged deeper, thrusting instinctively, and Ellen began to moan, but Albie barely heard her over his own panting breath. He moved faster and faster and the sudden rush of release took him by surprise. His eyes snapped open as his body pulsed and he smothered his own moans of pleasure against Ellen's throat. After his final spasm he collapsed on her chest, burying his face in her neck and murmuring endearments.

Then a horse in the stable coughed and he was about to pull away when Ellen held him back, saying, "Not yet," and began to move under him. This time it was slower and Ellen dictated the pace, telling him what she wanted. Albie was aware in some corner of his mind that he wasn't the first for her, but he didn't care. He watched the expressions flit over her face in the shaft of moonlight, and when she clapped a hand over her mouth to stifle a scream and shuddered beneath him, Albie came a second time on a tidal wave of pride.

*

Bert came to find Albie on the pier the next day, full of

apologies for rushing off the night before. "I was meeting a girl and I didn't want to be late. What did you want to tell me?"

Albie's face broke into a wide grin and Bert thumped him on the back, "You got a girl too?"

"Sort of," said Albie, glancing at George, who waved them away with the back of his hand. "You two go and chat over a cuppa – just make sure you bring me one back."

When they'd settled down in the tearoom with a cup of tea and a bun, Bert launched into a description of his Saturday night date with Alice. "She works for the milliner two doors down from our butcher's shop," he told Albie, "We went for a walk and sat on a bench on the prom."

Albie checked that the adjoining tables were empty before he asked, "Did you kiss her?"

"Twice on the bench and again on her doorstep," Bert confided, "Albie, she's so pretty and soft – I think I'm in love."

"That's a bit quick, ain't it? *And* you're a bit young."

"I'm only three months younger than you!" Bert said indignantly, "And I'm a working man now – got to look to the future."

Albie's smile faded – Bert sounded really serious. "Just don't rush into it — you don't want babies yet."

"Fat chance of that!" Bert laughed, "Alice wouldn't even undo her cardigan." He winked at Albie, "Did you get any further than that with your girl?"

Albie cursed the blush that raced up his forehead but merely said, "I got past the cardigan – but a decent bloke don't kiss and tell."

"Who is she, then – still that Ellen, or have you given in to Bessie at last?"

"Bessie Finch? Too pushy by half," scoffed Albie.

"Pushy is right — from what I've heard she'll undo more than her cardigan." Bert looked through the window at the helter-skelter. "Looks like your dad's getting busy so I'd best be off, but what was you all fired up to tell me last night?"

"I rode my horse!" said Albie, and told Bert every glorious detail of his ride.

"You want to watch out you don't get caught," Bert said when he'd finished. He dug his elbow into Albie's ribs, "Unless that's Farmer Finch's horse — reckon you'd be welcome to ride anything on Pinetree Farm, including Bessie!"

*

From the start of the season Gladys Daly picked fruit on Coppin Farm, and little Jimmy turned nut-brown from the long days in the open air. It wasn't long before Albie and John joined them in the fields, John wheeling the cart with Jimmy on board, and Albie riding his bike. They cheerfully bore the banter and ribaldry of the mainly female workers to fill their own quota of baskets. Most days Albie left at noon to work on the pier, unless there was a sudden glut of ripe fruit that had to be picked or spoil. On those evenings, while John and Gladys pushed their sleepy son home on the cart, Albie would go in the other direction to visit his horse, although there were too many people about for him to risk riding it again.

Among the fruit pickers was a group of gypsy women and children whom Albie watched covertly. He still hoped that one day he would recognize his own features on a man's face, but the men didn't come near the fruit-pickers. They were doing heavier work, clearing undergrowth in the pine plantations with sharp-bladed sickles, and although Albie knew their camp was on Pinetree Farm, he didn't go that way for fear of meeting Bessie, who still hovered round him like a troublesome wasp.

His love affair with Ellen occupied all the spare corners of Albie's mind. When the pier closed in the evenings George would often disappear to the tea-rooms, leaving Ellen to help Albie drag the mats inside the helter-skelter. They would kiss in the dusty shafts of evening light that crept through the gaps, but Ellen refused to take advantage of the pile of mats that lay so invitingly against the curved wall. "This is your dad's ride – it wouldn't be decent doing it here."

There were plenty of other places young lovers could go, and sometimes Albie took Ellen out of town on his crossbar to find an overgrown hedgerow or the corner of a barn, where they could make love in the twilit hours before bedtime.

But England's green and pleasant land depended on rain to keep it that way – there were occasions when the weather was inclement and the pier visitors scarce. Then Ellen would sit inside the helter-skelter with Albie and George, regaling them with stories of her foreign travels. She told them about the long train journey she and her father made in autumn through France and over the mountains into Spain, painting a vivid word picture of an exotic world of oranges and olives and rough red wine.

"You're a bit of a gypsy by the sound of it," George said one day, and Albie held his breath until Ellen smiled and answered, "I am, but not a real one – I ain't got the right blood."

Forgetting George's presence, Albie caught hold of her hand and kissed her ear. "I think my real dad was a gypsy," he said, and after that it was easy to tell her about his forays into the countryside in search of his bloodline.

When the wind blew cold and damp on an English summer day, Albie dreaded the coming winter and Ellen's inevitable departure. He remembered last Easter, when Ellen had returned with a deeply tanned face and her hair bleached almost white by the sun. Looking at the dull sky of a rainy Kent afternoon he was afraid that one day she might not come back at all.

*

At the end of July, when school broke up for the holidays, all the younger Daly children joined Gladys and Albie in the fields, picking strawberries and raspberries, followed by currants and beans. By saving every spare shilling they managed to accumulate enough money to put a down-payment on a van which John had spotted on his rounds. It was a flat-bed van, at least ten years old, and bore a few bullet-holes to bear testimony to its war service, but John was thrilled with it. "I drove one of these in France in the war," he told Albie. "Learned how to fix it too."

Ten pounds down and ten shillings a week for a year was the price they agreed, and before the end of the season John was able to join the other drivers taking boxes of fruit to the railway station for transport to London.

*

In August Luke Finch was making the most of the last weeks of the summer holidays. The hay in Bottom Meadow stood tall and golden in the sun, and hid Luke completely from sight as he crawled on his belly through the system of tunnels he had created by widening animal tracks. He was an Escaped Prisoner today, trying to evade the long arm of the law while he searched for the Real Baddy who had robbed the bank and framed him. A dagger was clenched between his teeth and one of Mum's head-scarves hung round his neck ready to be pulled up as a disguise.

At the sound of a horse and cart on the lane he flattened his belly into the ground – the slightest ripple could betray his whereabouts – but he remained undiscovered. Letting his breath out slowly he whispered, "Whew, that was close!" and moved forward swiftly to reach the shelter of the barn wall. Leaning against the warm wood, he shut his eyes for a moment and his tummy rumbled loudly. Days on the run had left him exhausted and if he didn't eat soon he would have to hold the farmer's wife at knife-point and demand food. Pictured on the inside of his eyelids he could see the remains of Bessie's birthday cake sitting on the larder shelf. He was about to crawl away through the hay crop when he heard Bessie say, "I brought you a piece of birthday cake," and his eyes shot open — had his sister read his mind? He looked all round but he couldn't see her, and then he heard Timmy Coppin say, "I thought your birthday wasn't till the end of the month."

"So that's why you haven't got me a present?"

"Oh, I've got you a present all right — all you've got to do is open it."

That Bessie and her presents! Luke had spent a whole week's pocket money on a pink ribbon for her hair and she'd just glanced at it and said she preferred green. Well, if those two were going to wrestle again there was no point in staying around. Luke slipped away from the barn and ran home to claim another slice of cake before Bessie gave it all away.

Bessie pushed Timmy's hand off her bosom and asked plaintively, "Aren't you going to stroke me first?" but Timmy simply pulled her hands down to his crotch. When Bessie sighed and began stroking him through the fabric of his trousers, he plunged his tongue into her mouth and tore at her buttons. Timmy had held himself back for so long that the news that Bessie was now sixteen had him throbbing with anticipation, and if he didn't get her knickers off soon he'd be spilling it into his underpants. Any notion of leading up to it properly flew out of the window - or in this case the barn door, he thought with a touch of hysteria. When Bessie fumbled with his buttons he knocked her hand aside to open them himself and poke his cock through the flies. "Look at him - he's ready for you," he said proudly, "Take a hold of him."

Bessie actually took a step back - it was so much bigger than she'd expected from the feeling of it through cloth - but the pile of hay caught her behind the knees and she sprawled on her back. Without pausing, Timmy lifted her skirt, dragged off her knickers and lunged at her. Bessie clamped her legs together and put her arms round him. "You do love me, don't you?" she insisted, searching for his mouth and the kisses that had always aroused her before. This Timmy frightened her. His hands were squeezing her breasts hard enough to hurt, and his eyes seemed almost angry as he pushed her legs apart with his knees. One of his hands moved down to between her legs and for a moment she relaxed – she liked the feeling of his fingers there – but then he wrenched one of her thighs up and drove himself into her.

"Stop it Timmy, you're hurting me!" she cried.

"It always hurts the first time – stop fussing," he said through gritted teeth, spread her other thigh as high and wide as it would go and plunged into her again. As he broke through the obstruction Bessie screamed, but Timmy kept thrusting. Every movement stabbed her with pain and rasped on her dry, un-aroused skin. She writhed under him and beat her fists on his chest, but there was no escape until he yelled loudly, pumped back and forth a few more times and collapsed on top of her.

Bessie was sore and sobbing and, far too late, Timmy tried to soothe her. "The first time always hurts for girls — you'll get to like it."

Bessie shook her head and felt hot tears slide into her hair. "It really hurt. It wasn't like I thought it would be."

Timmy looked at her in amazement. "What did you expect? No-one else has ever complained."

"No-one else?" Bessie shrieked, "You told me I was the one you wanted!"

"Well, yes," Timmy admitted, "I know I said that – and I meant it, honest – but you can't have expected me to wait. I mean – a man has his needs, and I'm here now, ain't I?" He tried to retrieve his mistake by kissing and stroking her, and Bessie was comforted by the familiar caresses, but after a couple of minutes Timmy stood up and buttoned his flies. "I'd better be going – and your mum will be wondering where you've got to."

Bessie sat up slowly and found her abandoned

knickers, but when she stood up to pull them on a trickle of liquid ran down her leg. "You've made me bleed! I told you it was hurting but you wouldn't listen!"

"That? That's nothing – just proves I was the first," said Timmy dismissively.

"Of course you were the first," Bessie cried, "I saved myself for you and now I'm sixteen we can tell my parents."

"Tell them what?" asked Timmy cruelly, "That we've been fooling around in the barn for a year and now I've fucked you?"

"Not that, no," said Bessie, winding her arms round his neck, "But you could come to tea and we'll tell them we're sweethearts."

"It's a bit soon for that – we don't want them guessing what we've been up to, do we? Give it a month or so and then we'll see," Timmy said, peeling her off his neck and backing out of the barn, "We'll talk about it next week, all right?" and he made his escape.

Half an hour later Luke took his egg basket into the home barn and a muffled sob drew him to the back, where he found Bessie curled up small in his secret hideout, weeping.

"What's the matter with you?" he asked.

Bessie rubbed her eyes with the hem of her dress and tried to stop crying — the last thing she needed was Luke telling Mum. "Nothing," she said, "Just girl stuff."

"If that Timmy Coppin hurt you I'll stab him with my dagger," Luke said fiercely, drawing the wooden knife out of his belt.

Bessie was horrified. She jumped up, demolishing the roof of Luke's hideout as she grabbed his shirt and hissed, "You've been spying on me again — what did you see?"

"I never seen nothing!" Luke cried, scared by her ferocity, "I only heard him say he had a present for you and then I came home."

Bessie relaxed her grip — if Luke had really left after

that remark she was safe. "All right, I'll forget it this once, but you stay off Coppin land from now on, is that clear?"

"But that ain't fair!" Luke wailed, "You go there all the time!"

"I do not! Anyway, I'm allowed to go where I want. You're only eight — I bet Mum doesn't know you leave the farm."

Luke hung his head, knowing he had lost this battle. "You spoiled my hideout," he grumbled, so Bessie helped him to rebuild it, hoping that any straw she picked up would explain her dishevelled appearance if her mother noticed. By the time they finished, she had persuaded herself that her reaction to what happened in Bottom Meadow had been silly — it was just the shock. Timmy *had* waited until she was sixteen, which proved he loved her even if he hadn't said so. Next Sunday she'd be ready for him, then he wouldn't need to go with other girls. She was a farmer's daughter and she shouldn't be babyish about sex. It was obviously Fate that Timmy was a farmer's son, and the Harvest Home party would be the perfect time to announce their engagement.

CHAPTER ELEVEN – 1928 – HARVEST HOME

Coppin and Pinetree Farms threw a combined Harvest Home every year, and at the end of September Albie received an invitation, along with all the other casual workers. "I ain't going," he told George, "That Bessie's bound to be there pestering me."

"We ain't seen her in a month," said George, "And there'll be hundreds of people to get lost in. Besides, it'll do you good to go — you've been like a wet weekend since Ellen went."

"Seeing that empty booth reminds me she's hundreds of miles away." Albie didn't add that every time he stacked the mats inside the helter-skelter he thought of the kisses they had shared, but he suspected Dad knew, especially when he said, "Bert all lovey-dovey with his Alice can't help, but it'll take your mind off things for a night." And so, for lack of any valid excuse, Albie agreed to go.

On the night of the party he and John padded the flat-bed van with an old mattress and took the entire Daly family in rattling splendour to Coppin Farm, where John parked in the farmyard with all the other vehicles. From there they walked through the copse to Bottom Meadow, and at the sight of half a cow and two pigs roasting on spits, Albie sniffed deeply - it had been worth coming after all. He and Bert and John hastened to join the group of men already clustered round the barrels of ale and cider, and Gladys Daly found herself abandoned by the barn with her other children. Most of the hay had been stacked outside the barn to make room for the dancing, and in the lee of this temporary hayrick Mabel Coppin was presiding over tables laden with huge brown teapots and jugs of lemonade.

"You're Gladys Daly, aren't you?" Mabel said, offering her a cup of tea, "I thought I recognized your brood from the strawberry fields. There are some kittens in the stables —

would they like to see them?"

"I'll take them, Mum — it will give you a rest," May offered, and shepherded the four younger ones away. Mabel poured Gladys a cup of tea and said thoughtfully, "That daughter of yours is a helpful girl — how old is she?"

"Fourteen next May."

"So she'll be looking for work soon — can she cook?"

"She cooked our tea every day while I was fruit-picking," Gladys smiled proudly. "May does wonders with the butcher's scraps our Bert brings home from work."

"I'll be wanting extra help in the house in the spring," said Mabel, "My present girl's getting married — I'll talk to May sometime tonight," and she turned away to serve another group of women with refreshments. Gladys went in search of her husband to tell him the good news that May was going to be offered work, but John was deep in conversation with potential customers, so she settled on a hay-bale in a corner of the barn to watch the dancing.

The sound of the musicians tuning up wafted round to the far side of the barn, where Albie and Bert were playing skittles against Pete and Brian Finch.

"Those two've been practising," Bert muttered as the brothers' score mounted, but Albie grinned and replied, "Wouldn't you practise if it were your party? I'm going to play my next shot differently – see if we can beat them that way." When his turn came round again Albie didn't take the usual run up, but simply planted his boots on the toe-line and bowled from there. He got six skittles with one ball and toppled the remaining three pins the same way.

"Them tactics ain't allowed," someone remarked from the crowd, but Pete Finch said, "Don't see why not as long as his toes don't cross the line," and they carried on playing. When the game was over, Albie and Bert's score was only a few points behind the Finches' and, with the promise of another game later, Pete and Brian took on the next pair of players.

Albie and Bert were heading back to the cider barrels when a familiar voice said, "Still playing dirty, I see," and Wally Biggins emerged from the shadows with his old sidekicks Fred Kelly and Timmy Coppin close behind.

"Thought that was you trying to stir up trouble at the skittles," Albie said, "Still need a gang to back you up, Wally? Afraid you'll get another broken leg?"

Wally took a belligerent step forward which Albie matched, and they were standing nose to nose with fists clenched until Bert said, "Leave it, Albie — we oughtn't to fight here." Albie turned away. Bert was right, of course, it would be bad manners to spoil the party by fighting, but when Wally sneered, "That's right, ducky — do as your lady-friend says," Albie's veneer of manners vanished and the former street urchin launched into battle.

Albie was no longer the small boy Wally had tried to bully at school and, although Wally was still the heavier of the two, he was flabby and unfit from days sitting at a factory workbench. Albie's initial rush pushed Wally back against the hayrick, a punch to the stomach doubled him over, and the scuffle would have ended there if Timmy and Fred hadn't also been drunk and spoiling for a fight. They leapt in with fists flying, Bert rushed to Albie's assistance, and the group of spectators abandoned the skittles to cluster round and watch.

Albie and Bert were holding their own against the gang of three until Timmy staggered under a particularly hard punch and his brother Ken joined the scrap. Now Albie and Bert were outnumbered two to one, but in the dusk it was difficult for the onlookers to distinguish who was fighting whom. It was only when the Finch brothers waded in to break up the fight that it became clear how uneven the odds were. Brian Finch hauled the Coppin boys off Bert by their collars and shook them. "Two onto one — you're a pair of sods and no mistake!"

"They started it," whined Timmy, struggling to break Brian's hold.

"Is that right?" Brian asked Bert, who had blood pouring down his face from a cut forehead.

"Wally's had it in for Albie since school," Bert hedged, and when someone else said, "That's true enough," Bert's evasion slipped by unremarked.

Meanwhile Pete Finch had dragged Wally and Fred off Albie's back, and an uneasy hush descended when he said, "He's not moving."

"You've killed him!" Luke screamed, tearing through the ring of people like a miniature whirlwind to kick Wally's shins. "You and your gang are stinking rotten cowards!" but then Albie sat up holding his head and croaked, "I ain't that easy to kill," a timely shout announced the roast meat was ready, and the onlookers dispersed leaving the Finches to deal with the aftermath of the fight.

Ken and Fred melted away with the crowd, but Pete and Brian took the other four combatants to the Coppin kitchen, where Brian fixed Bert's cut while Pete washed the dirt and blood from Albie's head. Wally and Timmy were holding wet cotton wads to their black eyes when Pete exclaimed, "This is a boot-print! Some bugger put the boot in – no wonder Albie was knocked silly."

Wally backed away from Pete's glare whining, "It weren't me!" and edged towards the door, but Brian blocked his escape, grabbed his leg and lifted it off the ground like a blacksmith inspecting a horse. "Does this one match?" he asked his brother, holding the boot towards the light, but it wasn't necessary to compare the metal toecap with the red weal on Albie's temple — Wally's guilt was written all over him. "Luke was right," Pete said in disgust, "You're all cowards. Wally - don't let me ever catch you round here again, and as for you, Timmy - your dad needs to know what kind of company you keep."

Leaving Bert to look after Albie, the Finch brothers frog-marched the other two back to Bottom Meadow, where they found Adam Finch dispensing beer. When he saw his sons manhandling Timmy Coppin, he waylaid them before too many people could see. "What's going on here, Pete?" he asked, "The last thing I need is a falling-out with Charlie Coppin." After Pete had explained, Adam said, "Too much drink caused this, I reckon, but it's best dealt with sober. Will you let me to sort out with Charlie?" When his sons nodded reluctantly he continued, "You can kick Wally out right now, and as for you, Timmy, there'll be no more drink for you tonight. I'll be round tomorrow to talk to your father."

An hour later, all Albie wanted to do was sleep. After the fight, the few mouthfuls of bread and pork he had managed to swallow had come up again on an acid rush of cider. When May dragged Bert into the dancing, Albie wandered away from the light and noise, looking for somewhere quiet. Eventually he found their van in the dark corner by the stables and climbed into the back, lay down on the old horsehair mattress and closed his eyes against the glare of the harvest moon. He was too woozy to notice, or to care, that Luke and Eddie Daly had followed him.

The two little boys, having agreed they'd die rather than dance with girls, had slipped out of the barn-dance when their mothers weren't looking. Pretending they were Just William and Ginger, they had tracked Albie through the thrillingly dark and spooky copse, and a minute after Albie settled into the back of the van they peeked over the tailgate to see him lying still and snoring.

"Probably drunk," said Luke, "My brothers snore like that when they've been to the pub."

Eddie bowed to Luke's superior knowledge – Bert was still too young to go to the pub – and they left Albie sleeping. A little later, after sitting in the driving seats of every vehicle they could get into and taking it in turns to beat the world land speed record, they drew Red Indian stripes on their cheeks with a lipstick they found on one of the dashboards and returned to the meadow.

*

Bessie couldn't bear it any longer. First Timmy had laughed when she wanted to announce their engagement, then he had turned down her suggestion that they should take advantage of her empty house to make love in a proper bed. Now, after being unfairly punished for a fight he hadn't started, he had brushed off her attempts to comfort him and left the barn with Kate from the dairy. She was sure all the other girls were laughing at her, the pork she had eaten earlier was lying in her stomach like a lump of dough, and the cider she had washed it down with was threatening to come back up. And then to top it all, when she went outside to have a decent weep in private, who should tug at her skirt asking "What's up with you?" but her little pest of a brother and his pal. She shook them off, hissing, "Go away and leave me alone," but then she noticed their faces and grabbed Luke to turn him to the light. "Have you been at my lipstick?"

"It ain't yours – we found this in a lorry," Luke said, "And we saw Albie snoring in the back of his van."

"You shouldn't be in the Coppin yard at all."

"And I bet Mum doesn't know you've got a lipstick," Luke shot back, and they ran off.

Bessie was still smarting horribly from Timmy's betrayal, and she definitely didn't want to see him return to the party with that after-sex look on his face. She wandered round to the barrels looking for her dad, but the smell of beer made her feel sick. The barn was full of music and dust and shrieks of people enjoying themselves – when she peered through the crush she saw that even her mum was dancing.

Bessie suddenly wished she was still young enough to be comforted by a cuddle, but if she asked for one Mum would want to know what was bothering her. She sighed heavily, hoping for sympathy, but nobody even noticed, and then she remembered Albie. He must be feeling miserable too if he'd gone to lie down – perhaps they could comfort each other.

Brightening up as the idea took root, Bessie crept away from the light of the fire and paraffin lamps. She met nobody in the copse or when she crossed the lane, and was able to nip through the gate by the stables and into the yard without being seen. The only sounds were of horses eating hay while they waited to take their owners home, the faint mew of kittens from one of the stables, and a gentle rumbling snore from the Daly's van. Bessie followed the sound and peeped over the side.

Albie looked so peaceful it seemed a shame to wake him, but she couldn't resist the sight of his broad chest rising and falling in the moonlight. She climbed silently over the tailgate and crawled up the mattress to snuggle into Albie's side, lifted his arm around her and rested her head on his chest. She'd never lain with a sleeping man before, and for a few moments she simply breathed him in. Albie smelled lovely – of fresh air and lavender soap rather than the farm-dirt smell of Timmy – and she could have stayed like that forever.

Albie's fall into unconsciousness when Wally kicked him had felt like thick black water closing over his head, and in his dreams he was still drowning — when he felt Bessie's body beside him he held on as if she were a lifebelt. Then the warm smell of horses and hay from the stables mingled with her soft hands on his chest and became a dream of Ellen, and without conscious thought he began stroking her back.

Bessie assumed Albie knew she was there, and she stretched up to kiss him. Her breasts in their thin cotton blouse tingled and she hoped Albie would touch them too, but then she thought that someone could come along at any moment – they didn't have much time. Timmy had taught her what he liked and she was adept at undoing a man's buttons — she opened Albie's shirt to rest her cheek briefly on his chest, then unfastened his trousers and slid her hand inside.

Albie's dreams were incoherent, and when Bessie's lips touched his, it was Ellen he kissed in his sleep. Half-concussed as he was, his young body still reacted to the cool air through his flies and a hand on his cock, and weeks of pent-up desire made him hard quickly. When Bessie climbed on top and drew him inside her, he responded automatically to her moves without once opening his eyes. Still only half-awake, he held back until he felt her shudder on top of him, and then he let his body surge into its own release.

"Ellen," he groaned, "Ellen love — my head hurts," and he reached up to pull her down onto his chest. He ran his fingers through her hair and then stopped. Something felt wrong, but it took him a moment to work out what. Instead of Ellen's thick straight hair he could feel curls, and his eyes shot open to see Bessie's face inches from his. Shouting, "What the hell are you playing at, Bessie Finch?" he shoved her off him with one sweep of his arm and scrubbed himself vigorously with the tail of his shirt. "Why are *you* here?"

Bessie had fantasized so often about Albie that she imagined she had a claim on him, and she had really thought he knew it was her in the back of the van. Then she had come with him inside her, which had never happened with Timmy, so they must be meant to be together. Even when he called her Ellen she failed to realise her mistake, because Timmy sometimes used the wrong name. It was the expression of horror in Albie's eyes that revealed the awful truth – he had actually thought he was making love to Ellen Ford, that common girl from the pier. She looked round in panic but to her relief they were still alone in their secluded corner. She pulled her knickers on clumsily. "I thought you wanted me!"

"What made you think that? I never said so."

"But you made love to me!"

"No I bloody didn't. I were knocked out and you fucked me unconscious. Now sod off and don't never come near me again!"

Bessie began to cry as she scrambled awkwardly down to the cobbles, and when Albie climbed down she thrust her face into his, snarling, "You fucked me too, Albie Smith, whether you like it or not," and ran off sobbing into the darkness.

Shuddering with disgust, Albie stumbled on wobbly legs to the yard pump and washed himself savagely, then stuck his head under the icy pump water. He couldn't bear to return to the van, and anyway he was wider awake than he had ever been in his life, so he made his way back to Bottom Meadow where he found that the party was winding down, John and Gladys were rounding up their tired children, and the whole ghastly night was over.

*

At Albie's fifteenth birthday tea a couple of weeks later, George and Bert went out into the back yard for a smoke and George took the opportunity to unburden himself. "Summat's up with our Albie but I can't put my finger on it," he confided. "At first I thought he was missing Ellen, but he's been worse since that fight at Coppin Farm. Doctor said there was no damage, so it ain't that." He was so agitated that he couldn't even roll a cigarette, and Bert offered him a Woodbine. George scraped a match on the wall to light it, dragged deeply and coughed. Thumping his chest with his fist he managed a weak smile. "Never could get on with ready-mades! Now — what about our Albie?"

"I'm as much in the dark as you," Bert said slowly. "I know he's missing Ellen but, like you say, it's more'n that." He leaned against the wall and watched the glow of his cigarette for a few moments. "Look, Mister Smith, you leave Albie to me. I should've asked him sooner but I've been too busy courting. I'll get to the bottom of it."

The next evening Bert appeared at the door holding his bike. "Come on Albie, we ain't had a ride for ages."

They rode in silence for a while, but when Bert turned down Farm Lane Albie put his brakes on. "I ain't going near Pinetree Farm."

Bert's ears pricked up at the panic in his voice — so it wasn't the scene of the fight that Albie was avoiding. "I was going down the other lane at the fork. Don't you visit your horse no more?"

It was true, Albie thought - he hadn't been there in weeks — and he allowed Bert to persuade him, though he didn't breathe freely until they'd passed the fork. The horse must have heard them coming because it was waiting at the gate, and when Albie rubbed its head it snorted with delight, then stood sideways on, presenting its broad back in a clear invitation.

"Go on, Albie, I ain't seen you ride it yet," Bert urged, so Albie climbed onto the horse's back, clicked his tongue and trotted round the field, returning with flushed cheeks and his eyes alight for the first time in a fortnight. Deciding now was as good a time as any, Bert came straight out with it. "Summat big's bothering you, Albie, and if you don't get it off your chest it'll fester. Come on — we been mates for long enough — tell me."

Sitting on the top bar of the gate with the big black head across his legs, Albie forced the words out more into the horse's ears than into Bert's. "That bloody Bessie Finch took advantage of me the night of the party."

"What d'you mean — took advantage?"

"I were knocked out, remember? Went to sleep it off in the van and she climbed on top of me. I thought it were Ellen and I didn't cotton on till it were too late."

"You mean you fucked her?"

"More like she raped me, the little cow, and I can't seem to scrub her off."

Bert had difficulty grasping the idea of a girl raping a bloke, and if he'd heard it from anyone else he'd have thought it was a joke, but he could see from Albie's face that this was no laughing matter. "Our Eddie says Luke Finch told him Bessie and Timmy Coppin have been at it like rabbits for over a year."

"So why'd she have a go at me?"

"Cause she's always fancied you — but that's Timmy's problem, not yours. I should forget about it if I was you."

Albie gave his horse a huge hug of relief and jumped off the gate. "Thanks, Bert, you're a pal - you won't let on to anyone, will you?"

"Course I won't," said Bert, slapping him on the back, "But you ought to tell your dad. It would let him rest easy — he's been dead worried."

"I couldn't talk to Dad about sex — he's too old!"

"Must've done it sometime, mustn't he?" laughed Bert, "One good thing — if you'd caught anything nasty you'd know by now."

Albie grinned his old cheerful grin. "I've been scrubbing it so hard it must be the cleanest cock around!"

Dot had a feeling Albie needed to talk to George as soon as he came into the kitchen, so she freshened up the pot and went upstairs, leaving George and Albie nursing cups of tea.

"Enjoy your ride, son?" George asked casually.

"I did that, both of them," Albie grinned, and told George about the carthorse.

"That horse must belong to Farmer Morris," said George, "His land meets Coppin and Pinetree at that corner - you be careful he don't catch you."

"I don't go much — this was the first time since that party." Albie stirred more sugar into his tea, and then took a deep breath and said, "Dad, something else happened that night — not just the fight." He clenched his jaw, but he couldn't hide the break in his voice.

George was appalled, and reached over the oilcloth to grip Albie's clenched fist. "Come on, son — spit it out."

"I had a bad head from the kicking and went to lay down in the van." Albie gulped, but now he'd started he was determined to finish. "I were dreaming about Ellen, you see – about being with her. . ."

"Making love, you mean?" George asked matter-of-factly and Albie relaxed a fraction — Bert had been right about Dad understanding. "Exactly – I were dreaming about that and there she was — or I thought she was — but when I opened me eyes it were Bessie Finch."

George's jaw dropped. "You mean to tell me she just climbed on top of you? When she knew you'd been kicked unconscious? That dirty little slut!" This was strong language from the usually mild George, but then he frowned. "Did she have any reason to think she'd be welcome?"

"No she bloody well didn't!" Albie cried, "Dad, you've got to believe me!"

"Calm down, lad, calm down — I do believe you, but I had to ask. Well, now you've got that off your chest perhaps you can start enjoying life again."

CHAPTER TWELVE – 1928 – THE LIE

A few days before Christmas Ruth Finch slid a tray of mince pies into the oven, straightened her back with an effort and caught sight of her daughter stretching up to hang the breakfast bacon back on its hook. Ruth's eyes narrowed and her brain shot into top gear. She'd assumed Bessie was simply putting on weight since the wet weather had curtailed her bike rides into town, but the shape outlined under the voluminous apron was unmistakable. Thinking furiously, Ruth put the teapot to warm on the range and took the square black tea-caddy from the dresser. "Sit down, Bessie — let's have a quiet cuppa before the men come in."

Bessie seized the chance for a sit-down with a sigh of relief that was not lost on her mother, sinking gratefully onto a form and resting her elbows on the oilcloth. The last week had exhausted her and opportunities for a rest had been few. Day after day standing on the hard flagstones mixing pastry or stirring enormous bowls of heavy, fruit-laden mixture for Christmas puddings; the kitchen full of steam when the puddings boiled in their cotton cloths; the range going full-blast as she and her mother baked bread and pork pies and cakes and hams for the food baskets that every farmhand expected as a Christmas box. The sickness that had plagued her for months, and that had been so difficult to conceal in the crowded farmhouse, had been replaced by aching legs and swollen ankles.

Bessie's thoughts had been circling like a rat in a trap for months and she knew she'd have to make up her mind soon. She still met Timmy every week, but lately she had begun to suspect he was bored with her. He didn't make any effort to excite her like he used to, but even he was bound to notice soon. She was beginning to show and couldn't hide it much longer, but she was afraid of his reaction to her news.

To add to her confusion, those few minutes with Albie

had been more enjoyable than an hour with Timmy. By carefully editing the events of that night, Bessie had spliced together a memory of kisses and passion and mutual orgasm. It was only because Wally's boot had knocked Albie silly that he'd shouted at her and thought she was Ellen. She only had to see him again to make it all come right.

Some of this maelstrom of doubt showed on her face as she sat at the table with her elbows in the film of flour, and her mother sat down heavily in her own chair, unsure how to begin. She waited for the tea to brew before pouring them each a cup, and decided on an oblique approach. "I've not seen your monthly rags on the line for a while, Bessie — what are you doing with them?"

Bessie looked up, startled, to see Ruth watching her with shrewd intelligence and knew there was no point in lying — it would have to come out soon anyway. "I've not needed them, Mum."

Ruth nodded and sipped her suddenly tasteless tea. "So you're expecting. How much longer were you going to wait before you told me?"

Bessie shrugged – an infuriating gesture that made Ruth's hand itch to slap her. "I was going to tell you next week — I didn't want to spoil Christmas."

"Too late for that now, my girl," Ruth said, beginning to lose patience, "You'll have to get wed before the month's out, by the look of you. Who's the father?"

Bessie stared at her mother dumbly while her entire future flashed in front of her. Married in a shameful rush and living on the next-door farm for the rest of her life — going to bed every night with Timmy Coppin, who she didn't even like very much. She shook her head at the thought, a movement which Ruth misinterpreted, and her careful composure evaporated. She jumped up so quickly that her chair toppled. "Do you mean to tell me you don't know? What have I done to deserve this?" and she swung her hand in a slap that had

Bessie clutching her ear. "I do know, so there! It was the night of Harvest Home — it's Albie — Albie Smith."

"What are you saying about Albie?" asked Luke, bouncing into the kitchen and sniffing appreciatively at the smell of baking, "Can I have a mince pie?"

"Dammit - the mince pies!" Ruth cried, flinging open the oven door to rescue them.

"Mum!" Luke gasped, "You said a bad word!"

"So I did, and there'll be more if you don't get out from under my feet," Ruth snapped, putting the hot tray on a board so she could ease the overcooked little pies onto a cooling rack. "And your hands are filthy — go and wash them."

Luke couldn't understand why Mum was so cross. Bessie was red in the face as if she'd been crying so it was probably her fault, but there was no need for Mum to take it out on him. He scowled at Bessie, who ignored him. With a face like thunder he stomped off into the scullery to splash his hands under the cold tap and sulk, though with no-one to see him there wasn't much point and he soon stopped. Sensing it would be best to keep out of the way, he hunkered down by the box in the corner to play with the puppies that had been born far too early to stay in the outhouse, and he was still there when his father and brothers came in for their afternoon tea.

"What's up with you, Bessie?" asked Pete, ruffling her curls.

She brushed his hand away. "Leave me alone, can't you?"

Pete was surprised — he had a soft spot for his baby sister and she was usually nicer to him. "Well, you're in a fine mood," he teased, "Wrong week, is it?"

"Peter!" Ruth scolded, but Bessie burst into tears.

Adam raised his eyebrows at his wife. "She's not usually this bad — sweetheart trouble?"

While Bessie howled and the three men frowned with

puzzled concern, Ruth said, "Well, I suppose you'll have to know soon — Bessie's expecting."

"She's what?" Adam's roar rang round the room and into the scullery. Luke dropped the puppy he was holding and ran to hide behind the door, peering through the gap by the doorjamb at the scene in the kitchen. Dad had pulled Bessie to her feet and was shaking her like a rag doll. "How could you shame us like this? You're only just sixteen and you're having a baby? I've a good mind to throw you out, Christmas or no Christmas!"

A baby! Bessie was having a baby! Ever since he'd learned how babies were made, Luke had realised that Bessie hadn't been wrestling with Timmy in the barn - she'd been mating. Consumed with curiosity, he had even watched them once though he hadn't seen as much as he'd hoped, but he had since witnessed the arrival of the puppies by peeping through this same gap and he had worked it out. His attention returned to the kitchen where Mum was crying now as well.

"You can't throw her out, Adam - where would she go?"

"To the man who got her this way, that's where! Who is he anyway - do you know?"

From his vantage-point Luke saw that Bessie was weeping noisily into Pete's shirt-front, but Brian was sitting at the table working his way steadily through the tray of mince pies — if he wasn't quick Brian would eat the lot. Luke slid round the door, careful to stay hidden, and grabbed a mince pie just as Mum sat back in her chair. He needn't have worried — Mum didn't even notice him.

"She says it was Albie Smith," Ruth said wearily, "At the Harvest Home party."

"That was three months ago! Even if she gets married now she won't get away with saying it's premature," Adam shouted, then he remembered something else. "Albie's only just fifteen - they won't be able to get wed!" He regarded his daughter with active dislike. "Give me boys any day — at least you know where you were with them. Bessie, get your coat on. Pete, stop fussing her and hitch Violet to the cart. Albie Smith might not be old enough to marry her, but he'll take responsibility if I have to beat it into him!"

Luke didn't understand any of this – Albie was a hero who had saved his life — why would Dad want to beat him up? "But Dad – I thought only married people made babies, so why is Bessie having one?"

Brian spluttered pastry all over the table and Adam glared at him. "What have you been telling Luke? Oh, never mind, I've got worse to deal with at the moment. Pete will drive us – Brian, you're in charge while we're gone."

*

Bert had delivered Dot's Christmas meat order early, in the certain knowledge that there would be tea and cake to keep him going till dinner, which could be hours yet with all the deliveries he had to make.

"There's just enough for another cup each," Dot was saying when a loud hammering on the door brought George to his feet. "All right," he called out, "No need to knock the door in!" and as soon as he'd undone the latch, Adam Finch burst into the room dragging Bessie with him.

During the half-hour ride into town Bessie's mind had been working furiously, weighing up the disgrace of having a baby out of wedlock against the possibility of marrying Albie when he was old enough. Albie would probably take her word that the baby was his, and if it came early and was fair-haired like the Coppins she could say it took after her. On the other hand, Coppin Farm was prosperous – they had their own motorcar and everything – while Albie only worked on the pier. That couldn't bring in much money, and what he did in the off-season she had no idea. But if she changed her story now, everyone would know she'd been with both Albie and Timmy and she'd be labelled a tart.

Ruth had sat silently beside her, also thinking. They'd seen nothing of Albie Smith since the day he came round to be thanked for saving Luke, and then he'd shown no interest in Bessie. Maybe they had been meeting on Sundays? No, that couldn't be right — Sundays were the busiest days on the pier. Bessie said it had happened at the Harvest party, when Albie had been knocked out in a fight — surely he wouldn't have been in a fit state to get her pregnant. And that was another thing that bothered her, now she had time to think about it – this was Bessie's first pregnancy and she shouldn't show this much if she was only three months gone.

With these thoughts churning in her head, Ruth had tried to stop her husband from barging in with guns blazing, but he wouldn't listen. Even before the wheels stopped turning he leapt off the front seat and hauled Bessie to the pavement, leaving Pete to tie Violet to a lamp post and help his mother down.

The minute he stepped over the Smith's threshold Adam pushed Bessie in front of him and started shouting. George barred the way to the table where Dot sat, but Albie and Bert scrambled to their feet, gazing open-mouthed at Adam's furious figure and Bessie's drooping one.

"Look what your boy's done!" Adam yelled at George, "No good ever came of picking a kid out of the gutter!"

George's chest swelled and he seemed to shed twenty years as he grabbed Adam by the lapels. Pulling him forward so that they were nose to nose, he growled, "How dare you barge into my house and insult my son!"

As the two men struggled they banged into the table and upset the crockery, so Albie helped Dot out of her chair, saying loudly and pointedly, "You go and sit in the rocker, Mum, you'll be safer there," and then he put his hand on George's arm. "Let go of him, Dad — this sounds like my problem."

Pete spun Albie round and snarled directly into his

face, "Too bloody right it's your problem — it's your baby Bessie's expecting."

In the awful silence that followed this bald statement Albie looked hard at Bessie, searching for the truth, but her eyes refused to meet his, darting instead around the small kitchen. This was clearly the only living-room apart from the even smaller scullery beyond the other door. With a table in front of the window, a range along one wall and a dresser against another, there was scarcely enough space for an ancient armchair and the rocker in which Missus Smith now sat, nervously pleating her apron. The whole house would fit into the scullery back home, Bessie thought wildly — how could she possibly live here?

She heard her father's voice as if from a great distance and her mother shoved her painfully in the back saying, "Bessie, answer your dad."

"Speak up, girl," Adam ordered, "Tell them what you told us — you were with Albie at the Harvest Home."

Bessie finally looked at Albie and shrank from his expression of dismay. Unable to form the words that would seal her fate, she took refuge in a fresh storm of tears.

"Oh for Heaven's sake pull yourself together, girl!" Ruth hissed. Infuriated beyond bearing, she caught hold of Bessie's arm and swung her round to slap her face but, to everyone's surprise, Albie pushed past the others and took Bessie in his arms, holding her awkwardly and patting her shoulders.

"That's enough," he said quietly, "What's done can't be helped. We only did it once and it weren't of my choosing, but no kid of mine is going to grow up without a dad — I'll marry her."

Dot flung her apron over her head and sobbed, rocking back and forth in a paroxysm of despair, and George sat down at the table, waving his hand wearily at the other chairs. "You'd all better sit down — we'll talk it over right here and now."

The Finches, deflated by Albie's capitulation, did as George suggested and Albie went to comfort Dot.

Bert, forgotten in the drama, leaned on the mantelpiece staring at Bessie. He'd seen his mum expecting often enough to know how big Bessie should be, and this wasn't right. "When did she say this happened?" he asked abruptly.

Pete answered him, "Harvest party, if it's any of your business."

"That's what I thought," said Bert, unabashed, "Albie told me how she crept up on him when he were knocked silly after that kicking."

"Shut up, Bert," Albie protested, mortified at the idea of that story coming out.

"Sorry, mate, but they've got to hear this," Bert insisted, without taking his eyes off the Finch family. "Albie were asleep in the back of the van and didn't wake up proper till after – he thought Bessie were his sweetheart – and that were the only time they done it."

Adam and Pete gaped at Bessie, aghast not only at Bert's revelation but also at the fact that they believed it. Ruth, having had her suspicions confirmed, demanded, "For once in your life, girl, tell the truth.Is what Bert says right – it was only that one time?" Bessie nodded miserably. "Right!" said Ruth, standing up briskly and dragging Bessie to her feet. "Albie, my daughter owes you an apology. Adam, Pete, we're leaving."

"What do you mean, we're leaving?" Adam demanded, "However it happened, Bessie's still expecting."

"I'm only too aware of that," Ruth told him grimly, "And I know I should have spotted it sooner – but this baby wasn't conceived at the end of September." She tugged Bessie's dress tight and forced her sideways on to the room. "As you can see, she must be at least four months gone – it wouldn't surprise me if it's already kicking – so by her own admission there's no way it could be Albie's."

Pete recovered first and rounded on his sister. "So whose is it? Do you even know?"

Bessie gasped as if he had struck her and started crying again, but Ruth remembered her daughter was only sixteen and still her little girl. She slid her arm round Bessie's waist and said more gently, "Come on, love – just tell us who the father is."

When Bessie continued sobbing, Bert decided he'd have to stick his oar in again. It was bad enough that Bessie had raped Albie, without all this hassle on top. "Reckon I can tell you who it is," he said.

Pete turned on him belligerently. "How would you know? Was it you?"

"Not bloody likely – me and my girl are waiting till we're wed. Your little brother told my little brother he seen Bessie at it in the barn with Timmy Coppin."

One glance at Bessie's face was enough to confirm what Bert said and Ruth gasped, "Luke saw them? But he's only eight!"

"He's a farmer's son, Ruth – he'll get over it," Adam said, and offered George his hand. "I must apologise for not getting at the truth before we came barging in. I'd ask you to keep Bessie's disgrace to yourselves if I thought for one moment she deserved such consideration."

George nodded wordlessly, knowing there was nothing he could say that would make Adam feel any better. Ruth bundled Bessie out into the street, Adam and Pete helped them into the cart, and they clip-clopped away.

After the Finches' subdued departure, the first to break the shocked silence in the Smith's kitchen was Bert, who punched Albie's bicep and let out a great shout of laughter. "Ha! Bessie Finch's got her comeuppance now. Timmy won't be best pleased – he likes his freedom too much – but I s'pose he'll have to wed her."

Dot heaved her bulk out of the rocker to do what she always did after a crisis — make a pot of tea — and George was beaming with relief, but Albie just stood staring at nothing.

"I've got deliveries to do," said Bert, "You going to be all right, Albie?"

"I'm fine, Bert, ta, off you go," and Albie sat at the table beside George, trying to work out why he felt so let down. Getting married this young was the last thing he wanted, particularly to Bessie, yet for that brief moment when he'd held her thinking it was his baby inside her, he'd been ready to take on the world. He sipped automatically at the tea Dot put in front of him and she stroked his hair like she used to when he was younger. That gesture of affection was all it took. Albie buried his face in her apron, breathing in her scent of lavender soap and baking, and swallowed the lump in his throat. "I'm sorry, Mum," he murmured when he could trust himself to speak.

"Hush, you've got nothing to be sorry for," she soothed, "Sounds like it was all her fault."

"Just be more careful where you sleep in future," said George briskly, "And open your eyes before your flies."

Albie slapped his forehead and exclaimed, "Shit! That story about me and Bessie will be round town in a flash!"

"No it won't, son — think about it - the Finches wouldn't want to smear Bessie's name any further by repeating that sorry tale."

CHAPTER THIRTEEN – THE FIGHT

The Smiths celebrated their usual Christmas with the family, and the only cloud left on Albie's horizon was the lack of any word from Ellen. That cloud lifted when, two days later, he came down to breakfast to find an envelope bearing a foreign stamp propped against the marmalade jar.

"You've got a letter," said Dot unnecessarily, taking the pan of bacon off the hotplate and sitting down to wait for Albie to open it.

"Knew she'd send you a card," added George, as eager as Dot to see the contents. The postman had handed the envelope over personally, impressed that this humble house had mail from abroad and commenting, "Late Christmas card, I shouldn't wonder — you can't expect a foreign post office to get it here on time."

"Feels like more'n a card," said Albie, turning the envelope over in his hands, "But there's no return address."

"She'll have sent a letter too — it'll be on that," said Dot, "Ain't you going to open it?"

Albie slit the envelope and pulled out a card. It was a highly-coloured depiction of the Holy Family, signed by both Ellen and Fred, which he placed beside the others on the mantelpiece, but the letter that was inside - several sheets of it - he slipped into his pocket. "John'll be round with the van soon," he said, "There's no time now to read letters," and Dot had to swallow her disappointment and finish cooking their breakfast.

After eating his midday sandwiches, Albie wiped his hands on his shirt and unfolded the letter. His eyes followed his finger across the page as he read about sunshine and strange-sounding food in places he couldn't pronounce. He was smiling until he reached the last page, then he had to read it twice before the truth sank in.

"*Dads getting too old for the boxing,*" Ellen wrote, "*So when the circus manager offered to take him on permanent as a rigger he jumped at it. We wont be coming back to the pier because after Spain we go to France and Germany and we wont be home in England till summer."*

When he read those words Albie thought that summer was better than nothing, but Ellen's last few sentences killed that faint spark of hope.

"One of the other riggers is called Mike and he is really nice. We have been courting for two months and he asked me to marry him and I said yes. I wont ever forget you Albie we had some good times together. I hope you find your gypsy dad. With love from your friend Ellen. xx "

Albie crumpled the letter into a ball and then smoothed it out to read again, hoping he'd misunderstood, but it was true – Ellen wasn't coming back.

*

The moment Albie got home, Dot brewed a pot of tea, sat down and asked, "What's Ellen got to say for herself?"

Albie summoned up a smile – Mum didn't know Ellen had been more than a friend – and read them the letter, only leaving out the part about finding his gypsy dad – he knew Mum wouldn't like that. George gave him a sympathetic look but Dot said cheerfully, "It's about time she was wed. Can't be much of a life trailing round with her dad."

She'll be moving all the time now with the circus," Albie pointed out.

"Then it makes sense to marry one of them and we wish her happy," George said robustly. "It was nice she wrote and told you — shows she thinks a lot of you, that does," and from the expression on his face Albie could see the subject was now closed.

"Never mind — there's always May," Bert said when Albie told him.

"Don't be daft, Bert — May's like me own sister! Besides, she's going to work on Coppin Farm and I ain't going near that place again."

"Oh for God's sake, Albie! You get too wound up about

things. You had a lucky escape and you should stop moping and start looking round for another girl — there's enough choice, after all."

"I'll never trust another girl – even if they love you they leave you."

*

But when spring arrived, with its surge of life evident in every field, hedgerow and garden, like any other young man, Albie's fancy turned to thoughts of girls, if not actually of love. He began to eye the workers and visitors on the pier, and even took a few girls for walks or to the pictures, but none of them could tempt him to go steady. Ellen had bruised his heart, his close call with Bessie had made him wary, and he earned a reputation among the local girls as a hard nut to crack.

One Sunday afternoon in summer, May Daly turned up on the pier with a group of pickers from Coppin Farm, and she stopped at the helter-skelter to say hello to Albie. When the well-built young man enfolded her in a hug the other girls looked on enviously and two of the boys scowled. Albie grinned and said into May's ear, "They think I'm your bloke."

"No harm in letting 'em think that," May answered with a mischievous twinkle, "Unless you fancy one of the girls?"

Albie surveyed the group. "The dark-haired one ain't bad-looking, but I've got two on the go as it is. What about you – got a sweetheart?"

"Two farmhands and a Londoner have asked, but I've told 'em I can't decide – besides, there's safety in numbers!"

George listened to this exchange and smiled ruefully. Albie was obviously well on the way to being heart-whole again, but it would be a while yet before they saw him settle down like Bert with a steady girl.

Walter Biggins watched Albie and May from behind a puffball of candyfloss and licked his lips – May Daly had filled out nicely in the year since he'd last seen her. When the

chattering farm group moved down the pier to the Penny
Arcade he followed them, admiring May's figure in her print
dress. No wonder Albie Smith fancied her, he thought, but a
gyppo's part-time money couldn't hope to compete with a
decent working man's wage.

Chinking the coins in his pocket, Wally hovered on the
edge of the group, putting in a word here, inserting a penny in
a machine there, and awaiting his opportunity to shine. His
moment came with the Try Your Strength machine, where his
weight was an advantage. He wielded the hammer to such
effect that the bell clanged loudly, drawing squeals of
admiration from some of the girls. Scooping up his winnings,
he announced grandly, "I'll buy all you girls a toffee apple,"
and walked back up the pier trailing his courtiers like a king.

As the girls bit into their treats, Wally edged closer to
May and slipped an arm round her waist. "Give us a lick," he
said suggestively, putting his cheek against hers. May cringed
and tried to break free, but Wally's arm tightened and he
wheedled, "Come on, May – I paid for it."

"Then you eat it," she replied and jammed the sweet
into his open mouth. Wally spat it out. "You ungrateful little
cow!" he yelled, grabbing May's arm, but he had forgotten the
toffee apple stall was directly opposite the helter-skelter.

May only just got out of the way in time as Albie's
furious charge carried Wally clear across the pier. A bench
caught Wally behind the knees and they both fell, but Albie
scrambled up first, pulling Wally by his shirt-front until they
were nose to nose. "Bullying girls now, Wally? Never could
pick on someone your own size, could you?"

Wally sprayed toffee-spit in Albie's face as he retorted,
"Bert Daly'll never be anyone's size – and now he's got
himself a girlfriend you've moved on to his sister."

From the lee of the helter-skelter George and May both
heard what Wally said. May covered her mouth in shock, but
George grunted approval when Albie swung his arm against

the side of Wally's head in a stinging slap. Wally retaliated by throwing a punch which Albie dodged easily. The fruit pickers, who had retreated to a safe distance at the first sign of trouble, returned to watch the fight and, in the centre of a growing crowd, Albie and Wally traded blow for blow.

Wally kept his fists up to protect his face as he had seen professionals do on boxing nights in the Pier Theatre, and his hobnailed boots beat a tattoo on the boards of the pier in an effort to emulate their dancing footwork. He got in a few punches, and he out-weighed Albie by at least a stone, but he worked at a bench in the furniture factory, breathing glue fumes and sawdust all day, and spent his evenings in a back-street pub — he was fat, fifteen and unfit.

Albie barely felt those punches that did find their mark. He had grown up on the streets, literally fighting for enough to eat, and he didn't know any rules. The combination of his outdoor life and his work moving loads had built up strong muscles on his sturdy frame. Albie's fighting method was simply to pummel his opponent until one of them ran out of breath or lost the will to carry on, and Wally's attempts to box properly fell on stony ground.

When Wally's hands dropped with exhaustion, Albie drew his arm back for the final punch but George called out, "No son — he's done for," and Albie stepped away.

He couldn't have picked a more humiliating way to end the fight. Even being knocked out cold would have been preferable, and as Wally's pals hauled him away like a sack of potatoes his mind seethed with hatred. One day, he vowed silently, he would have his revenge on Albie Smith.

Albie sensed the black thought and turned away, to see two gypsy men standing at the edge of the crowd. He walked straight over to them, still fired up from his fight. "You were watching me," he challenged.

"We were – and you've been watching our women out in the fields."

"Not like that!" Albie blurted, "And I don't mean no harm – I'm just looking for me father."

"So we've heard – but it seems to us you've got a good one here," the man said, nodding at George. He took Albie's arm in a strong grip and added, "You could end up in trouble by asking the wrong people. If you've got Roma blood your father will find you – one day."

"Everything all right, Albie?" George called, and Albie turned his head to reply, "I'm fine, Dad." When he turned back, the two men had gone.

PART TWO – 1935

CHAPTER FOURTEEN – 1935 - BLOOD

"Come on, Albie, I'll buy you a pint." Bert was so obviously bursting with some exciting news that Albie gulped down the last mouthful of his meal and grabbed his jacket off the back of his chair. As he pulled the front door closed behind him, Dot called out, "Mind you don't come home drunk!"

"I only did that once, over a year back," Albie said to Bert, "But Mum's never let me forget it."

"My mum's the same," Bert replied cheerfully, "Except I've done it more'n once!"

When they pushed through the swing doors of the King's Head the atmosphere hit them like a fist. Four or five dozen people filled the place with noise, and the damp from coats steaming in the heat of a coal fire, together with the smell of the beer-soaked wooden floor and cheap cigarettes, created a fug that the two friends inhaled with relish. Albie ploughed a path to the bar with his broad shoulders and they elbowed a space to lean against the counter. With a foot each on the brass rail they took long pulls on their pints.

"That's better!" Bert said, wiping his mouth on his sleeve, "I've got a real thirst tonight."

"So what's put that smirk on your face? You're like a cat that's got at the cream."

"I'm getting married!"

Albie spluttered beer all over the bar. "Dammit, Bert, you could've built up to that a bit slower!"

"Sorry, mate, but I'm that excited."

"Twenty-one's a bit young to get wed — is Alice expecting?"

"No she bloody well ain't!" Bert retorted, "But I s'pose folk are bound to wonder. No, the thing is, Mr Wallace has made me up to a proper butcher with more wages, and he says we can have the two rooms over the shop if I do 'em up. It's too good a chance to miss."

"Your mum and dad won't know themselves with you and May both gone."

"Oh, we'll only be round the corner," said Bert airily, "And May's home most Sundays."

"Will they manage without your wages?"

"They'll be all right. May brings baskets of goodies from Coppin Farm every week — there'll be enough food on the table."

"When's the big day, then?"

"Four weeks time — end of March." Bert grinned at the shock on Albie's face, "Thought we'd get wed before Easter so you'll be around to help me distemper the walls."

"What's wrong with Eddie doing it?"

"He's busy with his odd-jobs after school - besides, you're taller."

"Got it all worked out, ain't you?" Albie laughed and called to the barman, "Another pint for my mate here — he's getting married."

The man next to them muttered, "More fool him," but when Albie tapped Bert's tankard with his own and said, "Congratulations, Bert," everyone within earshot raised their own drink and Bert was soon surrounded by well-wishers.

Albie was edged out by the crush. He inhaled a waft of cheap scent and looked down at a hand on his arm wearing a clutch of garish rings. He tried to shake it off but the woman wheedled, her breath sour and boozy, "You got a girl too, dearie, or are you looking for company?"

"No thanks." She must be a stranger — the regular women knew it was a waste of time asking him.

The woman's grip tightened. "You could buy a girl a drink at least, couldn't you?"

As recognition dawned, Albie wrenched her hand off his sleeve and whirled round to face her. Peering into her drink-blurred eyes he hissed, "Don't you know who I am?"

"You could be the bloody King of Spain for all I care," she spat, "You've no call to be like that," and she tore her wrist out of his grip to go in search of easier prey.

Albie held onto the bar tightly, afraid to trust his shaking legs, and watched the woman who had been his mother for twelve years approach another man and leave with him through the side door.

Albie must have stood there for a good hour, sipping his beer and staring at nothing, before Bert lurched against him, slurring, "Think I might've had one too many."

Abandoning his own tankard, Albie said, "More than one too many by the look of you – it's time we was going."

When he steered Bert out into the street. The frigid February air embraced Albie like a blessing, and the need to hold Bert upright on the icy cobbles steadied his whirling thoughts. On the way back to the Daly's house he tried to tell Bert what had happened, but his friend was too drunk to give any sensible response, so he handed him over to John and walked slowly down to the promenade.

Leaning on the frozen iron railing, Albie watched the thin lines of white foam following one another in from the darkness to dissolve into the sand. It was still too early for the pubs to be emptying and on this cold night he was the only one on the promenade. He loved the sea in all its moods but, like George, he thought winter was the best time, when the town was left to the locals. The ceaseless push of the ocean against the land always had the power to heal, and he began to think more coherently. He had worked out years ago that his mother was a tart and the man who fathered him had probably been a customer. It was a shock to see her back in Thambay when he'd thought she was in London, but none of that was what had upset him. What had knocked him sideways tonight was that she hadn't recognized him – the woman who bore him hadn't even known her own blood.

After a long time gazing at the oily waves, Albie straightened his shoulders, sighed heavily, and went home.

Dot had gone to bed but George was still up, and it wasn't long before Albie had told him all about it. George's jaw tensed with disgust but for Albie's sake he merely said, "She probably still thinks of you as a scrawny kid — you've changed a lot since then."

"If she thinks about me at all — but she didn't even know her own son."

"You ain't hers, though, are you?" said George, "You're mine and Dot's - have been nearly ten years. She just happened to be there when you was born — no more'n that."

Albie went to bed comforted. Dad was right — Dot was the only mum he needed, and if that other woman couldn't recognize her own blood it was her loss, not his.

*

Bert and Alice's wedding was very much a neighbourhood affair. Bert's boss Mr Wallace donated a joint of beef, plus several pounds of sausage-meat with which Gladys Daly and Alice's mother made mountains of sausage rolls. Dot collected the ingredients from several friends and baked a fruit cake which the woman next door iced beautifully, and every neighbour who had been invited dropped off a few bottles at Alice's house to help with the bridal feast.

On the day itself, Albie stood at Bert's side in the church watching Alice's brother lead her down the aisle and listening to the murmurs of admiration from every pew. Alice's sprigged cotton dress and her hat covered with flowers transformed her dark prettiness into beauty — Bert was so open-mouthed with adoration that Albie had to nudge him into place beside his bride. Later, when the newly-married couple emerged from the vestry, the broad grin on Bert's face lit up the whole church. That was how a bridegroom should look, Albie thought, and thanked his lucky stars that he hadn't fallen victim to Bessie's wiles.

After Mr Wallace had wielded his Box Brownie to take pictures of Bert and Alice posed on the church steps, the bride and groom led the wedding party on foot through the streets, where housewives and the unemployed stood in their doorways to call down blessings on them, and a gaggle of children tailed the procession.

Albie was supposed to be escorting May, who was Alice's bridesmaid, but he lost her in the crush, and when he did find her he wasn't at all pleased to see her companion was Ken Coppin. Whenever Ken was in town he was with Wally Biggins, and everyone knew they were both still too free with their fists.

"What the hell are you doing here, Ken?" he asked, "You ain't one of Bert's mates," but May put a hand on his arm and begged, "Albie, please don't. I ain't had a chance to tell you yet — me and Ken are walking out."

This was a shock. May had been working as a maid at Coppin Farm for six years, and Albie immediately thought that Ken was just taking advantage of the hired help. It was on the tip of his tongue to say so, but May's eyes were imploring him not to make a scene, so he swallowed those words in favour of a warning, "Well, just you make sure you treat her right or you'll have me to answer to."

May dragged Ken away before he could respond, and as Albie watched them go he felt about ninety years old. He still thought of May as he had first seen her - a skinny ten-year-old in a too-short frock - and now she was courting. First Bert getting married and now this - it was about time he got himself sorted out, Albie thought. When he'd shaved this morning, the scullery mirror had shown him a grown man - one his own mother hadn't recognised - yet he hadn't had a proper sweetheart since Ellen. When the pier opened he'd have to make more effort to find one.

But the next woman to walk into Albie's life was far from the right age to become his sweetheart.

*

"Morning George – looks like being nice weather for the Easter weekend. Morning Albie – how's the delivery business?"

"Doing well, thanks, William – I've taken a few days off to help Dad open up the ride."

William had been the pier gateman for as long as Albie could remember, and nothing happened on the pier without him knowing, so they lingered for his usual start-of-the season news broadcast. "Bathing suit hire has gone," he informed them. Fred Ford's old pitch had had a chequered few years since the strongman left, and the bathing suit hire had lasted less time than most. William's expression said he had more gossip to impart so George obliged him by asking, "Who's taken it over?"

"This you'll never believe — management's let it to gypsies!" William shook his head in disbelief, "They offered Mr Campbell the whole season up front. Could hardly refuse, could he, the way things are? It's going to be a fortune-teller's booth."

George and Albie left William to pass on the news to the next arrival and headed for the helter-skelter. Their first task each spring was to scrub down and freshen up the paintwork on the ride after its winter in the salt spray, and over the years they had got it down to a fine art, but this year Albie worked his way up the slide with only half his mind on the job.

For five years, ever since the two men on the pier had warned him off, he had been more circumspect in his search for his father, but he had never ceased to hope. In another month or so there would be groups of gypsies arriving to swell the work-force on the farms, and he would once again search every face for some resemblance to his own. He'd have plenty of lonely evenings to do that now that Bert was married, but bike rides wouldn't be enough to fill the emptiness in his life. The news that the gypsies were actually coming to the pier seemed like an omen. This year was going to be special – he could feel the certainty fizzing in his blood like ginger ale. His fist clenched involuntarily and he nearly dropped his scrubbing brush, which pulled him up with a jerk – he'd better get on with the job in hand or Dad would be complaining.

George had started the morning inside the helter-skelter sweeping down the stairs, and then moved outside to beat the mats free of dried salt, dust and mouse-droppings. When Albie finished scrubbing the slide they broke off to share a Thermos of tea — the tearooms wouldn't open until Good Friday – and then Albie left George having a smoke and strolled down the pier. He took his time, greeting old friends engaged in their own refurbishments, but eventually he reached his target — the booth that had been Fred and Ellen's seven seasons ago.

The painted sign of a couple in bathing costumes, which had caused such ribaldry last season, was now propped against the doorpost, effectively barring entry to the booth. Sounds of hammering came from the dark interior, and then someone swore loudly, so Albie stuck his head inside to ask, "You all right?"

A weather-beaten young man looked up, sucking his thumb. "You'd think after all the pots I've mended I'd know how to use a hammer," he said, offering Albie his hand, "I'm Dan – I'm hanging curtains for my aunt Sofia."

As Albie's eyes adjusted to the dim light he saw a woman crouched beside an open chest. She pulled out a fringed shawl to drape over a small table and immediately the booth took on an air of mystery. Shutting the lid of the chest, she sat on it and peered at Albie. "Come in, Albert, I can't see you properly against the light," she commanded, so Albie moved aside the painted bathers and stepped inside to stand in front of the table.

The silence curled round him, and when Sofia took his hand he shifted uncomfortably, but he was held in place by the steady gaze of her black eyes. "We meet at last," Sofia said, so softly that Albie wasn't sure he had heard correctly, then she turned his hand palm upwards and put her own hand on top. He could feel his blood pumping through each vein under her cool touch and he was startled when she echoed his thought. "Blood," she said, "Roma blood. I think Mateo could be right."

Her nephew spoke from the shadows, making Albie jump. "From the look of him he'd be a Smith."

"He could be – they were always a bit wild," Sofia said with a smile in her voice. She released Albie's hand. "You can go now, Albert — we'll talk again."

Albie found himself outside with no clear idea how he got there, and walked back to George in a daze, mentally kicking himself. After all these years of looking, Sophia and Dan seemed to know who he was, but he hadn't asked a single question. He took the pot of red paint and climbed the stairs to paint the top cabin, occasionally catching a glimpse of Dan also wielding a paint-brush, but by the time he'd finished the cabin both Dan and his aunt had gone. It was only that night, when he was on the edge of falling asleep, that Albie thought to wonder how Sofia had known his name.

The next day was Good Friday, the start of the season. When Albie and George arrived at the pier they found Dan leaning on the rail by the helter-skelter, obviously waiting for them. George eyed him suspiciously. "What are you after?"

"Sofia wants to see Albert again."

Albie touched George's sleeve. "Won't be long, Dad," and he followed Dan, leaving George to open up alone. At the booth he was amused to see that the bathing couple had been transformed into a pair of sweethearts in modest clothes and commented, "That's a clever way to catch youngsters looking for love."

Dan pointed to the sign above the door that read, 'Gypsy Sofia can see your future'. "They can never resist having their palms read," he said, holding the door curtain aside for Albie to enter. The drapes had transformed the interior into an exotic tent, and when Albie's head touched the fabric ceiling the scent of spices drifted down.

Sofia was seated at her table, where a single candle cast her face into sharp relief and glinted from her jewellery. "Sit down, Albert," she said, waving him into a chair.

Albie sat and planted his hands firmly on his knees, determined he was going to ask his questions today come what may. "How come you know my name?"

"You have been watching us for years, so we made it our business to find out."

Albie felt the treacherous heat rising up his neck but continued doggedly. "You said I've got Roma blood – what's Roma mean?"

"It means gypsy – and if you *are* part Roma, I am here to find out."

"How are you going to do that? And if I am, then what? You planning to steal me?"

"You are far too large for that," Sofia laughed, "And you seem content where you are for now. If you have Roma blood you will find your own way to us in time. Now – go and explain to your father what's going on – he's worried you're going to leave him."

Dismissed again with only some of his questions answered, Albie returned to George and tried to explain what he didn't really understand himself.

"Does she know who your father is?" George asked cautiously.

"They said I look like a Smith, but I didn't ask which one – I don't reckon they'd tell me."

"There's a lot of us Smiths and I sowed my share of wild oats in my time," George said. "If I hadn't been married to Dot all them years ago I could've been your real Dad." He turned aside but failed to hide the break in his voice.

Albie caught his arm and pulled him back. "You're the Dad I picked and nowt's going to change that – not even if I find this other Smith."

George swallowed hard and ruffled Albie's hair as if he was a small boy again. "Glad to hear it, son, because if word got back to your Mum that you'd rather have a gypsy dad, there'd be Hell to pay."

*

As the season progressed, the stall-holders became accustomed to seeing Dan drive Sofia to and from the pier in a ramshackle cart hitched to a dappled pony, although many of them crossed their fingers as her colourful figure, clinking musically with jewellery, swept along the pier to her booth.

Dan had been right about people being lured by the desire to know the future, but it wasn't only courting couples who consulted her, for although the depression was lifting there was still political turmoil. At weekends, when the London trains disgorged scores of day-trippers, there was often a queue outside her booth.

Whether she had customers or not, Sofia was always standing in her doorway when Albie arrived on the pier after his mornings with John Daly. George told him one afternoon, "It don't matter if you're early or late, she always knows when you're coming. People are beginning to say she must be your mother."

"They'll never forget I ain't yours, will they?"

"It don't help when she picks you out all the time."

Albie knew what George meant. Once or twice a week Sofia would pause beside the helter-skelter at the end of the day to take his arm and command, "Hand me into the cart, Albert," and he could never refuse. Although he was aware of the raised eyebrows when they walked along the boards with her arm tucked through his, he was even more aware of the way his pulse seemed to beat more strongly beneath her hand. It felt as if his blood was just a tributary, like a stream flowing into the Medway, and if he had to put up with a bit of embarrassment to find out if he was part of the wide Roma river, it was a small price to pay.

*

By the middle of May Albie was restless and lonely. He only saw Bert if he went round to the two rooms above the butcher's shop where he lived, for with a wife to support Bert had no spare cash to go out. Sometimes Albie went to the pub with George and played dominoes with the old men, or challenged someone to a game of darts, but it failed to satisfy him. All his other old school friends had wives or girl-friends – even Wally Biggins was courting — yet here he was, still single, and as spring moved towards summer it irked him more and more.

The thought of Bessie no longer made him cringe, so it wasn't that. She was a mother of three now, though the gossip around town was that marriage hadn't put paid to her husband's philandering. As for Ellen, he had never heard from her again, but what she'd taught him hadn't exactly gone to waste. His big strong body attracted attention, and although he steered clear of girls in search of a husband, he occasionally accepted an invitation for a no-strings-attached romp. A couple of times he'd had to shin down a drain-pipe to avoid a returning husband, but so far he'd got away with it. The trouble was, it wasn't enough — he was a grown man and he should be falling in love.

There were still a couple of hours left of daylight when the pier closed, and one sultry evening he made himself a sandwich, got his old bike out of the lean-to by the lavatory and rode out of town. When it began to drizzle he actually relished the coolness on his face, but when the clouds thickened and the rain came on stronger he wheeled his bike into some woods to shelter under one of the big old trees.

He had just pulled the wax packet of sandwiches out of his pocket when he smelled smoke. Abandoning his bike, he pushed his way through the wet tangle of undergrowth to emerge, with startling suddenness, in a clearing.

Instantly he was surrounded by barking dogs, so he stood still to let them get his scent and while they sniffed he took in the scene. One brightly-coloured wagon, three canvas-draped ones and a couple of odd-shaped tents encircled the fire, where a shawled woman had frozen in the act of stirring a black pot suspended on a chain. He saw horses grazing beyond the circle and then a man strode towards him, calling the dogs to heel with a piercing whistle. Albie stood his ground and lifted both hands in a placating gesture. "Sorry, mate, didn't mean to disturb you."

The man relaxed visibly and said, in an accent strange to Albie's ears, "We did not think anyone would be out here in this weather."

Albie looked around with undisguised interest. There were faces peering over every half-door and between tent-flaps, as interested in him as he was in them. Although over the years he had met most of the gypsies who visited the area he didn't recognize this group, but after two months of seeing Sofia and Dan every day, these people felt familiar.

A woman leaned from a wagon and called something. The man turned to Albie. "My name is Josef – my mother invites you to share our dinner."

The invitation was unexpected but the food smelled so good that Albie said, "I'd love to, and my name's Albie."

Within moments he was sitting on the step of a wagon with a plate of stew on his lap. "This is good, what's in it?" he asked and Josef smiled, "Are you a gamekeeper?"

"Me — a gamekeeper? I'm a delivery-man in the mornings and afternoons I work on the pier — me and Dad do the helter-skelter." Something in the way Josef nodded told Albie that he already knew about the pier, but he'd learned from Sofia that asking a direct question seldom got him a straight answer. As the rain eased off more people emerged from the wagons and tents and he studied every face, but there was only one man old enough to be his father and all of them were too small. He turned to find his new friend watching him intently and asked the first thing that popped into his head, "How do you fit 'em all in?"

"We are accustomed to it, and in summer the children sleep under with the dogs," Josef said, pointing to the darkness between the wagon wheels. Albie thought that even in the bad old days he'd had a bed of sorts. On the other hand, if this stew was anything to go by, they were better fed than he'd been then, and the kids looked happy enough. There was one face in particular that he couldn't take his eyes off — a young girl, maybe seventeen, Albie thought – but more beautiful than any of the girls in town. He ate slowly, glancing at her more often than was wise, and each time he looked those black eyes were watching his. She's casting a spell on me, he thought, recalling how he'd lost his senses in Sofia's spice-perfumed booth, and decided he'd better go before he sank in any deeper. He shook his head like a wet dog and stood up, handing his plate to the nearest child. "Thanks for your kindness, Josef, but I'd best be off before it pours again."

"No more rain today," Josef said confidently, "And you must pay your respects to Abuela before you leave." He pointed to the steps of the most ornate wagon and Albie sized up the little door, protesting, "I'll never get in there!" but Josef nudged him up the steps until a bony hand fastened on his wrist and Abuela ordered, "Sit down."

Albie ducked under some hanging pots to sit on a small chair beside a lace-clothed table. He had never been inside a wagon before and he looked round with interest. A cupboard over the table held china behind glass doors and the walls between the lace-curtained windows were covered in pictures. A pot-bellied stove made the wagon cosy, and at the far end was a curtained-off bed. Not an inch of space was wasted, but now he was sitting down it didn't feel claustrophobic.

Abuela settled back in her chair still holding his hand and studied his face with sharp black eyes. Albie shifted uncomfortably under her scrutiny but she held him there, tiny though she was, as if her strength had become concentrated when her body shrank. Just when Albie was starting to wonder if her mind had gone she broke the silence. "So you are Albert. I am Clara but they call me Abuela, which is Grandmother in Spanish – our tribe escaped from a war in Spain a century ago."

"So that's why your names are odd?"

"They are not odd, they are just Spanish!"

As Albie blushed at the telling-off, Abuela continued, "Your life started bad but now you are with a good family."

Albie tugged his hand free of her grip. "You've been talking to Sofia," he said accusingly, but he stayed where he was when she spoke again. "You have the blood of your father – Roma blood."

Sofia had said the same thing – Roma blood – and Albie asked the question Sofia had steadfastly refused to answer. "Do *you* know who my father is? Where can I find him?"

"I believe I know, but you must find him yourself to be certain. You will do so before long – you have the same wandering soul."

"I ain't wandering nowhere — I've got a business here and a helter-skelter to run. Anyway, Thambay's my home."

"For now it is, yes, but soon the wind blows you to us." Abuela Clara sat back and flashed surprisingly good teeth in a smile. "Maria will wait."

This was a bit too weird for Albie's liking. What was the old dear on about? And who was Maria? As if he had spoken aloud, Abuela said, "Maria is my grand-daughter," and then she called, "Josef!"

Albie turned at a hand on his shoulder and followed

Josef out. Maria's dark eyes lifted to his as he descended the steps, but then he was distracted by a nudge in the back and turned round to see a large horse. It had wandered up on silent hooves and was looking at him as if to say, don't ignore me. It was the carthorse he had ridden as a boy, and he greeted the familiar face with delight, kissing the silky nose and pulling the ears while the gypsies watched with amusement.

"Friend of yours, is he?" Josef asked unnecessarily.

"He used to live down Farm Lane in Thambay – I had my first ride on him. I wondered where he'd gone. Perhaps he led me here."

Josef laughed, "It is possible — we took him in exchange for a season's work on Morris Farm when Abuela's old horse died."

"He ain't forgotten me, has he?"

"Horses have long memories, and you will see him again," Josef said confidently, "But now it grows dark — you must go."

So Albie said thank you for his meal, retrieved his bike and rode home. A small part of his mind dwelt on the incredible coincidence of meeting his black horse, but the majority of his thoughts were focussed on the memory of Maria's lovely face.

As soon as Albie had gone, Maria went into the wagon to kneel with her head in the old gypsy's lap and ask, "Are you sure he'll come back, Abuela?"

Her grandmother stroked her hair. "I am sure, Maria," she soothed, "He has a duty to his father, but he will return soon."

CHAPTER FIFTEEN – NORAH & THE FAIR

The start of school holidays brought the crowds to Thambay, and the usual scruffy urchins hung hopefully around the helter-skelter, but they were out of luck — it was impossible to sneak one of the heavy coir mats without being spotted by George's sharp eyes and sent packing. Occasionally Albie would see a boy who reminded him of himself and beckon the child forward for a free ride, but one afternoon his eyes were drawn instead to an old lady sitting on the bench opposite.

She was there again the following day, watching for an hour or so before sighing and moving off to the tea-rooms. Albie knew that look, though it was usually on the face of a penniless boy, and he could feel her need like an ache in his chest. She must be older than Mum, he reckoned, but she wanted a ride as badly as he had wanted one when he'd stood day after day in that very spot.

One quiet afternoon he made up his mind to talk to her and said to George, "I'll get the tea today, Dad — you want ginger nuts or rich tea?"

"I'll have ginger nuts," George said, taking some money from the tin, "Going to chat up that waitress again, are you?"

But once inside the tearoom Albie merely winked at the waitress, took his cup of tea and strolled over to the old lady's table. Putting his hand on a chair, he asked, "Mind if I sit here?"

Norah recognized the young giant from the helter-skelter and nodded. "By all means, young man, do join me."

Now he was here, Albie didn't know how to start. Maybe he'd got it wrong and all she wanted was to watch the kids, but then he remembered that look and plunged right in. "You want a go on the ride, don't you?"

Norah put her cup down carefully in the saucer. She was embarrassed that her longing to do something so childish was that obvious to this young man with the windswept curls, but she decided to trust the twinkle in his knowing eyes. "Silly, isn't it, at my age?"

"It ain't silly. The helter-skelter's a special ride, and I seen you looking all week."

"I've only been in Thambay for a month. I have retired to the seaside, you see, and I thought a stroll along the pier would be good for my arthritis. Then I saw the helter-skelter, and it looks such fun!" Fun, thought Norah — there's been precious little fun in my life so far — raising two boys only to lose them both in the Great War. She dragged her wandering thoughts back to the present and found Albie regarding her intently with the same grey eyes as those of her lost sons.

Albie didn't like seeing the old lady looking so sad. "A ride on the helter-skelter always blows the cobwebs away," he said, "You should try it."

Norah's face glowed for a moment, but then she slumped dejectedly. "I'd never be able to reach the top. I moved to a flat with a lift because I can't manage stairs any longer."

"Don't you fret about that — I'll get you up there."

All Norah's objections surrendered to Albie's persuasive tongue, and five minutes later George looked up to see Albie with Norah on his arm. "This lady here wants a ride so I'm taking her up – will you catch her at the bottom?" Before George's astonished eyes Albie picked up two mats and ushered Norah through the door.

With Albie's hand in the small of her back Norah managed the first flight, but on the tiny half-way landing she stopped and looked upwards in despair. "I can't manage it! I was foolish even to consider it at my age." Her eyes filled with tears, "I'm not even sure I can get back down."

"The only way you're going down is on a mat, missus!" Albie said, and he turned his back, "Hold tight to me – I'm carrying you up."

Norah didn't give herself time to dwell on how undignified she would look – there was no-one to see them after all – and when Albie crouched down she put her arms round his neck. With one arm clamping her to his back and the other holding the mats, Albie climbed the familiar stairs as if she was no weight at all. Norah was entranced as she breathed in the heady mixture of clean young skin and dusty wood and watched the pale archway above grow bigger and brighter. At last Albie lowered her gently onto the top landing and put her hand on the damp rail. "You hang onto that while I get your mat ready."

Norah took a deep breath of the salty air and drank in the scene. "I can see my flat from here!" she exclaimed.

Albie laughed. "My first time up here I thought I could see the whole world. Now, I'll give you a minute and follow you down. You'll need both hands – you want me to bring your handbag?"

Norah looked at the disappearing curve of wood polished by thousands of mats and suddenly she was frightened — what if her skirt blew up or she broke her hip? This was a ridiculous thing to be doing at her age. But then she looked at Albie, who had known how much she yearned to ride the helter-skelter, and saw on his face no mockery, only understanding. Meekly she surrendered her handbag, took his proffered hand, and lowered herself gingerly onto the mat. "Don't let me go yet!" she quavered, and Albie held onto the back of her coat while she tucked her good tweed skirt tightly round her legs.

"Keep your elbows in and your knees together, lean into the tower a bit and you'll be fine," Albie instructed, "The slide's a bit damp today so you won't go very fast."

Thank Heaven for small mercies, thought Norah. Albie started her off with a little push on her back and she let out a small unladylike scream, and then she was sliding. It felt more than fast enough to Norah, and she shut her eyes momentarily in fear but forced them open again. She was only going to do this once so she might as well enjoy it, and if she broke her neck at the bottom she would at least have had the experience. Heavens — she was going even faster! She risked a look up, but the clouds whirled past in a blur and she lowered her head hurriedly. Faster and faster she sped, round and round, her heart-beat racing, her hat straining against its hatpin.

Suddenly she realised what this feeling was that was surging up from her ribs. It was sheer exhilaration – she was having a marvellous time! She pulled the sides of the mat closer to her arthritic hips and flew round the final curve onto the pad, where George was waiting with out-stretched arms to ease her into a safe, if somewhat inelegant, landing.

He helped her to her feet. "You all right, missus? I was that shook when you went up, a lady like you!" then he scooped her off the pad just in time to prevent her from being bowled over as Albie shot off the slide to join them.

Norah straightened her skirt and re-pinned her hat with unsteady hands, smiling the widest of smiles at them both. "That was absolutely wonderful — I can't thank you enough." She fumbled for her purse, "How much do I owe you?"

"First ride's free, missus," said Albie, winking at George, "Same as mine was eight years ago."

Sofia commanded Albie's escort that evening, and as they walked to the road she asked, "What made you help that old woman?"

"Didn't think anyone was watching. She had the look – I always know that look. I could feel her wanting a go."

Sofia put a hand on his shoulder while Dan helped her into the cart. As she settled her skirts tidily, Albie was again held in place by the intensity of her gaze. "You felt her wanting," she said, nodding as if he'd confirmed a suspicion, "It's in your blood." She tapped Dan's knee, "Take me home, Dan," and they drove off, leaving Albie staring after them and wondering what it was that Sofia thought was in his blood.

Norah became a regular visitor to the helter-skelter after that. George would surrender his stool and sit on the pile of mats chatting to her, or when it was quiet he might join her in the tearoom for a cup of tea. Perhaps once a week, when she was certain no-one would see her doing something so undignified, Norah allowed Albie to take her up the spiral staircase of the helter-skelter. Those brief moments of weightless freedom never failed to raise her pulse, and she always landed laughing into George's careful arms.

One evening Albie winked at George over their evening meal. "Have you told Mum yet about your lady friend?"

"George Smith! What have you been up to?" shrieked Dot, but George smiled his broad innocent smile and described the little old lady who had fallen in love with the helter-skelter and came to the pier alone almost every day.

"Ain't she got no family?" Dot asked, and her soft heart was touched when George told her that Norah's husband had died young and she had lost both boys in the war. "I'll pop along tomorrow and have a cuppa with the old dear — she's probably fed up with listening to you."

The following day, after a comfortable gossip over tea and cakes in the tearoom, Dot announced, "I've asked Norah to dinner on Sunday — she says she usually grills a chop. Can you believe that? It's disgraceful – and I bet she don't bother with veg neither." The idea that Norah's diet was dictated by poverty never crossed Dot's mind — only common people were poor, and Norah was a lady.

So it came about that Norah was also adopted by the Smiths. She accompanied Dot to her church, declaring – with a silent apology to her incense-loving mother – that it was the same God with or without the fripperies, and her presence at Sunday dinner became a fixture they all enjoyed. Norah, who was five years older than Dot, had a fund of stories from her former life in London. She told them how she had witnessed soldiers marching off to war all proud and polished, and had seen the return of the pitifully ragged remnants. She had joined in the celebrations at the end of the war, and had seen demonstrations for women's suffrage, miners' rallies, and queues of the unemployed outside soup kitchens.

George was surprised but delighted to find a woman who could discuss politics knowledgably; they enjoyed many a heated argument from diametrically opposed positions that enhanced their friendship considerably.

But there were some matters Norah never discussed in front of George or Albie, preferring to keep those for wet afternoons in front of Dot's warm kitchen range. "After Lionel died I took in needlework to help feed my boys," Norah told Dot, who thus came to understand that poverty was no respecter of class. "Thanks to my mother I am a good seamstress and can mend lace so you would never know it had been torn." She dropped her voice. "Many of the garments I repaired were very intimate."

"Under-things, you mean, Norah?" Dot asked gleefully.

"Some of my customers brought little else, and I'm ashamed to say I used to wonder sometimes how they came to be damaged." Dot chuckled, fascinated by this glimpse into another world. "Women of a certain kind, I think they must have been," Norah added, "But they always paid on time, which is more than you could say for some of my other customers."

"That's the upper classes for you," said Dot, "Albie says they never pay as quick as us working class."

Norah hid a smile, content for once to be included in one of Dot's sweeping statements, and merely remarked, "Albert is very like his father in his views."

"That ain't surprising seeing as he's been hearing George's opinions for ten years."

"Only ten years?"

"Didn't they tell you? Albie's adopted."

"Well, that is a surprise – he looks so much like George.

Who were his parents?"

"Some woman who was no better than she should be. She abandoned him when he were only a lad," Dot spat, folding her arms across her chest as if to contain her anger.

Norah clutched the brooch that fastened her blouse. "Oh my dear! The poor child. He was fortunate that you took pity on him."

"We're lucky too – our grandson's gone on the fishing boats, so there'd be nobody to help George if it wasn't for Albie."

Norah coughed delicately. "I presume you do not know who his father was?"

"No we don't." Dot had spoken much more sharply than she usually did to Norah, and the two women sat in silence for a while to let the ripples subside before they started talking again — on an entirely different subject.

*

Norah couldn't work out whether it was coincidence or a touch of gypsy magic that prompted Sofia to approach her the next morning. She had just decided that George was too busy to stop for a chat and was turning towards the tea-rooms when Sofia called, "Will you share my tea today?"

"I shall be delighted," Norah replied. Her nursemaid had been a country girl who imbued her youthful charge with an interest in the occult which Norah had never outgrown. She entered the curtained booth with every sense alert, only to discover that there was no mystery or magic. As far as she could see the only atmosphere was the dust from a few drapes and a spot of incense. Sofia's crystal ball was obviously a fishing float, and there was even a touch of domesticity in the spirit lamp on which Sofia was balancing a kettle. But when she poured hot water into the pot and a fragrant scent joined the other perfumes drifting round the tent, Norah knew it would be very easy to lose one's senses in here.

Sofia sat opposite her, casually moving aside the glass

globe to make room for the tea-tray, and poured. "Norah – I think we are near enough in age to use first names?"

"Yes indeed, Sofia, and this tea is delicious."

"It is my own blend of basil and lavender – it both soothes and enlivens the mind. Now tell me, what is your interest in Albert?"

So this woman was not going to waste time beating about the bush, thought Norah. "My interest, as you call it, began with the helter-skelter, and I have since become a friend of the whole family. Your own interest is harder to understand."

Sofia looked at her guest shrewdly. It was clear that Norah was not at all unsettled by the low light, nor by the tea's third ingredient that she had neglected to mention. It would be a bad mistake to underestimate this tiny figure with pale blue eyes and wispy white hair.

Norah looked back steadfastly, seeing a sturdy and vigorous woman with black eyes, who would be a good friend but a formidable opponent. "Why do you single Albert out so frequently?" she asked, "It causes him embarrassment."

"Albert will have to become accustomed to that on his travels."

"I was not aware he had plans to travel anywhere."

Sofia reached across the bright cloth to take Norah's hand, and Norah felt as if her soul was being probed by this strange woman. The drapes seemed to sway without a breeze to move them, and the perfumes mingled in a sensual swirl that made her slightly giddy.

"You love him very much." It was a statement, not a question, and Norah felt no need to reply. "He has Roma blood, and one day soon he will find his way to us." Sofia released her hand and sat back, breaking the spell. "You must persuade Dorothy to let him go."

"With her prejudices that will not be an easy task."

"But you do not share those prejudices, I think."

Norah smiled reminiscently. "I spent many happy holidays here in Thambay when I was a girl. My father took me one day into a little cave under the promenade where a fortune-teller read my palm." Norah laughed. "She wasn't very good because she told me I'd marry a tall handsome man and have six children and many grandchildren."

Sofia took her hand again. "Instead of which you married a short man and had two sons – and then deep sadness."

"You are right – my husband died young and both my boys were lost in the war."

"Happiness will fill these last years of your life, Norah. You love Albert like a son, and you will live long enough to see his children. Your life is like his helter-skelter – a long climb carrying a heavy burden which becomes as nothing on the way down."

"You are right again – I had not thought of it like that. On the way up Albert carries the mat for me, and on the way down all my troubles seem to vanish."

Sofia pushed aside the tea-tray and pulled the fishing float towards her, polished it with a silk scarf and laid it on the table. The blob of glass on the bottom vanished into the folds of its silken nest, and as Sofia wove her hands over it in an intricate pattern, Norah felt at last that magic had come to the little seaside booth.

The pale green glass cleared to misty white and then became transparent, with patterns swirling inside like smoke. For a moment Norah could have sworn she saw the helter-skelter, but then it was engulfed by a huge wave, to be instantly replaced by a gypsy wagon. The wagon was painted in red and orange which morphed into flames, and both women watched as the crystal ball was rocked by explosion after fiery explosion.

"That does not look every peaceful," Norah said fearfully, "Are we seeing the future?"

"I am afraid we are seeing a war," said Sofia, covering the globe with the scarf. "I have seen enough to know Albert lives, but there are many deaths to come. Let us have another cup of tea and talk of a more cheerful future."

"I think ordinary tea will suffice this time," Norah said, casting Sofia a meaning look, "Shall we go to the tearooms?"

So to the astonishment and consternation of the waitress and customers in the tearooms, staid little Norah in her tweeds and flamboyant Sofia in her colourful shawls shared a pot of uncompromisingly English tea and a plate of cakes, obviously enjoying each other's company tremendously.

*

By the end of that summer, Norah and Sofia were firm friends, and often chatted over a cup of tea in the quiet lunch-hour before Albie arrived. They compared notes on the towns and villages around Kent where Sofia's tribe had camped and which Norah had visited with Lionel. Norah formed the impression that the difference in comfort between a travelling wagon and a bed and breakfast hotel was less than she had assumed.

Norah also grew closer to Dot, particularly when the damper days made a walk along the pier unpleasant. Albie and George often came home after a wet afternoon to find the two women with their feet on the fender and cups of tea at their elbows. There was also usually a piece of needlework in Norah's lap, for at Dot's instigation she had put cards in a few shop windows and was once again supplementing her income by sewing.

*

Norah was sitting on her tiny balcony one evening in August, making the most of the last of the daylight to finish a commission, when she heard the rumble of heavy engines like an army approaching. She almost dropped her work, but at the sight of the colourful trailers she relaxed, put aside her sewing — for which it was getting too dark anyway - and sat back to watch the arrival of the annual fair on the recreation ground.

The procession went on for so long that she fetched her supper and ate it outside as lorries and tractors pulled flat-sided trailers onto the grass, and she watched with fascination as the trailers unfolded ingeniously to display roundabouts, swing cars and dodgems. The ground was muddy from the morning's rain but it didn't seem to bother the riggers - they simply put down matting or boards and built on top.

The women were doing much the same, throwing down squares of canvas that were instantly colonised by children and dogs, setting up tables and chairs outside on the grass, lighting fires, preparing meals.

This is how gypsies live, Norah realised — making homes wherever they are — a nomadic life without a shred of luxury. Sofia says Albert was born to it and will find his way back in time, and it will be my job to persuade Dorothy to let him go. As she took her tray indoors she wondered how she would manage that, and her heart quailed.

The next afternoon Albie had been on the pier for a couple of hours when George commented, "Quiet today, ain't it? Where've all the customers gone?"

"Most likely at the fair - me and John saw 'em setting up when we drove past this morning."

George slapped his forehead with the flat of his hand. "Told you I was getting old! Fancy me forgetting that. You going along later?"

"Might do," said Albie, but his eyes sparkled — he'd never missed a fair yet.

"Go on, lad, you shove off now - seeing as there's nobody here I can manage on my own."

Albie didn't need to be told twice. "Ta Dad, and tell Mum ..."

"I know — you won't be home for your tea!"

When Albie reached the recreation ground the music from the merry-go-round set his pulse racing and, as he did every year, he bought a toffee apple to crunch, but somehow it didn't taste the same. He threw some hoops and won a little china cat which he tucked into his pocket to take home to Mum, and then he won a pretty pincushion for Norah, but after that the man shooed him away, saying, "You've got two prizes and no girl to give 'em to, so bugger off!"

Albie shrugged and wandered off, thinking he must have the glums worse than he thought if even a fairground man could see he was lonely. The swing-boats were full of courting couples, every horse on the roundabout seemed to hold a pair of lovers, and boys much younger than him strolled past holding hands with their sweethearts.

He was twenty-one now and still single, dreaming of a pair of black eyes he'd seen only once. Even the fun of the fair wasn't fun anymore and he turned away, deciding he might as well go home, then he saw the flicker of a fire and his heart began to thud.

He had never been able to find that clearing in the woods again, though he'd looked hard enough. He had even asked Sofia but she'd just patted his cheek and said, "Roma never stay long in one place." He had begun to wonder if he'd imagined the whole thing, but now instinct told him Maria was right here in Thambay. He strode across the flattened turf towards the fire and there they were — the very wagons and tents he remembered. They were even arranged the same way as before, and he stroked the black horse's flank as he passed by. The children crowded round him and Josef shook his hand as if they had seen each other only last week.

"It is good to see you, Albert," he said, drawing Albie inside the circle and pulling a pair of stools from beneath a wagon. Albie sat obediently, peering into the shadows.

"She is here," Josef said and Albie's heart beat faster when Josef continued, "She is brushing her hair — Abuela said you would come today."

"How did she know?"

"She always knows when a friend is coming."

"But you don't even know who I am – not really."

"Yes we do," Josef answered, "You are Albert Smith. Aunt Sofia thinks you are probably of Nate's getting, which makes you one of us."

Albie sat up straighter, forgetting Maria in his excitement. "You mean this Nate could be my father? Why didn't Sofia tell me? Is he here?"

"Calm down, Albert," Josef laughed, "You will meet him soon enough. Your paths will cross when they cross, but now you and I must talk before Maria comes."

So Albie and Josef talked, the older man probing gently but insistently until Albie had laid his whole life bare for inspection. Albie thought afterwards that Josef must have decided he was all right and made some sign, because after ten minutes Maria came out of one of the tents to join them.

Albie stood to greet her and she took both of his hands. "Welcome back, Albert," she said, her voice sweet and low. She pressed him back onto his stool and sat by her father's knee, watching Albie's face while Josef told him about their lives on the road – the fairs they met each year and the farmers who relied on their help for planting and harvesting the crops – and Albie talked about the helter-skelter and the deliveries around which his own life revolved.

They ate bowls of another savoury stew, the contents of which Albie remembered not to question, and it was dark before Josef stood up and said, "Abuela is expecting you."

Once again Albie ducked through the small door to sit under the scrutiny of those penetrating eyes. Abuela gripped his hand and for several minutes neither of them spoke, but Albie sensed that even the details he hadn't told Josef were being picked out like winkles from their shells. This suspicion was confirmed when she said abruptly, "You waste your seed on women not worthy of you." Albie blushed crimson and the old woman cackled, "You are young and only take what they offer, but now you will stop and save yourself for Maria." Albie's jaw dropped – Bert had courted Alice for years before they even got engaged, but Abuela was talking as if his future with Maria was decided already. He tried to think of something sensible to say but nothing would come, and then the old lady waved him out of the wagon.

Maria was waiting for him at the foot of the steps and strolled with him back through the fairground, her arm linked through his. After Abuela's remark, Albie was hoping for at least a kiss but they were not alone – at a word from Josef a pair of small boys had scrambled from beneath a wagon to follow them. At the edge of the recreation ground he stopped and slid his arms round Maria's waist, half-afraid she would vanish again. "Will you still be here tomorrow?"

"I will be here," she promised and stood on tiptoe to kiss him. In front of their little witnesses it was only a butterfly kiss, but it burned on Albie's lips and seared right down to his toes. His arms tightened involuntarily, but Maria slipped from his embrace and was gone.

The fair stayed in Thambay for two weeks and the gypsies remained camped nearby, waiting to dismantle the rides they had helped to erect. Each day they left the babies in the care of Josef's mother and went to pick fruit, and each evening Albie cycled over to sit by the camp-fire with Maria, Josef and the other adults. When it was time for him to go home to bed, Maria walked with him as far as the road, where they kissed briefly and sedately with their young chaperones giggling in the shadows.

Afterwards Albie always took the long way home so that the night air could blow the smell of wood smoke from his jacket, thinking about Maria and mulling over the stories he had heard beside her camp fire.

"It is not an easy life we live," Josef's father Mateo said

one night, "There is much prejudice against us, but there is also much freedom." There was a warning in his voice as he added, "Maria will never give up that freedom, even for love."

"Abuelo!" Maria scolded, but she didn't contradict him, and Albie's spirits plummeted — now he'd found Maria he couldn't bear the thought of losing her.

The second Saturday night Josef told him they were moving on the next day. "Our horses couldn't keep up with the fair's lorries — we are going south now to pick hops."

Albie gripped Maria's hand in desperation. "Dad's getting too old to do the ride alone - I can't just leave him."

"We understand that, Albie," said Josef, "Your duty is here now, but before long the wind will blow you to us."

Maria's hand tightened in Albie's - they both knew this was Josef's way of saying he approved of their love. Albie stayed very late that night and when he finally got up to leave, all the children were asleep. Josef shook Albie's hand and told him, "Maria will walk with you alone tonight."

After two weeks of learning about the gypsies, Albie knew Josef was breaking tradition to allow this, and he had to clear his throat before he promised, "She'll be back in ten minutes." He took one final look around to fix the scene in his mind before Maria tugged him out of the circle of firelight.

As they walked through the sleeping fairground under the thin light of a new moon, Albie turned the coins over in his pocket for luck. When they reached the road he lifted Maria's slight body off the grass to hold her against his chest while they kissed, this time as passionately as they wished. "You will come back?" Albie asked anxiously.

Maria whispered something, holding his face between her hands, and Albie laughed quietly, "You don't need to put any more gypsy spells on me!"

She shushed him with her fingers. "That was a promise - I will see you soon,"and she kissed him one more time, wriggled out of his embrace, and disappeared into the night.

CHAPTER SIXTEEN – STORMS

Without the alternative attractions of the fair the pier hummed with renewed activity throughout the rest of the holiday, and it wasn't until the children had gone back to school that Albie and George had a chance for a proper tea-break. The toffee apple man said he would keep an eye on the helter-skelter, so they went inside the tea-room to sit out of the wind.

"What happened, Albie?" George asked, "Out every night for a fortnight, coming home all glowing — then nothing, and your face like a wet weekend. Mum said I wasn't to ask, but this is just you and me — you want to tell me?" So Albie told him and, as it had all those years ago, George's big tattooed hand closed on his wrist. "Gypsy or no gypsy— if you love the girl then marry her."

"What will Mum say?"

"She'll find something wrong whoever it is, but you leave her to me. Now, when did you say she'll be back?"

"I don't know," said Albie bleakly, "Soon, she said — they all said they'd be back soon — but they've been gone weeks already and it seems a long time to me."

"So you won't be asking that waitress to the end-of-season party," George said, trying to inject a note of humour.

Albie managed a wan smile. "She'll have to find herself another bloke – I've asked Norah."

Norah was such a regular on the pier that her appearance at the party on Albie's arm caused little comment, though the waitress scowled – being ignored in favour of an old woman was an insult to her charms.

The pianist was bashing out a dance tune and the party was in full swing when the door opened and a gust of wind heralded the arrival of Sofia and Dan. The stall-holders were accustomed to her colourful clothes, but tonight Sofia was splendid in her extravagant best and glittered with jewellery. She stood poised for a moment, accepting the wide-eyed stares as homage, and then sailed through the assembly to drop anchor beside George and Albie. She greeted them warmly, complimented Norah on her hat, and then said to Dot, "You must be Missus Smith – Norah tells me you have been very kind to her."

Dot stared aghast at Sofia's proffered hand, and there was a beat of awkwardness before she gave it the briefest of touches and withdrew as if stung. Sofia's eyes glittered for a second, then she smiled wickedly, said, "Albert, I wish to dance," and placed her hand on his shoulder.

Albie could feel Dot's eyes stabbing as he swung Sofia into the room – he felt everyone's eyes on them – but he was helpless to refuse Sofia. The piano seemed to sing a different tune as they danced – the pianist looked amazed when the ancient tinny instrument took on the leaping sound of gypsy fiddles – and gradually the room filled with other couples who were unable to resist its siren call. Albie's feet followed the steps of a dance he was unaware he knew, and the lights of the pier tearoom flickered like flames. When the bewitched pianist finally lifted his hands from the keys and the music released the dancers, Albie was breathless and laughing.

"That's better," Sofia said, "You were too sad. Now take me back to Dan." When he delivered her to her nephew, Sofia pressed something into Albie's palm. "A talisman to keep you safe until we meet again." A smooth grey stone warmed his hand, a leather thong threaded through a hole in the centre. He couldn't put it round his neck here, not with Mum watching his every move, so he slipped it quickly into his pocket. When he looked up to thank Sofia, she was no longer there.

At the end of the evening he walked Norah home along the promenade. She tucked one hand into his elbow while the other held onto her hat to prevent it being snatched from her head by the blustery wind. At the door to her block of flats, when Albie bent to kiss her cheek, she said, "Sofia told me to look after you, Albert – what did she mean by that?"

"I don't know." Albie pulled the stone out of his pocket to show her. "She gave me this for luck – she must think I need all the help I can get." He said goodnight and went to the pub for a decent pint of draught to wash down the bottled stuff from the party. He was in his bed before midnight and fell asleep quickly, clutching the stone.

Later that night he was woken suddenly by his window rattling in its frame. He looked out to see the trees in the churchyard being blown almost horizontal and heard waves crashing over the promenade. A dreadful moaning sound built up and up – the roar of a dragon with the weight of the entire English Channel behind it – and his chest felt heavy with premonition. He went downstairs to make sure the house was secure, but George had beaten him to it and the kettle was already on the hob. They brewed a pot of tea and Albie was about to take a cup up to Dot when she appeared in the kitchen, clutching her dressing-gown closed as if afraid the howling wind would snatch it away. "A body can't sleep with that racket going on."

Albie hauled the clothes airer up to the ceiling so that they could sit by the open door of the range and be comforted by the sight of the fire. They talked in nervous snatches until about three o'clock, when the wind suddenly rose to a terrifying scream that catapulted Dot out of her chair and into George's arms. A giant gust shook the whole terrace to its foundations and then the wind died away to an ominous hum full of the echoes of things falling. The three of them looked at each other, their eyes wide with fear.

"We'd better check outside," said Albie but when George said, "No-one in their right mind would go out in this — you stop where you are," he was glad to obey.

When it was still relatively quiet after another half an hour, Dot said, "I'm for me bed — you coming, George?" and they all trooped upstairs for a few more hours of uneasy sleep.

The scenes of devastation in the watery dawn were horrifying. Trees lay across the roads; benches had been ripped from the pavement and flung into front gardens. The end house of their own terrace had lost its roof and half a wall had been torn right off — a double bed teetered on the brink of falling, the exposure of such an intimate item strangely indecent.

Albie and George fought their way through the debris towards the pier, and when they saw it was still standing they breathed a sigh of relief, but it was short-lived. As they got closer they saw a fishing-boat wedged high up in the pier supports, and the theatre roof had gone, along with half the decking and all the kiosks. But the worst sight of all was that of the helter-skelter lying on its side, shattered beyond repair, smack in the middle of the ruined tea-room.

Despite the early hour there was already a grim-faced crowd milling around the entrance, composed mainly of people who depended on the pier for their living, many of whom were in tears. At nine o'clock a town councillor arrived and told them the council would find the money to clear up the mess in town, but it would be months before they got round to the pier. Then the pier manager said they wouldn't be rebuilding the helter-skelter. Albie was horrified but George was philosophical. "I've had me pension for a year now, Albie, and you can always work full-time with John."

"No I can't, Dad – now Eddie's left school he wants more hours with his dad, not less. I'll probably end up in that factory with Eric after all." But even before Albie had finished his sentence another thought surfaced, and like a door opening in his mind he remembered Abuela's prediction – "The wind will blow you our way." A broad grin spread across his face and he thumped George on the back. "Could be that storm done me a favour! See you later, Dad – I've gotta go." He dashed home to retrieve his bike from the ruins of the lean-to, straightened the frame, pumped up the tyres and cycled out of town, only stopping briefly to check that Norah was safe.

The bike seemed to know the way, and soon he was leaving it under the very same tree that had sheltered him a few months earlier. It was no surprise to smell smoke, and the dogs greeted him like an old friend when he stepped into the clearing. A second later Maria was in his arms, and as they kissed he knew he couldn't let her go again. At last he became aware of a circle of small grinning faces, and Josef in the background with his hands on his hips.

"Here again, Albert?"

"Here again, Josef, and this time for good, if that's all right with you?"

"You haven't asked her yet!" said Josef with laughter in his eyes.

Albie, thinking back to the films to which he'd taken several forgettable girls, went down on one knee in the wet grass, took Maria's hand in his own and said, "Maria, I love you, will you marry me?"

She glanced at Josef to ask, "Papa?"

"Abuela says if you want him, you can have him – he *is* half Roma."

"Then yes, I will marry you, Albie," Maria said joyfully, and leaned forward to cup his chin and kiss him again in full view of her family.

Josef produced a bottle of wine as if he had anticipated the need, and after everyone had drunk to the occasion he said, "We will visit your parents tomorrow, Albert."

"Visit my parents?"

"Our tradition is that they should come here," Josef said, "But because of the weather we will go to them. We will be there at six o'clock."

"But we've only got a small house!"

"Smaller than our wagons? Do not worry, Albert, we will leave the children behind."

As Albie cycled back to town, the enormity of what he had started began to sink in. Maria's family would fill Mum's kitchen to bursting, but that wasn't the worst of it — telling Mum would raise a storm bigger than last night's.

Putting off the evil moment, he found John Daly and signed on at the Town Hall for a day's work, hauling bench seats and fallen chimneys out of people's gardens. The tribe would be clearing storm debris too, gathering every fallen branch from around their campsite, and Maria had told him they were moving to Coppin Farm tomorrow, where they would camp in Bottom Meadow and clear the storm-ravaged copse. "Logs for the farmer and small wood for us - that is the deal Papa made," Maria had said. "There will be early potatoes to pick up too - half of them will have been ripped out by the storm." So they'd have wood to burn, potatoes to bake, and the lee of the barn to shelter the wagons and tents, all a short bike ride away from Thambay.

And when they folded their tents to move on to the next farm Albie would be with them, walking beside one of the wagons leading a horse, with Maria beside him as his wife. As he imagined making love to Maria in the bender tent that would be their first home, the strange thought struck him that they'd probably be overheard by the horses, just like he and Ellen had been all those years ago.

"Come over here, Albie — you're the only one tall enough!" John's shout jerked him out of his reverie to hold up the roof of a prom shelter while some other workmen hammered a new corner-post into place, and as he stood there his gaze was drawn over the still-restless waves to the shattered pier.

He had heard the stall-holders planning to offer the Council their services to repair the pier before winter could make things worse, but he hadn't the heart to join them. Without the helter-skelter the pier wouldn't ever be the same - he didn't think even Dad would go there much now. Dad -

George Smith – it was odd to think his real name could be Smith after all.

John snapped his fingers under Albie's nose. "Anyone home? Buck your ideas up, Albie – you're not concentrating."

"Sorry, John – miles away." Albie shifted his superior height to another corner of the shelter, but as soon as he'd braced his legs to take the weight his mind was off again.

He thanked his lucky stars he'd already told Dad about Maria – that was one bridge crossed – but Mum would be mad as a bucket of crabs. She had paraded many local girls under his nose over the years, though none of them had taken his fancy, and she'd been dropping hints like leaves in autumn since Bert got married. He knew Mum hoped he would settle close to home, and he dreaded telling her that he'd be leaving Thambay to roam Kent and beyond with a tribe of gypsies. He heaved such a heavy sigh that John said, "Only another minute," but Albie barely acknowledged him. As soon as he'd finished work for the day he had to tell Dad and Mum and weather *that* storm, then clear up the mess and prepare the ground for tomorrow's meeting.

He sat in the reconstructed shelter with John and Eddie to eat his lunch, watching a few boys scavenging on the beach like he and Bert used to, obviously enjoying an unexpected holiday while the school roof was patched up. When he and Maria had kids they would be born in a wagon and sleep between the wheels with the dogs, their lullaby the sound of wind in the trees. They would do their scavenging in the hedgerows and pick tatties and fruit to help put food in the big black cauldron. He would have to teach them to read – him, who could hardly read till he was twelve — because they'd get no other book-learning, but they would grow brown and healthy in the open air, not picking up the diseases other kids passed round the schools in town.

By the time the work gang had fixed three shelters the dismal grey sky had darkened with the threat of more rain,

and Albie was home before five. Knocking the dirt off his
work-boots against the back wall, he could see Norah sitting in
the small armchair by the range and his spirits lifted slightly.
He should have remembered Norah knew how to handle
Mum. He gave his jacket a final shake, hung it in the scullery
and stepped into the warmth of the kitchen where Dot was
bustling about getting tea ready.

George looked up from his paper. "You coming with us
to the Town Hall tomorrow to ask about the pier, son?"

When Albie didn't answer immediately, Norah lifted
her head from her sewing. He gave her an agonized look as he
said, "Not me, Dad. I'll help, of course, but I've got other
things to do." George's shrewd look and Dot's suddenly still
hands told him they'd noticed his tone of voice so he
ploughed on. "I'm getting wed."

Dot's knife fell with a clatter as she rushed to hug him.
"Albie! I thought I'd never see the day – who is she?"

George dropped his paper on the hearth and heaved
himself out of his chair to shake Albie's hand.
"Congratulations, son — it's that Maria, I suppose?"

Dot pulled back to search Albie's face. "Maria? I don't
know any Maria. What ain't you telling me, Albie – have you
got a girl pregnant?"

"God, Mum, no! Maria's a good girl – her people don't
do that sort of thing."

"Her people? What is she – a foreigner?"

"Sort of — way back," said Albie, casting a hunted look
at George, who took pity on him and said it for him. "They're
travelling folk, Dot — Maria's a gypsy."

Dot's shriek of dismay was as bad as Albie had feared,
and the woman next door banged a saucepan on the wall
shouting, "You all right, Dot?"

George bellowed back, "Nothing to do with you,
missus!" and guided Dot into her chair, where she flung her
apron over her head and rocked back and forth, wailing.

Norah patted her hand. "Calm down, Dorothy – you will give yourself palpitations."

"Palpitations? He's broken my heart! How could you, Albie? The boy I nursed in my own bosom taking up with a gypsy!" George snorted with laughter and Dot turned her venom on this fresh target. "What makes you think it's funny, George Smith?"

"Sorry, pet, but I can't get my head round the picture of Albie at your bosom. He was a bit big for that when we got him!"

"Oh, you know what I mean – I've been nursing a viper in my bosom!"

Norah bit her lip and her eyes were twinkling as she said, "It seems that congratulations are in order, Albert dear."

"Thanks, Norah," Albie said, hoping Norah's influence would calm Mum down, but Dot hadn't run out of steam yet.

Her eyes narrowed and she pointed an accusing finger at her husband. "Talking of vipers – you knew about this gypsy girl and you never told me!"

"And get yelled at like this before I needed to?"

Albie sat at the table, relieved things were out in the open and happy for Dad to take the heat for a while, but Mum soon rounded on him again. "You won't get a landlord to take a gypsy — or did you think you could live here? I ain't having her in my house."

"We don't want to live here, Mum – we're going to live with Maria's family," Albie stammered, "They're coming round to meet you."

"How exciting," Norah said cheerfully, "I hope I will be invited? And we will of course be polite to them for Albert's sake, won't we, Dorothy?"

George leaned forward to grip Dot's agitated hands. "Of course we will — guests are guests whoever they are. When are they coming?"

"Tomorrow," said Albie helplessly, "At six o'clock,

after they've set up camp at Coppin Farm."

How they got through the rest of that evening Albie could never quite recall. Dot was too distraught to do more than rock and weep at the thought of Albie living on the road with a tribe of gypsies, so Norah dished up the stew that had been simmering on the hob. Unfortunately no-one remembered the potatoes, which caught the pan and filled the kitchen with smoke, sending Dot into a fresh storm of tears.

Around nine o'clock George said brusquely, "Dot, that's enough now, give it a rest," and Dot was shocked into silence. George led her towards the stairs but paused with his hand on the banister to say, "Albie – you'll see Norah home, won't you?" He gave Dot another push towards bed. "I'll sort your Mum out while you go and drag Bert out for a pint – I reckon you need one."

When Albie pulled the door shut behind them, Norah tucked her hand through his elbow saying, "I want to hear all about your Maria." Albie put his big hand over hers and matched his stride to her short steps to walk her home, pouring his excitement and dreams into her receptive ears. When they reached Norah's block of flats she stood on the steps and held Albie's face in her small, gloved hands. "Maria sounds lovely, Albert, and I shall be there tomorrow to meet her."

"I dread to think what Mum's going to do," Albie said, leaning forward for her kiss.

"Dorothy will behave — I intend to speak to her in the morning," Norah said, sliding her key into the lock, "I shall see you tomorrow, Albert – now go and celebrate with your friend."

*

Albie was awake at dawn and sat up slowly, nursing a sore head from too many pints the night before. Looking out of his window he saw a soggy grey day that would make moving the wagons difficult and considered going to help them, but decided against it — he would need the money from work to pay for the wedding. He dressed and went downstairs, dreading what mood he would find Mum in. Dot was in her usual place at the range and he said, "Morning, Mum," on his way to the scullery to wash, but she didn't reply. He could see eggs in a pan, so he sat at the table and poured himself a cup of tea, watching her out of the corner of his eye. A moment later Dot slammed his breakfast down in front of him without a word, and Albie wondered how on earth Norah was going to change Mum's attitude in a day. He ate hurriedly in an atmosphere thick with resentment, grabbed his work jacket and escaped.

But at five o'clock he arrived home to find Norah and Dot making sandwiches. Norah actually winked at him as he stood staring, but Dot snapped, "Don't just stand there taking up space, Albie — bring the bedroom chairs down. Your Dad's gone for beer and Eric and Hilda will be here soon with some sausage rolls."

Albie was so relieved that he kissed them both and tried to hug Dot but she pushed him away. "Don't think you can get round me that easy, but I ain't having them gypsies think I'm too ignorant to be civil." She cut a sandwich into four with savage emphasis. "Now get a shift on - you've got to wash yet and put on a collar."

*

When Josef hitched his horse and cart to the lamp-post at exactly six o'clock, heads were silhouetted against every window in the street to watch — the neighbours knew by now that Albie Smith was going to run off with the gypsies. Eyes widened as he helped Abuela down from the cart as if she was a real lady, and widened further when George Smith ushered them into his home just like he would ordinary people. The second the front door closed there was a concerted dash to be nearest the window, but Dot knew her neighbours well and had drawn her curtains firmly together. Their curiosity had to be satisfied by taking it in jealously disputed turns to press an ear to the pane and relay the conversation to the others.

Eric and Hilda backed nervously against the dresser as the kitchen filled up, and Dot would have joined them if George hadn't pinned her firmly to his side. Norah caught a glimpse of Maria before she shrank back into a trio of other women and she thought, the girl is as nervous as we are, and no wonder – the hostility in here is palpable.

With everyone standing, the small room was packed. Albie knew he'd have to start the ball rolling or this meeting was doomed before it got off the ground. He drew Josef forward. "Dad, this is Maria's father Josef."

George shook Josef's hand. "George Smith — and this is my wife Dorothy."

Hearing her husband use her full name helped Dot to stand her ground, and when Josef offered his hand she touched it briefly, aware of Norah watching her. Then Albie introduced Eric, Hilda and Norah, after which Josef presented his family. "My grandmother Clara — my parents Mateo and Lydia — my brother Theo and his wife Emily — and of course, my daughter Maria. Maria, pay your respects to Albert's parents." He gave Maria a little push that propelled her into the centre of the room, where she bobbed a curtsey and murmured, "Mister Smith, Missus Smith."

Nobody had ever curtsied to Dot in her life, and she was too taken aback to do more than nod, but Norah came to the rescue by saying, "Shall we all sit down?" Dot sank into her rocking chair as if her legs could no longer hold her and Abuela took the armchair opposite, leaving George holding centre stage in front of the range.

"Albie says him and your Maria want to get wed," he began, looking directly at Josef. "His mum and me were a bit surprised but..."

When he floundered to a halt, Josef interjected, "You do not understand our ways, so you are worried for your son."

"Couldn't have put it better myself," said George. "Now if Albie and Maria was to settle in town, we'd be happy." He could feel Dot glaring and hurried on, "More than happy — she looks a decent, respectable sort of girl — but this moving around from pillar to post don't seem right to us."

"And your ways seem strange to us," Josef replied, his voice rising, but his father Mateo coughed a warning and Josef took a breath before continuing. "Our travels are not random, Mister Smith. We are rarely more than two days from our next stop, and many farmers expect us every year."

There was a long pause and then Dot burst out with, "I still don't see why you had to pick on our Albie. I thought you people only married your own kind by jumping over a broomstick."

Her tone was far from polite and this time it was Mateo's voice that began to rise. "Albert chose us, Missus Smith — he is not a child to be stolen. As for broomsticks..."

Abuela silenced him with a gesture. "Albert – I believe you have a question for us?"

Albie still wasn't used to the way Abuela could read his thoughts, but he gave her a half-smile and asked, "When will me and Maria get a wagon?"

"Emily's father asked the same thing," Mateo said, "I think he was afraid he would have to buy one. You will start off in a tent like everyone else – Josef will buy you a new piece of canvas." He grinned and winked so vigorously that his earrings flashed gold in the gaslight. "Everyone goes deaf at bedtime, Albert," and Albie cursed the blush that never failed to catch him unawares.

"There'll be no talk of bedtimes in my house," said Dot severely, "And if there must be a wedding it'll be in church or not at all." She folded her arms across her best frock and glared at the old woman sitting opposite.

Abuela responded by straightening her back and lifting her chin. "Before there is talk of a wedding – in church or no –

we agree a bride price."

"Bride price?" squeaked Dot, "You mean he's got to buy her?"

There was a sharp intake of breath and Abuela's black eyes flashed. "We do not sell our children, Señora Smith, but if Josef gives his daughter to Albert, Albert must give something to show he values her – this is our way."

"That sounds like a dowry," Hilda said, thinking of the historical romances she borrowed from the library and read avidly. "I thought the girl's parents paid that."

"You mean they buy her a husband?" Mateo asked pointedly, "After feeding and clothing her for years?"

"I'd never thought of it like that," Hilda admitted, "But it *was* hundreds of years ago — nobody does that now."

"Well, we do," said Mateo in tones that brooked no argument, and another thick silence blanketed the room.

Albie caught hold of Maria's hand. She felt the tension in his fingers and squeezed to reassure him. She should have warned him that negotiations were always like this in her family. Albie interpreted the squeeze as his cue to intervene. "I'd like to say something," he began, then paused for Abuela to acknowledge him with a nod before continuing. "Maria told me the bride price is paid 'cause her family is losing her, but they ain't going to lose her. I'll be working for the family along with Maria." Mateo and Josef exchanged a look and Mateo began to speak, but Albie continued doggedly. "I ain't finished. Bride price or dowry — whatever you want to call it — you're welcome to me fifty quid of savings. But I'll tell you this — me and Maria are getting wed regardless, and if you can't agree tonight then we'll just run off. It's up to you – all of you." He put his arm round Maria's shoulders and she nestled into his side, staring defiantly at her family.

Josef, Mateo and Theo were on their feet instantly, shouting — George and Eric tensed ready to defend Albie if it came to fisticuffs — and Dot, lacking an apron, just prevented herself from throwing her skirt over her head as she rocked and wailed. Only Abuela and Norah remained calm, exchanging a smile at the determination on Albie and Maria's faces. The neighbour with her ear to the window hissed, "There's a fight starting!" and half-a-dozen others fought for positions beside her in time to hear one voice cut through the racket. "Basta! Enough!"

Even Dot stopped wailing at the tone of authority and in the ensuing silence Abuela delivered her verdict. "Albert is correct. We do not lose Maria and so the bride price is not necessary. You agree, Josefito?"

Slowly Josef nodded but said, "He could help pay for the wedding, though."

"That sounds fair enough," said George in relieved tones and shook Josef's hand to seal the bargain. Albie scooped Maria up and kissed her soundly, Eric fetched the beers from the scullery and put them on the table, Josef and Theo delved into their deep pockets and produced bottles of wine, Hilda brought her sausage rolls in on a tray, and Norah whipped the damp cloth off the sandwiches.

Josef poured the wine into Dot's best glasses, insisting wine must be drunk as a toast, and the chink of glass on glass almost concealed the black cloud of disapproval emanating from Dot. The neighbours in the street were astounded – and more than a little disappointed – to hear, not the anticipated free-for-all, but a chorus of voices wishing Albie and Maria a long and happy life together.

CHAPTER SEVENTEEN – 1935 – PREPARATIONS

When Josef stood, cap in hand and respectful, in the farmhouse kitchen and asked permission to hold a gypsy wedding in Bottom Meadow, Farmer Coppin was within a breath of refusing when May Daly, who was mixing a batch of pastry at the table, asked Josef, "Is it your daughter that's marrying Albie Smith?"

Josef glanced at her and said, "Yes, miss."

May turned the full force of her bright blue eyes on Charlie Coppin and pleaded, "Oh please, please do let them! Albie's our Bert's best friend and it would be such fun!"

Charlie couldn't resist her sparkling face – not for the first time he thought that his good-for-nothing son Ken was luckier than he deserved to have hooked such a prize — and he turned back to Josef. "I suppose there'll be hundreds of you?"

"A fair number, señor," Josef admitted, "If word reaches them in time."

"It's going to be soon, is it?" Another shotgun wedding, by the sound of it, thought Charlie, and he would never know how fortunate he was not to have voiced the thought.

"Before the end of next month, we hope," Josef told him, "After the potatoes are picked up we go to Ruxley for the winter, and they want to be married first — Albert's people all live here."

With May gazing at him, Charlie yielded. "Fair enough – you can use Bottom Meadow – but if there's any damage you'll have to put it right."

"There won't be any damage, señor, I will see to that, and we are grateful to you," said Josef and, with a quick smile at May, he left to relay the good news.

*

Meanwhile Albie and Maria were sitting on the edge of a shiny settee in the church minister's study, holding hands tightly and staring at him aghast.

"Can't you christen me now?" Albie stammered, embarrassed to the roots of his hair yet again, "I'm sure my mother meant to get me done, but somehow she never."

"It's not that simple, Albert, not when you're an adult," the minister told him sternly, "You should have instruction first."

"But we ain't got time!" Albie cried, "We've got to get wed this month!"

"Is there any particular reason for such unseemly haste?" the minister asked wearily.

Albie grasped his meaning from the way he was looking at Maria, but held onto his temper. "No, there ain't, but Maria's folks are moving on soon and we want it done quick."

The minister still hesitated, pursing his lips and staring at the pair in front of him. Mrs Smith was a regular member of his congregation, but wasn't there some doubt about her large son's background? And this disturbingly attractive girl was pure gypsy.

Abruptly Maria stood up. "Come on, Albie — if he doesn't want to marry us, he won't. We'll just make our promises in front of the tribe."

"Then we'll be married?" Albie asked — could it really be that simple?

"That's our way," Maria assured him, "Papa married Mama like that," and they would have left there and then if the minister hadn't stopped them by saying hastily, "Perhaps we could forego the instruction in the circumstances. As long as one of you is christened I can marry you. Albert, could you rustle up some godparents? Two will be sufficient."

"I suppose so," Albie said doubtfully, "What would they have to do?"

"Just stand with you and promise to make sure you grow up God-fearing."

"Oh well, if that's all!" Albie laughed, "Seeing as I've grown up already and Mum's put the fear of God in me many a time! When can we do it?"

The minister made a pretence of consulting his diary, but in fact he was keen to get it over with before his wife found out. "Come tomorrow afternoon at three — we'll do it then."

"And the wedding?"

"Would the twenty-third suit you? Saturday the twenty-third at two o'clock? That will give me just enough time to post the banns."

*

Bert fell about in hysterics when Albie asked him to be his godfather. "You're not expecting me to hold you over the font are you?"

"It's no laughing matter, you arse," Albie growled, grabbing Bert by the lapels, "And if you tell anyone else you're a dead man! It's just that I can't get married in church without it and Mum's in a bad enough mood as it is - I daren't tell her we can't have a church wedding."

"All right, I'll keep it to meself, but you owe me for this. Godfather indeed! But didn't you say you had to have two?"

"I'm going to ask Norah."

Norah, predictably, wept when Albie asked her to be his godmother. "Oh my dear boy, I would be delighted! Tomorrow, you say? I will brush my best hat."

"Better save that for the wedding, Norah," Albie advised.

"Oh no," Norah said firmly, "I shall be purchasing a new hat for that occasion."

So the next afternoon Albie stood with Maria, George, Dot, Norah and Bert at the rear of the town church, nervously twisting his cap. The minister so rarely baptized an adult that he said, "Name this child," and George had to stand firmly on Bert's toe while Norah answered in her clear voice, "Albert

George." Albie bent awkwardly over the font for his head to be sprinkled with holy water and then the minister stood back.

"Is that it?" Albie asked.

"That's it – not too bad, was it? Now, once you've shown me your birth certificates I can post your banns in time for the twenty-third."

Albie blanched. "I'll bring 'em in in a day or so," he said hastily, grabbed Maria's hand, and escaped.

Neither Albie nor Maria had the birth certificates required by the minister before he would marry them, but here Albie's new godmother proved her worth. Norah made telephone calls to various offices which resulted in Albie being registered as Albert George Smith, son of George and Dorothy Smith, born October 11th 1913, claiming that his registration had been overlooked due to his mother suffering from childbed fever.

"It's only a little white lie to simplify matters," Norah told Dot, who was afraid of officialdom in all its forms, "And if anyone should ask – which they could never have reason to – Albert was a change-of-life baby. You are just the right age for that to be credible." Dot was flattered enough to agree, although when Albie was born she would have been forty-four and well past the change.

Maria's certificate was obtained by yet more telephone calls, in one of which Josef spoke to a farmer who knew the Perez family and was prepared to remember Maria's birth on his land eighteen years earlier – "Though we'll be working that farm for nothing next year," Josef grumbled. Maria was the first member of the tribe to have a birth certificate, and she went every day to Abuela's wagon to gaze at the ornate sheet of paper on which she could read only her name.

*

That Sunday Albie and Maria went with Dot and Norah to church, holding hands tightly while the banns were read between 'Albert George Smith, bachelor of this parish, and

Maria Perez, spinster of the Parish of St John the Evangelist, Sidcup'. After the service Albie took Maria back to Coppin Farm on his crossbar, leaving Dot and Norah to walk home to prepare the Sunday dinner.

The moment they left the churchyard Norah launched into a severe lecture. "Dorothy," she began, in a tone her sons would have recognized, "You are behaving very badly and extremely foolishly with regard to Maria."

"*I'm* behaving badly? You've got a nerve, Norah Barnes, when it's Albie who's running off with the gypsies!"

"No-one at church can have failed to notice your grim expression, Dorothy – it was more suited to a funeral than to the reading of your son's banns."

"Well, did you see the state of her? Wearing that coloured headscarf and great hooped earrings like a common tart!"

"Hardly common, my dear. Unless I'm very much mistaken those earrings were solid gold. And I am surprised you looked at her for long enough to see what she was wearing. As I said, you are being extremely foolish."

Dot banged her front door open and strode across the kitchen to slam the kettle down on the hotplate. George woke up with a start from his fireside snooze and scurried to refill the coal-scuttle, out of range of the approaching storm. Norah was the only one capable of dealing with Dot when she'd dug her toes in, but she couldn't half wind her up while she did it.

Norah unpinned her hat deliberately slowly, waiting until Dot had a cup of tea in her hands before returning to the attack. "You will lose Albert completely if you're not careful, Dorothy — is that what you want?"

"I ain't got a choice, have I?" Dot wailed, a tear oozing down her face unchecked.

Norah hardened her heart – this was no time for patting hands and sympathizing. "Of course you have a choice. The girl has been well brought up – no, please do not interrupt me

– her respect for her elders will make her an excellent daughter-in-law. She obviously adores Albert and will be a good wife to him, and I have absolutely no doubt that she is a virgin." Dot gasped at this indelicacy, but Norah ploughed relentlessly on to deliver her clinching argument. "And when she has babies, whether they are born in a bedroom, a wagon, or a tent, they will be your grandchildren."

George came back in on cue to add, "Legitimate, too, now Albie's officially our son. It'll be nice to hold a baby again."

He couldn't have said anything more calculated to soften Dot's attitude. As she fetched the teapot from the range she said to the wall, "I s'pose she could come to dinner next Sunday after church," and turned just in time to catch George giving Norah a huge conspiratorial wink.

*

Three weeks later Albie leant his bike against the gate to Bottom Meadow and drew Maria into his arms, grateful for the darkness. Five minutes was the most they would get before Maria's small cousins began to trickle out of the shadows. He and Maria might be two days off getting married, but they still had to spend their evenings in the firelight under the watchful eyes of the adults. He lifted Maria onto the top bar where she perched like an exotic bird, threading her fingers through his thick curls. Albie leaned forward to kiss her nose, feeling her small ribs move with each breath under his big hands. Maria stroked his evening stubble and kissed his mouth, but when he tried to deepen the kiss she held him off, laughing, "I don't want Papa to see my face all red from your whiskers."

"I didn't have time for a second shave today," Albie said ruefully. He rested his chin on her head and asked, "Ain't anyone coming to our wedding?" He had expected there to be dozens of wagons in the lee of the barn or dotted around Bottom Meadow, but he could see only one fire.

"They'll be here," Maria told him confidently, "When Papa went to tell Sofia, Dan had already gone to spread the news."

Albie shook his head in wonder. "She probably knew we were getting wed before I did. Did she see it in her crystal ball?"

"More likely in the fire," Maria answered matter-of-factly. "That's where Abuela and I saw you before you found our camp that first time."

"You too?" Albie chuckled, lifting her to the ground as two little boys materialised out of the darkness, "You never let on you had the sight."

"I was afraid it would scare you off," said Maria, watching him admiringly as he tossed a child onto each shoulder with no visible effort.

"It'd take more'n that to put me off you," Albie replied, "Though I'd better watch what I get up to if you can see me in the fire!" He flashed his teeth in a grin and galloped off with his yelling passengers towards the wagons.

*

Luke Finch was on his way back to Pinetree Farm after making an early delivery in town the next morning, so he was the first to see a line of wagons moving down the lane. Luke was sixteen now – well past his games of let's pretend — but the horses' breath mingled with the mist that billowed over the fields and hedges in ghostly waves, giving the procession an air of mystery and magic that took his breath away.

The man leading the first horse broke the spell by asking, "Are we right for Coppin Farm?"

"You're here for the wedding? Coppin Farm's next to ours. I'll show you the way."

Later that day Adam and Luke drove their cart up to the barn in Bottom Meadow and gawped at the ordered chaos that was the gypsy camp. There were a dozen fires burning, each with its ring of wagons and tents, and the festive spirit had pervaded the area to such an extent that the mist had retreated. A pale sun glinted off painted wood and hanging water-pails, and lines of washing snapped in a drying breeze. Swarms of children were picking over the nearby field for any potatoes missed the previous week, while the adults caught up with family news and cooked cauldrons of food for the wedding party.

"Who's in charge here?" Adam asked, and was directed to Josef who, as father of the bride, was the host of this gathering. Luke dropped the tailgate of the cart and dragged two carcasses to the edge while Adam told Josef, "These are my wedding gift to the happy couple. My son here wouldn't be alive today if it wasn't for Albie hauling him out of the sea when he was a nipper. Your girl's got herself a good man."

"We know that, señor, and we're grateful for the meat," said Josef, beckoning some of his cousins to offload the carcasses. "You'll be at the party tomorrow?"

"Wouldn't miss it for the world," replied Adam, turning his horse back towards home, "And if your kids want to pick over my potato field next they're welcome to what's left. Luke will show them where it is."

While Luke was directing the wagons, Albie was coming down the stairs of his house, yawning after a rare lie-in. He found Norah a calm presence in the kitchen, sewing a filet of lace onto Dot's best frock while Dot made pastry. Hilda was there too, filling the strips of pastry with sausage-meat, and Albie stood uncertainly, wondering what to do with his day.

Dot wiped her forehead with a floury wrist and told him, "Alice is doing your breakfast today. Get along there quick before Bert eats it all."

Albie looked at the array of trays waiting to go in the oven. "I thought we were just having cake here tomorrow — are we feeding an army?"

"You might have decided to have your wedding party

in a field," Dot snapped, "But I ain't having the neighbours think I'm too mean to put on a spread." She plonked a huge lump of pastry on the table, raising a cloud of flour, and picked up her rolling pin.

Albie winked at Norah, grabbed his jacket and cap and escaped to the relative peace of Alice's kitchen, where he found Bert still in his braces.

"What you doing home on a weekday?" Albie asked.

"Couldn't leave you to mooch about all day on your own, could I?"

Alice put a plate of bacon and eggs in front of him and headed for the door. "I'm off to the shop to finish trimming your mum's hat, Albie, so you two can amuse yourselves," she said, and on a draught of cold air she was gone.

Albie ate his breakfast and shared Bert's newspaper, but they were both too restless to sit still for long, so they set off to walk along the seafront. When they were nearly at the damaged pier Bert stopped and turned round quickly. "Sorry Albie — I should've gone the other way."

"It don't worry me now, mate," Albie said, leaning on the salt-damp promenade rail, "And it's always good to have a look at the sea."

Bert rested his elbows alongside Albie's, watching his friend's face and trying to guess at his thoughts. "Sad, ain't it?" he ventured at last.

"I dunno. If it'd happened a year back I'd've been knocked for six, but not now."

The worst of the debris had been cleared, and a casual glance showed only a pier closed down for the winter. Tarpaulins covered the roofs of the theatre and tearooms, awaiting milder weather and the ministrations of builders, who would be paid from the Disaster Fund set up by the town's businessmen. The kiosks had been repaired and boarded up and it all looked neat and tidy, but the profile of the pier had been irrevocably altered by the loss of the helter-skelter — it wasn't the same place now.

Albie turned his back on the scene and started walking again - walking always helped him to think. "It's like that book I read when I were a kid," he mused aloud, "You get to the end of a chapter, stick in a bit of paper and close the book, then the next night you start again and the story goes a different way."

"What are you on about, Albie - what book?"

"Treasure Island, it was called. Reckon my life's like that."

"Like a treasure island?"

"No!" Albie laughed, "Like a book. The pier's finished for me and I'm moving to the next chapter."

"Not before we've had a pint," Bert said firmly, steering him towards the nearest pub, "If you're going to talk about books I need a glass in me hand!"

CHAPTER EIGHTEEN – 1935 – THE WEDDING

The morning of the wedding was sharp and cold, but most of the Smith's neighbours turned out to watch the gypsy procession arrive at the church. It was a cheerful crowd, the hard-core disapprovers having stayed indoors, and Maria's family put on a fine show for them. They had left the big horses and wagons at the farm, but the ponies pulling the brightly painted and freshly scrubbed carts were buffed to a high gloss and their harnesses jangled with ornaments. Men and women alike wore bright clothes and jewellery – exotic splashes of colour against the dark bricks of the church – and Maria's white dress shone like a dove amongst birds of paradise. When Josef lifted her from among her aunts and cousins to set her on the ground as if she were made of porcelain, even the doubtful among the onlookers had to admit that Albie Smith had snagged himself a beauty.

The stir of their arrival spread in a wave from the west door. Albie, sitting tensely in the front pew, grabbed Bert's forearm in a grip that made him wince, stammering, "She's here!" and stepped out to watch the vision that was Maria waft down the aisle, her white dress gleaming in the dim church. His heart seemed to fill so much of his chest that he couldn't breathe and his blood pulsed in his ears, drowning the murmurs of admiration from the guests. Albie gripped the carved end of the pew to anchor himself against the tide of emotion – part love and part fear – as the moment approached for his leap into the unknown, but then Maria smiled at him and the world righted itself.

Norah hissed in Dot's ear, "Dorothy Smith – smile now or I'll never speak to you again!" George winked at her gratefully and put his hand over Albie's white-knuckled one on the pew-end, swallowing a lump in his throat at the naked adoration in his son's eyes.

"At least she's wearing white," Dot muttered through

gritted teeth, and Norah pinched her arm to silence her. She recognized the quality of Maria's gown. It must be at least a hundred years old, she thought, and meticulously cared for between generations of brides, for the antique lace had none of that yellow tinge it could so easily acquire if neglected. How the gypsies managed it under their primitive living conditions she couldn't begin to imagine. And that veil was a genuine Spanish mantilla, held in place by a comb that must in itself be worth a small fortune. This simple uneducated girl was walking towards her marriage in an unremarkable church, in front of ordinary common people, wearing a bridal outfit for which a debutante would give her eye-teeth — and all Dorothy could remark on was her lack of flamboyance!

Albie stepped forward in a trance of delight to stand in front of the minister, whose appreciation of the drama of the occasion led him to deliver the traditional words with more meaning than usual, and the silence as Albie and Maria exchanged their vows was profound. When the minister pronounced them 'man and wife together' Albie lifted Maria's priceless veil to give her a kiss that held the promise of the night to come, and the church erupted with a cheer hitherto unheard within its sober walls.

After the newlyweds had retired to the vestry to sign the register, the congregation, townsfolk and gypsies alike, chattered freely, and greeted their return with another tumultuous welcome that caused the minister to wish all weddings could be as joyous. The bridal pair's progress to the west door was delayed while every member of Maria's extended family kissed her and shook Albie's hand. Even Dot, walking slowly behind them on George's arm, preened as friends and neighbours admired the new red hat that set off her tan coat to perfection and managed, by the merest whisper of a shade, not to clash with Norah's purple one.

Bert's boss Mr Wallace took his photographs, wishing that his Box Brownie was capable of capturing the rainbow of colours displayed on the porch steps, after which Dot bustled George, Eric and Hilda away to make sure the house was ready to receive visitors, leaving the wedding party to make their triumphal progress through the busy Saturday streets.

Housewives going home from the market rested their heavy baskets on the pavement to lift children for a better view of the colourful procession; shopkeepers lounged in doorways, their customers momentarily distracted by the spectacle; a chimney-sweep jumped onto the step of Josef's cart to kiss the bride for luck; and the townsfolk who turned away in disapproval at this marriage between two cultures went un-noticed in the wave of good will for Albie, son of George and Dot Smith, and his stunningly beautiful bride.

*

"I don't remember asking all these people," Dot said as she made yet another pot of tea, "Eric – chase them kids off the sausage rolls and then go and find out who Albie invited."

It had been hard enough keeping track of all the comings and goings from the start, although only Maria's immediate family had come to the house, but then George had had the bright idea of unlocking the back gate. Now the yard was full of men knocking back bottles of beer as if they were going to close the brewery tomorrow, and there were kids everywhere. Even Norah and Abuela, tucked into a corner on the only chairs that hadn't been taken upstairs, looked alarmed at the crush, and Dot feared for the safety of the cake that sat in ornate splendour on the dresser.

Eric collared Albie in the back yard. "Mum wants to know who you invited as well as this bunch of gypsies."

"The only ones here 'cause I asked them – apart from Maria's family," Albie replied with heavy emphasis, "Are the Dalys and Ken Coppin."

"I never knew he was a mate of yours."

"He ain't, but he's May's bloke. Now I'll get Josef to help us get rid of these free-loaders – who did Mum ask?"

Dot came over to point out the uninvited guests and soon mere nosy neighbours had been weeded out, light-fingered children had been sent packing with a clip round the ear, and one of Josef's swarthier cousins was guarding the back gate. The small house was still full, but now even the most casual observer could see the clear division between the two groups of guests.

In the kitchen and scullery the local women sipped cups of tea with little fingers raised, watching the gypsies out of the corners of their eyes. They admired each other's best hats, pulled from the tops of wardrobes to be brushed and newly trimmed for today, and noted complacently how their fair and powdered cheeks differed from the dark, weathered faces of the gypsy women. The women of Maria's family were equally complacent, although only her aunt Emily was used to houses like these. They thought Dot's neighbours' dresses were sadly plain and their faces pasty, and they knew that the gold and gems which glowed richly against their own dark skins showed up the other women's jewellery for the cheap imitation stuff it was.

Outside there was a similar male chasm across the back yard. Although George and Albie crossed and re-crossed it to chat with equal bonhomie in both camps, there was small chance of any inter-mingling. The locals were drinking beer straight from the bottle as they considered real men should, while the gypsies shared the wine they had brought, which to the townsmen marked them as cissies. No-one was foolish enough to say so, naturally, with a dagger stuck in every ornate gypsy belt. Ceremonial daggers, Albie said they were, but they looked sharp enough to do some serious damage, and Ken Coppin quietly voiced the opinion that they were probably illegal.

Only Norah and Abuela, marooned on their little island of calm, crossed the communication divide. Norah leaned forward, instinctively cupping her good ear against the babble of small-talk, to comment, "At least you will have room enough for everyone to spread out in the meadow tonight."

"Many guests bring good fortune," Abuela replied serenely, shifting her chair to make room for Eric and Hilda to move the wedding cake to the table, "So many people here show this is a house of love."

"You are right, of course," agreed Norah, wondering how old this woman was, "Though I doubt Dorothy sees it in that light."

"Dorothy sees many things in a wrong light," said Abuela, "But she will learn — and I have seventy-four years." Her sharp black eyes twinkled at Norah, full of glee at the success of her mind-reading demonstration.

There was a flurry of movement to watch Albie and Maria wield the big carving-knife for the ceremonial cake-cutting, and then Dot and Hilda cut it into portions and passed it round on a variety of borrowed plates. Eric opened Norah's gift of a bottle of sparkling wine and shared it out by the thimble-full to the assembled guests, and then Bert made a short, red-faced speech and proposed the toast.

Abuela touched her glass to Norah's, saying, "Albert will be happy with us — do not fear for him."

"Fear is too strong a word," Norah protested, "Although I will miss him quite dreadfully."

"He is not lost to you while you have him in your heart – and you must care for Dorothy now." Norah caught a glimpse of Dot's bleak expression as Albie and Maria fed morsels of rich fruit cake between each other's lips. Abuela was right and her duty was clear – Dorothy would need her more than ever after today.

The afternoon light was fading fast when Josef unhitched his patient pony from the lamp-post and prepared to depart for the second half of the celebrations. Maria made a respectful curtsey to her new in-laws before Albie lifted her aboard and turned to kiss Dot. "That were a lovely cake,

Mum," he told her and then shook George's hand. "Are you sure you'll be all right in John's van? We can send the cart back if you'd rather."

"We'll squash in somehow," George assured him. "Norah's coming too, remember, and I can't see her in a gypsy cart, can you?"

"Why not?" Albie laughed, pulling Norah closer for a hug and a kiss, "After all, we seen her often enough on a helter-skelter mat, didn't we?"

*

Gladys Daly, squeezed into the cab of the van with John and Dot and Norah, instantly forgot the discomfort of the door-handle digging into her hip at the sight of the torches and fires. "It's like the Harvest Home parties," she said to Dot, "Though it's still light when those start — this looks much more romantic."

"Hmmph!" Dot muttered, "Going to be a sight colder than harvest-time."

"There are so many fires that you will think it is summer," said Norah, "And if you haven't put on warm undergarments you have only yourself to blame."

Gladys smothered a giggle at the shocked expression on Dot's face and John guffawed. They had long ago learned that Norah, although definitely a lady, was not afraid to mention unmentionables.

"Here we are," John said, pulling on the hand-brake and jumping down into the cobbled farmyard to lift Norah down while George helped Dot. The rest of the Daly family tumbled out of the back of the van where they'd been cocooned in blankets against the November air.

A small boy with a torch led them through the copse over a layer of straw that covered the mud, and they arrived in Bottom Meadow to a blaze of firelight. A piercing whistle from their escort brought Josef and Albie hurrying to greet them, and the next moment George, Dot and Norah were surrounded. George put a protective arm round Dot, Josef escorted Norah, and they progressed towards the largest fire through a path formed by what appeared to be every adult in the meadow, each one determined to shake their hands.

"They are treating us like royalty!" Norah exclaimed, "And I am not even a relative — I feel such a fraud."

"You're part of the family, Norah," George replied firmly, shaking yet another calloused hand, "And seeing as we're out-numbered a hundred to one, I'll thank you to stick with us!"

As he said this, the corridor of welcome widened to reveal Abuela, her tiny, neat figure posed statue-still on the narrow platform at the rear of her caravan. With impeccable timing she took Mateo's hand to descend the steps and say, with her clear voice resounding in the hush, "George, Dorothy and Norah, we are happy to welcome you to our fire."

Chairs had been placed for them a comfortable distance from the fire, with the tall wooden wall of the barn to shelter them from the light breeze that whipped sparks up into the miraculously clear dark sky. Maria darted in to kiss their cheeks, glasses of wine appeared in their hands seemingly of their own volition, and with the merest flick of her fingers Abuela signalled for the music to start.

Albie had been practising for this moment for weeks under Maria's tuition. He drew her into his arms and, sweating profusely with nerves, danced with his bride for a full two minutes in front of his astonished family and friends. A change of rhythm brought other dancers into the ring and Albie relaxed – he had managed not to trip over his own feet or to tread on Maria's gown. When Maria kissed him and disappeared on an errand of her own, George raised his glass saying, "Well done, lad!"

Albie held his hand out to Dot. "Mum, may I have this dance?"

"Oh, I couldn't – not with my feet!" she said, frowning

at the swirling dancers. Albie's face fell and George glowered, but Norah shot Dot a withering look and stood up.

Tossing the pansies on her hat, she held out her hand. "I promised I would dance at your wedding, Albert, and this music is irresistible." So Albie held Norah's bird-like figure in his strong young arms and they whirled off together, laughing as they tried to imitate the other dancers.

Dot watched them sourly but George swallowed a reprimand, knowing that if he said anything to wind Dot up tonight she was quite capable of storming off in a huff. Inching his chair closer, he groped for the hands that lay clenched in her lap. "You put on a good show this afternoon, Dot — everyone said that cake was one of your best."

Slowly her fingers unwound to clasp his. "I'm surprised there was enough to go round with all them people. Whatever possessed you to open the back gate?"

"There was such a queue for the lavvy that the men used the alley. It's just that every time the gate opened, more people came in than went out."

Dot let out a shriek. "George Smith! How could you? What will the neighbours say?"

"Not much, seeing as it was them doing it," George assured her, concealing a smile – once again the chance for a good scold had cheered Dot up.

Ten minutes later Abuela clapped her hands for the music to stop and a group of women appeared with Maria in their midst. They removed Maria's veil to unplait her braids, releasing the strong, curly hair to flow down her back in a shining blue-black waterfall. Then her grandmother Lydia handed Dot a bright headscarf, saying, "You must cover Maria's hair with this dikla now she is married."

Dot, caught in the limelight, was unable to refuse. She draped the scarf over Maria's head, twisted the ends and tied them in a double knot beneath her chin. The guests applauded, Maria bobbed another curtsey, and Dot's reward when she returned to her chair was a broad grin from her husband and a nod of approval from Norah.

Josef whispered in Abuela's ear and she clapped her hands again for him to be heard.

"Before we eat there is time for the wedding gifts," he announced, and Mateo led into the arena a brown and white pony pulling a blue cart. Albie and Maria stood speechless with delight while Josef told everyone, "The pony is my gift to my daughter and her husband – a husband who is more Roma than he knows."

In the laughter which followed this remark Albie's eyes were drawn across the circle and there, smiling directly at him, was a broad-shouldered man standing half a head taller than his neighbours. With a shock of recognition Albie knew where he had seen that face before – he shaved its double every morning in the scullery mirror. He had found him at last – the man who had given him his wandering blood. His father Nate Smith had come to his wedding.

Maria tugged at his hand — Josef was speaking again. "The cart is a gift from Adam Finch and his son Luke, in gratitude for the life Albert saved." Adam raised a hand in salute as Josef continued, "There are other gifts inside the cart," and Luke Finch popped up holding a large canvas roll.

"That's our wedding present," George called out, "Josef told me what to get — it's a tent – and Eric and Hilda got you a set of towels."

"They're in here somewhere," said Luke, scrabbling through the parcels to read their labels, "And this one's from Norah."

"Those are sheets and pillow-cases," Norah said, "Two sets of good cotton ones." The bedding had cost her a whole pound, but it was worth it for the pleasure on Albert's face and the kiss from Maria.

An oil lamp came next – John and Gladys Daly's choice – then Luke held aloft a shiny galvanized bucket and a pointed shovel. Bert shouted, "That's from me and Alice so you can dig you own lavvy!" and there was a roar of delighted approval.

Josef gave the bucket to Albie, saying, "Hold that," and the men of the tribe crowded round to shake Albie's hand, kiss Maria, and drop money into the bucket.

As Albie voiced his thanks over and over again he was thinking that, instead of starting out with nothing but a bed in a shared tent, he and Maria were rich. They had their own pony and cart, their own tent and enough money to see them through any hard times.

When the cry went up that the meat was ready, Abuela told him to hide the bucket of money in her wagon, and while he did so Josef unhitched the new cart. Putting the pony's reins in Albie's hand, he winked and said, "Release her in the field with the other horses — and take your time."

Maria slipped her hand into Albie's and his pulse began to beat faster. She was his wife now — the escort of small boys had vanished — and as they walked across the meadow they were alone in the dark with only the pony for company. Albie stopped and Maria snuggled her head under his chin, sliding her arms round his waist and pressing her whole body against his. He tilted her head back to kiss her. "Where can we go?" he whispered, willing the pony to behave.

"Somewhere clean," she giggled, "I'm wearing the family wedding gown."

Beyond the barn scores of people were silhouetted by the fires over which the meat had been spread-eagled on old metal bed-frames, but behind Abuela's wagon, where the shadows lay deep and black, they found the barn door ajar. They tied the pony to the wagon wheel and slipped inside the barn. Hay filled it to the rafters, soft and dry and clean, and they pulled down a few bales to create a nest for two, crawled inside and fell on each other hungrily.

The scent of hay brought back to Albie his own first

time and he tried to hold back, as Ellen had taught him, to be gentle with his virgin bride, but Maria's hot Spanish blood had been constrained for too long. She yanked his jacket open to stroke his muscles through his shirt and urged, "Quick! Make me yours now before someone comes."

"But I want to make love to you properly!" Albie protested, un-buttoning his flies nevertheless as his body responded to her urgency.

"And you will," promised Maria, lying back and lifting her lace skirts carefully aside, "We'll make love all night and for many nights to come, but for now..." she reached up to draw his head down to hers, "For now, just do it!"

Albie needed no further urging. He spat on his hand and parted her thighs, moistening her with gently probing fingers and, as her tongue snaked between his teeth, he eased himself into her. Maria lifted her hips to meet him and dug her heels into his buttocks, drawing him further in until he met an obstruction. He pushed harder and she gasped, but when he would have pulled back she cried, "No – don't stop now!" so he slid one hand under the small of her back, kissed her hard and lunged, and he was through. Three firm thrusts were all it took for his pent-up desire to burst out of him in a flood, and Maria forgot the brief pain in the delicious sensation of him pulsing deep inside her.

Albie collapsed on top of her, pressing her down into the sweet-smelling hay, and as they lay entwined he pleaded, "Couldn't we just stay here?"and began to move again in the warmth of her. Maria, who had been on the verge of saying that it was time they rejoined the party, adjusted her rhythm to match his and after a few moments, on a rising moan of delight, she discovered what it was that made other couples cry out with fulfillment in the night.

Later, after Albie had released their new pony into the pasture and helped Maria to pick strands of hay from her dress, they wandered nonchalantly into the crowd and helped themselves to platefuls of the food for which they now had ravenous appetites. Their absence had not gone un-noticed, and their self-conscious re-appearance drew a few knowing smiles, but no-one commented apart from Bert, who muttered, "All right?" in Albie's ear and received an ecstatic, "Oh yes!" in reply.

Abuela smiled complacently. Some of the family had objected to Maria's marriage, but Abuela's own parents had been half-blood and she had over-ruled the critics. Besides, it was obvious to anyone with half an eye that Nate Smith must have fathered Albert, so he was half-blood too. By taking Maria's virginity immediately, Albert had secured his bride and the dissenting voices had been silenced — no-one else would take Maria now.

Mateo nudged George in the ribs. "If your son's father *is* Nate Smith, Albie and Maria are related by more than this marriage."

George took a gulp of beer to moisten his suddenly dry mouth. "How's that?" Ever since Albie had told him about this other Smith he'd been afraid there'd be some kind of announcement at the wedding. He soon discovered his fear was unfounded — Mateo simply wanted to air his knowledge of the family relationships.

"I am Maria's grandfather," he said, "And my father's brother was Nate Smith's grandfather, which makes Maria and Albert cousins."

"And all the others you call cousins too? There's scores of them!"

"My mother had four children who lived, then we had three children each, and our children have all got at least two." Mateo counted on his fingers until he ran out of hands and then waved vaguely at the figures passing to and fro. "The rest are Mother's brother's and sister's families, and my brothers' and sister's families."

"Stop – I'm lost already!" George laughed, and turned

his attention to Dot, grateful that she obviously hadn't heard Mateo talk about Albie's gypsy father. He looked at her barely touched plate and asked solicitously, "You not hungry, love?"

"The rice tastes funny," she said, passing him her plate.

"It's cooked with garlic and herbs," said Norah, who was tucking into her own with relish, "I think it's delicious – Rosanna has promised to give me the recipe."

"You seem to know everyone already," Dot said resentfully, "Who's Rosanna?"

"Abuela's youngest son's widow," replied Norah, who was beginning to sort out the tangle of Maria's family, "Her youngest took Georgie off for a beer."

"I hope our Georgie ain't overdoing it," remarked George through a mouthful of rice and stew, "He ain't used to boozing."

"He's seventeen, George," Dot reminded him, "And he *is* your grandson – he'll have been going to the pub for a year or more."

When the meal was finished and the music started again, Dot and Norah disappeared to use the farmhouse lavatory and Abuela moved to sit by George. "We may not get the chance again, George, but we must talk. Maria will need you one day – not soon but one day – and Dorothy must learn to love her as a mother should."

Fear clutched George's heart. "I don't like the sound of that — is something bad going to happen to our Albie?"

Abuela gripped his forearm – sometimes the blessing of sight could be a burden. "He does not die, but when he goes to war you must care for Maria and her babies."

George's spirits sank to his boots – if she was right, all this talk of another war was not just so much hot air. How many of the young men milling around Bottom Meadow tonight would survive the next one? "Are you sure Albie'll be safe?" he asked.

Abuela gazed at him and he shivered as those black

eyes probed his soul. "I see you would give your life for him," she said at last, "But he will not die."

When she would say no more, George went to join his elder son by the beer barrels, but even there the conversation was about the general election that had just taken place, the re-armament of Hitler's Germany, and whether there would be another war.

An hour or so later Hilda found them still there. "John's ready to take you home," she told George, "And Eric and I should go too, but I can't find Georgie."

"Right — I'll look for him," Eric said wearily, but Georgie was nowhere to be found. Eric searched for him, at first good-humouredly, then with increasing impatience and finally with real concern. He even entered the barn and hauled one angry young man off his partner, but there was no sign of his son anywhere. When Albie joined the hunt they discovered that Eddie Daly was also missing, along with two gypsy lads.

"They'll be boozing somewhere," Albie said cheerfully, but Eric had reached the end of his patience. "You and your bloody gypsies!" he yelled in Albie's face, "Mum said no good would come of it and this proves her right. Our Georgie would never have gone off drinking if you'd married a girl from a decent family!"

"What – like Hilda's?" Albie retorted, "If her dad's not in the pub by six they send out a search party!"

"You leave my wife out of this!" Eric threw a punch that landed on Albie's chest, Albie hit him back, and the next minute they were rolling around on the trampled grass having a real scrap. The fight drew a crowd immediately, but before it could get totally out of hand, George waded in and got Albie in an arm-lock while another large man encircled Eric's neck with a rock-like forearm, saying fiercely, "You touch my boy again and you're dead!"

George's head shot up at this threat to his elder son and he found he was looking at the face of Albie twenty years on.

White teeth flashed in tanned skin as Nate acknowledged the recognition in George's eyes, and when George said, "That's my other son – let him go," Eric was instantly free.

"What the hell were you two fighting about, today of all days?" George demanded.

Albie shrugged. "Nothing much really — just a joke that got out of hand."

"Is that right, Eric?" George asked suspiciously.

"Like Albie says, it were nothing. I'm just worried I can't find our Georgie and someone said he's drinking with some gypsy lads."

"That'll be Matt and Alfredo," said Nate instantly, "Young hooligans, that pair, and I can guess where they'll be." He led the other three to the stables and there, with an inquisitive horse nosing their recumbent bodies, lay the four stray boys. Nate picked Alfredo up and tossed him over his shoulder, Albie took Matt, and they disappeared towards the wagons while George and Eric dumped the other two in the back of John Daly's van.

"What did that gypsy mean when he called Albie his boy?" Eric asked.

"Dunno, son — must be 'cause Albie's part of the tribe now," George replied, "Come on, it's time we were all in bed."

Albie and Nate dropped their burdens by Mateo's fire, where the boys' mothers wrapped them in blankets and shooed the two men away with resigned gestures.

Nate showed Albie a bottle he had retrieved from Alfredo's pocket, ""There's two-thirds of this left — shall we finish it off?"

Albie glanced towards Abuela's wagon where Maria was talking to her great-grandmother. "She'll understand," Nate said, sitting on a bale of hay and passing Albie the bottle, "And you won't rest easy till we've talked."

Albie sat beside him and took a swig. "No wonder the boys got so drunk!" he gasped, "This is strong stuff."

"Hedgerow spirit always is," Nate laughed, "You'll get used to it."

Albie stared at his boots, noting absently that the high gloss of this morning was now smeared with mud — Mum would have a fit when he got home. Then he remembered that Mum wouldn't see them - he was living here now. Living in a tent in a field, and tomorrow he would stow that tent in his new cart and move on somewhere else — his home now was wherever Maria was. Excitement surged through his blood - blood inherited from the man sitting beside him. "Do you even remember my mum?" he asked, hating the childish tone in his voice but unable to hide it.

"I remember a pretty girl making eyes at me in the cherry orchard," Nate said gently.

"So you weren't a customer?"

"God, no! Never paid for it in my life - there are always girls who fancy a gypsy lover. Is that how she ended up - on the streets?" Nate touched Albie's arm briefly. "You poor kid. I didn't know about you till Sofia told me, and you were a grown man by then."

Albie heard the regret in Nate's voice and felt comforted. His father was simply a man who liked women and took what was offered - exactly as he had been doing until Maria came along. "Well, I soon learned to look after meself," he said, "Then Dad and Mum adopted me, so I didn't do too bad in the end."

"You turned out all right," said Nate, ending the conversation by standing up, and without warning he pulled Albie to his feet and hugged him. Albie closed his eyes - for a brief moment he was a small boy in his father's arms — but then the adult re-surfaced and he broke away. Nate chuckled. "Go and join your bride. We're leaving early tomorrow but we'll meet again at Ruxley - we'll have all winter to talk."

By midnight the final pair of headlights had made its unsteady progress back to town, and the torches that had lighted the way along Coppin Lane were extinguished.

In Bottom Meadow the remainder of the meat was strung up high out of the reach of foxes, and the barbecues had been smothered with dirt — only the banked fires glowed to show where the gypsies were still camped. Tomorrow the long trek to the winter camping grounds at Ruxley would begin, and only a few diehards remained out of bed, talking in low murmurs that reassured rather than disturbed the sleepers.

The lace wedding dress, with a few wisps of hay still clinging to its delicate fabric, hung in Abuela's wagon to await its meticulous cleaning, after which it would be folded away in a linen cloth to be brought out next spring for Maria's cousin's wedding.

And in their brand new tent, pitched a discreet distance from the others, Albie and Maria lay on a straw-and-heather-filled palliasse covered by Norah's gift of cotton sheets, making love with all the fire and passion of their shared gypsy blood.

PART THREE - 1939

CHAPTER NINETEEN – AUGUST 1939 – PINETREE FARM

Early in August 1939, Albie was walking beside his pony Blossom at the tail of a small convoy of wagons on its way once again to Thambay, counting off the familiar landmarks as he went. In the four years since he and Maria were married Albie had slotted into the gypsy life as if born to it, living on the move between hop-farms, fruit orchards, and pea, bean and potato fields. On pre-arranged dates they would meet up with the Davies Fair – tomorrow they were due to set it up in Thambay – and each winter they gathered with other tribes to spend the winter at Ruxley.

It was during Albie's second winter at Ruxley that their son was born. They named him Josef for Maria's father, although everyone called him Joey. Joey was two and a half now and rarely still, but he was asleep at the moment in the cart beside Maria, who was expecting another baby soon.

Now Albie was a family man, the shadow of war loomed large. It would be a relief to spend a few weeks at Pinetree Farm, where Adam Finch had cleared a corner of one of his pine plantations and covered it with gravel to create a campsite for them.

The convoy slowed in Farm Lane and Albie led Blossom through the gate which Adam was holding open.

"Where's Luke?" Albie asked him, parking his cart by the hedge and beginning to unhitch Blossom, "It's always him opens the gate for us."

"Somewhere in the wilds of Scotland flying aeroplanes with the RAF," Adam said with evident pride. "Under this Military Training Act he had to do something, and he's always been fascinated by aeroplanes."

"Don't seem possible he's old enough," Albie said, remembering the skinny child he had pulled out of the sea.

"Daisy must be missing him." Luke had been courting Eric's daughter since meeting her at Albie and Maria's wedding.

"They got engaged on her birthday," Adam said, "But Scotland is a long way away and he doesn't get home often. His mother's taken it really hard too – from his letters he seems to be having a whale of a time, but she's terrified of what will happen when war comes."

"Ain't we all?" Albie replied quietly, trying not to wake Maria – despite being close to her time she had driven for part of the night while he slept. He took Blossom across the lane to the pasture and removed her harness, stroking her soft nose in apology for the long trek. The Finch horses looked up to whinny a welcome and Blossom trotted in to join her old friends.

The four wagons had already been parked in their customary square when Albie lifted his bike from the cart and helped Maria gently down. After checking that they were unobserved, he stroked her swollen stomach and said, "I'll make the fire while you go for eggs and milk, but walk slowly. I'll be gone when you get back – we saw the Fair lorries on the road an hour ago."

Maria kissed him gratefully – bending down to start a fire was difficult at the moment — and set off towards the farmhouse with Joey. She carried her big basket filled with the small ones that she had woven out of reeds at their last stop – Ruth Finch was always happy to take the little baskets in exchange for produce. Joey trotted beside his mother collecting pine-cones, happy to be free again. He hated being cooped up in the cart, but his legs tired too quickly when they let him walk. The tribe had covered a lot of miles since yesterday morning. They had been anxious to reach Pinetree Farm before the baby came, because a delay on the road meant money lost to the tribe, and with the threat of war hanging over them everyone was saving as much as they could.

After ten minutes' walk Maria was sitting in Ruth

Finch's yeast-fragrant kitchen sipping a cup of tea while Joey buried his nose in a beaker of frothy milk.

"That baby's going to be born here, by the look of you," Ruth remarked as she placed eggs carefully on a layer of straw in Maria's basket.

"Another two weeks, Rosanna says. We're going to call her Clara after Abuela."

Ruth didn't even ask how Maria knew she was carrying a girl – after having the Perez tribe on their land each summer she had learned not to be surprised by their intuition. "How is your great-grandmother?"

Maria's face fell. "Abuela died last winter. My cousin Matt caught the flu in the potato fields and then we all got it. When Olivia's baby died, Abuela said she couldn't let the baby go alone, so she died the next day." She stared into the flames licking up round the big black kettle. "We burned them together."

"Poor Olivia – how old was her baby?"

"Three months – but she's expecting again now."

"Rosanna must be devastated to have lost her grandchild – and I am so sad to hear about the old lady. I shall never forget the sight of her descending the steps of her wagon at your wedding. I suppose that lovely wagon will be ashes now."

"In fact it isn't – we still have Abuela's vardo," Maria said, easing her aching back in the cushioned rocking chair. "She said more people were coming and we would need it. She was so insistent that Grandfather gave in, and when she died he and Grandmother moved in to share the vardo with Rosanna."

"And did more people come?" asked Ruth, fascinated by this further glimpse into gypsy life.

"Four of them," Maria answered, wiping Joey's mouth with a cloth. "About a month ago Philipe and Estelle walked into our camp one day with their children. They said the Nazis were rounding up Roma people and sending them to camps like the Jews, so they sold their horse and wagon to get places on a boat. They arrived with nothing — they didn't even speak English - only French."

"How on earth did they find you?"

"Estelle has the sight."

I should have guessed, Ruth thought — that sixth sense again. Hadn't Rosanna told her only last year that Luke would fly the nest? She bit her lip - 'fly' was the operative word.

"Luke will come back to you," Maria said, touching her hand, and then she heaved herself to her feet, picking up her basket and the milk-churn ready to leave. "The others will be over to start work after breakfast."

"Pete and Brian will be in the bush field — the currants ripened beautifully in last week's sunshine. And tell Albie to collect these newspapers later — there are far too many for you to carry." She gave Maria a fresh hot loaf and pressed a warm biscuit into Joey's hand. "If you need any help when the baby comes, just send someone over to ask."

"I have family to help me, Missus Finch, but thank you."

As she watched them cross the yard Ruth thought, growing up in a tent hasn't done that child any harm. He's clean and well-behaved, and it's a crying shame that Dot Smith doesn't appreciate her own grandson.

At the end of the day Albie appeared to collect the pile of old newspapers. "I won't sit down," he said when Ruth offered him tea, "I'm covered in grease from the fairground." He scanned the headlines in the top papers and remarked gloomily, "Everywhere's the same — war, war and more war."

"Dreadful, isn't it?" said Ruth, "Still, at least you'll turn those newspapers into something useful. I put some magazines in there too." The women of the tribe spent the winter making papier mâché trays and boxes which they painted with traditional Romany designs, while the children wove paper strips into fruit punnets – every member of the tribe contributing to its income.

"Maria'll like the magazines," Albie said, "Her reading's coming on a treat."

"Well, when she's read them they'll make colourful punnets and I'll take as many as they can make. Selling currants in the market is so much easier if they're already weighed up." As Albie turned to go she added, "Have you visited your parents yet?"

"Thought I'd ride over after tea with Joey on the crossbar. He's learned to say 'Nan' now — that should please Mum."

As she took more loaves from the oven, Ruth hoped Albie was right.

Albie was crossing the farmyard when Adam hailed him. "Albie - is that engine grease you're covered in?"

"Yessir - why?"

"Because if you know about motors perhaps you could fix my tractor."

"If I can fix a fair ride I reckon I could fix a tractor – let's have a look at it."

The tractor sat in the home barn, covered in the dust that drifted down constantly from the roof. Adam shooed a couple of chickens off it. "Leave anything standing still for a day and they'll roost on it," he said as the chickens flapped away protesting loudly. "Now, Albie, what do you think?"

Albie slowly circled the tractor, poking here, sliding a hand in there, lifting the engine cover to peer inside. "Got any tools for it?"

Adam pointed to a chest in one corner. "See what you can find in there. Pete *would* buy the damn tractor — I'd sooner stick to horses myself."

Albie lifted a broken harrow off the chest and raised the lid, then seized a metal toolbox with a grunt of satisfaction.

"This'll be it — I'll be back tomorrow with Ricardo to give me a hand."

"Splendid!" said Adam, "That bloody Fordson cost me a fortune and packed up after only two years. If you can't get it going again I'll take it out of Pete's wages."

"From what I've heard, your sons don't get any wages," Albie said and went off laughing to collect his own small son.

*

Maria had scrubbed Joey till he shone, but after half an hour on the crossbar his hair was as wild and curly as ever when Albie carried him into his parents' kitchen. George dropped his paper on the rug and jumped up to take Albie's hand in a crushing grip. "When I saw the fair arrive I knew you wouldn't be far behind," he said, ruffling Joey's hair. "This can't be Joey! He's a real little man now. Give him to me, Albie — I've been looking forward to this for months."

Joey went to George's big hands willingly, and studied his face with eyes as black as his mother's. "Bampa?" he said.

George beamed. "Grandpa is right, young feller-me-lad – glad you remember — and that's Nan by the fire."

"Nan," Joey repeated and bared his baby teeth in a grin so like Albie's that Dot was surprised into an answering smile before turning away to the range. "You'll be wanting a cuppa, Albie."

"Yes please, Mum – and you're looking well."

"I'm as well as can be expected," she replied and Albie sighed – if she'd at least talk to Joey it would be a start.

"Has Maria had her baby yet?" George asked.

"Another two weeks," replied Albie, "Hardly seems possible we ain't seen you since the spring."

"What have you been doing since the hop-vine training?"

Albie grinned – Dad loved showing off his knowledge of the tribe's routine. "We've been mostly picking fruit, but we met the fair in Faversham and then came to Pinetree to catch up with it again, so here we are."

"We can always count on you coming at the start of August," smiled George, "Regular as clockwork, the fair is, and you with it."

"I like the fair," Albie admitted, "Reminds me of the pier, though God knows what'll happen to it if there's a war. Some of the Roma boys we know are in training camp already and two have joined the Merchant Navy. That reminds me, how's Georgie doing?"

"Studying for his Mate's ticket," said George with obvious pride in his grandson.

"Our Georgie, studying?" laughed Albie, "He's no more a reader than me!"

"This is different, he says," Dot said, joining the conversation at last, "And being in the Merchant Navy will keep him safe. It's a reserved occupation, according to the wireless."

"Like farming," added George, looking meaningfully at his younger son, "Good thing the minister put you down as a farmhand on your marriage lines."

Albie glanced at Joey, but the child was totally unaware of the sudden tension in the room. "I ain't opting out, Dad. If war comes, I'll fight to keep the Germans out of England. They've already put thousands of Austrian Roma people in concentration camps. I don't fancy me and my family being next."

George's knuckles tightened briefly on the arm of his chair. "How's the other Mister Smith?"

Dot made a disgusted sound but Albie was used to that, and at least she'd stayed put - the first time Dad had asked about Nate, Mum had stormed out. "He's very well, Dad. We met a month ago outside Canterbury."

"I thought you only saw him at the winter camp."

"As a rule, yes - the Smith tribe usually works further east — but they decided they'd be safer away from the coast.

Nate says the Government are even using Dover Castle as part of the defences."

"But that's hundreds of years old!"

"They built things to last back then, Dad, and we might as well make use of what's there."

Dot's cup clattered in her saucer. "That's enough of that talk – there ain't going to be a war."

George leaned across the hearth-rug and patted her knee. "Say that as many times as you like, Dot, but you can't stop it."

"I could do if they'd let me run the country."

"Reckon you could 'n' all, my love – reckon you could."

*

Albie and Ricardo pushed the unwieldy tractor out into the sunshine of the yard the next morning and set about working a miracle with the set of tools that had come with the tractor. Joey and Ricardo's son Pedro were drawn irresistibly to the wonderful machine, and while Albie and Ricardo dealt with the seized-up engine, the two little boys were put to work digging dried mud from between the deep treads of the tyres.

At lunchtime Pete Finch came back from felling pine trees to be confronted by the sight of the tractor engine lying in several pieces on the cobbles beneath an ingenious hoist made from scrap metal. He stormed into the kitchen. "What's happened to the Fordson? I was going to get the bloke from the garage over to look at it."

"You've been saying that for months," his father pointed out, "Now calm down – Albie and Ricardo are fixing it."

"Wrecking it, more likely — have you seen the state it's in? That tractor's worth a fortune!"

"Not sitting in the barn covered in chicken shit, it's not," Adam retorted, "And I never wanted to buy the bloody thing anyway."

"It'll do the work of four horses," Pete said defensively,

"I only hope those two know what they're doing."

"So do I, son, so do I, because we're going to need it *and* the horses to work the farm when war comes."

*

Little Clara Smith was born two weeks later on a baking hot day, much more easily than Joey who had been, at a hefty eight pounds, a large first baby for his diminutive mother. When Albie was presented with his tiny daughter he kissed her head, promised he would always look after her, and then kissed Maria saying, "I hope she'll be as pretty as her mother."

"She's pretty already!" Maria scolded, "And our other babies are going to be born in the summer too — raspberry tea helps the birth along much better with fresh leaves."

"Our other babies? Ain't two enough for you?"

"Two or three more should be enough," Maria said, reclaiming Clara and putting her to her breast, "So you be sure to come back to make them."

When Adam and Ruth Finch approached the campsite later, having been invited to help celebrate baby Clara's arrival, Ruth gave a little skip at the sound of the fiddle. "Listen to that, Adam - it brings back happy memories of the wedding. Was it really four years ago?"

"Those were happier times," Adam replied, squeezing her hand, "We didn't suspect there was going to be a war then."

Later, sitting on the steps of Abuela's old vardo later with Mateo, Adam looked at Matt and Alfredo sharing a bottle and asked, "When will your grandsons be joining up?"

"They won't," Mateo replied brusquely, "As far as this government is concerned we Roma don't exist. People will eat the food we grow and drink the beer from hops we train, but the police won't even let us stay one night on common land. Why should we fight for them?"

"But they'll have to fight when they're called up," said Adam.

"That won't happen," Mateo said confidently, "We are not on any official lists."

Which of course was true, thought Adam. No birth certificates, and married for the most part over a camp-fire, the gypsies were a hidden race that people ignored or reviled unless they were useful. As he had too until recently, he reminded himself. He looked around him at Mateo, his two sons, five younger men including the Frenchman, and a handful of women. A strong team, used to working together, and he had a farm to run. "What will you do when war comes?" he asked carefully, anxious not to spoil this opportunity with the wrong word, "Would you consider staying here?"

Mateo sat up straighter and regarded Adam thoughtfully. "On your land, you mean? We have to earn a living and fruit-picking won't last forever."

"There's more to farm work than fruit-picking."

The other men moved over to join them, drawn by what was clearly a serious discussion, and listened closely while Adam elaborated, becoming more enthusiastic as his initial impromptu remark grew into a conviction that this was the way forward for Pinetree Farm. "War is coming, without a doubt. I've got one son in the RAF already, and although farmers are exempt, my younger hands are champing at the bit to go and fight. The Government says I've got to plough up my pastures to produce more food – lots more – but I'll be left with half my usual workforce. I'd rather have you than a bunch of land girls, so how about it?" He looked at them all eagerly, but Mateo was not to be rushed.

"This is a big thing you are asking of us," he said gravely, "To stay in one place is not our way — we need to discuss it before we decide. Josef, Theo, what do you think?"

Josef had spent the weekend packing up the fair and had heard the owner talking of putting the rides into storage early because of the uncertain times. Half of the small sideshows had disappeared already, and many of the riggers had volunteered for the army, hoping to pick up a trade. "If there is work for us here, I think we should stay — the horses can pull a plough as easily as a wagon," he said.

Albie and Ricardo added their votes to stay on Pinetree Farm, but Theo was less keen. "If farmers are looking for workers we should go to Emily's people," he said, "And my son Matt needs a wife — he's not going to find one here - not a Roma one, anyway."

The discussion bounced back and forth all evening and for several days afterwards, but eventually a decision was reached — one that saddened them all.

The tribe whose ancestors had travelled from Spain a century earlier, and who had made a living in England together ever since, picked fruit as a group for the last time that summer. At the end of August Theo and Emily and their son and daughter packed up their wagon to move south to Emily's father's hop-farm. With them went the French refugees and Rosanna's younger son Alfredo, who refused to be parted from his lifelong friend Matt.

CHAPTER TWENTY- WAR

The day after Theo's group left, Albie drove his cart into Thambay to buy petrol for the tractor and seed for the newly-ploughed four-acre pasture. He found the farm merchant's store buzzing with news.

"Those damn Germans have invaded Poland," the storekeeper was saying as he walked in, "So much for peace in our time!"

"Hitler really pulled the wool over Chamberlain's eyes," said another man, "Bloody politicians! Whatever possessed him to say we'd help Poland? It's hundreds of miles away."

"But there's nothing between the Germans and us except sea," said Albie and then, remembering the fear that had driven Philipe and Estelle to leave their possessions and flee, he added, "We don't want them over here — the Nazis don't like anyone who's different."

"All your lot would be goners then," someone remarked from the back. Albie's hands tightened on the counter and there was a shocked pause, but when he said nothing an older man broke the tension. "I fought the Germans in the last war and mark my words, they'll try to invade us next. I'll be cleaning my old rifle when I get home. If they want to take England they'll have to get past me first!" His speech was stopped by a hacking cough that spoke of gas in the first war but no-one laughed at his fighting spirit. They all felt the same — if they were too old to join up they would still defend their country, with bare hands if necessary.

Many of the farm merchant's customers went home that day to dig their own guns out of storage, while Albie returned to the farm with the cart full of seed corn and potatoes, two large cans of petrol, and a roll of blackout material. Ruth had confessed she should have made her curtains weeks earlier, but hadn't been able to face the task

until she had Rosanna and Lydia to help with the sewing –
there were six bedrooms in her farmhouse and every window
had to be blacked out.

The old men's memories of the trenches in the Great
War had only stiffened Albie's resolve to fight. Their reaction
to the threat of the Germans – whom they thought they had
defeated in the last war — occupying their land, found an
echo in his own heart. The very idea was unthinkable.

He walked beside Blossom to ease her load, looking
fondly at the hedgerows on either side of the lane. They were
thick with brambles, the fruit turning black in the sun, and the
ditches were lined with cow-parsley and tall grass that
hummed with insects. He stopped to let Blossom crop some of
the sweet juicy stems and leaned on an old, grey timber gate
for a smoke, gazing at the stubble of a wheat field and
thinking that at least this winter there'd be flour for bread.

Skylarks sang way out of sight and he closed his eyes to
absorb the sound, locking the peace of the moment away in his
memory and hoping he'd be around to hear the larks sing
again next year. Maria was sure he'd be back to make more
babies but he wasn't convinced – the stories he'd heard this
morning had rattled him. Blossom snorted, snapping him back
to the present. "Brooding won't do any good," he scolded
himself, picked a few blackberries to eat, and hastened back to
the farm to relay the latest news.

The big wireless in the farmhouse kitchen was never
turned off after that, and Adam said anyone was welcome to
pop in and listen. One news bulletin after another plunged the
entire farm into frenzied activity and a sombre mood of
dreadful anticipation.

When the Finches and all their workers gathered in the
kitchen to listen to the wireless that Sunday, they heard the
official announcement that their country was at war with
sadness, but also with a sense of relief that the waiting was
over. Pete Finch summed up their thoughts in one terse

sentence. "This time we'll hammer those German buggers so far into the ground they'll grow roots!"

*

Two weeks later Albie and Bert joined the queue at the Town Hall to volunteer.

"How's Maria taking it?" Bert asked, "Alice is bawling her eyes out."

"Maria's gone all quiet on me," Albie replied, "She says I'll be safe but she still tried all the arguments. They don't want men over twenty-one, farmers don't have to go, Joey and Clara need their dad — but when I asked her if she wanted the Nazis to come over here and throw our babies in a camp, she shut up. In a way that's worse than the yelling."

"They ain't going to be very safe in that campsite when the bombing starts, Albie."

"I ain't told you, have I? What do you think I've been doing these past two weeks? I've been building a shelter with Josef and Ricardo."

"What, an Anderson, out there? Didn't know they issued 'em to gypsies." Bert's smile took the sting out of his words but he was right — only proper households were entitled to official protection.

"Made one ourselves out of timber," Albie explained proudly, "Great solid tree-trunks like an underground log cabin. The kids think it's wonderful."

"Ours is in the back yard of the shop," Bert told him as they reached the head of the queue, "Mr Wallace says Alice and little Susie can stay in the flat for the duration. Meat is bound to be first in line for rationing, so he don't think it's worth taking on another full-time bloke. Dad's going to help out in the shop and keep my job open for when this lot is over."

"What about his delivery round?"

"He don't reckon he'll be able to get the petrol."

"NEXT!" The recruiting sergeant was surprised when

the ill-matched pair insisted on staying together – the weather-beaten giant and his gingery, slightly-built friend – but he gave them consecutive numbers as they requested, sent them for the very cursory medical, and they were soldiers.

*

"Call the boys down for breakfast, love," Gladys Daly said to her daughter the following morning.

"I ain't got time, Mum, I'm running late as it is," said Jane, gulping down her last spoonful of porridge, and she hurried out to join the scattering of neighbours also on their way to work.

Gladys sighed and shouted up the stairs, "Porridge on the table!" May had married Ken Coppin and now lived on the farm, but Gladys liked to give her four remaining children a decent breakfast before the day's work, and she hated to see it spoiled.

When there was neither sign nor sound of her sons after a further two minutes, she turned off the gas under the porridge and went upstairs to discover the boys' room was empty. She stood for a moment in the doorway, catching her breath and shaking her head at the unmade double bed all three boys shared, and at the mess on the floor. Where on earth had they got to? For them to go without their breakfast was unheard-of – you'd think after their long day yesterday they'd be starving.

They'd got all wound up by Bert's announcement that he'd joined the army, and then in the evening there'd been that military band playing its rousing marches in the market square, all polished instruments and flash uniforms. All three boys had been talking very late last night until John banged on the wall, and they should have slept like logs.

An awful premonition clutched at Gladys's heart and, forgetting her bad hip, she hurried downstairs, slung her coat on over her apron, and ran to the Town Hall in her slippers.

A bunch of men and boys milled about beneath the

colonnade where the food stalls were on market day, and Gladys heaved a sigh of relief when she failed to see her sons. Then a door opened, a uniformed soldier called "Next!" and as a group of men went inside the hall, Gladys caught sight of Eddie's unmistakable mop of ginger hair. She pushed through the door just as it was closing and grabbed his sleeve.

"Just what do you think you're doing?" she cried, ignoring the sniggers from the other men in the room.

The sergeant at the desk looked up. "Is this your son, madam? He's just signed up."

"Don't you 'madam' me!" Gladys retorted, "And you can just un-sign him. You've already got my Bert and you're not having any more of 'em."

"You're too late, madam," the sergeant said, not without a touch of sympathy, "There's a war on and we need all the men we can get."

"Men, maybe, but not children!"

"They're young men, madam, and you should be proud that your sons are willing to defend their country."

"Sons?" shrieked Gladys, suddenly terrified, and a swift look round confirmed her worst fears — Billy and Jimmy were there too, doing their utmost to blend into the background. "You ain't signed all three up, have you?"

"Daly, Edward, Daly, William, and Daly, James - yes, madam, all three."

"And how old did they say they were?"

The sergeant consulted his list. "Edward's nineteen, William and James are eighteen — twins, apparently."

"Well, you can cross 'em off again," Gladys said severely, "Eddie's only eighteen and these two ...." she glared at her younger sons, who shifted from foot to foot looking horribly embarrassed, "These two are sixteen and fifteen and no more twins than – than you and me!"

The sergeant was reminded forcibly of his own mother – the only person who could still reduce him to a quivering wreck – and he crossed Billy and Jimmy off his list saying, "Take them home, Mrs Daly — the war will be over before they're old enough."

"Come on, you three, you've got jobs to go to," ordered Gladys, turning on her heel triumphantly in a circle of amused faces. But the army had the last word after all.

"Only those two, madam," the sergeant said, almost apologetically, "We'll be keeping Edward."

*

A week later there was a letter for Eddie containing a postal order and instructions about which train to catch to the barracks. He dashed round to the butcher's shop to discover Bert had received an identical one. Albie's letter arrived at George and Dot's the next day – Smith being after Daly in the alphabet – but when Albie and Maria arrived for Sunday dinner and opened it, his instructions were the same. He had three days left to organize his affairs before his body and soul became the army's.

Maria was always uncomfortable in the Smith's home — Dot's monosyllabic presence cast a pall over her sensitive spirit — but after learning the contents of Albie's letter she was even quieter than usual. Albie had run to Bert's to compare notes and was now back talking earnestly to George; Joey had finished his dinner and was on the floor playing with a box of bricks. Maria was struggling to eat one-handed while dealing with a grizzling baby, and only Norah noticed her silence. Pushing her own plate aside she said, "Give Clara to me, Maria – I will hold her while you eat your dinner."

"You've hardly touched yours, Norah," said Dot, "Is something wrong with it?"

"It is as delicious as always, Dorothy," Norah hastened to assure her, "I simply seem to have lost my appetite of late."

Maria handed Clara over gratefully and tucked into her food – Albie's mother was an excellent cook, which was strange in such a bad-tempered woman – while Norah put the baby over her shoulder and patted her back gently. A minute later there was a little juicy burp and Clara spat a dribble of curdled milk down the back of Norah's good Sunday frock.

Maria was half-way out of her chair when Dot said, "Maria — stay where you are and finish your dinner — I'll deal with this." She passed George a damp cloth telling him, "Wipe Norah down before it sinks in," and plucked Clara from Norah's grasp. As she wiped the baby's tiny chin, Clara gripped her finger and smiled a wobbly smile straight into her eyes. "Did you see that?" Dot asked the room at large, "She smiled at me!"

Maria sat down again with a bump and a surprised glance at Albie, who for a moment was too astounded to speak — this was the first time Mum had touched either of his children. He opened his mouth to say, "It's only wind," but shut it again with the words left unsaid. If a windy smile was what it took to melt the ice in Mum's heart, thank God it had happened before he went off to war. Dad's promise to watch out for Maria and the children would be much easier to keep if he didn't have to fight Mum at every turn.

When it was time to go, Albie offered Norah a ride in the cart - he'd been so engrossed with George that he'd hardly spoken a word to her.

"What a treat!" Norah said gaily, and Albie helped her into her coat, but when he lifted her over the tailgate his hands almost met round her waist.

"Norah! You're thin as a rail. And you didn't eat your dinner — are you ill?"

"I have no time to be ill, Albert," Norah said in a tone of voice that effectively closed the subject.

When they drew up outside her block of flats Norah offered them a cup of tea which, to Albie's surprise, Maria accepted. Normally she was anxious to get home before dark.

The moment they entered the three small rooms that comprised Norah's flat, Maria opened the long windows overlooking the promenade, and stepped out onto the balcony that was barely big enough for the tiny table and two chairs it held. "Look, Joey — you can see Daddy's pier from here."

"And I can see my flat from the top of Albert's helter-skelter," Norah said, and then frowned, "That can't be right — the helter-skelter has gone, hasn't it?"

Albie heard the tremble in her voice and hastened to cover her distress. "Years ago, Norah, but I still look for it every time I come to Thambay. I'll never forget my first ride on the helter-skelter."

"Neither shall I, Albert," Norah said, diverted by the memory, "And I have you to thank for that experience. I would never have had the courage or the strength without your help."

When they left half an hour later, Norah kissed Joey and Clara and held Maria's hand tightly. "I hope you will bring the children to visit me while Albert is away?"

Maria nodded wordlessly and fiddled with Joey's scarf while Albie wrapped his godmother in his customary bear-hug. Norah leaned her head on his broad chest, filling her lungs with his smell of the outdoors and woodsmoke, then she pulled away with a shaky laugh. "Look at me, silly old woman that I am! I shall not be at the railway station on Thursday, Albert – there is bound to be a dreadful crush – but I will be thinking of you." She gave him a gentle push, "Take your family home now, my dear, and God speed."

As they turned the corner, Albie waved to Norah who was standing on her balcony. She returned his wave as gaily as a young girl to her lover but Albie shivered with foreboding. "Why do I feel so bad?" he asked Maria as they drove home through the autumn lanes, "I'll get leave after Basic Training — I'll come and see her again then."

"Saying goodbye is always sad," Maria said, wrapping her shawl more snugly around both her children, partly to protect them from the chilly breeze but chiefly to ward off the shadow she had sensed when Norah held her hand.

CHAPTER TWENTY-ONE – BASIC TRAINING

On Thursday morning the gilding on the Victorian railway station's ornate ironwork shone in the steamy gaslight, and the smell was of coal smoke, ancient soot and damp clothes. The hiss of steam and blasts of heat from the polished railway engine gave the impression that it was straining at the leash, impatient to be gone.

Porters pushed trolleys piled high with the leather trunks of the well-to-do topped by poorer men's cardboard suitcases, but war was no respecter of income, and all this luggage would soon be jumbled together in uneasy proximity in the guard's van.

Men and boys crowded the platform, some wearing tailored suits and velvet-collared coats, others in patched trousers, worn jackets and hand-knitted scarves, but the apprehension on their faces was the same.

Mothers and wives and sweethearts, whether in smart hats or faded shawls, kissed and hugged their men, issuing instructions to be careful and promises to be faithful into ears deafened by the racket that echoed round the station. Some were tight-lipped, some were weeping, but all for once were classless in their shared fear for sons, husbands and lovers.

While Bert and Eddie said goodbye to their own family, George gripped Albie's hand hard enough to hurt and said, "You come back safe, son."

Dot gave him a greaseproof-wrapped package of gingerbread and kissed his cheek with lips that trembled despite her resolve, then stepped back to hang onto George with a brave smile while Albie said goodbye to Maria. He pressed her head to his heart so fiercely that he was sure he felt her blood mingling with his, then he kissed her swiftly and pushed her into Josef's arms. "Take care of her," he croaked, before turning away to locate Bert and Eddie and claim their seats on the train.

His eyes were so blurred with unshed tears that he was lifting his suitcase onto the rack before he felt a wave of ice wash over him, and looked down into the pale eyes of Walter Biggins. Neither of them had time to react before everyone was jostling for space at the window for a final word or wave. The guard walked the length of the train — "Mind the doors!" — the last doors were slammed shut, a whistle blew, a green flag fluttered, the train jerked, stopped, jerked again and they were moving.

The station echoed to a thousand voices calling: "Goodbye! Write every week. Remember to wear your vest. I love you. Goodbye! Don't forget to feed my pigeons. Kiss the baby for me. Come back safe, you hear? Goodbye!" Yet over it all Albie could sense Maria's love following him - a thread of gold that no distance could break - and through his shirt he clutched his talisman. The little leather bag held the stone Sofia had given him, and last night he had added three locks of hair - one each from Maria, Joey and Clara.

When she snipped the curls Maria had promised for the hundredth time, "We will be thinking about you every day, Albie - you will have the whole tribe keeping you safe."

Albie had smiled sadly in the darkness of their tent and replied, "But what about Bert and Eddie? Who'll be watching them?"

"You will, of course. You are Roma, my love - trust your instincts and you will all be safe."

Last night he had believed her — last night, buried deep in her body, he had been invincible - but today at the station he had felt her fear, and its echo still trembled in his heart.

With an effort that was almost physical he pushed the fear away and looked around the carriage, noting that he obviously wasn't the only man engrossed in his own thoughts, but eventually a few throats were cleared, cigarettes were lit. Albie tried smiling at Walter Biggins. "It must be four years since I've seen you, Wally."

"It can be another four years for all I care, Gyppo," Wally replied, lit a Capstan and blew the smoke deliberately into Albie's face. There was a collective intake of breath from the other eight men squashed into the carriage – Albie and Wally were both big men, and there was scant room for a fight. Bert quickly dug his own cigarettes out of his jacket and stuck one between Albie's lips, saying, "Leave it, Albie."

"You're right, Bert – he ain't worth dirtying my hands on. Besides, any punch'd sink right into that belly."

Albie flicked a match with his thumbnail to light Bert's cigarette and his own, all the time staring contemptuously at Wally, daring him to take a swing. At last Wally dropped his eyes and Albie took in the other faces. Most of them were strangers but they were all headed to the same place — he might as well get his piece said and over with. "For them as don't know me," he said, catching each pair of eyes in turn, "I'm a gypsy and proud of it – but the next man to call me Gyppo had better be prepared to fight."

*

"*Sunday October 1st.*
My darling Maria," Albie wrote, "*I have to send these clothes home. We got our uniforms today and theres no room to keep them here with 12 of us sleeping in Hut 4. The trousers are horrible and scratchy just like the mattresses which are just sacks of straw. The boots are hard they hurt when we do marching every day but dont worry I will get used to them.*

Bert and Eddie are in the same hut as me. Eddie cried a lot for his mum so did Titch Harris but they are pals now and have stopped. And youll never gess whos in the next hut to us Wally Biggins. Him and Green from our hut are pals. Wally watches me all the time it makes my neck itch but dont worry Berts got my back.

I really miss you a lot I cant tell you how much. When I cant sleep I want you with me I cant wait to see you again. Sometimes I wish Id not come I could of stayed home a bit longer but Im here now and Id better not moan too much they read our letters. Im sending this letter to the farm. Mum will read it if I send it to hers. I hope you were all right today at mums she cant help the way she is tell dad I will rite to them soon.

Kiss Joey and Clara for me and say hello to Josef and the others.

From your loving husband Albie.XXX

*

Maria only went to George and Dot's for Sunday dinner because she had promised Albie, and it felt wrong to be there without him. She collected Norah on the way, and the old lady filled any awkward silences by talking politics with George.

The Sunday after Albie's parcel of clothes arrived at Pinetree Farm there were no silences to fill – as soon as they had eaten, George read aloud their own letter from Albie.
Tuesday October 3rd
Dear Dad and Mum, Well weve been here 4 days and weve got our uniforms now tin hats and all. This little spiv Green in our hut made friends with the stores clerk so ours fit better than most but Greens still a nasty piece of work who makes snide remarks all the time."

"There's always one," George commented, "Useful but a pain in the arse."

"George Smith!"

"Sorry love," George said sheepishly and returned to Albie's letter.

"We have to spit-and-polish our boots so the Sarge can see his face in them but Darby used to be a boot boy in a hotel and hes given us a few tips. We call Darby Joan you can guess why."

"Darby and Joan – that's a good one," George laughed, and Dot said, "They're all used to having their boots cleaned for them. Perhaps they'll appreciate their mums and wives more now."

"That boot-boy Darby appears to be a resourceful young man," Norah said, "I taught my own sons to sew before they went overseas, so they are probably helping their fellow soldiers just as Darby is doing."

George and Dot exchanged a look of concern — these

'moments' of Norah's were occurring more often lately. George raised an eyebrow at Maria that telegraphed the question, "Have you noticed?"

Maria nodded but only said, "What else does Albie write, Dad?"

"Titch Harris and Eddie are best pals now. Jones the medic looks after them so all of hut 4 call him Auntie. He says he don't mind hes been called worse."

"Isn't it kind of him to look after the homesick boys?" Norah said and George kept his suspicions on that subject to himself. If the younger lads needed mothering then a nancy-boy was better than nothing, and they'd come to no harm in a hut full of soldiers.

"Weve learned how to take a rifle apart and clean it and put it all back together. Corporal Blake made us do it blindfold in case we have to do it in the dark when we fight the Germans. I was good at that cos Ive learned how to find my way round in the dark in camp. I can hit the target now and Ive used a sten gun and a bren gun. The best shots are Paddy Obrien and Toff Steele. Paddy couldnt read when he joined but hes having lessons now and we all help him."

"Albie will be good at that too," Maria said shyly, "He taught me from newspapers."

George beamed. "Did he now! That's how I taught him to read."

"Only after he learned from the baby books with me," Dot reminded George sharply.

"I also taught my sons to read yet they have not written to me once," Norah said sadly, "Please continue with Albert's letter, George."

"There ain't much more. He just says, *"The other chaps in hut 4 are Allcock, Thompson and Corporal Blake."* Then he sends his love to everyone, including you, Norah, and that's it."

George folded the letter carefully and slid it back into its envelope – Maria suspected Albie's parents would treasure his letters as much as she did hers. When George stood up to put it behind the clock, she took Clara into the scullery to change her nappy and he followed her out there.

"Me and Dot are worried about Norah," he whispered, "She ain't right, is she?"

"I visit her every time I go shopping," Maria said, "Her mind comes and goes but she's safe enough for now. Papa's aunt couldn't be trusted with a pot of hot water, and we had to feed her like a baby in the end."

"Hell's bells! I hope it doesn't come to that," George exclaimed, and Dot called out, "Not in front of the children, George Smith!"

Maria pinned Clara's clean nappy and wrapped her up again. "That won't happen to Norah — her body will give up before her mind goes completely."

"You really do know these things, don't you?" George said, glancing at the scullery door to make sure Dot wasn't listening. "Do you know when? And what should we do?"

Maria simply smiled and kissed his cheek. "There's nothing we can do – and I don't know when – but she's a good soul and she will go peacefully." She returned to the kitchen and began wrapping Joey's small torso in a large scarf against the cold October wind.

Dot stared. "I knitted that scarf for Albie years ago and you're still using it?"

"Of course," Maria said, "There's plenty of wear in it yet. Now I must take Norah home or we won't be back before dark."

Joey planted a kiss on George's bristly chin and then held his face up to Dot. "You want a kiss too, Nan?" he asked, and another splinter of ice melted when Dot felt his soft lips on her cheek. She patted his curls – really the child was quite clean in spite of living in a field. "See you next Sunday," she said, and tucked the ends of the scarf she had knitted for Albie's first Christmas into the back of his small son's trousers.

*

The very next day Maria again made a nest of blankets in the cart for Clara, sat Joey beside the baby with strict instructions not to move, and drove into town. The rain of the past week had eased off to a mere dampness in the air and the countryside smelled fresh and clean – of fallen leaves already starting to rot down to feed next year's growth – of coal and wood smoke drifting from chimneys to blend with the low clouds – of newly-turned earth and grass roots in ancient pastures ploughed up for the first time on government orders.

As usual it had taken her ages to catch Blossom, who would come at Albie's first whistle but not at hers. The pony's ears had drooped visibly when she found only Maria at the gate, although once she was between the shafts she had gone with her willingly enough. "You're happier when you're working, aren't you, Blossom?" Maria said as they trotted along the lanes, and Blossom's ears twitched. "I'll find something we can do," Maria promised her, "We're both used to being on the move and it will ease the waiting."

When Maria hitched Blossom to the usual lamp-post and lifted the children down, Norah came out onto her balcony and called down, "Maria, how lovely to see you again. If I drop the key, would you mind letting yourself in?"

As soon as they were inside the flat, Norah put the kettle on the gas in the kitchenette and asked, "Is Albert coming later?" Maria frowned but Norah brushed her hand over her face as if to remove a cobweb and continued, "No — how silly of me — he went away." She turned to face Maria, "My boys went away too, you know — both of them. They are soldiers now, like Albert."

Maria laid Clara on the carpet and took the teapot from Norah's hands. "You sit down and let me do this," she said and Norah obeyed meekly as a child, but as she watched Joey run a toy car around the pattern on the carpet the fog lifted from her mind. Maria sensed the difference in her and seized her chance. "Norah, will you help me write a letter? It's Albie's birthday on Wednesday and I'm no good at writing."

So Norah wrote a letter to Maria's dictation in the clear script she had used for seventy years. When Maria left an hour later she went straight to the Post Office, where she used a pen from the counter to add a carefully written few words of her own, before buying a stamp and sliding the letter slowly into the letter-box.

*

"Monday October 9th
My dear Albert," Albie read two days later, *"Maria has asked me to write to you on her behalf to wish you a happy birthday. I shall add my own good wishes to hers now, so that the remainder of this letter can be solely at her dictation. Happy birthday, my dear. Do please take great care of yourself and return unharmed to those who love you. Farewell, my dear Albert, from your loving Godmother, Norah."*

Albie smiled as the familiar image arose of Norah, in her tweed skirt and felt hat, sliding round the curve of the helter-skelter. Five years ago, that was, and she'd been an old lady even then. He shook his head fondly and returned to his letter.

"My darling Albie, I hope you have a happy birthday with Bert and Eddie. Papa says to tell you he will drink your birthday wine as well as his, but I won't let him because he will snore and keep me awake."

So Maria and the kids were sleeping in the wagon with Josef — Albie was pleased about that.

"Papa is working on Coppin Farm to stop Ken from telling the Town Hall we're here. I told Papa he is too old to be sent for a soldier, but he is afraid they will think he is Italian and lock him up. Papa mended Mr Coppin's car for free so I think he is worried for nothing."

That bloody Ken Coppin! If he weren't married to May, Albie would have killed him long ago.

"Grandmother and Rosanna made black curtains with Mrs Finch and she gave them some clothes so now we've got lots, even some things for Joey. We had to turn them up for his little legs but

they will fit him for ages."

*"Clara is very greedy and getting fat and she smiles a lot now
at everyone. We had dinner with your Dad and Mum on Sunday
and your Mum had to talk to me because you weren't there. Your
Dad came to the farm in Bert's Dad's van to see us and give me your
letter. I am happy you like the other soldiers."*

Thank God Mum had got over her sulk and started
treating Maria right — pity it had to take a war to do it — and
Dad was keeping his promise to visit Maria. He'd probably sat
on the wagon steps for a smoke and a chat with Mateo. He'd
have cuddled little Joey and Clara as well, the lucky sod.

*"It rained a lot last week and it was very muddy. Papa and
Grandpapa had to dig the drain bigger from the wooden shelter but
it's all right now. Ricardo made a wood floor for his and Olivia's tent
too so their bed won't get wet."*

*"We are all working hard in the fields to grow food, mostly
potatoes and cabbages. Everyone is well."*

*"Olivia's baby was born safely and they have called him
Nicholas. Give my love to Bert and Eddie but keep most of it for
yourself. I wish you were here and not there. My heart is empty
without you."*

"With all my love from your wife, Maria."

After *"everyone is well"* Maria had inserted in her careful
capitals – *"But not Nora who is getting very old."*

Albie's mental picture of Norah on the helter-skelter
was replaced by an image of his last sight of her, tiny and frail,
waving from her balcony. Her writing in the letter looked
steady enough, but Maria wouldn't have put that extra bit in if
there was nothing to worry about — those few words were a
warning.

15th October,

My darling wife Maria,

*Your letter made me see Pinetree clear as if I was there I wish
I was. Its good you moved into Josefs wagon but promise me youll go
in the shelter when war really starts. I said all along that drain
should be longer but they wouldnt listen. I know you call it a rabbit*

hole but it will keep you safe.

Thinking of rabbits I could do with a plate of your rabbit stew right now the army food is horrible. We think they start boiling the cabbage at breakfast time and Bert says the meat is horse that died of old age. Toff Steeles mum sent him a food parcel which he shared round. There was a tin of tiny eggs in salty jelly and meat paste called patty and some mouldy cheese I didnt fancy. Its a shame you cant put mums Sunday dinner in a jar.

It was kind of Mrs Finch to give you clothes I wonder if the trousers you took up for Joey were Lukes. Bet he will soon grow into them.

I must tell you a funny thing happened on my birthday. Marching to the mess hut it was really windy and I got this feeling there was danger so I stopped the others and then a wopping great sheet of iron roof crashed down it just missed us. Green said only a gippo would of known and I shut him up but hes right and I must of got it off Nate. Seeing the future will come in handy when we go to war if we ever do. Bert says hes going to stick to me like glue cos Im a lucky beggar and the others have started calling me Gippo. I cant stop them but I dont mind really.

What you wrote about Norah had me worried. I know shes not good and Ive got this feeling I wont see her again. Next time you see her give her a big kiss from me and heres some more for Joey and Clara and you XXXXXX

I cant wait till I see you again. Your loving husband Albie
Ps. And give Blossom a pat from me as well.

CHAPTER TWENTY-TWO — MILK ROUND

Maria put the letter carefully away in the glass-fronted cupboard in her father's wagon where she kept their birth certificates and marriage lines. She had only learned to read at Albie's insistence, but she was glad now that she could read his letters herself.

While she fed Clara her mind kept returning to his final remark about Blossom, and when she had finished she popped her head over the half-door of Lydia's vardo. "Can you mind the children for a while, Grandmother? I'm going to the farm."

"It will be a pleasure, dear," Lydia replied, bundling up her sewing, and she hurried to Maria's wagon to watch over the only grandchildren she had left now that Theo had broken with Roma tradition and gone to live with his wife's family.

Ruth Finch was busy checking eggs in a bowl of water before putting them in a crock of isinglass, and was happy to accept Maria's help with the tedious task. When the crock was safely stored next to the others in the walk-in larder, beneath shelves laden with preserved fruit, chutneys and jams, the two women shared a pot of tea.

Finally Maria plucked up the courage to ask her question. "Blossom needs to work, Missus Finch, and so do I, to take our minds off the waiting. Two days a week shopping aren't enough — can we do the dairy deliveries in Thambay for you?"

Ruth sat back and stared at Maria's eager face. "What about your baby? She's only two months old — won't she need feeding?"

"Olivia can feed her if she needs it while I'm gone — she's got plenty of milk."

So Maria and her cousin nursed each other's babies, thought Ruth — how sensible - but she still demurred. "I wouldn't want you to get noticed by the authorities — you're not actually here officially."

"They won't trouble me," Maria said complacently, "I got my identity card the same time as Clara's birth certificate. The Town Hall thinks we're living with Albie's mum and dad. I've got a ration book too, and one for Joey. Albie's dad registered us with their grocer."

"You're a godsend, Maria," Ruth said with feeling, "Those milk-churns are heavy and I'm not getting any younger. You can start tomorrow."

Ruth was filled with admiration — Maria was making the transition from a nomadic life to a settled one more easily than she had anticipated. As a nursing mother she would be getting extra rations, but the tribe would have fared badly on so little without their steady jobs on the farm. Adam paid the men a farmhand's wages – just short of two pounds a week – while their womenfolk helped her in the house and dairy, taking their wages in produce. Even Maria's grandfather Mateo, a man of Adam's age, earned his way by persuading his horses to pull the farm machinery rather than wagons. So Pinetree Farm benefitted from a steady workforce while other farms struggled, yet somehow those unofficial workers mysteriously vanished whenever a Ministry official appeared.

Maria and Blossom and their little blue cart soon became a familiar sight in the area, delivering dairy produce, eggs and vegetables, and Maria would usually pop in for a cup of tea with Norah before she drove home with the empty churns. Sometimes Norah was her old self, but more frequently as the weeks progressed her mind slipped back twenty or thirty years to when her husband and sons were alive. Her conversations jumped about like a flea circus and she rarely concentrated for long enough to write Maria's letters, so Maria asked Ruth to help her. Her weekly letters were full of the everyday incidents that brought the tribe's life vividly alive for him but also hinted at the heart-breaking decline in Norah – Maria knew the ending was inevitable and she didn't want it to come as a shock to Albie.

*

Halfway through December Ruth began preparing for
Christmas — the house had to be spotless and the larder full,
because Luke had been given leave. She recruited Maria and
Olivia to help her, and they were delighted to spend their
mornings in the warm farmhouse kitchen, baking cakes and
pies while their children made pastry shapes and the babies
slept in the adjoining parlour. Albie's latest letter had said that
he was coming home for Christmas too, and every time Maria
filled a pie she wondered if it was the one Ruth would give
her to celebrate his home-coming.

One morning the three women were happily mixing
and chatting when Maria stopped suddenly and said, "I have
to go — Norah needs me," removed her apron and rushed
out. For once Blossom came at her first whistle and backed
docilely between the shafts of the cart, then she caught her
mistress's sense of urgency and trotted rapidly into Thambay.

Maria barely took the time to tie the reins to the lamp-
post before running down the area steps to knock on the
caretaker's door. A minute later he let her into Norah's flat
with his pass-key, and stood suspiciously in the open doorway
while she tapped on the bedroom door calling, "Norah." A
feeble moan answered her and she hurried into a bedroom
stuffy with sickness, caught one of Norah's agitated hands and
said, "Norah, I'm here - Maria - you're safe now."

The caretaker peered round the door to say with
ghoulish interest, "The poor soul looks bad — should I get the
doctor?"

"Yes please — and Mister and Missus Smith from
Middle Street, number fourteen." When the man still lingered
she spoke more sharply, "Go quickly or they'll be too late!"

He stomped off muttering, "It's come to a pretty pass
when I 'as to take orders from a bleedin' gyppo!" and took his
time collecting his coat, but then he remembered that gypsies

could put a curse on you and he ran all the way to the doctor's. A few minutes later he arrived panting on the Smith's doorstep and delivered his message with a hand already held out for a tip, but George and Dot simply brushed past him and rushed out.

It was half an hour before the doctor arrived at Norah's and George met him at the door. "You're too late — she passed away five minutes ago." The doctor tried to push past but George refused to budge. "You only live round the corner so what took you so long – finishing your dinner?"

"There is no call to speak to me in that tone," the doctor blustered, "Let me through, my man — you are not qualified to pronounce anyone dead."

His attempt to assert his medical authority shrivelled as George's large chest swelled visibly. "Dead is dead whoever says it. And I'll have you know I'm nobody's man, least of all yours, so you can bugger off back to your dinner."

"What about my fee for making the call?"

George shot him a withering look, pulled a shilling out of his pocket and dropped it into the out-stretched palm saying, "Even that's more'n you're worth!" and the doctor, who usually charged a guinea, decided he'd be safer at home and scuttled off.

The little flat was very quiet apart from Dot sobbing beside the bed. Maria sat on a stool nearby, watching as Norah's spirit brushed George and Dot's faces with a farewell kiss. The three men waiting by the window must be Norah's husband and sons, Maria guessed, come to show her the way home, and she had to smother a smile when Norah took the older man's hand and winked at her. The old lady's face had relaxed, and the puzzled frown that had haunted her last few months had gone. She looked again like the woman who had danced and flirted at the gypsy wedding, and Maria was happy for her. George and Dot had been with her at the end, which was only right, but Maria nursed a secret she would only tell to Albie, whom Norah had loved best: in those quiet minutes before the others arrived, the last word Norah had spoken was "Albert".

*

"When's this funeral, Private Smith?"

"Thursday the twenty-first, sir, it says in the telegram."

"Well, you're due for leave from Friday, so you won't miss much if you leave two days earlier, I suppose. Your godmother, did you say?"

"Yes sir."

"I'll put her down as grandmother – looks better on the paperwork."

"Thank you, sir."

"I assume you'll be needing a rail warrant?"

"It would help, sir. I've sent all me money home to the wife."

"Mind you're back on the twenty-sixth with the others, preferably sober."

"Yes sir, thank you sir."

"Off you trot, then. Oh, and Smith?"

"Yes sir?"

"My sympathies. Fond of her, were you?"

"Very, sir. Grand old lady, she were. Took her first ride on me helter-skelter when she were pushing seventy, and danced like a girl round the fire at me wedding."

"Danced round the fire? So it's true then, what they call you?"

"Gyppo, you mean? Yes sir, that's me."

*

It was weird travelling without the other members of the squad. The carriage was packed — soldiers and airmen in khaki and blue; women lumpy in layers of clothing against the cold in the un-heated train; a child who grizzled constantly until its mother gave it a heel of bread to chew — but at least Albie had a seat. The corridor was solid with troops, each man taking up another man's space with his enormous kitbag, and the air was thick with tobacco smoke.

After many stops and starts, half of them in the middle of nowhere with nothing to look at but starkly bare trees, fields heavy with frost under a pale sun, and isolated chimneys trailing streamers of smoke, the train finally pulled into Albie's station. He hauled his kitbag onto the platform and through the ticket-office to the street, where a whinny of welcome from Blossom alerted him to Joey's small running figure. He dropped his kit to toss Joey in the air — his son had grown and his hair had been recently trimmed, but the same smile flashed and the arms around his neck were heart-achingly familiar. Albie swallowed the unmanly lump in his throat and held Maria against his chest with his free arm so he could inhale the clean warm perfume of her hair. "All well?" he asked and, "All well," she answered, "Clara's at home with Olivia." Then Josef shook his hand and took his kitbag to throw it into the back of the cart, and Albie climbed in to sit with Maria and Joey clasped firmly to his sides.

"Straight home, Albie?" Josef asked.

"No – I think I'd better go round to Dad and Mum's first."

Dot wept when she saw him in uniform, and George gripped his hand and told him, "We were with Norah at the end – Maria sent for us. She went so peaceful, just like the lady she was."

Dot let out a fresh sob. "Seems like we knew her all our lives, but it was only five years."

"D'you want to see her flat one more time?" George asked suddenly, "Some lawyer bloke's coming to the funeral so it'll be your last chance. Dot brought Norah's handbag home to keep it safe, so we've got her keys."

"Norah's at the undertaker's and I gave the place a good clean-out," Dot added, "There's nothing to worry you there."

"Well, if Maria and Joey can stay here in the warm, I think I will have a look," Albie decided, "Just to say goodbye."

Josef drove Albie and his parents along the promenade to Norah's block. A blustery wind was whipping the sea into breakers that boomed against the sea wall and Albie took great lungfuls of the salty air that he had missed so much – there was no knowing how long it would be before he could do so again.

While George and Dot trundled upwards in the lift Albie took the stairs, bounding up them two at a time on legs strengthened by months of marching drill. Finding the door to Norah's flat ajar he stopped dead, half-expecting her to appear, but then he shook his head to dispel the stupid notion, pushed the door open, and found himself face to face with a stranger. Albie wedged his solid army boot against the man's attempt to slam the door in his face and demanded, "What the hell are you doing?"

The lift gates clanged open and George stormed out. "That's the new caretaker – Wally Biggins' uncle Fred – but he's got no right to be inside Norah's flat."

"He's got no right to be having this either," said Dot, snatching a small marquetry box from the man's hand and opening it to inspect the contents. "This is Norah's jewellery box. It had better all be here or you're in trouble."

"Thieving's obviously the Biggins' family business," said Albie. "Wally got caught last week going through another chap's stuff." He shook his prisoner as if expecting more loot to drop from his trouser legs. "How did you get in anyway?"

"He's got a key," said George, pushing past the two of them, "He let Maria in the day Norah passed away. Albie, you hang onto him – I'm going for the police."

As Albie dragged the caretaker back into the flat the man whined, "I ain't stealing nothing – I were only going to keep it safe."

George hesitated, thinking that if nothing was missing

there wasn't much point in getting the coppers involved, but Dot knew Norah's place as well as her own. She stood, four-square and seething with anger, looking round the walls. "The mirror's gone off this wall, and that little table Norah used to put her cup of tea on."

"That settles it then," said George, "Police it is – I'll send Josef up to keep you company."

Albie smiled grimly and pulled the man's jacket halfway down his back, effectively pinning the flailing arms. "He won't give me no trouble, Dad – I learned a few tricks in the army I wouldn't mind practising given half a chance."

While George went to fetch a policeman, Albie and Josef searched the caretaker's unsavoury person and found a pair of silver-backed hairbrushes in his jacket pocket.

"Looking after these too, were you?" Albie sneered.

"Those were Norah's wedding present from her husband!" Dot cried. "She said she'd never part with them even if she was down to her last shilling." She narrowed her eyes at the man. "Where's the mirror and powder jar what goes with 'em? What else have you nicked?"

When Biggins remained stubbornly silent, Dot toured the flat ticking items off on her fingers. "It's like that game we play at Christmas," she said to Albie, "Remember what was on the tray before and you'll know what's been took away. There's a picture and three silver photograph frames gone out of the bedroom, and two pictures from in here, and a tapestry footstool Norah stitched herself." She checked the drawer in the kitchenette last of all and stood staring at it for a long time. "Empty," she said softly, "All her lovely Apostle spoons have gone." Her shoulders sagged briefly, but then she strode across the small room and swung her arm in such a resounding blow on the caretaker's ear that he fell over. "You horrible little man! Poking your dirty thieving fingers through Norah's things! I s'pose they've all gone down to uncle's by now?"

But he hadn't got round to pawning all the things he had stolen. Dot insisted on helping the policeman to search his basement flat and they found everything except the side-table and the cutlery.

When Biggins was hauled off to the cells, Dot rejoined her husband and son with her nose wrinkled in distaste. "You wouldn't believe the stink in that place – the next man'll have to get it fumigated!"

*

Moments after Josef had unhitched Blossom, the rest of the tribe arrived from their work in the fields, eager for the midday meal that had been simmering all morning in the cauldron. Albie shook hands all round and then sat on the back steps of the wagon to eat every scrap of his share with relish, finishing on a sigh of contentment. "You remembered what I said in my letters, Maria — nothing beats a rabbit stew!"

CHAPTER TWENTY-THREE - FUNERAL

Norah, typically, had paid a small monthly sum for years to ensure that her funeral would not be a burden on anyone. She had no family, but the simple coffin and hearse were followed by many mourners on foot - the friends whom Norah had collected in Thambay saw her decently laid to rest.

The only car, chauffeur-driven, contained a thin, elderly man who was clearly the expected lawyer, and Dot told George he should invite the man to the house along with everyone else. Thus Mr Wetherby of Curtis and Wetherby sat in George's armchair in a smaller house than he had ever before entered, sipping a cup of tea but refusing a ham sandwich - "You're very kind but I'm afraid my digestion is not good" - and taking in the scene that explained why Norah Barnes had been so happy in her declining years.

Albert Smith was the man Mr Wetherby was most interested in. Albert and his parents George and Dorothy were people about whom Norah had written with genuine affection. Those of their neighbours who had attended the funeral were no different from the common people he encountered in London, but the gypsies had been a surprise — Norah had never mentioned them. Albert Smith's wife was obviously one, and with her family, a Mr John Daly and his, some farmers and a scattering of neighbours, the house was groaning at the seams.

Norah, the widow of Mr Wetherby's old university friend Lawrence Barnes, had been at least a class above these people, yet in every conversation he overheard - and his hearing was acute even if his limbs were failing - she was obviously remembered as one of them. He heard one neighbour say that her lace curtains would never again be mended as well as Norah had done them; another spoke of her light hand with pastry; and one of the gypsies recalled fondly how the Norah whom Mr Wetherby had always considered staid had danced at Albert's wedding. Clearly Norah Barnes had discovered a lighter side of her nature in this company, but he found it difficult to believe his ears when Albert and George talked about their first meeting with her. Surely a lady of Norah's advanced years would never have ridden a helter-skelter?

Mr Wetherby's chauffeur Roberts stayed outside in the car despite Dot's urging to join the guests in the house. The gleaming Rover had drawn a crowd of urchins like a magnet dropped in a tin of nails, and he didn't trust any of them not to nick one of the wing mirrors. The youths Billy and Jimmy Daly were even more fascinated, and under Roberts' watchful eyes they inspected every shining inch of the wonderful car.

"I'm going to have one of these when I'm older," Billy declared.

"You'll have to nick it then," Jimmy laughed, "You'll never earn enough to buy one."

"Then I'll be a chauffeur," said Billy and asked Roberts, "How can I learn to drive?"

Roberts sized up the boy – red hair, skinny, could be anywhere between sixteen and twenty. "The army would teach you — are you old enough to join up?"

"Not for a year and a bit. Me and Jimmy tried it once but Mum split on us."

"That's mothers for you. Well, you could try again when you're eighteen."

"The war'll be over by then," said Billy gloomily.

Roberts shook his head. "According to the papers it's hardly got started. Before this lot's over they'll probably even call me up, bad leg and all!"

*

In a corner of the scullery Mabel Coppin put a motherly arm round her daughter-in-law. "You're awfully quiet, dear – is something wrong?"

"I'm fine, Mum, don't fuss," May snapped, but as she

pulled away she winced. A dawning suspicion made Mabel grasp May's wrist and slide her sleeve up. When she saw the clear imprint of a hand in bruises, her suspicion turned to a dreadful certainty. "Ken did this, didn't he?"

May wrenched her wrist free and tugged her sleeve down again. "Leave it, Mum — it's nothing much."

"Nothing much?" Mabel gasped, "Nothing compared with what? How long's this been going on?"

May shrugged, biting her lip to stop it trembling, and Mabel was appalled. May Daly had been such a lovely, bouncy addition to the family when she married Ken, and now she was reduced to this pale shadow. What made Mabel's heart beat fast and furious in her chest was the appalling knowledge that her own son was responsible. Charlie had always been harder on Ken than on Raymond and Timmy and Mabel had tried to shield him, but now she saw that Charlie was right to be severe. Ken's cruel streak that she had dismissed as boyish mischief, had found a new target once the gloss had worn off his marriage. She could have wept with grief for the little boy she had loved, but she had to be strong for May and her little son Frank. She forced her voice to remain steady. "Tell me everything, my dear — we can't let this go on any longer."

May had held her shameful secret in for so long that once she started crying she couldn't stop, and that was when Albie found them. He had always had a soft spot for May, and now he pulled her against his chest and raised an enquiring eyebrow at Mabel. "Why's she crying like this? She weren't that close to Norah. Is she expecting again? Maria gets weepy at first."

"It's not that, Albie."

Albie tried another guess. "She needn't worry about Bert and Eddie. They're fine — they'll be home tomorrow."

Mabel looked at his worried face and forced the admission out. "It's our Ken — he's been hurting her."

"He's been what? I'll fucking kill him!"

George was sitting in the kitchen with Mr Wetherby when Albie's roar of rage catapulted him out of his chair and into the scullery. "Albie, I won't have barrack-room language in this house!"

"Sorry, Dad, but I'm that angry. Ken Coppin's been beating on our May."

From Mabel's expression of shame, George could see it was the truth, and called John Daly over to hear the bad news.

"We'll take you both back to the farm now and sort him out," John said through clenched teeth.

Mabel put her hands on his chest, as if she could stop him physically, and asked, "Will you let me deal with it if I promise to keep May safe?"

"You ain't kept her safe so far," John pointed out.

Mabel winced, but May leapt to her defence. "It's not her fault, Dad — I never let on."

"That's as maybe," said John, "But dealing with Ken is a man's job."

"I know that," Mabel said sadly, "Which is why his father - and if need be, his brothers - will see to it that he never hurts May again."

Her determination was so clear that John yielded, but Gladys said, "We'll keep May with us till you've sorted Ken out."

"No, Mum," May said, "I can't stay in Thambay — I've left Frank playing with Joey."

"Then that's where you'll stay tonight," Albie said firmly, "You and Frank can sleep in the wagon with us." He looked at Mabel, "I'll come over to see you tomorrow first thing, and if Mister Coppin ain't dealt with Ken by then, I will."

The neighbours had gone when they went back into the kitchen, and Albie would have taken Maria and May back to the campsite then if Mr Wetherby hadn't stopped him. "If I could speak to the Smith family alone for a few minutes I should be grateful," he said to the remaining guests, "I apologize for intruding on your grief, but I doubt I will be able to drive down from London a second time with petrol in such short supply."

So Josef and his parents took May back to the campsite with them, the other guests departed, and the Smiths were left alone with the lawyer.

Mr Wetherby arranged some papers on the table and asked if they would all please sit down, but Dot said, "Not till that chauffeur of yours has come in for a warm. Albie, tell Billy and Jimmy to mind the car."

When Roberts was seated by the fire with his hands wrapped gratefully round a cup of tea, Mr Wetherby cleared his throat. "I must first explain that Mrs Barnes was an old friend. She specifically requested me to read her will today, here in this house, although I would not do so under normal circumstances."

"Will – what will? Norah didn't have nothing to leave," Dot said scornfully.

"Please, Mrs Smith, let me speak," said Mr Wetherby, and Dot subsided with a sniff.

"Mrs Barnes – Norah – was the widow of my best friend," Mr Wetherby told them, "And therefore she and I have always kept in touch. She asked me not to burden you with legal terms – 'All that long-winded nonsense,' I believe were her exact words – so I have prepared a brief summary."

"That sounds like Norah, all right!" muttered Dot, not quite under her breath, "So get on with it!"

Roberts spluttered over his tea, thinking that if only more of his employer's clients were as forthright as Mrs Smith there'd be a lot less hanging about. Mr Wetherby pushed his glasses back up on his nose and read.

"'To Mrs Dorothy Smith I bequeath' – that means 'leave'," he added hastily, " '- my jewellery box with all its contents, and *my sewing box in memory of our happy hours stitching together by her fireside.'"*

"Well I never!" said Dot, dabbing her eyes, "Bless her — she didn't have to do that. George! To think we nearly lost that jewellery box yesterday!"

"'To Mr George Smith I bequeath the bookcase containing all my books to remind him of the many discussions we enjoyed.'"

"Her books?" exclaimed George, "What – all them encyclopaedias?"

"'All my books' would mean precisely that, Mr Smith," Mr Wetherby assured him.

George sank back in his chair, stunned at his good fortune — a whole set of encyclopaedias would keep him happily occupied for years. He and Dot were both delighted, not only by Norah's gifts but by the fact that they'd been remembered in a proper written will, read out by a grand London lawyer. Although pleased for his parents, Albie was hoping that whatever Norah had left him wouldn't take up as much space as a bookcase.

Mr Weatherby continued. *"'To my dear Godson Mr Albert George Smith I bequeath all my other property and possessions with my love and thanks for persuading an old woman that life could still hold some adventures'."* Mr Wetherby removed his glasses and looked at Albie. "All of Mrs Barnes' other property and possessions, young man — they're all yours."

"Yes, but what is?" asked Albie, "Would that be her furniture and stuff? We couldn't fit much in the wagon, could we, Maria?"

"If I might put in a word, Mr Wetherby?" said Roberts, taking advantage of his length of service. "I don't think Mr Smith quite appreciates what you mean by 'property'."

"Ah, I see, thank you, Roberts," said Mr Wetherby: "Mr Smith, Mrs Barnes has not merely left you her furniture — she has left you her flat."

"The flat?" Albie gasped, "You mean it were Norah's – not rented?"

Mr Wetherby allowed himself a fleeting smile to cover his relief as the last vestige of suspicion vanished. This family had loved Norah Barnes for herself, not for her money which, although meagre, was obviously more than they had. "I handled the purchase of the flat for Mrs Barnes when she sold her house in London," he told them, "The difference left her with a small income – very small – which just covered the expense of maintaining it. That income will also devolve upon you once probate is completed."

Albie stared at the lawyer wide-eyed. "What would I do with a flat? We've got our wagon."

Maria clutched Albie's hand. "I don't want to live in a flat, Albie," she said tremulously, "I couldn't breathe in a flat!"

This reaction was not at all what Mr Wetherby had expected. He glanced helplessly at Roberts, who interpreted the look correctly as a plea for help and said, "May I suggest a solution, sir?" When Mr Wetherby nodded, the Smiths turned to face the chauffeur. "With a war on," Roberts said, "No-one knows what's going to happen next week, let alone next year. Why not leave any decision until the war's over? You don't have to move into the flat — just hang onto it till things have settled down."

"Leave it empty, you mean?" asked Albie thoughtfully.

"You could do that," said Mr Wetherby, taking the reins back into his own hands, "Or you could rent it out. Either way, I would be happy to deal with the details while you're away, if you're agreeable."

"Then that's what we'll do," said Albie, squeezing Maria's hand, "We'll leave it empty for now and decide later, 'cause I ain't got time before I have to get back."

As Mr Wetherby began shuffling his papers together, Dot found her voice. "Is it Albie's now? 'Cause if it is, it'll need looking after. You can't leave it collecting dust for months on end – Norah'd never forgive me!"

"We've still got her keys, Dot," George remembered.

"We'll keep an eye on the place for Albie," and with Mr Wetherby's agreement, that was how it was left.

Billy and Jimmy had fended all comers off the Rover, and to their astonished delight Roberts gave them each half a crown before he drove Mr Wetherby back to London.

*

It was dusk by the time Albie let Blossom free in the paddock, where she headed straight for the three-sided shelter and the net of hay that hung there. Albie swapped his uniform for his own comfortable clothes and joined the other men round the fire, with a sigh of relief that he could now relax for the remainder of his leave. Then he saw May sitting on the wagon steps hugging her young son, and remembered there was one more thing to sort out before his conscience would be clear.

Early the next morning he walked past the pine plantation and along Coppin Lane to the farm. Raymond Coppin was hitching one of the carthorses to a wagon and raised a hand, but his expression was unapproachable and Albie merely sketched a wave in return. When he knocked on the kitchen door, Charles Coppin himself opened it – he seemed to have aged ten years since Albie last saw him.

"This is a dreadful business, Albie," he said, "I always knew that boy of mine was a bad'un, but I never thought he'd stoop to this. He's brought shame on the whole family." He sat down heavily, pointing to another chair in invitation, but Albie was too agitated to sit.

"What've you done about Ken, Mister Coppin? 'Cause if you ain't sorted him out…"

"You needn't worry about Ken any more," Charles said, smoothing his bald head with a weary gesture that revealed badly grazed knuckles. "I gave that worthless son of mine a taste of his own medicine and a choice — he could work as just a farmhand and sleep in the men's cottage, or he could join up. Timmy drove him into town first thing this morning, so he'll soon be fighting Germans instead of his own wife."

Albie sat down then, all his pent-up aggression draining away, to be replaced by sympathy for the defeated man in front of him. Mabel joined them, looking just as dreadful, and asked Albie, "Will May and little Frank come back to us? This is their home."

"You'll have to ask May that, Missus Coppin. Her mum said she could squeeze them in, or they can stop with us if she wants — it's up to her."

But May went back to the farm later that day — it was the only home Frank knew and he missed his own bed and his toys. After supper Mabel knocked on the door at the end of the passage that led to Ken's part of the house, and stood uncertainly on the threshold until May said, "Come on in, Mum, we're just having a cuppa." Mabel walked through to the kitchen to find her other daughters-in-law Bessie and Jennifer at the table, and her grandchildren playing by the range, in an atmosphere that already felt lighter. A thought slid into her mind uninvited, and however much she later tried to shift it, it wouldn't budge — the longer Ken stayed away the better it would be for all concerned.

*

"This war's changing everything already," Albie complained to Maria that night. "I've just got used to Christmas at Ruxley and now Dad and Mum are expecting us to go round to theirs."

"It will be nice for Joey," Maria said, "He'll love that tree your mum's decorated."

"But what about your dad?"

"He'll be surrounded by family, and we'll be back before dark. Now stop fretting and kiss me – Clara's asleep and Papa took Joey to sleep with him for a reason," Maria said, snuggling into Albie's shoulder and winding her fingers through the mat of hairs on his chest, and Albie forgot everything else as he made love to his wife in the soft sheets and curtained privacy of the high bed in their wagon.

So on Christmas Day 1939 Albie and Maria, for the first time in their four years of marriage, joined George and Dot in church, and then went back to Middle Street for dinner. Albie described life in the training camp in more detail than in his letters, trying to inject a touch of humour into his stories, but it was a poor effort. War was the uninvited guest at their table, and although everyone avoided raising the subject of Albie's imminent departure it was on all their minds.

They ate roast beef and plum pudding and exchanged gifts and played with Joey's new Dinky cars, but after they had shared a pot of tea and forced down a slice of cake, Albie looked at the darkening sky and said, "Maria, we'd better get a move on — that looks like snow." He was right — they got home just as the first flakes began to fall, and hurried inside the cosy warmth of the largest wagon, to finish Christmas Day with Josef and the rest of the tribe over a few bottles of Rosanna's elderberry wine.

<u>CHAPTER TWENTY-FOUR – JANUARY 1940 – LETTERS</u>

The train back to camp was crowded with men and kit, packed in so tightly that Albie elected to stand — even the swaying corridor was preferable to being penned in a stuffy carriage stinking of sweaty uniforms and wet boots and fear of the unknown. His heart ached with the memory of Maria's tearful black eyes at the station, and he had no idea when he would have home leave again. The train had been chugging through the frozen countryside for half an hour before Bert's voice penetrated his doleful reverie. "Want a smoke, Albie?"

Albie took the offered cigarette and leaned towards Bert's cupped hands to light it just as the train slowed down at a level crossing. A surge of instinct prompted him to wipe a clear space on the steamy window and peer through. For a second he thought he must be dreaming and rubbed his eyes, but they weren't deceiving him — waiting to cross the track was a gypsy wagon with the familiar painted designs and dangling pots. He tugged on the leather strap to drop the window, ignoring various cries of protest.

As he leaned out into the frigid air, the smoke from the engine parted like a curtain to reveal Sofia sitting on the wagon and Nate leading the horse. "Albert, take care, son – we'll be watching you!" Nate shouted, and Sofia raised her fingers in a good luck sign. Then the train jerked forward and they vanished into the smoke as if they had been merely apparitions.

When Albie shut the window there was a chorus of disgruntled remarks.

"What the hell was all that about?"

"Only some bloody gypsy wagons."

"That was Gyppo Smith's family giving him a send-off."

Albie, biting back a grin of delight that other men had seen them too, raised his voice to shout, "That you, Wally?

You'd better hope they ain't put a curse on you."

When it snowed again during the night Albie thought of those wagons. The middle of winter was a bad time to be on the road and he had assumed Nate and Sofia were at Ruxley. There was only one reason for them to have been at that crossing, which was to wish him Godspeed. He hoped fervently that they had found a sheltered spot before nightfall.

*

Albie's intake had completed their basic training before Christmas, and now they could march in step – even young Titch Harris with his two left feet. They knew how to fire and clean a rifle, how to keep their kit in order, how to scrub a barrack-room floor, and how to follow orders without wasting time asking questions that never got answers anyway.

When they returned from leave they were moved to Dorset to await mobilization, where the Sergeant worked his platoon harder than ever — apparently the army didn't consider basic training was enough to mould them into a fully trained fighting force. Despite the newspapers writing about the 'Phoney War', other battalions had already gone to fight the Germans, yet they were further away from the war than they had been before Christmas. They were bored — the Nazis were bombing ships practically on Britain's doorstep and getting off scot-free and they were itching you have a crack at them. Albie, along with the other eleven men in his squad, fretted under weeks of tension, being held on constant standby, powerless and frustrated.

The only entertainment was driving lessons, which were restricted to men strong enough to heave the big steering-wheels of the lorries round. The other men in the squad learned how to maintain the vehicles, from their wheels and engines to their canvas roofs.

*

"John Daly done me a favour teaching me to drive the van," Albie wrote to Maria in late January, *"Thompson and Steele drove on*

civvy street too – Toff Steele even had his own Rover. It gives us a head start on Paddy O'Brien and Allcock who were picked to learn just on size. Allcock kept getting his left and right mixed up and one day he took the porch right off the barracks. Wally called him Cockup which was funny till he started crying. But Tommy sat him down with some sardine tins for pedals and made him keep at it till he got it right. That shut Wally up. I aint told you have I we have to share with Wallys squad now. The barracks are bigger than the spider hut we had at basic training. The Hut 4 squad bagged one end but its not nice knowing Wallys sleeping in the same room.

Did you read in the papers about the Russian tanks stuck in snow in Finland? Here in Dorset weve got snow lots deeper than we get at home and we are freezing. I hope your keeping warm enough.

How are you doing with the rationing? Its probably no worse than winter camp we never got much food there did we. I miss your stew with herbs and fresh veg. The food here is really bad youd think the army could find proper cooks and real veg not tinned.

Kiss Joey and Clara for me XXXX and heres lots more kisses for you XXXXXX from your loving husband Albie.

*

Dot went to Norah's flat every week to dust and run the sweeper over the carpet, enjoying looking after the delicate furniture, but she resented the fact that Maria also had keys. One Sunday over dinner she demanded, "Have you been taking things from the flat?"

Maria looked up from spooning mashed carrots into Clara's mouth. "Just a few clothes, Mum – Alice needed a winter coat and she hadn't got enough coupons."

"That coat would've fitted our Daisy – you got no business giving it to Alice."

George sighed heavily and broke in to keep the peace. "Dot – Maria can do what she likes with Norah's stuff — Norah left that flat and everything in it to her and Albie."

Dot slammed a saucepan down so hard on the table that Clara started to cry. "She can clean it herself then! She's in there all the time, wasting the electric."

"Only on Thursdays, Mum, and I don't put the light on."

"So why go at all? And what's so special about Thursdays?"

"I promised Albie I'd be there then," Maria said, looking at George in desperation – any hint to Dot that she actually *saw* Albie would cause an enormous row.

George intervened again. "Maria — seeing as Olivia looks after the baby, why don't you leave Joey with us on Thursdays? We'd love having him and you'd get a bit of peace to have a think about Albie." He winked, proving to Maria he guessed there was more to her quiet time than just thinking, but Dot was successfully diverted. Joey had begun to carve his own little niche in Dot's heart, and having him to herself for an hour or two would help to make up for those years of Albie's life she had missed.

From then on Maria dropped Joey off with his grandparents on Thursday mornings before making the Pinetree deliveries, after which she went to the flat, cleaned round quickly and then sat on the balcony on one of the little wrought iron chairs. At the campsite she usually did her seeing in the fire, but at Norah's she found that simply watching the push and pull of the waves beyond the promenade was enough to connect her with Albie.

Once she was sure he was safe and well she spent the remainder of her time sorting through Norah's wardrobe and chest of drawers piece by piece. She had no qualms about re-using Norah's possessions, knowing she had hated waste of any kind. Clothes and linen she took home to be worn, or to be unpicked and re-knitted or made into patchwork. Although Dot was too generously proportioned for Norah's clothes, Maria gave her a fur tippet, saying, "This would look lovely with your brown coat."

"It's too posh for every day," Dot said, unable to conceal her pleasure as she wound the soft fur round her neck,

"But I suppose I could wear it to church on Sundays."

Eventually all that remained was one hat — the splendid purple creation which Norah had worn to the wedding. Maria hung it on a hook on the living-room door, and each time the door moved, the hat pervaded the atmosphere with a hint of lavender and a strong sense that Norah might appear at any moment.

*

January 26th

Dear Albie, Ruth wrote for Maria. *We are all well and working hard on the farm. They need us now half the men are in the army. Blossom comes every time when I whistle and she is much happier working. She knows most of the delivery route now so I can just sit and keep Joey warm and not worry about the reins.*

Rationing doesn't bother us much because we get butter, eggs and milk on the farm. All we need to buy is sugar and flour. Joey would be happy if I didn't get his cod liver oil but I tell him it will make him big and strong like his daddy.

Grandpapa said we should use the bomb shelter now just in case, so Papa and Ricardo made the entrance longer like a tunnel. They made some sleeping shelves so there is room for us all to sleep, but Rosanna says she won't leave her vardo for any one, not even Germans.

Ricardo set lots of snares in the cabbage field so we have rabbit nearly every day. Mrs Finch's pig had babies and we've got one to fatten up in our camp. The meat will taste lovely because all the herbs we use will flavour the swill. I will send you some dry herbs so your cook can put them in his stew. Clara is happy with Olivia and Joey says he likes cooking with his gran while I do the farm deliveries, so when I'm at Norah's flat on Thursday mornings you can imagine me on my own now.

From your loving wife Maria xx

Albie laughed when he read that last sentence — finding a quiet minute during any day to imagine Maria was impossible. When the squad weren't training or driving or delving into the bowels of an engine, the Sergeant found plenty of often meaningless tasks to keep them occupied. Albie could hardly go to him and ask for time off to think about his wife — you were supposed to do that at night and hope the others didn't notice. Even so, on the Thursday after he got Maria's letter, Albie's driving lesson went like clockwork. His feet moved in the correct sequence, the gears slid smoothly into place, and the sharp pain between his shoulder-blades eased when he tried working with the steering-wheel rather than against it. The huge lorry, with its wheels that took two men to lift, obeyed his every command that morning, and when he jumped down from the cab at the end of his hour, Sergeant Davis actually clapped him on the shoulder and said, "Well done, Smith."

Albie was walking back to his hut when he heard the roar of an engine behind him, and leapt into a doorway a split second before a lorry thundered past, with Wally in the driver's seat and a white-faced instructor hauling frantically on the steering wheel. They missed Albie by inches.

*

Albie and Bert were on guard duty together that night. When they'd circled the armoury a few times, Albie stopped in a corner out of the wind and lit two cigarettes, cupping them carefully in his hand, and passed one to Bert.

"We didn't ought to smoke at all, let alone right by the ammo," Bert said, but he still dragged deeply on the cigarette. "Shit! What did you put in these – your socks?"

"Best I could get – there's a war on, you know!"

"About bloody time we was in it then."

They smoked in silence for another minute and then Bert said, "We had Wally Biggins' lorry in the M.T. Section this morning."

"What was wrong with it?" Albie asked, "He damn near ran me down after my lesson."

"He said the accelerator was sticking, but Eddie and me worked on it for hours and couldn't find nothing wrong."

"So it probably wasn't an accident – it didn't feel like one. I'd better watch my back when Wally's around. Still, the Sarge was pleased with me today — I reckon Maria must've put a spell on me."

"Wish she'd do the same for our Eddie," said Bert, "If we don't go to fight soon I'm afraid he'll go AWOL."

"What's up with him - still homesick?"

"Like you wouldn't believe! Mum couldn't keep him in the house before, but now he misses it summat fierce."

"Titch Harris is just as bad — I heard him crying again the other night but Auntie shut him up before he woke anyone else."

"Tell you what — let's take them both out and get them drunk."

"Not bloody likely – we'd all end up in jankers. Saying that – I can hear the sergeant's boots — I'd know them anywhere!"

They hurriedly pinched out their cigarettes and pocketed the stubs, and when the sergeant appeared they were innocently stamping their feet to warm them up. The sergeant shone the faint light from his pencil torch over the ground, sniffing suspiciously, but he couldn't find any ash to justify putting them on the charge he was certain they deserved.

"You and your gypsy ears!" Bert said when the sergeant had gone, "Saved our hides again!"

*

Feb 4th
Dear Alice, We have been here a whole month now and theres nothing interesting to do except the driving. Im freezing and I wish I was home with you in our warm bed. The barracks is so cold our boots freeze to the floor in the night. Outside its worse and weve got extra guard duty in case the IRA pinches our ammo. How can Irishmen be on the same side as the Germans? The men who do extra duty lose a nights sleep but still have to work the next day but Albie helps me out when Im too tired. He is the best mate in the world and

I know Im safe when hes around.

Waiting to go is boring and we all wish they would let us fight it can be Germans or Russians we don't mind just let us get at them. Eddie dont cry so much now he is pals with Tich Harris. Wally is a pain teasing them all the time but we got our own back on him last night. When he was asleep we lifted the mattress with him on it and put it under his bed. You should of seen him at Revally he was so mad he was spitting nails.

I hope you and little Susie are alright and she aint forgetting her Dad. Lots of love and kisses from Bert xxxx

Febuary 10th
Dear Bert, You must wear 2 prs of socks to keep your feet warm. I am sending you some I nitted from an old scarf you cant get new wool for love nor money. You cant get much beef neither and the bangers are full of gristle but your dad lets me have extra when hes got it and Mr Wallace aint looking. I might get more coupons soon I think Im pregnant again you don't know your own strenth. Your dad says you must be stronger than you look cos meat is heavy but hes glad hes working. Hes 47 so they wont take him for a soldier even if he wanted to go.

What you done to Wally made me smile and I wish Id seen him but take care he dont hurt you back. He might of heard about his missus going off with the grocers boy and be in a bad temper.

Maria give me a nice warm coat of Noras and a skirt. I made a frock and jacket for Susie out of the skirt, theres none in the shops. I wish you was here to see us looking all lovely and posh.

Love and kisses from Alice xx. ps. And a kiss from Susie xx

*

Feb 10th... Dear Wally, I have gone back to Mums. The rent man says you havent paid for weeks and I aint got the money. He took our things instead of rent and threw me out. I don't want to see you again I have another man friend who treats me right. Love Doreen.

"The bloody tart!"

Walter Biggins' roar of outrage shook the hut, lifting all the other heads from their own letters, but although everyone guessed what had happened, only Green dared to ask.

"I was only a couple of weeks behind with the rent and the little cow gets herself another bloke," Wally told him, then lowered his voice to add, "I was counting on our little plan to put me back in pocket."

"Well, you'll be able to keep it all to yourself now, won't you?"

That happy thought took the edge off Wally's ill humour, but he still needed someone to blame and he decided he must be suffering from a gypsy curse as all his bad luck seemed to happen when Albie Smith was around.

His opportunity for revenge came the next night when all the men from their hut were marching along the country lane to the wash house for a bath. The lane was lined by tall overgrown hedges and was very dark before the moon rose. Green was in the lead while Wally guarded the rear, each man carrying a slit-beam torch to warn other traffic of their presence.

On the return journey the men were relaxed from their baths and, with no sergeant to bellow at them, took the opportunity to have a smoke. The march deteriorated into a stroll until they were strung out over a hundred yards with Albie the last but one — the only soldier between him and the dark, empty road was Wally.

Albie was thinking about Maria. In their four years of marriage he had always known instinctively where she was even when he couldn't see her, but now he was too far away. He felt lost without the knowledge that she was just round the corner. Today was a Thursday, the one day when he knew where she'd be, but he'd been too busy all morning to stop and spend time with her. She would be putting Joey to bed now, he thought – tucking him into a bunk bed in the shelter behind the wagons.

As he walked along the lane in Dorset, Albie was suddenly struck by the feeling that Maria was just on the other side of the hedge. Even as he was chiding himself for the stupid thought, a bramble swung out and caught his sleeve. Cursing, he stopped to untangle it, but each time he unwound one bramble another one caught him and, try as he might, he couldn't get out of the hedge.

Wally had dropped back until he was quite a distance from the other men and a good fifty yards behind Albie. When he heard a vehicle coming round the curve, he hid his torch under his jacket and backed into the hedge, muttering, "Let's see if gypsy magic can save the bugger this time."

Albie was still fighting to get free of the brambles when he heard the low growl of an engine, then a pair of dimmed headlights was practically on top of him and a fifteen hundred-weight truck lumbered by. It was so close that he felt the draught of its passing, and then the hedge let him go. He ran into the road yelling, "Lorry coming!" and the other men dived for the ditch in a flurry of arms and legs and flying wash-bags.

Later Wally claimed that he had waved his torch at the lorry and it had gone past before he realised the torch wasn't working. "The switch must've caught on my pocket," he said, all innocence and apology, and although Albie knew he was lying, he had no proof.

*

February 24th
Dear Maria, The King came to inspect us today and just to see him made all the bull worth while. Hes smaller than I thought and didnt have a crown but he had a uniform with lots of medals which proves hes a soldier like us. The sun shone for him which it aint for weeks so perhaps that's a good omen. We was 2 men short cos Wally Biggins and that stupid ass Green got put on a charge for trying to nick stores. Green wrote to a mate to meet him with a van but the army reads all our letters so they got arrested. It serves them right for stealing our food. I know we took rabbits sometimes not asking first but thats different.

We painted all the lorries this week with new camerflage so we reckon we must be leaving soon. We only have little slits of light so God knows how we will see in the dark when we dont know the roads. I aint got time to write more everyones really busy.

I hope Joey and Clara aint forgot their Dad. XXXX Love and kisses from Albie XXX

<u>*March 8th*</u>

Dear Albie, Ruth wrote again on Maria's behalf. *It was lovely to get your letter and I'm so proud you met the King. Did he shake your hand? He is braver than some people who have gone into the country in case of bombs, because he is staying in London with the Queen and he says he won't let the Princesses be evacuated either. Mrs Finch says she doesn't have to have any evacuees because Kent is not safe enough but don't worry about us. Mr Finch says the Germans only want to destroy the factories not the farms.*

Everything is rationed now but we are all right. We had a warm spell and Papa caught two hedgehogs. Our piglet is getting fat. Papa made a harness for it and Joey and Pedro take it for a walk every day to eat acorns. I think they will be very sad when we eat it. Joey hasn't forgotten you. I see him looking for you everywhere we go and his Grandpa talks about you when hes there. Clara is nearly as fat as the piglet and her hair is curlier than its tail.

Ricardo made a brazier out of metal so we can have a fire in the bomb shelter which is good because its damp being underground. I will be glad when the war is over and we can sleep in the wagons again like Rosanna. We see aeroplanes quite often but Mr Finch says they are all ours like the ones Luke is flying and they will keep us safe.

Your eyes are used to the dark so you will be fine on those foreign roads. I am sure you will go soon.

With love from your wife, Maria.xx

<u>*March 20th*</u>

Dear Dad, That letter you sent on to me was from Mr Wetherby the solicitor like you thought. He says hes going to retire cos hes too old to face another war and if London is bombed he dont want to be there. So he wants to rent Norahs flat for the duration and his man

*Roberts has put in for the caretaker job at the flats. Mr Wetherby
says he will pay the rent into a bank so Ive asked him to make sure
Maria can get at if she needs to. So it looks like its all arranged.
Maria will have to stop going there after Easter. She can sit on the
pier instead on Thursdays.*

*Our brigade is going to fight at last so I will be home on
Friday for embarkation leave and I will see you on Sunday to say
goodbye. Love to Mum XX your Son Albie.*

*

From the moment he stepped off the train in Thambay, Albie
refused to discuss the war. He cuddled his children while
Maria drove him home, changed out of uniform immediately
he arrived at the campsite, and headed out into the fields
where Josef and Ricardo were planting early potatoes. They
waved a greeting but continued working as Albie pulled a bag
of seed potatoes from the trailer.

He located an empty trench and bent to the familiar
task. This was what he would be fighting for – this patch of
earth, this way of life. He planted his sackful almost savagely –
each seed potato a promise that only English mouths would
eat the crop. Poor little Finland might be defeated already but
he was going to do his damnedest to make sure that didn't
happen here.

He walked home at dusk, with his back aching and his
hands ingrained with Kent soil rather than engine grease, to
sit contentedly by the fire with his family, listening to the
crackle of wood and the chirrups of birds roosting.

Sunday was the most difficult day, and it took all of
George's tact to keep Dot off the subject of the dangers of war,
but for the remainder of his leave Albie simply hoarded
memories – the sights and sounds of the farm and the camp,
the touch of his wife and children, the scents and flavours of
England itself – to sustain him against whatever faced him
across the Channel.

CHAPTER TWENTY-FIVE – APRIL 1940 – FRANCE

"It's no worse than when we went fishing that time with your Uncle Keith," Albie said, holding Bert's belt to stop him falling overboard as the troopship lurched into another trough.

"I were sick then too, remember?" Bert said before heaving more of his breakfast over the side.

Albie parked his whey-faced, shivering friend under the pitiful shelter of a companionway and left him there while he walked the deck. The dark grey waves lifted and fell all the way to a horizon almost as grey, needles of spray lacerated his cheeks and the deck was slimy with spume and vomit, but Albie pulled in deep lungfuls of the salty wind and laughed with sheer joyful exhilaration.

"What you fucking grinning at, Gyppo?" snarled Wally Biggins, who was huddled against a bulkhead with Green. When the battalion received the order to move, both the miscreants had been given the option of staying in jail or re-joining their unit. At the time it had seemed an obvious choice but, after losing their own breakfasts before the ship had even left Southampton, they were now regretting their decision.

Eddie and Titch Harris were nearby under the care of Auntie Jones, adding their contributions to the mess on deck, but the rest of the squad were down below.

Albie eased the webbing on his shoulders for the hundredth time, bracing his legs to ride the pitch and roll as if he were standing on the front of a moving wagon, and constantly straining his eyes south for his first sight of France — Maria had been right when she said he'd be there soon.

Platoon Sergeant Davis, who had only kept his own stomach under control by a supreme effort of will, rounded up his green-faced men on the quay in Cherbourg. His familiar voice shouting, "Get a move on, you sorry bunch of tossers!" got them into acceptable formation to march off the quay into the town and, as their legs re-adjusted to solid ground, the men began to take in their surroundings.

Although Cherbourg was only ninety miles from Southampton, this place looked totally alien to the troops. Tall grey narrow buildings with shuttered windows gave the impression that the town was turning its back on the foreigners. A woman scuttled past with a stick of bread under her arm and her shawl tightly held across her chest against the wind: a man pedalled a creaking bicycle along a side street and disappeared through an archway: even the one thin cat they saw turned its tail and ran. The shop fronts and advertisement signs were strange as well, and the fact that some of the words were almost familiar seemed like a deliberate attempt to confuse.

"Even the air smells funny," Bert muttered when a waft of cooking gusted from the only place that looked open – a Café de Poste.

Albie sniffed appreciatively. "Mmm – garlic – Maria puts wild garlic in a stew."

"Don't talk to me about food or I'll be chucking up again."

"Not now, you won't — you ain't got nothing left to chuck!"

They marched right through the town to the open country beyond, where the lack of hedges added to the general air of bleakness. Fields were sprouting spring growth but were otherwise empty – the soldiers seemed to be the only living souls under this foreign sky.

Eventually they turned off along a track already churned to mush by army vehicles, and headed towards a corrugated iron barn — shelter at last. The barn still smelled strongly of the cows it had recently housed, but the cooks had set up a field kitchen under an awning close to the entrance. After their hour's march the soldiers' sea-sickness had been replaced by such a ravenous hunger that even the ubiquitous army stew smelled good.

Inside the barn the men milled about uncertainly — all except for Albie, who took one look and headed unerringly for a corner where a few bales of hay were stacked. Corporal Blake, acknowledging Albie's superior experience in making himself comfortable in all situations, commandeered the area immediately for his squad. Eating irons came out and they consumed the bully beef stew with more relish than it normally warranted, after which they split open the hay bales to insulate their bedding from the mess on the floor. The twelve men who still thought of themselves as Hut Four settled down to check their equipment and dry the rain and seawater from their battledress as well as they could. Then, trying to block out the uncomfortable knowledge that they were in a foreign land within reach of the enemy, they slept.

*

"Pack your kit - we're going in ten minutes!" Sergeant Davis's bellow had them scrambling to their feet the next morning, furiously assembling their kit and rolling blankets that seemed to have developed minds of their own overnight.

When they formed up ten minutes later there was a definite air of dishevelled haste that would have earned the whole squad a spell of jankers back at the barracks, but the sergeant merely did a quick head-count, snorted in disgust and gave the order to climb into their allotted places in the lorry.

"Where the hell are we going, Corp?"

"Fucked if I know — ask the Sarge."

"Didn't he tell you?"

"Me? I'm just an oik like the rest of you."

"Well, I ain't about to ask him."

"Then shut up - we'll find out soon enough."

With Albie and Tommy Thompson sharing the driving they headed south and soon lost sight of the sea, their only remaining link with home. The grey skies of yesterday had cleared to a perfect spring blue, and with the canvas screens of the lorry rolled up, the squad had an uninterrupted view of the country around them as it slid past at twenty miles an hour. Patches of forest broke up the monotony, but they saw hardly any sign of life other than their own.

Bert waved his arm at the arrow-straight road lined with thin trees. "It'd be like shooting fish in a barrel if the Jerries aimed a gun along here!"

"The Jerries are way over in Belgium," Joan Darby said, "Didn't you see the maps in the papers? They're hundreds of miles away, and the Maginot Line'll hold them back."

"So they tell us," said Toff Steele darkly, "I wouldn't trust anything the French say."

Titch Harris pointed a shaking finger at some isolated farm buildings. "How do we know they're not full of Germans?"

"We're closer to England than we are to Belgium," Auntie told him, patting his knee, "We're safe enough here," and Titch relaxed a little at the comfortable nursery tones.

"At least in England there were people around," Green said nervously as they drove through an eerily shuttered village, "All this emptiness is spooky."

"You just ain't used to being in the open yet," Albie called from the cab, which had the desired effect of raising a laugh.

Then their lorry bounced over yet another pothole and Green yelled, "Watch what you're bloody doing, Gyppo! We're sitting on a pile of ammo back here."

"Don't know what you're worried about, Cyril," Albie yelled back, "You've got no balls to get blown off anyway."

The little spat between the regular antagonists eased the growing tension and the men began to look around with interest – for most of them it was their first time abroad.

Eddie gestured at the landscape already scarred by the tracks of thousands of tanks and lorries. "What do the Jerries want this god-forsaken place for anyway?"

"It's not all as bad as this," said Toff, remembering the France of winter evenings in Parisian night-clubs and long, languid summer days on the wide white sands of Le Touquet. "The French produce the best food and wine in the world. German food is all stodge and pickled cabbage – probably what makes them so miserable – so they're bound to want a change of diet."

"And from France it's only a short hop across the Channel to England," added Tommy, "I can see Calais from my house in Folkestone. It's only twenty-five miles away — an hour's drive on dry land."

After that, everyone sat in silence for a while, absorbing this sobering thought. Miserable as the crossing from home had been, it had only taken a few hours and had stripped away the life-long sense of safety unique to an island race. Tommy's words had brought home to them, as no newspaper article or army lecture so far had done, that if they did nothing to stop them, the Nazis could launch a fleet of ships from every port in France and over-run England in a day.

*

April 3rd
Dear Maria, Just a note to say Im in France somewhere. Everyone was sick on the ship except me and then we slept in a French barn on some hay. It made me think about you and me in Bottom meadow. Since then Ive used my one man tent. There would be enough room for you as well but its no use dreaming.

Travelling in this lorry is noisier than being in the wagon but not much faster cos we have to stay behind the Armoured Division. They churn up the road so we have to get out a lot and push which is worse when its raining. The mud spits up all over us and we are cold and dirty all the time.

France aint like England. For one thing theres hardly any people and theres no hedges the fields just go on forever. I can smell garlic in towns it reminds me of your cooking.

Kiss Joey and Clara and remember to look in the fire every day to see if the German planes are coming so you can go in the bomb shelter. From your loving husband Albie XXX

April 5ᵗʰ
Dear Son, I know you cant say where you are but I can guess from what I read in the paper. I read one of Norahs encyclopaedias every day and Ive got to F for France now. I pinned a map on the wall to see where the countries are. We are proud of you Son and our Georgie in the Merchant Navy. With Churchill in Defence now things will get better they couldnt be much worse. The pier has got barbed wire all over in case the Germans come but theyd have to get past me and my mates first. Fred and Wilf made spikes out of wood and Ive got my garden fork they wouldnt like that up them. We tried to join the Local Defence but they said we are to old which is a dam cheek. I am not 70 yet and Ill try again but tell them Im 60 that should do it.

Everything is on ration now and Mum aint made a cake for ages not even for her birthday. We wont buy black market stuff it aint right. Mum says its good for me to lose my belly ha ha. Maria brings food from the farm on Sundays which helps and Mum is clever at making good dinners with scraps as you well know.

We still miss Norah but Mum says she might ask Mr Wetherby to Sunday dinner instead.

Look after yourself Son. Mum sends her love. From Dad
*

"What's the hold-up, Corp? We've been stuck here for ages!"

"I'm just off to ask, lads – stay put."

Half an hour later they were still there, with thick forest on both sides and their engine switched off, when Corporal Blake came back from the front of the line. "It's one of the big gun-carriers – something's gone wrong with the engine and they can't fix it until a new bit arrives."

"Bloody hell! How long's that going to take? I don't remember passing a garage!" Joan's joke didn't deserve the hysterical laughter it received but it broke the tension, and when the Corporal said a motorbike courier should be with them by the next day, the men tumbled out of their lorry to grab a smoke.

Finding himself momentarily surplus to requirements, Albie strolled off the road onto a track that disappeared into the trees. Beyond the noise of the battalion the forest sang its siren song of solitude, and his entire body relaxed. Instinct told him that no danger lurked in the green shade, and after a quick wave to Bert he wandered off into the trees, his feet sinking gratefully into the leaf-mould of decades.

Soft grey mist drifted between the tree-trunks and stray sunbeams shone on broad swathes of knee-high ferns. Tiny butterflies flashed their wings, bees clung to the undergrowth soaking up the first warmth of the day, and faint animal scurries shifted the stems of grass, brambles and ferns.

The long months of soldiering drained away until Albie was simply a gypsy again — his ears and eyes on the alert, not for enemies but for food. Four years of roaming the lanes and woods of Kent had taught him how to live on what nature provided, and instinctively now he stepped softly, his heavy army boots as silent as moccasins. The small round pellets of rabbit dung were everywhere, and he followed an almost imperceptible track to a bank of drier earth with the tell-tale bare patches of a warren.

He lowered his body to a crouch so gently that not even a leaf rustled, and then whistled one piercing note. Immediately there was the urgent thump of a rabbit-foot signalling danger and the inhabitants of the warren dashed for the safety of their burrows – all except one fat doe that ran straight into Albie's out-stretched hand, squealed briefly and died with his fingers round her throat.

"Now you need mushrooms and herbs." Maria's voice was so clear that Albie glanced over his shoulder, but then he smiled – this was Thursday, so Maria was sitting on Norah's balcony watching him. He pulled a fan fungus from a tree, searched until he found some wild thyme, and on his way back to the road he caught the distinctive scent of garlic and found a patch of it – Maria wasn't just watching, she was helping him. He blew her a kiss.

When he emerged from the trees the field kitchen had been set up, and he begged a pan from one of the cooks.

"Our food not good enough for you?" the cook asked, eyeing the rabbit, "And who are the flowers for – your girlfriend?"

Albie's fist tightened – Wally had said much the same in the school playground years ago. But then he spotted the man's grin – he had meant no offence. "This is just garlic and herbs for rabbit stew — you want some?"

"Too fancy for me, mate, but you carry on — if you get a bellyache that's your problem."

The cook watched with amusement and then with increasing interest as Albie deftly cleaned and jointed the rabbit, then browned it in his borrowed tin with an onion and stirred in the garlic. When he produced some dandelion roots and the fungus from his pocket the cook gasped, "You're not going to use them, are you? They could be poisonous!"

"Been eating these for years and I ain't come to no harm yet," Albie said, washed them in a bucket, and broke them into pieces to add to his pan. A dash of water, a pinch of salt and the herbs, and as the aroma spread a small crowd began to gather hoping for a taste, but they were out of luck. When it was cooked Albie gave a spoonful to the cook and took his creation over to where Bert and Eddie were sitting, smugly certain of their share.

"Almost as good as Maria's," was Bert's verdict, and when the three of them showed no signs of dropping down dead, every member of Hut Four demanded a taste next time Albie caught a rabbit.

The lift in morale engendered by this little incident hadn't gone un-noticed. The next day, after the replacement part had arrived and while the gun-carrier was being repaired, the officers arranged target practice in the forest. On the battalion's second night beside the road there was a choice between the regular army beef stew and a dish that Toff Steele christened 'Rabbit a la Roma'.

*

Day after day the Infantry Brigade trundled further east towards Belgium to join the forces already stationed there. The rank and file only registered the names of the major towns they drove or marched through – the villages were too similar to remember. They met no opposition – in fact the troops were hailed as saviours, in particular where the Germans had bombed obviously civilian targets.

Somewhere outside Rouen it started raining heavily and the squad was keeping dry by riding on the load of ammunition. They had been sitting there for a couple of hours when Allcock called to the driver, "Slow down a minute, Paddy, while I take a piss." This was standard practice - if the convoy had halted every time a man needed a toilet break they would never have made progress. Allcock jumped down to urinate in a handy ditch and then raced ahead of the lorry to catch it as it went past, fumbling with his fly buttons as he ran.

Just as Paddy drew level with him, Albie, sitting in the back, felt an icy hand clutch his spine. He leapt from his seat shouting a warning, but the lorry lurched into a deep pothole and swerved towards Allcock, who spotted the danger too late. The huge front wheel ran over his foot and he fell, too shocked to scream. Albie banged on the cab roof yelling "Stop!" and the big Irishman jammed on the brakes, managing to avoid by inches crushing the rest of Allcock beneath the back wheel.

Once Auntie Jones had established that only his foot was broken, Allcock was carried off to be patched up, but Paddy was distraught. He handed over the driving to Joan Darby and rode in the back, telling his fellow soldiers time and again, "I didn't expect that feckin' puddle to be that deep

— and I never even saw Allcock."

"It's lucky Gyp did," Tommy remarked, "You'd have killed the boy if he hadn't stopped you."

Paddy crossed himself twice in his agitation. "Thanks be to God he did - with him around we've got the angels on our side."

Bert looked across at Albie, whose expression was unreadable in the dim canvas light, and thought it was just as well only he was the only one who had noticed Albie warned Allcock *before* the lorry hit the pothole. If Albie wanted to keep his gift quiet, his best mate wasn't going to open up that can of worms.

*

A few days later Bert rushed round the back of the squad's tent waving a letter from home. He found Albie sitting in the sun holding one from Maria, but instead of reading it he was staring across the campsite.

"Alice says Maria reckons this one's a boy!" Bert cried, waving his letter in front of Albie's face. "Albie! You all right, mate? You look like you've seen a ghost."

Albie pointed to the lorry where the sack of letters was still attracting a crowd of soldiers. "Look over there - ain't that Ken Coppin? Shit — he must be Allcock's replacement."

"I ain't having that bugger sleeping in my tent," Bert said at once and dashed off to find Corporal Blake: "Corp - we can't have that new bloke in with us - can't you do a swap?"

"He's been assigned to us, Daly, and he'll soon fit in."

"But Corp - he's my sister's husband and he's been beating her up." Bert's face was as red as his hair with fury.

Corporal Blake's heart sank to his polished boots - the squad had got along so well until now. "There's nothing I can do, Daly. We needed a twelfth man and now we've got one."

When Ken Coppin jumped down from the lorry and landed in the middle of a crowd of men hoping for letters, he felt like a new boy at school. After months of waiting for embarkation and a fortnight marching across France, everyone else here knew their roles in this drama, but Ken was fresh out of Basic Training and didn't know what to do. The driver pointed him towards the right tent but abandoned him when he heard the post clerk call his name, so Ken dumped his kitbag by the one empty camp-bed and sat down. Everything was neat and ordered, like the barracks had been, but it was disconcerting having only a canvas roof. Ken was used to solid buildings – the sides of this tent were rolled up to chin height and didn't even give the illusion of safety.

He shuddered involuntarily, feeling very sorry for himself. Farmers were exempt from fighting, and until May had over-reacted to a little slap or two he had been tucked away quietly in Kent, where the greatest danger he had faced was that of being trampled by a carthorse. He jumped up hopefully when a few men trickled in and one said, "You must be Allcock's replacement," but they were all more interested in sitting on their own beds and reading their letters. Ken hovered uncertainly until he felt a hand on his shoulder, and turned round to find he was nose to nose with Bert Daly.

"Welcome to the war, Coppin – seems you're in our squad," Bert said, showing his teeth in a parody of a smile. Ken tried to step back but stumbled when his cot hit the back of his legs, and Bert's hand on his chest sent him sprawling. The other men watched and wondered, until Bert turned his back contemptuously on the newcomer and told them, "This here is Ken Coppin, everyone. He's married to my baby sister, and he thinks using his fists on her proves he's a man."

"He won't find any women round here," said Toff, "If there were any I'd have found them."

Bert ignored his attempt at humour. "I'm telling you all here and now, he's got fair warning," he said with savage emphasis, "The minute he gives me an excuse, I'll have him for what he done to May."

"And if Bert don't, I will," Eddie added.

Albie didn't say a thing – he didn't need to. The expression in his grey eyes was cold as the steel helmets they wore. Ken knew he had more to worry about than flimsy tent walls. From now on three implacable enemies would be sharing his daily life – it wasn't a comfortable thought.

He was queuing up at the mess-tent for his meal a while later, as far from the Daly brothers and Albie Smith as he could get, when a voice bellowed, "Ken Coppin!" and a moment later he was shaking hands with his old friend Walter Biggins.

"God! It's a relief to see a friendly face," Ken exclaimed.

"What you doing here, Ken? I thought farming got you out of fighting in the war."

Ken wasn't about to tell Wally how his brothers had frog-marched him to the recruiting office and forced him to sign up, but he'd had plenty of time to invent a story. "Dad and my brothers can do the ploughing," he said, "I fancied a bit more excitement than staring at a horse's arse all day."

"It's bloody boring here an' all," replied Wally, poking suspiciously at the stew the cook was ladling into his mess-tin, "But now you're here we might liven things up a bit."

Ken smiled for the first time since he'd been bundled out of his own home by his brothers. "Anything special in mind, Wally?"

"Not yet, but you must meet my pal Greene — I'm sure we'll think of something between the three of us."

*

By the end of April the British Expeditionary Force, of which their Infantry Brigade was a part, was very close to the Belgian border, helping to strengthen the French defences while they waited for permission from the Belgians to enter their country.

The German army was surging towards them at an alarming rate and a constant stream of refugees flowed past, heading for the French coast. The lucky few had vehicles in which they had a chance of out-running the enemy — if they could keep them from becoming bogged down on the army-ruined roads — but the majority were on foot, pushing handcarts, bicycles or prams laden with bundles of possessions. There were very few young men — they had stayed behind to defend their country — but old men, women and children plodded west — thousands of grim-faced, dust-smeared people fleeing the certainty of death or domination for the hope of freedom elsewhere.

In an off-duty moment, Albie and Toff were having a quiet smoke and watching the endless procession.

"My jam arrived today," Toff said suddenly.

"What jam?"

"My mother got some black market tins," Toff said, pulling a letter from his pocket, "Listen to this - she says, '*He charged me an extortionate price and was a dreadful little man, not at all the sort of person I am accustomed to dealing with. I hope you appreciate my sacrifice.*' I can almost hear Mother telling the ladies at her Bridge Club how daring she was. She posted the tins to Cherbourg and they were sent on by the indefatigable British Post Office."

"Lucky you - I'll swap you a spoonful for some of my fried mushrooms," Albie offered.

Toff gestured at the passing refugees. "How can I spread jam on my bread when these people have no bread at all? I'm going to give it to one of these women."

It was hard to choose one exhausted woman out of so many, but Albie pointed out one mother with a young boy who were pushing a pram from which two other small faces peered over piled bundles. "How about them - her kids'd love the jam."

Toff was moving towards her when he saw another soldier approach them holding out a tin, so he stepped back.

"That's Green," Albie said, "He's up to something."

They saw the woman's face light up at the sight of food but then they heard Green say, "What'll you give me for this?"

and realised with a jolt of disgust that he'd been raiding the stores again – he was up to his old thieving tricks but now he had added a new and vicious twist.

Green grabbed the woman's breast, his intentions clear as day. She slapped his hand away, spitting "Non!" but she couldn't take her eyes off the food, and her children were pleading for her to take it. When Green slid the tin under the bundles in the pram and pulled her arm, she slumped in acquiescence and patted the older child's head, clearly leaving him in charge while she paid the price for feeding them. Green pushed her against the nearest lorry and lifted her skirt while other refugees walked by averting their eyes – it wasn't the first time a mother had fed her children this way.

Green had just undone his fly when Albie's arm clamped his windpipe shut and his erection was slammed painfully against a sharp metal mudguard. The woman scurried off to lose herself in the crowd, the stolen tin of beef safely hidden in her pram.

"You despicable little turd!" Albie hissed in Green's ear, "I'd kill you but you ain't worth the trouble." He put his knee in Green's back and squeezed his throat even tighter, but Toff warned, "The Sarge is watching," so Albie reluctantly allowed Green to squirm free.

Buttoning his fly over his throbbing groin he said hoarsely, "You'll wish you *had* killed me before I'm done, Gyppo — you can't watch your back all the time!"

"Maybe not, but his mates can," Toff said, "I saw what you did, Green, and Gyp is right - you *are* a disgusting pile of shit."

"Who're you calling names?" Green sneered, "You've got tins in your own pockets - I can see 'em. Planning on giving 'em away, was you?"

"As a matter of fact, I was," said Toff, "And they're not stolen either. My mother sent me these, but I thought these people's need was greater than mine."

"Yeah, right, like I'm s'posed to believe that!"

"I really couldn't care less what a rotter like you believes," Toff said and strode off to find another family to receive his jam.

Green, thinking he was free and clear, ducked underneath the lorry for the sack he had stashed there, but Albie grabbed it. "What've we got here?" he asked loudly as half a dozen more tins clattered onto the ground – right in front of Sergeant Davis.

"I see the rats have been at the stores again," the Sergeant said resignedly, "What else have you stolen, Green?"

"It wasn't my idea, Sarge," Green whined.

"So whose was it?"

Albie only had to twist Green's arm slightly to extract the information that Wally and Ken were involved, and a search of their belongings unearthed enough loot to confirm his story. Wally and Ken were livid that Green had ratted on them, but there wasn't much the army could do to punish the culprits out in the field. Before long their mutual hatred of Albie, Bert and Eddie had re-established the unwholesome alliance.

To his fury, Green had also acquired a nickname – partly from the sergeant's remark and partly from Wally and Ken – within days everyone was calling him 'Ratty'. The name suited his features as well as his personality, but it was fitting in another way too. The trio of petty criminals was like a dead rat under the floorboards – the source of a bad smell that was difficult to ignore but impossible to remove.

While they waited for the real war to reach them, Wally, Ken and Green's private war of attrition was a constant irritation and danger to those they held responsible for their ill fortune. Every time Albie, Bert or Eddie tried to catch an extra forty winks after a night of guard duty, they would be disturbed by a sly kick to their rickety camp-beds. After several plates of stew were sent flying by seemingly accidental stumbles, Albie and the Dalys learned to sit with their back to a tent-pole and eat quickly and warily. Eddie, whose target shooting was only passable at the best of times, nearly shot a fellow soldier when Ken nudged his elbow at a crucial moment, and Bert hobbled for days after Ratty dropped a shell on his foot.

One day Albie found the webbing on his pack cut through to a few threads. If he had lifted it in a hurry, as they might have to do if an order to move came suddenly, the strap would have snapped completely. Instinct told him that Ratty had done it – that and the gleam of triumph in the man's eyes – but he sewed the strap up securely with string and said nothing, resolving to check his gear more carefully in future.

Wally slept in another tent so they were spared his presence at night, but to Albie's heightened senses Wally's hatred was a physical thing. It was only because his instinct for self-preservation was on high alert that he foiled what might have been a real attempt on his life.

The squad had spent a morning digging new latrines – a tedious, smelly but necessary task – and for most of that time Ratty had contrived to be standing guard over the other men's rifles. Several times Wally Biggins stopped beside him, ostensibly for a smoke, and each time the skin tightened between Albie's shoulder-blades. He couldn't work out why, unless it was because Wally ignored him rather than taking the opportunity to kick dirt in his face.

When the task was done, Albie retrieved his rifle and went for a meal, still feeling uneasy, and on impulse he used his hour's break to clean his rifle. Inside the barrel was a pebble, one of the millions that littered the ground, but this particular pebble had been shoved down the barrel several inches, hard enough to stick. Albie poked it out with a cleaning rod and held it in his hand. Without proof he couldn't report it as sabotage but he could make sure Wally knew he knew. He rubbed Wally's little death-wish pebble in something he found growing on a rotten log, and slipped it into Wally's supper that evening.

Wally spent most of the following day squatting over the newly-dug latrine and told Ken, "With the enemy getting nearer by the day we'll soon have our chance for real revenge on Albie Smith and those bloody Dalys."

Meanwhile Ken, deprived of a wife to bully, took great delight in launching verbal sniping attacks, aimed almost exclusively at Bert and Eddie. His constant digs wore away at their nerves, but his *sotto voce* remarks passed un-noticed by anyone else until one day the situation escalated into violence.

The men were relaxing after supper, some lying on their beds smoking, others sitting outside in the last of the daylight. Eddie had just re-read a letter from his mother and folded it into his wallet, surreptitiously wiping away a tear. Ken, always alert for any sign of weakness, sneered, "Girlfriend dumped you?"

"He doesn't need a girlfriend," Ratty said, "He's got Titch."

Eddie flung himself at Ratty so suddenly that he caught him off guard, and in a second they were wrestling on the grass. Titch dived in to help Eddie and was in his turn attacked by Ken, then Wally joined in and the two eighteen-year-olds were overwhelmed. Wally started laying into Titch, Ratty tightened his arm round Eddie's throat, and then Ken said, "Let's see what Daly's boyfriend likes so much," and yanked Eddie's trousers down to his knees.

With a howl of rage, Bert flung himself onto Ken's back and Albie practically broke Ratty's arm as he wrenched it away from Eddie's throat, but the damage was done – Eddie had been humiliated in front of scores of onlookers. As he hastily covered his nakedness an angry pink flush highlighted his freckles, and it took a valiant effort not to cry.

A wave of paternal protectiveness washed over Albie. Eddie had been only Joey's age when he'd first seen him – one of a row of pinched faces tucked into the bed in Bert's cold kitchen. Now, as Eddie shrugged off Bert's attempts to comfort him, he didn't look much older.

CHAPTER TWENTY-SIX – AWOL

Eddie and Titch were sitting against the concrete wall of a bunker the next night, smoking a final cigarette in the warm darkness, and for once they had the spot to themselves.

"Did you hear about the Germans taking Norway?" Titch asked idly, "Auntie Jones says there was the most enormous flap about it and Chamberlain's resigned. When are we going to get our chance to have a crack at the Nazis?"

"Maybe never," Eddie replied, "We might as well have stopped at home for all the good we're doing here."

"Well, I wish I'd never bloody volunteered!" Titch grumbled for the umpteenth time, "That Wally gave me a bloody nose and all this waiting's boring. At least I got Sundays off at home."

Eddie peered round carefully before whispering, "I s'pose we could un-volunteer."

Titch's eyes gleamed and he drew hard on his cigarette. "You mean we could ask to be sent home? Would they let us?"

"Course they wouldn't, stupid!" Eddie hissed, "And keep your voice down. No, we'd have to just go. It would get us away from Ratty and Ken Coppin."

The two boys leaned back against the bunker staring at the stars, contemplating the enormity of what Eddie had suggested.

"What about your brother?" Titch asked, "You wouldn't leave him?"

"Bert's got Albie so he don't need me – hardly notices I'm here." Eddie crossed his fingers as he said this because he knew he was being disloyal, but his longing for home over-rode everything else. "We'd have to sneak off quiet-like. If we go right now we can be well gone before anyone even missed us."

The sentries were watching for intruders, not for anyone leaving camp, and Eddie and Titch knew their routine so they were able to slip past unobserved. Once they were out of earshot they settled their small packs more comfortably and broke into a steady jog. It was early May — in Kent there might still have been a chance of frost, but on the Franco-Belgian border spring was more advanced and the night was balmy.

When they reached the first patch of woodland they slowed to a walk, over-awed by the vast silence — the two town-bred boys had never been alone in the countryside at night and it was an eerie experience. When a pale grey shape swooped out of the darkness on a whisper of sound, they both yelled with fright.

"Shit! What was that?" Eddie gasped, trying to see where it had disappeared to.

"Whoo-oo!" came the answering call and Titch laughed nervously, "Just on owl."

"D-didn't know they was that big," Eddie stammered, "It's got no right scaring me like that!"

As soon as they were clear of the pitch-black woods they jogged again and had covered several more miles before they saw the lights of a camp ahead.

"What now, Titch?" Eddie whispered, "Friend or foe?"

"You sound like my mates and me playing war," Titch giggled.

"This ain't a game though, is it? They could be Jerries." Even if the camp was British, they were deserters now, Eddie realized with a jolt of fear – they were in trouble either way.

"We'd have heard if the Jerries had got into France, wouldn't we?" Titch said.

Eddie dragged him off the road into the shelter of a grassy bank, whispering, "We can't be sure, but if we keep our heads down we can get past without them spotting us."

The two friends crept along bent almost double, relying on the darkness to hide them, but when Titch stumbled over a clump of brambles a sentry only yards away demanded, "Who goes there?" and there was the click of a rifle being cocked.

Eddie dropped flat on top of Titch, pinning him down, and they lay scarcely breathing for endless minutes until another voice said, "It must have been that fox again, Private Arnold — stand easy," and two sets of army boots walked away.

Eddie and Titch didn't dare to move for another half an hour, but eventually they disentangled themselves and crawled away. When they could no longer see the lights of the camp they stopped to smoke a cigarette in their cupped hands, each boy wondering why he had embarked on this escapade but reluctant to admit it.

The faint light of pre-dawn found them exposed on the open road without even a ditch to conceal them, and Eddie said, "Where the fuck are the woods when we need 'em?"

Titch pointed across the fields to a roofless ruin. "That house can't possibly be inhabited – we'll hide up there."

When the sun rose fully the boys were safely hidden within the broken-down walls.

"This is better, ain't it, Titch?" Eddie said, lying with his head pillowed on his pack and gazing up at the clear blue sky, "No-one shouting at us or nothing," but a gentle snore was his only answer — after a night of jumping at every sound, Titch was out for the count.

*

"Please, Corp, don't tell the Sarge," Bert begged, "Me and Albie'll get 'em back."

"Can't do it, Daly. Both ginger-nobs missing from the platoon would be too obvious."

Bert knew he was right — no-one had had a haircut for weeks and the red hair of the Daly brothers shone like beacons in the May sun. "Well, let Albie go and I'll run round so they think there's two of me. Go on, Corp, you know how Albie is — with his nose he'd find a darkie in a mine at midnight."

"Well — I can't actually give him permission, but after

what happened to those two lads yesterday I'll look the other way."

"Thanks, Corp – you're a star."

So Albie walked purposefully out of camp, relying on the maxim that if you looked as if you were supposed to be doing what you were doing, no-one would question you, and was soon hidden by a bend in the road.

Corporal Blake gave Ken Coppin a list and sent him to Brigade HQ with orders not to return until they'd given him everything on it, and when Sergeant Davis arrived with the day's assignments the rest of the squad never stood still for long enough to be counted. To the sergeant there seemed to be a ginger-headed Daly on both sides of a lorry, helping a big chap who could have been any one of the drivers, and when he asked where Harris was, Auntie said, "Urgent toilet call, Sarge," and that was that.

Meanwhile Albie was following his instinct — where else would two homesick boys go but west towards home? The road was busy enough for a soldier who seemed to have a purpose not to cause comment, and he passed unmolested.

The plight of the refugees affected him deeply – he saw groups of black-clad nuns escorting groups of frightened children – he passed a woman hobbling on a wooden leg, and an old man pushing a pig in a wheelbarrow. There were pregnant mothers and old people and hundreds of children. He scanned faces for a while, thinking the boys might have joined them, but then he remembered they would be some hours ahead and lengthened his stride.

At midday he joined an army food queue and made such appreciative noises that the cook gave him a second dollop out of sheer gratitude. Pleased with his small triumph, Albie covered his full mess tin and walked away before some officer could notice him and assign him a task.

An hour later he stopped suddenly, instincts on full alert. The stretch of road was deserted and he wondered for a moment whether Maria was sending him a warning, but the birds were singing un-disturbed, and if there were any Jerries concealed in that nearby ruin they would have fired by now. He looked around. Eddie and Titch couldn't have got much further than this in the dark. He'd bet they were laid up waiting for night, and he'd have chosen that ruin himself. There was a faint track through the healthy crop in the field and, holding his rifle ready just in case, he followed it.

When he peered through the doorway he found the runaways fast asleep. They looked scarcely older than Joey, lying there with their hair tousled and their faces pink from the sun, and far too young to be facing death. If he had thought they had any chance of getting home Albie would have left them there, but instead he sat on a portion of fallen wall and kicked Eddie in the side. "Wake up, sleepyhead."

Eddie sat bolt upright and scrabbled round for his rifle before he remembered he'd left it behind in camp, and then his eyes focussed enough to realise who had kicked him. "Shit, Albie, you scared the life out of me!"

"I meant to, you stupid bugger — if I'd been a Jerry you'd be dead by now."

Titch sat up rubbing his eyes and said without a trace of surprise, "Oh, it's you, Albie. Is that food I can smell? I'm starving."

"Didn't you even bring any food?" asked Albie, watching his second helping of dinner disappear, "How was you planning to stay alive for four hundred miles?"

"Four hundred?" Eddie gasped, "Didn't know it were that far!"

"We'd've made it, no problem," said Titch confidently, "We practically walked across France to get here so we can walk back."

"We rode a lorry most of the way, stupid," Eddie said.

"Should've thought of that before you suggested it then, shouldn't you?" said Titch.

"You was the one always saying you wanted to go home."

"Well, yes, but it's your fault we're in dead trouble now."

"You came willing enough — I ain't taking all the blame."

"Shut up, the pair of you!" Albie snapped, "On your feet on the double — we've got to get back before Sergeant Davis misses us."

After a quick brush down and a drink of water from Albie's flask - they'd drunk all theirs and hadn't thought to look for more - Albie herded the two strays back onto the road and forced them along in double time. As Albie was the only one armed, he marched them briskly like prisoners past any other soldiers, and on the only occasion they were stopped he just said, "Runaways, stupid little sods - the sergeant's waiting for 'em," and they were allowed to continue.

*

Sergeant Davis frowned. Despite the fact that all the work was getting done there didn't seem to be as many men as there should be. Corporal Blake had said that morning they were all present and correct, but every time he tried to count heads the buggers moved. There were two redheads - he'd seen one a minute ago on the top of that bank and there was the other one now carrying a sack of spuds. That big chap with the non-regulation blue handkerchief round his neck must be Smith, and Jones had his head inside an engine - you could tell from the shape of his bum. Harris was over by the tent - no he wasn't, that was the new man, Coppin, who'd just driven back from Headquarters.

"Where's Harris?" he asked aloud and, as if by magic, the little spiv Green materialized beside him. Ratty had been waiting hours for his opportunity. The others had deliberately not told him what was going on, but a lifetime of keeping his eyes peeled had taught him how to winkle out a secret, and when he'd seen that thick Irishman wearing Gyppo's scarf it had been ridiculously easy to make him tell. He couldn't actually go up to the Sarge and say, "Hey, Sarge, guess what?" but no-one could blame him if the sergeant asked him a direct question. With a malicious gleam in his eye he said, "Harris, Sarge? Him and Daly have gone a – aargh!" Corporal Blake had dropped a bit of engine on his toe – a heavy bit.

"Sorry, Green," the corporal said, "Didn't see you. I thought I sent you to help Daly with that lorry? Get a bloody move on — and take this with you."

The sergeant's gaze followed Green as he hobbled off with the engine part. For a brief instant all the men were still enough for him to see that one Daly was missing, and Harris and Smith seemed to be absent as well. "You're three men short, Corporal," he said.

Corporal Blake's lungs seemed to have frozen. The squad had covered for the three men for most of the day, but if their absence became official, not only would Harris, Daly and Smith be in deep shit, so would he. He squinted hopefully west where the setting sun was just sinking in a blaze of fiery colour behind some trees, and was struck by inspiration. "Sent them for firewood, Sarge," he said, and walked smartly away to make sure Green was kept occupied — all he could do now was pray.

Eddie and Titch's steps slowed to a reluctant crawl when the camp came into sight. Albie had marched them along so fast that they'd had no breath to talk, but now Eddie asked fearfully, "What's going to happen to us when we get back?"

"Buggered if I know," Albie said with a marked lack of sympathy, "Bert and the rest said they'd cover for us but it's been a whole day – and if them other three cottoned on they're bound to have talked."

Titch stopped dead in the middle of the road clutching his belly, said, "Gotta go!" through clenched teeth, and dashed into the woods to squat behind a fallen tree. At the sound of his friend's bowels emptying explosively Eddie turned pale green and ran to heave his guts into the ditch.

Albie was left standing alone, staring after them and wondering how he could get them into camp unseen. The woods were back-lit by the setting sun as if they were on fire, and he realised he'd been given his answer. Fire – firewood – carrying a load of firewood they could march boldly into camp and no-one would question them. When Eddie and Titch had voided their terror he made them lift the awkward branched end of the fallen tree and hefted the trunk end himself. A few minutes later they staggered into camp out of the sunset, in full view of anyone who cared to look, and dropped their excuse on the woodpile.

Corporal Blake was there to meet them. "You don't know how lucky you are!" he muttered when Albie cocked an enquiring eyebrow. "The Sarge only realized you'd gone an hour ago and I told him you were collecting firewood." Eddie and Titch were edging away but he stopped them with a growl, "You two deserve to be shot – which as deserters you would've been but for Smith." He held finger and thumb an inch apart. "You came this close, and I'm going to make sure you're too busy to think from now on. Report to me after supper."

"I've got bellyache, Corp," Eddie groaned, "Couldn't eat a thing."

"Me neither," said Titch.

"You've been collecting firewood for a couple of hours so you're hungry," said Corporal Blake severely, "You'll eat the same as everyone else or I'll shove it down your stupid throats myself. Now wipe that sick puppy look off your faces and fuck off!" As Eddie and Titch trotted off the corporal punched Albie lightly on the arm, "I never believed in this gypsy luck crap till now, but I hope it lasts – I've got a feeling we're going to need it."

CHAPTER TWENTY-SEVEN – MAY 1940 – ACTION

Two days later a lightning raid by German gliders and paratroopers captured the 'impregnable' Fort Eben-Emael and the so-called Phoney War was over. The battalion erupted into frantic action, and the Hut Four squad was transformed from a group of bored and disgruntled labourers into the soldiers they had been trained to be. They were crossing the border into Belgium at last.

"Thompson, you drive," Corporal Blake ordered, "O'Brien can navigate."

"We'll never get there if Paddy's on the maps," Ratty said.

Paddy scowled – it was true that he'd struggled with orientation lessons, same as with the reading, but there was no need to keep reminding everyone. "I never get it wrong now, Ratty – I'll get us there."

"Yeah – but only if there's signs saying 'This way to the Nazis'."

Albie dumped a box of ammunition in Ratty's arms. "Shut up, Ratty – you're tongue's so sharp you'll cut yourself one of these days." As he turned to take another box, Ratty stuck his hand accusingly under Albie's nose. "Look what you done – you and your gyppo curses!" A deep gash ran across the ball of his thumb, blood already flowing through the dirt and soaking into his jacket cuff. He scuttled off to get it bandaged and didn't return until the lorry was loaded, after which he climbed aboard and sat on one of the ammunition boxes as far away as possible from Albie.

Together with the French army, the British Infantry followed the throaty rumble of the tanks across the Belgian border, eager to meet the enemy and drive it back into Germany. Their objective was less than thirty miles away, but their leaders hadn't anticipated the renewed flood of refugees that clogged the road, and progress was painfully slow. At times they were moving at a mere walking pace, but the tanks' movement was inexorable and the refugees had either to give way or be mown down. Many bundles of possessions were ground to rubbish beneath tank-tracks, but the Belgian hands that waved from the ditches were more often open in encouragement than clenched in anger. If the soldiers who had crushed a bed-frame or a prized clock could drive the Nazis out of their country they would be forgiven anything.

At dusk the army made camp in a field, set watch and turned in, still without sight or sound of the enemy.

*

In the early hours of the morning Albie woke with a start. For a moment he forgot where he was and swung his legs out of bed, thinking he had heard thunder and Joey would be scared — but when his feet touched trampled grass he remembered. The sound came again and it wasn't thunder, it was bombs – lots of bombs dropping out of the night. He could also hear the cough of answering guns, but when no-one raised the alarm he lay down again.

Staring into the semi-darkness of the army tent, Albie sent his mind back to the thought of a moment ago, trying to imagine Joey sleeping in the wagon with Maria and Clara while Josef lay on a mattress between them and the door, but the image wouldn't come.

"Silly – we're in the shelter!" Maria's sleepy voice told him and now he could picture them, snug beneath the roots of the pine wood — Maria, Joey and Clara tucked into a double bunk at the rear of the shelter with the rest of the tribe snoring nearby. Albie sighed contentedly and drifted off to slide into the bunk with them, Maria's silky back against his chest and his face buried in her herb-scented hair. His arm encircled them all – baby Clara nuzzled into her mother's milky breast, and beyond her the skinny limbs of his sleeping son. Albie knew that Maria wove a charm around him daily, but his sense of security was strengthened by the dream, and he slept peacefully until Corporal Blake banged on the tent pole.

"Right, you lot – take yourselves down to the river in twos to wash – and be quick about it. We're breaking camp after breakfast to be ready to move again later today."

"What about that bombing last night, Corp?"

"Miles away, lad, miles away – and our lot saw the buggers off."

Albie stripped off and ran to the water's edge, his brown forearms and neck in stark contrast to his pale torso. He threw a stone in to gauge the depth and then jumped, knees to chest, to land bottom first in the river. He surfaced grinning, shook his head like a dog coming home after rain, and looked for Joan Darby, his swimming partner, but Joan was standing on the bank looking nervous. "I'm not jumping in there – I can't swim."

The idea that someone couldn't swim was strange to Albie, born at the seaside, but he stood up to demonstrate he was only chest deep, so Joan stripped and waded cautiously in. This was their first chance for an all-over wash for some days but, even with guards posted, Joan felt vulnerable naked and he soon scrambled ashore.

Albie swam out to centre stream and turned, treading water. The sun sparkled off the ripples, and in the shade cast by his body he saw fish darting through the weeds on the river bed. Birds called in the trees, willows trailed their tresses in the current, a duck stuck its tail in the air as it grazed by the far bank, and a church clock struck the quarter. Albie drew a deep breath, recalling mornings like this before the war when the whole tribe would swim together, and then the splash of another body hitting the water reminded him they were only allowed five minutes.

Swimming quickly back to shore, he was tensing his shoulders to heave himself out when someone grabbed his hair and pushed his head under water. None of them had had haircuts since leaving England and Albie's curls were tough enough for his attacker to get a good grip. Thinking a German must have sneaked up and overcome the guard, Albie scrabbled for purchase on the rabbit-cropped turf, but it slid out of his fingers. He dug his toes into the river-bed and shoved, lifting his body enough to snatch a breath before the hand pushed him back down, but he had seen enough to know it wasn't a German – Wally was trying to drown him.

The words of the unarmed combat instructor rang in his head – "Move with your opponent, not against him." Bracing his feet against the bank, Albie gripped Wally's wrist in both hands and shoved off with all his strength. It worked like a dream, and Wally somersaulted into the river fully clothed. When he surfaced, blowing like a whale, Albie was waiting, and the platoon was treated to the spectacle of the two men standing up to their waists in the river trading punches, Wally wearing sodden battledress and Albie stark naked. After letting them slug it out for a couple of minutes, Sergeant Davis bellowed, "Stop fighting and come here!" When they stood in front of him dripping wet, he looked them up and down and demanded, "What was all that about?"

"Just a bit of fun, Sarge," Wally said hastily, "No harm meant."

"Smith?"

"Like he says, Sarge – no harm done," but Albie knew that when they went into battle, the Nazis were not the only enemy he would have to watch out for.

The battalion drove another forty or fifty miles into Belgium that day and set up camp in another field in the dark. They could hear the drone of unseen planes overhead and the far-off thump of bombs drifted in on the wind. The war felt much closer now and that morning's carefree swim seemed part of another life.

As soon as they arrived, Sergeant Davis assigned each squad a length of canal to guard. The whole country was criss-crossed with canals and rivers which the Belgians had thought would stop the enemy, but the Germans had overcome with humiliating ease one obstacle after another, landing gliders, building bridges and crossing rivers with alarming speed and efficiency.

"They caught us all with our trousers down," Corporal Blake told his men, "Belgians, French and Brits — and your luck doesn't extend to canals, Private Smith," he added with a heavy-handed attempt at humour, "One big canal the Jerries took today was called Albert."

At daybreak the war finally caught up with them. While the opposing armies did their utmost to knock hell out of each other with massed tanks and bombers, the squad from Hut Four manned their anti-aircraft gun. Once they were dug into position they only stopped firing when the ammunition was slow to arrive. Open breach, load shell, aim and fire – an endless repetition – open breach, load shell, aim and fire. After a few hours, when one group of men's hands were so tired they could hardly hold the shell or pull the lever, another group would take over – open, load, aim and fire.

The men on either side of the gun wound the aiming handles until their shoulders froze solid, and even Ken Coppin and Ratty Green were glad to let Auntie Jones massage the knots out of their muscles. The hot shell cases ejected from the breech struck legs which would be bruised for days, and the men trampled the cases into the mud of their dugout to make a floor. By the end of the second day the walls were lined with shell cases too, and when anyone was relieved for a few moments he would collapse on a pile of them to sleep with the sound of the gun as his lullaby.

When the battle was over and the opposing armies retired to lick their wounds, the Hut Four squad returned to the tent that, after five months away from England, seemed almost like home. They were filthy and red-eyed and totally spent but no-one had been injured, which most of them attributed to Albie's presence. Let other soldiers clutch their rabbit-foot charms or sweethearts' ribbons – Hut Four believed that Albie was the magic charm that would get them out of this mayhem alive.

Alive maybe, but not necessarily in good health — their clothes were crawling with fleas and lice, and their feet were in an awful state. Albie made a foray into some woodland at dawn and brewed up a bucket of herbal foot-wash, while Ratty, who had once again befriended the stores clerk, persuaded him to part with clean socks for them all. They washed the mud of the dugout from their rotting feet, soaked them in Albie's herbal concoction, and pulled on their clean socks. The difference this small miracle made to morale was immediate, and they lay back on their camp beds wearing expressions that wouldn't have been out of place in the Ritz.

"Anyone know when we'll get fed?" Tommy asked, but nobody answered.

"I could sleep for a week," Albie said, but no-one heard him.

"I never knew noise could hurt like that," said Eddie, wiping a trickle of blood from his ear, but no-one heard him either – the incessant pounding of the gun had perforated their eardrums, and every single one of them was deaf.

*

The north end of the Allied line held out for two more days, but when Holland surrendered after the bombing of Rotterdam, and the Germans obviously had the upper hand further south at Sedan, the order was given for the British to withdraw.

The roads were chaotic. Tanks, armoured cars and ordinary vehicles vied for space with horse-drawn carts, bikes and footsore pedestrians, and this time the troops were going in the same direction as the refugees. Tanks were trundling along behind horse-drawn carts driven by stubborn peasants who saw no reason to move aside. Plodding pedestrians glared at soldiers riding in the trucks, their expressions clearly asking why they should get out of the way so that the army could flee faster than they could. But when the German planes screamed down from the sky the refugees ran, jumped or rolled into ditches, behind walls, into any cover they could find, while the soldiers tumbled from their lorries to man their guns.

After one such attack, Albie climbed back into the driver's seat to manoeuvre the lorry past a burning tank, but had to slam on the brakes when a soldier leapt from the turret right in his path. With awful, ponderous inevitability two wheels of the heavily-laden lorry slid into a ditch, dragging the Bofors gun behind it. Albie jumped from the cab unhurt but he could see daylight under the roadside wheels – to have any chance of getting the lorry out of the ditch they would have to lighten the load. The squad unhitched the Bofors and hauled it back onto the road, then unloaded their remaining ammunition boxes and man-handled the lorry out of the ditch. Bert crawled underneath to check for damage while the rest of the squad prepared to re-attach the gun.

Albie was at the rear of the lorry, wiping mud and weeds from the towbar, when he heard Maria scream "Albie!" and there was the roar of an accelerator being floored by an army boot. He didn't even look – he simply jumped aside, and with a split second to spare missed being crushed between the tow-bar and the bonnet of another five-ton truck. When he picked himself up it was no surprise to see Walter Biggins driving the other vehicle. There was no doubt about it this time – Wally had driven at him deliberately. Albie had a foot on Wally's running-board and his hand on the door before he saw that the crash had shoved their stricken lorry into the ditch again, and remembered Bert had been underneath it. He slid into the ditch yelling, "Bert!" expecting to see his friend's mangled body and prepared to lift the whole thing off him if necessary.

Then Bert's cheerful voice called, "Over here, Albie –

I'm all right – but I seen Wally drive at you deliberate and I'd swear to it in court."

"What court?" said Albie, "I don't reckon any of us will get out of this alive – here comes another plane."

So they turned their gun towards the sky once more, with bombs falling and bullets screaming on all sides, machine-guns clattering, and the air solid with noise. Then one of their shells hit its target and the plane went into a nose-dive trailing black smoke, hit the ground with a satisfying whoomph and exploded in a fountain of dirt and flame.

"Got the bastard!" the corporal crowed, "Well done, lads – now get this lorry out again."

"It ain't worth it, Corp," said Bert, "One look told me the drive-shaft's buggered."

"Then we'll take this one," the corporal said, pulling open the door of the apparently empty cab beside him, and a body fell out onto the road.

Albie stared at the blood-covered face and swallowed hard – it was Wally. He'd known Wally for fifteen years — argued with him and fought with him in the playground, on the pier and in the fields of Thambay – murderous enemy though he was, his death was still a dreadful shock. Bert and Eddie came over, alerted by Albie's silence, and as the three of them sketched a farewell salute to their old adversary, Ratty shoved his face right up to Albie's. "You've killed 'im – you and your fucking gypsy curses!"

Corporal Blake grabbed his collar and forced him to look at Wally's wound. "He took a bullet in the neck, you idiot – and if he hadn't driven deliberately at Smith he wouldn't have been there, would he? Now let's hitch the Bofors to the back and get going before another bloody plane arrives."

But Bert had to break the bad news. "This lorry's knackered too, Corp – there's petrol all over the road — we'll have to walk."

*

Hauling the anti-aircraft gun was painfully slow work and they were an easy target for the attacking Stukas. Armed soldiers and unarmed civilians alike were shot at by one plane after another, but in the hours after losing their lorry Hut Four brought down six more planes, and the charmed circle that surrounded Albie continued to deflect the strafing bullets.

At times Albie was sure he could hear the Nazi pilots laughing as old men, women and children dropped in their tracks, to lie in the road until someone pushed them aside like bundles of rubbish. In the appalling racket of thumping guns and screaming planes, the squad was even grateful for the deafness that muffled the smaller sounds of the injured moaning in the ditches.

Night came at last. Trying to snatch some sleep inside the doubtful shelter of a bombed-out building, Albie and Bert huddled together for warmth, chilled to the soul by fear and by the suffering they had been forced to ignore in their own fight for survival. Eddie slept with his head in his brother's lap and Bert whispered to Albie, "Poor kid cried himself to sleep – he's terrified."

"We're all scared," Albie replied, "Eddie's got nothing to be ashamed of." He looked around at the men sprawled among the fallen tiles and splintered furniture that was the debris of some family's life. Paddy and Tommy were sharing a burst mattress and snoring loudly; Joan and Toff were propped against a stove that still held a residue of warmth; Ken and Ratty were tucked into opposite corners with their chins sunk into their chests, while Auntie was leaning against a year's-worth of soot in the big fireplace, with Titch using his legs as a pillow.

"Where's the Corp?" Albie asked.

"Under the gun with the Sarge, and the camouflage net over the lot," Bert told him. "This war's made some strange bed-fellows, ain't it?"

CHAPTER TWENTY-EIGHT – VAL

Albie woke stiff-limbed and ventured outside in the faint dawn light to empty his bladder. Unbelievably, there were birds just beginning to stir in the nearby trees and he stood still for a moment to listen. Then he heard another sound and spotted a strangely familiar shape. Certain his mind must be playing tricks on him, he moved towards it, talking softly.

A dappled horse turned wide frightened eyes in his direction and tried to rear, but it was held fast by traces tangled in a wrecked cart. Albie stroked the horse's trembling neck and talked it into calm. A quick glance at the torn bodies in the cart was enough to show him why the poor creature was in such a state – it had been imprisoned all night next to the blood and spilled guts of its owners. Albie cut the traces and led it away to eat some grass and drink from a bomb crater. Ten minutes later he took his new companion back to the ruined building and his squad.

"What the bloody hell do you want with a horse, Private Smith?" Sergeant Davis asked.

"To pull the gun, Sarge — she'll be a great help."

"What makes you think you can handle a strange horse?"

"Everyone knows I'm a gypsy," Albie said, tugging the horse's ear, "We talk horse language."

"Well, I suppose it's better than pulling it ourselves," said the sergeant, and with Albie stroking its nose and murmuring love-words, the horse stood calmly while the squad cobbled together a harness with which it could tow the gun.

They christened Albie's horse Val after Toff told them the French for 'horse' was 'cheval'. She hauled the platoon's heavy gun steadily behind the retreating tanks and, although she quivered at every blast, with Albie's strong arms round her neck and his voice in her ear, she held still enough for the gun crew to fire their weapon without unhitching it. In gratitude for her help, every man in the squad kept his eyes peeled for horse-food, frequently coming back from a swift dash into a field carrying a bunch of grass cut with a bayonet or an armful of hay filched from a barn.

Sergeant Davis's platoon was miles behind the main body of British troops by now and way out of reach of the Catering Corps. The men had to find food where they could and, following Albie's example, Squad Four soon learned to forage in roadside fields for maize cobs and root crops that could be boiled up at night or, at a pinch, eaten raw. Albie had an instinct for which bombed houses would yield chickens or ducks, often finding them ready-killed by bomb-blast, and on one momentous occasion he even discovered a whole pig, roasted to mouth-watering perfection in its own sty.

The entire platoon ate well that night, and as Sergeant Davis licked grease from his fingers he remarked to Corporal Blake, "I don't know what we'd have done without Smith and his horse. He's popular with the others in the squad too, isn't he?"

"Every squad should have a gypsy, Sarge — he's lucky, and that's worth sticking close to."

*

On the edge of the charred thirty-mile-wide corridor between Amiens and Arras, through which huge detachments of German motorcycles were roaring at alarming speed towards Abbeville and the coast, Albie's luck and Val's strength kept the squad together and unharmed. Whenever one of the low-flying enemy planes zoomed overhead spitting death, there was always a ruined house or the arches of a market hall for them to hide with their gun and fire back. Time and again a wall was blown to rubble, or an entire building collapsed, seconds after they had moved on. Tanks exploded, RAF fighters shot down German planes mere yards from their positions and other soldiers died, but still the Hut Four squad remained unscathed.

Their appearance was a far cry from the spit and polish of the barrack-room. Bloodshot eyes peered wearily out of stubbled faces, their uniforms were filthy with dried mud, dust and gun-grease, and they wore the same underclothes for days on end. Skin rashes and flea-bites were a constant irritation they were too exhausted to scratch, and after a few days even the most fastidious among them got used to the stink of his own body. Any food that came their way they ate on the move and they hardly slept at all, making do with snatched cat-naps in ditches, against rough walls, sometimes on a pile of ammunition, and always with that gnawing fear that even gypsy luck couldn't last forever.

*

Val had been with them for a week when the British troops began to advance south, attempting to close the German-held gap between themselves and the French, and fighting for every yard they took. There was a stand-off mid-morning between a British tank and a German road-block that gave the squad a few minutes respite. Tommy – a Catholic who'd never missed Sunday Mass until he joined the army – took the opportunity to slip inside a church to say a quick Hail Mary. He emerged a moment later with a thunderous expression on his normally placid features, shouting a string of obscenities.

"What's up with you, Tommy?" asked Ratty from the shelter of an ornate buttress where he was smoking a cigarette, "That don't sound like prayers!"

"Those fucking bastards must've known it was a church!" Tommy told him, "Whacking great tower and everything. Bloody sacrilege, that is – dropping a bomb straight through the roof."

"It's only another building, for God's sake."

"For God's sake! That's the fucking point, you tosser. The priest's lying by the altar with a socking great lump of masonry on his head and there's a dozen bodies blown to bits around him. They were saying Mass when the Jerries got them."

"They'll have gone straight to heaven, then, won't they?" said Ratty carelessly, and Tommy threw a punch that knocked the smaller man off his feet. Tommy had taken a step to follow through when the all-too-familiar scream of an approaching Stuka split the air.

Corporal Blake yelled, "Get down – it's coming straight for us!" and for a split second everybody froze, unable to believe their time had come. Then Albie heard Maria shriek his name through the clamour of sound and he dived for cover, taking Tommy and Ratty with him in a flying tackle. They fell between a buttress and the church wall and Albie lay with his face pressed into the earth, holding his helmet over the back of his head. In the plants beneath his nose he smelled lavender – Norah's scent – and then the Bofors gun took a direct hit and exploded.

When the plane climbed back up into the sky, the moans of injured men were drowned out by the screams of a horse in agony. Albie was several yards from the church, running to help Val, when Sergeant Davis roared from inside the porch, "Stay down – he's coming round again!" and Albie threw himself back.

Eddie had been near the gun when the Stuka attacked. He survived the plane's first run and the subsequent explosion, but he was still out in the open with only Val's thrashing body as cover. Toff was lying dead beside him, and Eddie was frightened enough by Toff's sightless stare without the horse screaming directly into his ear as well. Giving the returning plane a terrified glance, he made a dash for the safety of the porch, and Corporal Blake, with his stomach shredded by shrapnel from the exploding gun, dragged himself after him. But the pilot had seen them, and loosed a stream of bullets that finished off Corporal Blake, put a merciful end to Val's sufferings, and practically sliced Eddie in two. Albie watched in horror as Eddie's helmet was blown off, and his red hair flamed briefly in a sunbeam before it was extinguished by a cloud of dirt.

Bert howled with rage and raced outside to drop to his knees beside his brother pleading, "Eddie, don't die, please don't die," but he was too late. Eddie Daly, who would have been nineteen in June – not even old enough to vote but old enough to fight for his country — was dead. Bert knelt in the rubble, cradling Eddie's body and shaking his fists at the empty sky until Albie pulled him to his feet. "He's gone, mate — you can't do nothing for him."

"I ain't leaving him lying by a dead horse," Bert said, so they carried Eddie inside the church and laid his body beside a large and solid tomb.

"What am I going to tell Mum?" Bert cried, "I were supposed to look after him!"

"It weren't you that killed him, Bert, and he weren't the only one who died."

A dozen bodies lay sprawled by the altar, the black- and grey-clad villagers congregated in death around their priest in his lace-trimmed surplice. The resemblance to a morgue increased when they brought the bodies of Toff Steele and Corporal Blake to lie beside Eddie's, and then Sergeant Davis counted heads and asked, "Where's Harris and Jones?"

"Having a cuddle somewhere, I shouldn't wonder," said Ratty with a smirk.

Paddy's huge hands closed round his throat and lifted him clear off the ground. "Keep your dirty mouth shut in God's house."

"Drop him, O'Brien – he's not worth being put on a charge for," said the sergeant, and Paddy let him go just as Auntie came into the church supporting an ashen-faced Titch.

"He took a bullet in the side, Sarge. I've fixed him up as well as I can but I can't get it out. He says he can walk."

"I'm afraid he'll have to," said the sergeant, "We can't

leave him here."

"I'll carry him, Sarge," said Paddy.

"It could be hours before we find some proper medics," the sergeant warned.

"Ah, he's only a tiddler, God love him — I've caught fish bigger than him back in Ireland."

Sergeant Davis almost smiled – this was a good team. He wanted to keep the remainder together, but they needed a leader, and the obvious choice was Smith, despite his lack of education. "Smith - you're Corporal Smith now and this is your squad. Any questions, anyone? Good. Corporal Smith, take your men and find another gun and a vehicle. And Smith?"

"Sarge?"

"I'm sorry about your horse."

CHAPTER TWENTY-NINE – THE FARMHOUSE

Corporal Albie Smith's squad hadn't been able to find a vehicle or another Bofors gun, but they had rescued two three-inch mortars, along with their ammunition, from beneath some bodies in a ditch.

They were now on the edge of the retreating army, hiding in ditches or the shadows of trees and aiming their mortar-bombs at German infantry rather than at planes. At times they were less than a mile from the enemy, and with the mortars weighing them down their progress was dangerously slow. It was rare for them to have a moment like this – marching along with nothing to fire at – and they were making the most of their opportunity to put more distance between themselves and the Germans.

"What you got there, Albie?" Bert hadn't spoken a word since the previous day, but watching Albie's hands working at something as he walked, he couldn't resist asking.

Albie looked quickly round to make sure they were unobserved. "I'm plaiting a bit of Val's tail to go in my talisman."

Bert peered into the little bag made from a scrap of leather. "And what's that other hair?"

Albie had never outgrown his tendency to blush and he did so now. "Curls off Maria, Joey and Clara. I've got some lavender from that church too, 'cause I felt Norah was there, and that's Sofia's lucky stone."

"We could use a bit of luck to find us a lorry," said Bert, his practical streak resurfacing, "Paddy's carried Titch since yesterday without moaning once, but even he's got his limits."

Albie's charm must have been a powerful one, because an hour later they spotted a medical vehicle making a dash for the coast, and they flagged it down by the simple but effective method of standing in the middle of the road.

"Get out of the bloody way or I'll run you down, you

stupid fuckers!" yelled the driver, but then he felt a chill on his neck and found Albie's broad figure looming on the step beside him. Suddenly his feet seemed to be frozen on the pedals and his hands were unable to shift the gearstick. While he struggled, cursing, Paddy mounted the back step of the truck with Titch in his arms and pushed the canvas flap aside. His large silhouette made the medics and wounded alike shrink back instinctively, and Paddy eased his burden down into the resulting space as tenderly as a mother, saying in his warm Irish brogue, "There you go, Titch, plenty of room for a tiddler. You'll be grand now."

The troops with transport pulled ahead again during the course of that day and Sergeant Davis's platoon was left to protect the rear. At nightfall they found shelter at an isolated farm where Albie's squad commandeered a stone barn.

Albie lay down holding his lavender-scented talisman to his face and fell asleep as if he'd dropped off a cliff. The clamour of war was replaced in his dreams by the quiet creaking of his wagon bowling along a country road and the clop-clop of horses' hooves. The black clouds thrown up by exploding French earth softened to a pale grey mist swirling through peaceful English woodland, and his nostrils were filled with the scent of herbs and freshly-mown hay instead of the stink of sweat and blood and rotting flesh.

That first deep sleep was disturbed when the watch changed, and when he fell back into his dreams he found himself in the ruined church. Dad and Mum were there, and Norah – Albie could smell her lavender perfume. A minister splashed his head with water and on the far side of the font Bert laughed, "Me — a godfather!" Then Maria wafted down the aisle, her lace gown trailing over rubble, and Albie was waiting by a stone tomb on which Eddie lay, clasping his rifle like a knight with a sword. Then Maria was in his arms and they were dancing to the strains of a gypsy fiddle, but the tune rose to a crescendo and became the whine of a descending bomb. After the explosion, all that was left was a heap of masonry and a scrap of lace stained dark with blood.

Albie jerked awake, sweating, to the renewed boom of a heavy gun and he and his men scrambled outside. Beyond the farmhouse was a small hill behind which the sky was brightening, but they were dismayed to see a plume of smoke a mere couple of miles distant.

Sergeant Davis barked his orders. "Corporal Smith! Take position by that small building north of the farmhouse," so they grabbed the heavy sections of mortar and ran. The sergeant sent the rest of his platoon racing along the road to defend the village that was just visible on the skyline, while Albie's squad crouched by the brick shed, one mortar on either side, three men to each mortar. Small though it was, this shed was the only cover between the advancing enemy and the British soldiers on the road to the village, and they would defend it for as long as they could.

Leaving Albie in charge there, Sergeant Davis took Joan Darby and Ken Coppin up the little hill to reconnoitre. Lying concealed in the thin woods that crowned it, they saw one of the smaller German tanks, flanked by soldiers, bumping through a crop of chest-high wheat. It was heading straight for the road and the British troops still visible in the distance. Sergeant Davis said to Joan, "Tell Corporal Smith to fire two hundred yards north of his position exactly three minutes from now – you can count the seconds on the way back to him. Coppin – you and I are going to stop that tank."

Joan wriggled back out of sight and raced to the farm, counting seconds with every step, leaving the sergeant and Ken lying in ambush – two men against an entire German squad and a tank.

Ken was a farmer's son, and the sight of that tank carelessly crushing a decent crop of wheat made him angrier than anything had done for weeks. When the tank was level with their position and Sergeant Davis said, "Now!" Ken shot off like a clay pigeon from its trap. His helmet flew off as he ran, and his hair was such an exact match for the ripe wheat that the Germans didn't see him until he was among them -- he had cut one man's throat and injured another before he died. Sergeant Davis was close behind him, but he was shot in both legs at point-blank range and fell. Undeterred, he rolled deliberately in front of the slow-moving tank, pulled the pin from a grenade and blew himself up just before the tank-track crushed him into the wheat.

Instantly the tank turret swung round and fired at the only sizeable building in sight – the farmhouse — but flames from the caterpillar track began licking up the sides of the tank, and a moment later burning soldiers spilled out of the turret. The German foot soldiers were using the tank as cover when a mortar soared with deadly accuracy straight into the open turret, destroying the tank completely, and a second one blew the remaining soldiers into fragments. Corporal Smith had followed Sergeant Davis's instructions to the letter.

They couldn't find any trace of Sergeant Davis, but they buried Ken Coppin's body in a shallow grave beside the shed and stood with heads bowed while Tommy said a prayer. Then they all stood looking at Albie – he was in charge now.

"We'd better try and catch up with the others," he said.

Ratty piped up immediately, "They're miles away by now and we ain't got transport."

For once Albie had to acknowledge that Ratty was right, but Joan peered into the shed, asked, "Would this do?" and Albie and his remaining six men crowded inside to stare at the oddest vehicle any of them had ever seen.

If it had ever been a thing of beauty, the evidence now lay under layers of mud and chicken droppings. A topless, backless box of a cab perched behind the engine, there were no bumpers or headlights, and the open back had obviously been created by taking a saw to whatever bodywork had originally been there. Paddy rubbed the paintwork of the door with his sleeve and they read 'Marc's Glacès' – their new vehicle had started life as an ice-cream van.

"I think it's a Renault," Tommy said, "They're known for being reliable and I reckon it still goes — someone's used this steering wheel recently."

"The tyres are a bit worn but they'll do," said Bert, giving them a kick, and while Ratty lifted the remaining half of the bonnet to see whether the engine looked all right, Albie tapped the tank.

"Still some petrol in there, too. The Sarge said we're only about thirty miles from the coast – it might get us there, but we can't just steal it."

"Don't reckon they'll be needing it now," said Bert, "The Jerries got the farmhouse."

He was right — what was left of the farmhouse was burning fiercely. Shutters that had been closed against the night air glowed red in the grey stone walls and, as they ran towards it, the ancient dry timbers of the roof caved in with a groan, cutting off abruptly the screams of those trapped inside.

"Let's just go," Ratty said nervously, "They're all dead now."

"And there'll be more Jerries along any minute," Bert added.

Looking at the fiercely burning building, Albie knew they were right, yet instinct pulled him towards the farmhouse. "You get the car going while I check the outhouses – I'll only be a minute."

"I'm with you," said Bert and Paddy grunted, "Me too," so the three men raced to the farmyard and circled the house. Bert tugged on a shutter, but when it burst into flames in his hands he dropped it hurriedly. Paddy darted through the smoke to fling open an outhouse door and released a pair of terrified goats, one singed cat and a fluttering, cackling cloud of chickens, but the living quarters were a mass of impenetrable flames.

At the sound of an engine coughing into life and Auntie's voice, soprano with urgency, calling, "Come on, Corp, we've gotta go!" Paddy and Bert started to run back, but Albie hesitated. Beneath the roar of the inferno he had heard a tiny cry from the goat shed, and with a shock he realised it was the whimper of a baby waking to be fed. He dived inside the shed and searched rapidly in the light of the burning ceiling, but found nothing. Then he spotted boots poking out from beneath a long brown skirt.

The woman's head and upper body had been crushed beneath a beam, but Albie pulled aside the burning straw and there, hidden in the folds of her skirt, was her baby. It looked about two months old – a tiny creature with a fuzz of blonde hair and its mouth open ready to howl again for food. Albie snatched it up and tucked it into the front of his battledress, dodged another falling beam, and dashed across the yard just before the walls of the farmhouse rumbled and collapsed.

The Renault was already moving, and Bert leaned over to drag Albie into the back. The instant he was aboard, Tommy put his foot down to drive them along the rutted farm lane to the road. Ratty was wedged in the cab between Tommy and Joan, leaving Auntie and Paddy to bounce around on the straw in the back with Bert and Albie.

"I got us some dinner," Paddy said proudly, pulling aside his battledress blouse to reveal the slit yellow eyes of a small goat. "I hope you know how to cook this, Corp."

Albie laughed out loud and revealed his own prize. "And I hope that's a female, cause how else am I going to feed this baby?"

"Holy Mary Mother of God!" Paddy exclaimed, "Where'd you find that?"

"In your goat shed," Albie told him, "Its mum was squashed under a beam."

Paddy crossed himself. "Born in a stable? Sweet Jesus!"

"Not in a million years," said Albie. "Born in Belgium, I'd guess from its mum's clothes, about two months back." The van lurched from the farm track onto the smoother surface of the road, and Albie laid the baby across his lap to un-pin the soiled rag from its bottom.

"Well, now we know it's not Baby Jesus!" laughed Auntie, "It's a girl, and a very dirty one. Do you know what to do, Albie?"

"Sort of — I seen it done often enough," Albie said doubtfully, but Bert came to his rescue. "I done Susie's a few times — give her to me."

So the four soldiers in the back of a chopped-up ice-cream van cleaned the baby girl's bottom, and Bert fashioned a nappy out of an army-issue vest. Paddy wrapped the wriggling goat firmly in a shirt and the baby, after a few false starts, decided goat milk was better than nothing and suckled hungrily.

When she was full and her eyes drooped shut, Albie tucked her back against the warmth of his chest and looked at the others. Every one of them had a soppy grin on his face – he probably had one too – but saving this baby wouldn't be much use if they got her killed. Seven men and a baby were in a foreign country, racing for the coast with the enemy in hot pursuit, and it was up to him to get them there. "Paddy, you watch the east – that's that way," he said, "Auntie the west, and me and Bert'll watch the back. Tommy, can't this bloody ice-cream van go any faster?"

"Not unless you want to stop while we tinker with the engine," Tommy answered over his shoulder, and that was that.

CHAPTER THIRTY – THE ROUNDABOUT

The nearest village was a pock-marked ruin. Every house along the main street had its shutters hanging down or blown away, several roofs were burning, and the inhabitants had vanished — either hiding or dead. Bodies lay sprawled everywhere – British and German and French. Leaving Auntie curled protectively round the baby, Albie and the rest of the squad checked every doorway and window for snipers while Tommy drove past the heaps of rubble and burning vehicles.

Ten tense minutes later they left the village, and as the van picked up what speed it could, Paddy pointed a shaking arm eastwards and yelled, "Jerries!" On the skyline a row of tanks was lurching across the open fields, and when they saw more of them in front, Tommy swung the wheel hard left to drive into a side road lined by a double row of poplars.

"These skinny trees won't hide us," Bert said as they sped through the stripes of shadow.

"There's a thicker patch a hundred yards on if we can make it in time," Tommy answered, hunching over the steering wheel to encourage a few extra revs out of the protesting engine, and somehow they did make it. When the rumble of tanks grew louder they abandoned the van to crouch among the trees, but the Germans disappeared north along the wider road and the little group remained undiscovered. Tommy had switched off the engine so that the noise wouldn't betray them, and it took several hard swings of the handle to start it up again, but eventually it caught and they piled in hurriedly.

Albie sat in the cab beside Tommy. "Keep going north," he told him, "If we're not quick we'll get cut off."

The narrow road wound between fields seemingly untouched by the war - possibly because no vehicle wider than their own could have made it - but it was headed roughly in the right direction. Although he was constantly on the lookout for potholes, Albie still watched the country on either side, where distant explosions proved the battle still raged. Half an hour beyond the ruined village he grabbed Tommy's arm exclaiming, "I don't bloody believe it – look at that!"

Tommy shook his hand off, saying, "Nearly had us in a ditch then, Corp — what's up?"

Albie looked a second time and snorted at his own stupidity. For a moment he'd mistaken the burning shell of a windmill for a helter-skelter — the lack of sleep must be getting to him. "Never mind me, Tommy," he said, "Must be seeing things."

Bert tapped his shoulder. "You ain't the only one Albie – I mean Corp," he said, "Could've swore I seen the sea."

But Bert wasn't mistaken - Albie too had caught a glimpse of the sea - they were nearly there. Tommy tore his eyes away from the welcome sight just in time to wrench the van round a blind corner between two mossy walls, and what he saw made him screech to a halt. "Another town, Corp, though it looks deserted — shall I chance it and drive straight through? If we stop the van we'll never get the awkward cow going again."

"Better not," said Albie, jumping out of the cab, "You keep her running while we recce." He passed the little bundle of baby to the medic. "Auntie, take care of her. Bert and Ratty — you're with me. Joan and Paddy — you're on guard."

Taut with even more tension now that the coast was so near, they clambered over the piles of rubble, checking everywhere, but the war had done its worst to this once peaceful little town and moved on. It was just as it seemed - totally deserted. The town square with its Hotel de Ville, pavement café and stone fountain was strangely untouched, and as vacant as if its citizens had been spirited away. The three men shivered in the eerie silence — not even a dog stirred.

"At least there's food," said Ratty, and slipped into the bakery to emerge a moment later with several long loaves sticking out of his battledress blouse. Feeling slightly guilty, Bert broke the lock on the café door to liberate a few bottles of wine, but then a shutter banged with a noise like a gunshot and they dived for cover. They stood with rifles raised for a couple of minutes but nothing else disturbed the silence.

"Let's get out of here," Bert whispered, "This place gives me the willies."

"Me too," said Albie, "But the van won't get through the way we did. You two take those side roads back and find a way for Tommy to get to this square — the road's clear in front."

Once they had gone, Albie went to check behind the Hotel de Ville — it was a solid enough building to hide a tank and there could still be Germans here. The cobbled alleyway opened out abruptly into another, smaller square and there, as abandoned as the rest of the town, was the roundabout from Thambay pier. First the helter-skelter that wasn't and now this! Albie shook his head in sheer disbelief and wondered briefly whether he was hallucinating, but when he touched the flared nostrils of his favourite horse Blaze, the wood felt solid enough. Forgetting the danger of distractions, he yielded to the temptation to climb into the saddle. Hearing the motor begin to whine into action, he gripped the twisted pole in anticipation of that first jerk of movement, but then the whine grew impossibly loud and his world went black.

*

The men in the van ducked instinctively when the shell whined overhead to burst in the town centre. Auntie curled into a tight ball round the baby and Paddy just caught the goat's back legs before she could escape, but there was no following fire. After a moment they guessed it had been just a stray shell and Bert dashed back down the side road screaming, "Albie!" Tommy ground the van into gear to follow him.

Bert's heart hammered painfully in his chest when he saw the wreckage. Red and gold scraps of timber covered the cobbles, and smack in the centre of the square, heaped around the mechanism of the roundabout, lay a mound of horribly lifelike dismembered horses. He knew that Albie wouldn't have been able to resist the roundabout, and that his friend lay somewhere beneath that heap of broken horses – splintered wooden horses from which wisps of smoke drifted up, hinting at fire to come.

Flinging aside his rifle, he tore at the nearest section of wreckage yelling, "Albie, where are you? Come on mate – answer me!" Joan jumped out of the van to help him, and Paddy tied the long-suffering goat tightly in his jacket, shoved it at Auntie and ran to add his muscle to the race against the growing fire. Tommy kept the van's engine running, praying that the petrol would last out. Only Ratty stood unmoving, watching the potential pyre with a satisfied smirk.

"Why the fuck aren't you helping, Ratty?" Joan yelled.

Ratty took a deep breath – that hated nickname was the main reason he wouldn't lift a finger to help Gyppo – and called out, "I'm standing guard!"

Joan shrugged and grabbed a horse's head just as the centre of the pile flared up fiercely with a whoosh of sound. "That'll be the motor fuel," he yelled in Bert's ear, "It'll all go up in a minute. We'll have to leave it — the Corp can't have survived that shell anyway."

"I ain't giving up," Bert said stubbornly, "I know he's still alive."

"The Corp's got a gypsy charm round him," Paddy added, so the three of them searched with greater urgency as the flames licked nearer.

Then Bert shouted, "Albie! He's just there – I seen him move!" and with a strength born of desperation Paddy hauled a horse, its pole and an entire section of planking away, allowing Bert and Joan to lift Albie out of his prison and carry him to the van.

Albie's shoulder was broken – crushed by the head of the roundabout horse that had kept the weight of the rest of the wreckage off his body. Auntie could do no more than strap his arm to his side and give him a shot of morphine, but as soon as the drug began to take effect, Tommy put his foot down hard and drove as he'd never driven before.

In years to come, Tommy would describe the van to his motoring cronies as a pathetic apology for a vehicle. He wouldn't have admitted under torture that he had enjoyed driving it, but he told his wife that the challenge of getting seven men, a baby and a goat through hostile territory in the face of imminent death had been the greatest thrill of his life. Even when a tyre burst he kept them on the road, and Paddy's strong arms did duty as a jack while the team of army-trained mechanics made short work of changing the wheel for the one miraculously bolted to the side.

With only a few miles still to go the engine began coughing and Tommy warned, "We're nearly out of petrol."

But Joan had been hotel-trained to anticipate needs and he fished a length of hose from the back. "Found this in the shed – thought it'd come in handy."

"I don't see no petrol station," Ratty sneered but Joan said, "There's enough abandoned vehicles around," and he was right – it wasn't long before they found an overturned lorry from which they could siphon off a gallon of fuel.

In the crush of thousands of troops pouring into the funnel of the road to the coast, they should have been hard pushed to get through, but it wasn't so. Possibly it was the strange picture they made in their cut-down ice-cream van that caused the lines to part for them, or the tinkling tune with which the original owner had replaced the horn. It might even have been the sight of the goat's head peering out of Paddy's battledress or, as they claimed later, gypsy magic, but it was

Tommy's driving that got them to the beach.

He steered the little van round many obstacles — smashed walls and abandoned lorries, tipped-up carts with the bloated bodies of their horses still attached, medics carrying stretchers, and men — thousands of soldiers, British and French — all moving with identical defeated expressions towards the dubious safety of the beach and the possibility of transport home. A few more soldiers climbed aboard the van, doubling the load, and a second tyre burst on some unidentified bit of debris, but Tommy drove on, with Joan helping him to hold the wheel against its tendency to veer sideways. Both of them cursed every pothole and bump, their hands were slippery with sweat, but they kept going with a grim determination not to be beaten.

When a waft of ozone crept through the smell of unwashed humanity on the road, a line of dunes concealed the ocean itself, but their destination was clear from the number of planes swooping constantly over their heads like obscene seagulls.

"We could be heading for trouble," Joan remarked laconically.

"Looks that way," replied Tommy, "Oh well, in for a penny in for a pound," and he raised his voice to a shout, "Hang on in the back!" slammed his foot to the floor and drove straight for a gap in the dunes, where protruding scraps of metal burst two more tyres and the van slewed to a standstill.

CHAPTER THIRTY-ONE – DUNKIRK BEACH

Tommy had quite a struggle to let go of the wheel, he had been gripping it so hard for so long. He fell out onto the sand and patted the remaining half of the bonnet affectionately. "You're a good old girl," he said, knowing he would never again experience a drive that exciting. Then he crawled up the last few yards of dune, lay beside Joan, and thought he was unlikely ever to get the chance. "Jesus wept! Will you look at that fucking mess!"

"Not much point in rushing, was there?" Joan sounded almost resigned to the inevitability of death on that broad expanse of sand. "We'll never get out of that alive."

Bert added his own comment in a mincing falsetto, "Tommy dear, couldn't you have found us a quieter bit of beach for our picnic?"

The port installations burning fiercely in the distance formed a hellish backdrop to the massed troops on the beach. Injured or exhausted men sprawled in the sand, too weary to move even when the Luftwaffe planes screamed overhead dropping their bombs. Vehicles and armour were the only shelter from the explosions, and around each one huddled clumps of soldiers hoping that the metal would protect them.

Bert returned to the van where Squad Four and the seven other men they'd collected in the last mile stood waiting for leadership. There was nothing else for it, thought Bert – he'd have to rouse Albie. Climbing into the back, he shook Albie by his good shoulder. "Albie, we're here – time to wake up!" Albie was still in a drug-induced sleep, with Auntie and Paddy sitting protectively on either side of him, but he was needed, so Bert shook him again. "Corporal Smith, your men need you!"

Finally Albie fought his way up through the morphine. "That you, Bert?" he muttered, struggling to his knees, and he allowed Bert and Auntie Jones to help him out of the van. The men grinned with relief. If it wasn't for the Corp they'd never have made it this far, and they needed him to get them safely through this final horror.

It was Joan Darby who found a shovel to dig a sort of cave in the sand, and Paddy O'Brien who wrenched the remaining bodywork off the van to shore it up. Auntie Jones emptied his small pack and tucked the baby inside it, then put her right at the back of their foxhole. Albie, wobbly from loss of blood, managed to stay upright long enough to make sure his squad was still together, then he handed over command to Tommy Thompson and lay down next to the baby under Auntie's watchful eye.

Several times through that long afternoon Paddy, who refused to be parted from the goat, crawled in beside Albie to feed the baby. Handfuls of coarse dune grass were all Paddy could find to feed to his charge, but she ate it eagerly and her milk kept flowing.

*

When night came, some of the troops on the beach clustered around a few field kitchens, but it was obvious there were too many men for too little food and, with superstition their only remaining defence, the Hut Four squad were reluctant to leave Albie's side. Then Bert remembered the wine he'd liberated from the roundabout town and found his booty still concealed under the straw in the van. Ratty was out-numbered and forced to give up his bread, but when Albie pressed the crust it was rock-hard.

"It needs wetting," he said, looking speculatively at the goat, but Paddy read his mind.

"That milk's for the baby."

"Use the wine," Bert said, knocking the top off a bottle, so they chopped the bread into lengths with a bayonet and gave each man a piece which Bert soaked with the dark, sour wine. As fourteen men sucked their bread dry and passed it back for more wine, Bert remarked to no-one in particular, "I feel like Jesus feeding the five thousand!"

"Pity you aren't," said Tommy, staring out over the stranded army, "There must be ten times that number out there."

"Bloody quiet for that many," Albie remarked, pointing out what they had all tried to ignore. Now that the Luftwaffe's attack had ceased, an ominous blanket of silence had fallen over the sands. The normal buzz of chatter one would expect from so many men was replaced by a barely audible murmur.

"It sounds like that cat's-whisker wireless me and my brothers listened to under the eiderdown," Bert said, and then stopped when he remembered there was one brother he would never share a wireless programme with again.

Three bottles of wine didn't go far between so many, but the men slept heavily after their unaccustomed alcohol and woke with sore heads when the first bombs of the morning dropped. Rumour had spread of an attempt to rescue them, and they watched the horizon for the longed-for ships while even more troops poured onto the beach. Some of the new arrivals drove their lorries and armoured cars all the way to the water's edge and even into the sea itself.

"Stupid buggers are trying to drive home!" Ratty sneered.

"They're making a pier, arsehole," said Bert, "Anyone with half a brain can see that!"

"Who're you calling arsehole?" Ratty threw a wild punch at Bert, who dived low and threw him to the ground.

"Albie shouldn't've bothered saving your miserable hide back at that church!" he said, raining blows on the thin face, but Ratty squirmed free and whipped a knife out of his belt.

"Come and get it, lover-boy. Your Albie's magic didn't stop 'im getting blown up, did it? Or your kid brother."

With a howl of rage Bert knocked him flying, and they were grappling on the sand when Ratty thrust his knife at

Bert's side, but a heavy boot stamped on his wrist and Tommy said severely, "Save it for the Jerries, Ratty, because if there's any more of that we'll leave you here."

Ratty got up clutching his wrist and backed away. "Fucking gyppo-lovers, the lot of you!" he shouted and ran off.

After their wine of the night before the men were horribly thirsty, but they emptied their water-bottles in the first hour and the sight of the waves lapping the shore was torture. Albie and a man with a broken leg suffered more than the others due to loss of blood, but they could do nothing except lie and wait for rescue.

By now all fourteen men knew about the baby and donated spare underwear to be used as nappies. The tiny girl in Auntie's pack was a focus that helped to distract them from the mounting panic on the beach, and one father passed round a creased photograph of his own child.

Later that afternoon Ratty slunk back, his pockets bulging. He had tried to attach himself to several other groups but been driven off, so he had returned to the only safety he knew. Hut Four re-absorbed his presence with resignation, and no-one had the energy to question where he had obtained the cigarettes he handed round with uncharacteristic generosity. Albie guessed they had come from the pockets of the dead, but smoking eased the hunger pangs and he could hardly tell Ratty to put them back.

*

The second night there wasn't even any bread and wine for them to share, and the soldiers lay listlessly around their little dugout, watching the dark waves for the promised rescue.

Albie and Auntie's other patient were both shivering violently and burning up with fever, so Paddy milked his goat into a mess tin and persuaded them both to drink, watched enviously by the other men. From the expressions on some faces, Paddy had a feeling he'd be wise to guard his goat carefully.

Auntie had commandeered everyone's first aid packs, and at midnight he divided the last shot of morphine between the two injured men. Bert noted the absence of any more syringes and asked, "What happens tomorrow?"

Auntie shrugged, refusing to meet his eyes as he repacked his depleted medical kit and said, "We'll have to trust the Corp's luck for that." He and Bert went outside for a smoke as the patients drifted off to sleep and when they checked later, the man with the broken leg was muttering in delirium, but Albie's pulse was beating steadily and his forehead was cool.

*

Albie opened his eyes and peered into the dawn gloom of the dugout. He'd been dreaming of Maria – he could still feel the caress of her hair against his cheek – but the eyes that looked back in the faint gleam of light were blue instead of black. Of course — the baby. Maria had always said she wanted lots of babies and she was going to love this one as if it was her own. Albie could see it so clearly in his mind – Maria waiting to meet him and the baby girl turning those clear blue eyes on her new mother. The image was so vivid that he sat up too suddenly and bumped his head on the van door that was serving as a roof. The sound and Albie's curse woke Auntie, who had been dozing in the corner.

"You all right, Corp?" he asked, checking Albie's bandages, "You've stopped bleeding at last."

"I'm fine, Auntie," Albie assured him, "And I'll be even better when you can hand me over to the doctors at home."

"Had a premonition, did you?" Auntie asked, catching Albie as he swayed, "You stay put till they come, Corp," he ordered, easing him back down, and reached past him to see to the baby.

Albie wasn't the only one to have a premonition that morning. A spirit of renewed hope rippled across the beach like a breeze through corn, and lines of men began snaking down to the sea before first light. Even the inevitable Stukas failed to scatter them for long, and when they roared away to re-arm, the line simply reformed, each fit man supporting an injured comrade.

The engineers were so busy they hardly noticed the planes. Every gun and vehicle had to be disabled and every tyre slashed to ribbons – if they couldn't take them home, the Nazis weren't going to use them either. If the enemy had descended then in force, the entire army – British, French, Polish and assorted others — would have been sitting ducks but, inexplicably, the Germans didn't come.

When the black silhouette of the first ship was spotted, a wave of hope washed up from the water's edge to lap over Hut Four's shelter in the dunes, and in moments only the original squad remained. Joan made a seat of crossed hands with Auntie to carry the unconscious man with the broken leg, and Bert stuck his shoulder under Albie's armpit.

"Where's the baby?" he asked and Paddy said from behind him, "I've got her, along with her milk bottle. You can have her back when we get to England."

"I'll find us a place to wait," Tommy said, "Ratty – you'll have to help Bert with the Corp," and he led the squad to join the shortest line he could see.

The first launches to touch the sand were swamped by frantic soldiers, but officers fought to regain control, even resorting to punching those who refused to obey, and gradually order was restored. The lines of men waded out into the surf, the furthest from shore having to swim as the tide came in faster than they were being picked up. Many, weighed down with packs and rifles, drowned with rescue in sight, their bodies floating face-down and bumping against the living as they waited their turn.

There weren't nearly enough ships for them all and with a sense of cold despair they knew it. Then the miracle happened. A flotilla of small craft appeared, manned by fishermen or weekend sailors – there was even a paddle-boat that had made its way over from Margate — and the lines of men moved faster.

Albie, leaning on Bert and Ratty, shivered when he felt the cold water on his legs, but the sand was firm so he merely braced against the swell and waited, dopey from the remnants of morphine on an empty stomach.

As soon as he felt the Corp take his own weight, Ratty ducked quietly underwater and slipped away to surface beside a sailing boat and scramble aboard.

"Hey – you – no queue-jumping!" said a stern voice, but Ratty scuttled to the blunt end and pulled his tin helmet over his face like a child playing hide and seek – if he couldn't see anyone they couldn't shift him. The skipper shrugged and helped others aboard, and when the little boat was full to the gunwales he trimmed the sail and pointed her into the swell. As the prow rose to the first wave Ratty raised his head to find he was looking straight into the accusing eyes of Bert Daly, standing up to his chest in the surf and still supporting Albie.

"So that's where you got to, you selfish fucker!" Bert said.

"It's every man for 'imself now," Ratty answered, and turned his face away.

The sail filled in the stiff breeze and the boat tilted towards home, but a minute later a German shell flew clear over the beach and struck the sail-boat, which sank instantly. The crew and most of the passengers swam the few yards back to shore but Ratty Green, his arms tangled in the anchor rope no-one had had time to stow properly, drowned in only ten feet of water.

Bert and Paddy watched it happen without moving a muscle and smiled grimly, then they heaved Albie into the next boat, helped by a wave that lifted the big man at just the right moment. Once on board, Paddy stared at the ungainly barrel of a body and the huge, rusty-brown sails and asked, "How can something this big get so close to shore?"

"I seen one of these once on the river near London," Bert said, "It's a Thames barge – practically flat-bottomed."

There wasn't much room for the three of them — the hatch-cover took up most of the deck space. As more men poured aboard they were told, "Get below and look lively," so Bert went backwards down a ladder, guiding Albie's feet, into a vast, dark hold.

The inside of the barge was saturated with linseed oil from its regular cargo and smelled like furniture polish – a homely, comforting smell. Bert propped Albie against a curved wooden wall and slid down beside him to await his fate. Paddy followed them down, goat, baby and all, and wedged himself against a timber on Albie's other side. "Did you see what happened to Ratty?" he asked Bert.

"It happened right in front of my nose," Bert replied, "Serves the bugger right, but it's another one of our squad dead – I reckon Albie's gypsy magic stopped working when we lost Eddie." Forgetting he was talking to an Irishman he added, "I dread telling Mum we left Eddie behind in a Catholic church."

"She won't mind what kind of church it was – and I reckon the Corp's luck did hold out. He was buried under a fecking roundabout, God love him, and still dug out alive."

The barge lifted on a wave and lurched as it turned for England. The goat bleated at the sudden change of movement and the baby wailed once and spat her last meal down the front of Paddy's chest. He scrubbed at the stain, telling the baby, "Sooner your dad wakes up the better," but Albie was too far gone to hear.

*

Albie dreamed he was rocking in the back of the cart, catching up on his sleep while Maria drove through the night to the next farm. He rolled when the cart hit a rut and a moment later he was in the kitchen, where Mum was polishing her rocking-chair – the smell of linseed was very strong. The chair sounded like it needed oiling – the whole room was full of its creaking. There was a trace of dust too, which was odd, because no dust was ever allowed to settle in Mum's house. Perhaps he wasn't at Mum's at all.

He frowned at the effort of trying to solve the puzzle and shifted irritably in his sleep, but then his hand touched coiled rope and he smelled the sea. Ah – he knew where he was now. Rope and polish and sea and dust could only mean one thing — he was on the pier, sitting on a pile of coir mats, safe inside the warm dusty belly of the helter-skelter.

END

Made in the USA
Columbia, SC
25 September 2018